Sweet Surrender

LOYAL WYNYARD

Sweet Surrender

Contents

Sweet Surrender

2010 John Thornton, Look Back at Me
2011 John Thornton Meets Miss Hale
Mill Owner
2011 Margaret With The Red Book
2012 John Thornton's Unfolding Dream
2012 First Comes Death
2012 Forever Champion
2012 I Killed Him
2012 A Comedy of Eras
2012 Margins of Her Heart
2012 Northern Ways
2013 My Soul to Keep
2013 M'Lady
2013 The Courtship of Margaret Hale
2014 Sweet Surrender

Acknowledgement to my Readers

Thank you to all that have written letters and told me of your love of these stories. That has inspired me to write more.

I love the characters of John and Margaret and wish to have them falling in love over and over again.

Sweet Surrender

Chapter One

1852: Milton, England

Margaret didn't think she could swallow the lump that had formed in her throat during her walk to Marlborough Mills. She massaged her neck, as if it were some remedy to ease the tightening muscles. It might have an effect eventually, but nothing could relieve her embarrassment. All pride had gone. Even Dixon was looking for more work.

Margaret was a pretty young woman of twenty-two, educated and brought up as the daughter of a gentleman, a clergyman, now recently passed. Her mother, also deceased, had been a Lady in the most proper sense, but married below her level of society because of the love she had for Richard Hale. Margaret's brother, Frederic, was somewhere in Europe, on the run from the British Naval court martial system, for mutiny on the high seas.

A close family friend, Mr. Adam Bell, who would be Margaret's guardian and provider, was nearing his end of life. He had taken it upon himself to see the colonies that his academic life had taught him much about. He traveled quite often and had never received the news of the passing of his lifetime friend, Richard Hale. Had he known, his immediate actions would have been to return to England and secure Margaret's financial future. However, that seemed likely to be far off, as it had been three months since she last heard from him.

Margaret was now nearing the end of the finances left to her. She had her maid, Dixon, and herself to keep going.

Dixon was taking in ironing and washing to help. Margaret had been depressingly busy selling pieces of the household items and the few family heirlooms with which she could bring herself to part. She was preparing to leave this comfortable flat that she had shared with her parents for over two years and to move to the outer edge of the Princeton district, known as the poorest section in Milton.

John Thornton, owner of Marlborough Mills, happened to look out of his office window and spotted Margaret Hale walking through his factory gate. The gateman tipped his hat to her, remembering her from past visits to the Thornton family. John felt the immediate ache to his heart. He thought he was over her rejection of his proposal the previous year. He had not seen nor heard of her since Mr. Hale's funeral, who had been a good friend to him.

What could she want and why was she walking?

She could not want to visit his mother, who was plainly not in accord with Margaret's attitude towards living in an industrial town. John left his office and walked down the outer steps to greet her. Immediately, he noticed her demeanor had changed, having seen her at her father's service and looking poorly then, as well. She looked pale, drawn and thinning in the face. Was she sick? There must be some urgency to her visit, he thought.

"Good morning, Miss Hale." John didn't ask her how her health was, as it was visible. "It is nice to see you again. It must be lonely for you and Dixon in that large flat. What can I do for you?"

"I need to speak with you, if you can spare a few minutes. I will be brief."

"Of course. Would you prefer the office or my home?"

"It does not matter, Mr. Thornton. Whatever suits you?"

"Shall we retire to my home and have a cup of tea?"

Margaret hesitated, remembering Mrs. Thornton's attitude towards her, but she had already said, it didn't matter where.

"You needn't worry, Miss Hale. Mother is out."

"I hope she is well."

"She is getting poorly. Pain in her joints has slowed her down, and she no longer helps me in the mill. Dr. Donaldson tells me there is nothing to be done, and it shall become worse over time."

"I am very sorry to hear this news. It must be disheartening to see her decline. I remember that vividly with mother and father."

"Yes, I suppose you do," John said, opening the door to his home.

Margaret proceeded first through the door and climbed the stairs to the parlor with some effort. She remembered the room and the adjoining dining room well; very little had changed. "Your home is still as lovely as I remember it."

"Please sit, Miss Hale. Can I offer you some tea?" he asked as Jane, the housemaid, came into the room.

"No, thank you, Mr. Thornton."

John had indicated a chair to her before he sat. "What can I do for you, Miss Hale?"

Margaret lowered her eyes, searched for the handkerchief in her bag, and tried to swallow the lump again. "Mr. Thornton, please forgive me as I may falter," Margaret said, pausing to take a deep breath. "It is with great humility that I have come to Marlborough Mills to see if there is any employment available." She took another deep breath once she had said the words and stifled a sniffle. She looked up proudly, reaffirming to herself that she had the resolve. Surprisingly, a small panic ran through her as she became trapped in his gaze on her.

John Thornton's slate blue eyes were piercing her. She felt weakened. Her resolve fled. Never had she expected the feelings that rushed over her at the moment. There was no accounting for it.

"Please forgive me, Mr. Thornton. I should not have come. How silly of me to bother you. I will waste no more of your time." Margaret stood and headed towards the steps leading out of the house.

"Miss Hale! Please! Can I not answer your questions or ask another?"

"No, Mr. Thornton. Once again, I find myself interrupting your life with silliness. I'll see my way out."

"Silliness?" John repeated. "Is that all you thought you meant to me?" He wished he hadn't said that.

Margaret descended the steps quickly and fled the house. She picked up her dress hem and began to run as the tears fell. She thought he would try to follow because he was a gentleman. She swiftly headed into the direction of the Princeton district, assuring herself that he would not think she would take such a path home.

After searching for Margaret outside his gate, John walked back towards his office. His best friend and now partner, Nicholas Higgins, walked up beside him. "John, was there some problem out there? I saw you running."

"The strangest thing just happened. How long has it been since you have seen Margaret Hale?"

"I've been quite remiss, I must confess. I saw her at her father's funeral, but have not followed up with her since. Why? Did you see her?"

"Yes. Let's go upstairs."

John and Nicholas headed up the office steps.

Coming through the door, Nicholas asked, "Did you just now see her?"

"Yes. She had no carriage." He paced the room as Nicholas frowned and waited for John to continue. "She came asking if work was available. I must admit I was surprised seeing her again and then she asks about employment. Perhaps her home is lonely with little to do, and she is trying to find work for Dixon."

"What else could it be, John? Do you want me to go around and see her?"

Avoiding the question, his mind was elsewhere. "She said something about bothering me with her silliness again and then fled the house. I couldn't get her to listen to me," John's voice was rising. "She was saddened, I could tell. When I looked at her, it was as if she had had some revelation. She blurted out those words of silliness and hastened away. She never waited for an answer."

Nicholas could see John's far-off look as he struggled with the brief visit.

"John, sit down. I understand this is confusing, but you look like you have been struck dumb. Did all of this Miss Margaret stuff, from a year ago, come rushing back? I thought you were well and truly over her."

"I *am* over her. Surely, I am."

"Well, something just happened to you. You look lost," Higgins offered.

"I must admit seeing her and having the opportunity to speak to her came as a shock. That was quickly followed by a question on employment, which seemed very unlikely. After that, she announces she's being foolish once again and flees that house … without a carriage, no less. Doesn't all that seem odd?"

"Yes, it does. There is only one way to sort it, and that would be that one of us should call on her. I think I am the one to do it. No telling if it was seeing you again that sent her off."

"She said she would falter," John whispered.

"She what? Asked Nicholas.

John cleared his throat and came back to himself. "Yes, she said she would 'falter,' and said she was coming with 'great humility' to ask about employment."

"Great humility? That is an odd statement by Margaret."

"Yes. My thoughts, too." John walked to the window and looked out—searching his mind.

"Perhaps Peggy and I will take a ride to her home this evening to say hello."

"It should be my place to do that. I am the one she came to see. You could be right, though. She may have some memory or embarrassment of our relationship, a year ago."

Turning from the window, he sat on his desk edge and folded his arms. "Nicholas, she will know I sent you if you do it tonight. Why not send her a note, asking to come calling?"

"She would hardly expect that from me," said Nicholas, "but I will do it. It's proper that I should. I will let you know the outcome."

With that, John and Nicholas settled into their accounting of the day's productivity.

Margaret stopped running, as she was starting to draw attention to herself. People wanted to assist her. She slowed and looked about at the sickening poverty around her. Little did she ever think that she would become one of these people. The small flat, which she had secured with the last of her savings, was on the very fringe of this poor and hungry area of Milton. Unless she or Dixon found suitable work, other than working at a weaving machine, she could sustain them for about four months. Margaret thought of Mr. Bell. Would he return to London soon? She had sent several notes there, never knowing if his college would forward them to him or just let them accumulate until he returned. If he had ever received word of her father dying, he would have been to Milton by now. Margaret remembered the inheritance that Mr. Bell had promised her father that he would leave to her on his death. Surely, he would come to her aid now, if he knew.

Dixon had started to take in laundry and ironing, which would help in the future. It paid a mere few pence more than standing at a weaving machine. As Milton's industrial town began to blossom into an international trading city, more jobs were opening up. Margaret was still hoping she could find some clerical work or perhaps be a governess. Why she ever thought that Marlborough Mills would have any such position was beyond her reasoning at the moment. She walked home slowly, thinking about the effect that John Thornton had on her. She felt besieged when those eyes of his, looked upon her again.

Margaret was uneasy about her feelings. She never felt the draw of the man when he was in her company. He seemed arrogant and prideful ... much too straightforward of a man to her liking. "A northern gentleman," she thought. That conversation came back to her. John had said he was probably not considered a gentleman such as the ones from whence she came, and she had agreed at the time. After a year, she now understood the northern gentleman better, the one that never sought status, but never took the opportunity to apologize for her behavior. She could have turned down his proposal in a friendlier manner. Margaret remembered telling him that she didn't like him. How awful that sounded to her now. It hadn't taken her many months after that to realize she had been wrong. He wasn't asking for her hand out of obligation, for her help when the rioters were at his door and she stood between them. He must have truly meant the words that he shouted at her that day. "I want to marry you because I love you." How those words had haunted her.

She cast him aside that day, and there he stayed. She knew she deserved his disfavor.

Margaret reached home after her hour's journey. "Dixon, I didn't ask him. I couldn't. He looked at me and I ran. I don't know what I was thinking."

"There, there, miss. You remembered him as once being a friend to this family. He and Mr. Higgins have been your only friends since moving here. That's all it was. You were thinking of asking a friend. That's why you were going to ask him for employment in the first place."

"Well, I never got the words out. He looked at me. I was startled at his gaze. Something happened. I told him I was silly for being there and ran. He's sure to think me a fool."

"Do you have a care what Mr. Thornton thinks of you?" Dixon asked. "There was a time when you didn't."

"Yes, I know. I've done nothing but think about that in these past long months."

"And you made a mistake back then, didn't you?"

"Dixon, you are not to be so curt with me. And no, I don't know if I made a mistake back then. I understand his feelings now, but I never knew my own. That was a time when I knew little of the northern ways, or about living in a mill town or even the ways of men. I have learned a lot since then, but as to feelings for the man, I cannot say. Father admired him, you remember. He thought John Thornton a brave and honorable man. I cannot say I have heard any words to dispute that, since then."

Margaret could not help but notice all the precious parts of her life that were now sold. Pieces of her memory had been paid for and taken away. They were gone forever. What good did it do to remember happier times? It would only make her adjustment to the future that much harder.

"What will you do tomorrow?" asked Dixon. We will have to move the following day."

"I will once more go over the bundles and trunks to see we are prepared. The linens are off of the beds, are they not?"

"Yes, miss, only a blanket to sleep under tonight and tomorrow night. The packing left will be the food that we haven't eaten, and there won't be much of that. We will have soup for lunch and dinner tomorrow. We will split an egg in the morning, and finish the bread."

"You can have the egg, Dixon. Right now, I don't feel hungry. I think I will go up and have a lay down."

"Miss Margaret, you must stop missing your meals. I know it is not a sickness, but I don't want you to eat little so that I can have it."

"Come wake me in an hour."

"Yes, miss."

Margaret went to her room and lay across her bed. She had been worrying about her situation and dealing with it for many weeks—nothing else was in her thoughts until now. Seeing John Thornton again had emerged an unknown vulnerability. She had felt flushed, embarrassed, and a bit light headed. Margaret could not understand how to deal with it, or why she ran. It was suffocating her. She took stock of herself as she lay there, realizing she had no ill feelings now, only sorrow. What had come upon her? Mr. Thornton had only spoken a few condolence words at the funeral. That was all there was between them, since she sent him away nearly a year ago. For a long time, Margaret felt she had made a mistake that day of his proposal, not so much in rejecting him, but the way in which she said it, in the words she used. Lying there, she determined that she had never apologized to him, and there she was today prepared to ask him for help. He must have thought her mad. How presumptuous that was.

Margaret went back downstairs to her writing desk that still remained. She owed John some explanation for her behavior today or he may come to inquire of her. Facing him again, was something she was not yet prepared to do, or so it seemed.

Those eyes . . . .

Chapter Two

Mr. Thornton,

Please forgive my behavior that I displayed yesterday. It is unlikely for you to believe me, but I wanted to apologize for the way I rejected your proposal, almost a year ago. I have come to learn the ways of a northern gentleman. I know I came to feel your proposal was sincere, and not one of duty as a gentleman to protect my reputation from my own actions. I know the hurt that I have caused us.

That difficult time has passed, and I hope happiness can be found in moving forward with your life. I shall never forgive myself. All of the words that were left unspoken came to me suddenly, as we spoke. I was not prepared for that–hence my hasty departure. Please disregard my statement about employment. I know I was in error to seek you out. Continued good fortune in your successful mill operations.

Regards, Margaret Hale.

Early the next morning, Margaret took her note to the gateman at Marlborough Mills. She continued from there further into the industrial area, intending to speak with other mill masters about employment. She was aghast at all of the mills that had been built in the last year. "Surely, one of the masters could use an educated clerk," she said to herself, as she walked the long, dusty road. Many men stared at her as she passed, making her feel unsafe. Her plan was to visit five factories, then return home and make final preparations for the wagon and two men coming in the morning.

Not wanting to be too close to Marlborough Mills, Margaret walked down to the newer factories, where most would not remember her from the rioting at John's mill and home. The first factory she visited was called Griffin Mills. She asked the gatekeeper where the office was, and it was pointed out to her. She knocked on the door that had "office" painted on it. There was no answer. Margaret tried the door handle, and it was open. Calling inside brought no response, but she entered and found a chair to wait. As Margaret looked around the sparse room, she felt there was not enough income to pay a clerical worker. The master would be doing his own bookkeeping. As she decided to leave, two men came in through the door talking about one of the machines. They were taken aback to see a woman in the office.

"I'm sorry, sir. I was directed here to ask about employment. I feel I have made a mistake and shall be on my way."

"Wait lass," said the owner, wondering about her motives. She could be working for someone else and just looking for something. "Please have a seat. Andrew, I will see you later about that machine."

Andrew smiled at him as if there was some other reason for his boss dismissing him so quickly. That made Margaret nervous. She looked at her surroundings and felt she could call for help if the man advanced on her.

"My name is Cecil Griffin, owner of this mill. And you are …?"

"Going to leave now if you don't mind."

"I do mind, Miss …?"

"Miss Hale."

"Why, may I ask, do I find you here?"

"I was looking for employment."

"I find that hard to believe, Miss Hale," said Cecil Griffin.

"I can understand that. That is why I think I have made a mistake and am now taking up your time."

"Were you looking for mill work?"

"I was looking for clerical work. I am not fit for the sheds."

"I see. You must have some form of education to be looking for clerk work."

"I do."

"You don't seem to be the type of lady that needs to work. Certainly, there is a man in your life–a father, brother, husband–who is bringing in an income."

"There once was, but my father passed away several months ago, and my benefactor is somewhere in the Americas. I have come to the end of my funds and must seek employment which can benefit from my education. It appears to me from your sparse office that you do your own bookkeeping. I would be obliged if you knew of any other mill master who could afford someone such as me."

"Your story sounds plausible, I guess. Where do you live?"

"I will be moving tomorrow to a flat that is more suitable to my position at the moment. I shan't think that where I live should bear any relevance to my abilities to work."

"You speak well."

"Thank you. I would like to continue my journey if I may."

"Miss Hale, I am a mill master, but not a new one. I am new to Milton and this building. No, I do not have a permanent position available, but I could pay you for two week's work while I seek out other situations for you. I have not had time to set up my books and accounts in a proper manner as yet. Does that sound like something you could do for me?"

"It would depend on the salary for the work, the hours, and ultimately your respect for me and my education."

"You don't ask for much, do you," Cecil laughed. "When could you start? You say you are moving tomorrow." Cecil mentioned a salary figure. Margaret felt it was far beneath what she would be asked to do.

"I do not believe I can start at all, sir; not at that salary."

"Excuse me," he laughed. "I have never hired a clerk before. I am unsure of the wage for someone such as yourself."

Margaret countered with an honest figure for her work.

"What? That's a man's wage."

Margaret folded her arms and said nothing.

Cecil was finding her boldness very enticing. "Miss Hale, you drive a hard bargain. I may be able to squeeze it into my opening expense budget. What needs to be done will take two weeks, I believe. I will pay you that salary for the first week. Then we will talk about the second week. Can you start in three days, on Monday?"

"What would the hours be, sir? We have not settled all of my concerns."

"Can you be here by 8:00 a.m.? You would not tell me where you live, so I don't know how far you will have to come."

"Yes, that time is agreeable. I will wish to leave by 6:00 p.m. or an hour before dark."

"I will agree to that and perhaps even earlier. There may be a couple of nights when I will ask for more hours so that I know you are underway. I will see that you arrive home safely on those nights. I see that look on your face. We will not be alone."

"Are you married, sir?"

"No, but that doesn't mean I am not a gentleman."

"Very well, Mr. Griffin. I shall see you in three days."

Cecil dropped in his chair behind his desk, as she left. He felt like a storm had just blown through his office, and he laughed to himself. He stood and walked to his window just to make sure he hadn't dreamt the last few minutes. She was walking out of the factory compound. He spotted Andrew, his foreman who had walked in with him, and now was paying a bit too much attention to her as she left.

John had been in his office for half an hour when the gateman came through the office door.

"Excuse me, Mr. Thornton, but Miss Hale, I believe it was her, delivered this note for me to give you."

John stood, taking a note from him. "When did this happen?"

"Twenty minutes ago, sir. I had a wagon coming in as she left. I had to check it against its manifest."

"Did you see which way she went?" John asked, immediately checking the signature before reading the note.

"Yes, sir. She walked further into the mills. It looked a bit strange to me—a woman like that, headed that way, alone."

"I will walk back with you and see if I can spot her." John still hadn't read the note. He only cared that he catch up with her. "Yes, you are right, it is strange."

John trotted ahead of Ewan through the gate. He looked in the direction of where Margaret had journeyed, but did not see her. He whistled for Branson to bring the coach.

Margaret had already passed Marlborough Mills heading home when John's carriage finally pulled out onto the roadway. He never found her, and she never knew he was searching for her.

As Branson was returning to his master's home, John unfolded the letter and read it. From all his actions and words over the last year, this note should have had little to no effect on him, but it did. Memories flooded back. His heart quickened. She was using words like *apologize*, and *understand*, and even *sincere*. He was determined not to slip back into his old thoughts of her. In his hands was a note that he had always hoped would come. Some understanding by her had finally been met. That was all he had wanted as the days, weeks, and months went by. She had come to him about employment for someone, and the conversation was interrupted. He had no fault in that. John had waited for the day when Margaret Hale changed her attitude. The day had come, and now he was more unsettled than before. He wasn't sure he could set this revelation aside and go on as before.

Margaret, exhausted, returned home with a bit of good news to tell Dixon. If Margaret could prove herself in that temporary position, perhaps a more steady employment may come from it by some other master.

Dixon and Margaret had their second night of soup and bread. There was a last walk through the flat and talk about remembered happenings in each room. It was a melancholy night, but Margaret was glad to have new memories to take with her. Both went to bed early as the morrow would be early and long hours.

Nicholas was sitting at his desk when John arrived with two cups of coffee.

"Good morning, John. Anything new with Miss Hale?"

"Yes. She left a note with the gatekeeper. Here it is," John said as he passed it to Nicholas.

There was quiet in the room as it was being read. John paced patiently waiting for any word from his friend. Nicholas handed it back to him.

"Well?" John inquired.

"Well what? I am not sure what you expect me to say. I know we have talked about her seeing or understanding your real feelings. It appears that she now understands what you were about, a year ago. I should think you would feel some triumph in that. I don't see you smiling, though."

"It . . . it just doesn't feel like it's enough. Can you understand that?"

"I think I can understand that you want to see her again. Perhaps, you hope she will return to you. She has stated what you have wanted to hear, hasn't she? What do you expect or want to happen?"

John sat and reflected. "You're right, Nicholas. I think I would have preferred for her to tell me to my face rather than in a letter, though."

"Apparently, it was never her intention to apologize when she arrived yesterday. She says so in the note. All the unspoken words came to her and she wasn't prepared for that."

"I can't put my finger on it, but it was more than that."

"I think you *wished* it was more than that."

"Well, what is this rubbish about employment?"

"I don't know, but I hope to soon. I sent a note to her yesterday, asking to come by. I am sure she will feel it is in regards to your brief meeting yesterday. She'll think I am coming to speak for you, I suppose. Do you want me to talk for you?" Nicholas asked, knowing John would decline.

"No. Of course, no one needs to speak for me. I intend to put this all behind, and consider that part of my life closed. I did receive what I had always hoped for, which gives me little satisfaction now."

"What about Elaine, your Mother's apparent favorite choice for you?"

"There are no changes there. Mother isn't like she once was. She saw how Miss Hale, and her opinion of her, had affected my life. She vowed to stay out of my personal affairs. It has been better, I must admit."

"Until she hears the name Margaret Hale once again."

"Nicholas, I think we have exhausted this subject. However, I would be interested in the original reason for her visit two days ago."

"I will let you know what I find out," Nicholas smiled. He knew John well enough to know there would be a reawakening ahead.

Several neighbors gathered around the door at Margaret's flat when they saw the furniture and few boxes being loaded onto a wagon. They inquired to Margaret about her moving. She was too embarrassed to say where, but let it be known that the flat was now too much for them, with her parents gone. That seemed to quell the onlookers. No one pushed her for a new address.

It was late morning and the men were setting the last of the contents on the wagon, when the post came. Margaret accepted the letter, opening it quickly. She hoped it was from Mr. Bell. It wasn't, but hearing from Nicholas Higgins was good news, too.

Margaret's face dropped.

"What is it, Miss Margaret?"

"It seems Mr. Higgins and his wife would like to come and visit with us. I cannot let that happen. I don't want them to know where we have moved. I will write a note tonight, asking for some postponement. Actually, I don't know what I will say. Let's just get on the other side of town and unpack."

Andrew walked into Master Griffin's office that morning. "Mind if I ask why that young lady was here yesterday."

"It seems she can offer a service of bookkeeping because she is educated."

"She's a pretty one, she is. I think I saw her somewhere before yesterday."

"Yes. I saw you eyeing her as she left. You leave her alone. I can use someone to help set these books up correctly, and I don't want anyone scaring her off. Now, you will be in and out of this office, so make her feel welcomed and nothing more than that. You understand?"

"Yes, guv. Anything urgent today?"

"No. I will ride into town for some supplies so she can start on Monday. Otherwise, just walk the sheds and keep the machines running."

"Aye guv."

John arrived at Mill 2, the following days, about mid-morning. Nothing further had been said about Margaret Hale since yesterday. His night had been restless, thinking about how pale she had looked and wondering why. He assumed she was still in her bereavement stage, which must be the reason for her sickly complexion. He would have to see if Mr. Bell had been in Milton lately.

John wandered through the sheds, which was his daily routine, but very few came up to him with issues. He hadn't realized he was wearing his furrowed brow and frown look. One of the foremen caught up to him.

"Did you see anything wrong, guv?"

"No. Why do you ask?"

"You're frowning. I can see the workers moving away from you today."

"I am sure you are imagining that."

"Perhaps, I am, but they aren't."

John looked at the workers who were close by. They looked almost frightened of him. "I see what you mean. I have had other things on my mind, but didn't think it was affecting my disposition. I am sorry. Please explain to anyone who asks that nothing is wrong."

"As you say, boss."

John skipped the other sheds and left for home. He could tell by the look on his driver's face that he too, saw something in it.

"All right, Branson. What is it?"

"Nothing, gov."

"Say it, so I can go on. I am frowning. Is that it?"

"If you say so, sir."

"What do you say, damn it?" John blustered.

"You appear to be in a mood of sorts today. You look worried. Is the business doing well?"

"Yes, Branson. The business is doing very well."

"Is it Miss Hale?"

"No. What makes you ask that?"

"Well, sir, it's been since she arrived on the property two days ago, that I have seen a change in you."

"There is no change and there is no Miss Hale returning."

"I am sorry to hear that."

"I do not need your sorrow, Branson." John turned towards his front door.

"What time do you want to leave tonight, sir?"

"Leave? Tonight?" John was lost.

"Yes, sir. You have an evening planned with your young lady, Miss Hawkins."

"Oh. Yes, that. I will be ready by 6:45 p.m."

Branson knew then that Miss Hale had impacted his guv, just as she had before. He knew John Thornton had never ushered her out of his heart. Apparently, he hadn't realized it, yet.

Sweet Surrender

After the wagon men had set the furniture in the tiny flat, there was little to unpack. Dixon was busy in the kitchen, where most of the boxes were taken. A few boxes of linens and clothing sat in rooms to be put away, but Margaret was depressed and wasn't up to it. It soon was clear that she had kept too many things and the small rooms were overcrowded with furniture pieces. Margaret couldn't bear to give up most of it, hoping soon that her arrangements would change. There were four rooms plus a kitchen. The loo was outside, but close. At least in these flats, she would not have to share that with the neighbors. The realization of their predicament was a ball rolling downhill towards her and she could not stop it. She was grateful that she would have two weeks of a decent salary, beginning next week.

Margaret squeezed around a chair to get to her writing desk. Opening it, she saw that papers, and ink and pens had shifted around. She tidied it and began a note to Nicholas.

Dear Nicholas and Peggy,

It was nice hearing from you and your invitation to visit. Just today, Dixon and I have moved into smaller quarters, as the flat was too large for the two of us. Perhaps you would not mind giving me a week or two to settle. I will write to you when this smaller flat is in order.

I haven't heard from Bessy since you sent her off to school. That is something that I am glad she decided to do, but I miss her terribly. I hope all of you are well. I will have to stop by and see Mary, too. I imagine she is cooking like a chef by now. I expect her to open a restaurant soon. Thank you for your friendship. I have but few.

Take care. We are doing well. Looking forward to seeing you soon.

Regards, Margaret

"John. John! What is bothering you tonight? You are paying no attention to me. Is something wrong at one of your mills?"

"Elaine, I am sorry. I have not been myself today. I am worried about an acquaintance, I once knew."

"Can you speak about his problem to me?"

"He is a she, actually."

"A she?" Elaine interjected.

"Yes. Is there something wrong with that?"

"Just what is this worry you have for her?"

"Elaine, please adjust your tone of voice. She is just a friend I haven't seen but once in over a year. That one time was at her father's funeral, and I only spoke of my condolences."

"I'm sorry. Go on."

"Two days ago, she came to the mill and was going to ask me something about employment. We never got into a conversation before she fled the grounds. My concern is that she looked sickly, and she left on foot. Also, asking about work is something I would never have expected to discuss with her. There is too much of a mystery here for me."

"And what do you intend to do about it?"

"Nothing, but Nicholas Higgins, a longtime friend of hers, will contact her. If she is in need of help, he and I will assist her."

"Of course you will. Is that settled now? Can we have our own conversation or should I wait until this situation is resolved in your mind?" Elaine said with indifference.

"Elaine, what is the problem?"

"There's no problem. May I ask what kind of a friend she was to you?"

John paused, wondering whether to reveal his personal life or not. Since they had been seeing each other for several months, he felt she was entitled. "I had asked for her hand a year ago. She turned me down, in no uncertain terms. That's all there is to say."

"I do not believe that is all there is to say. There is more I wish to know, if you would be so kind."

"I will not be so kind. What is it, you must know?"

"What is she to you now?"

"I cannot even be sure we are friends. I would think we are not."

"How does she compare to me?"

"Elaine, it is inconceivable that you ask such a question."

"But you feel you want to help her?"

"No. Not really. I would like to solve the mystery if there is one. If she is in dire need, which I doubt, Nicholas and I will help. Now, that brings us to the end of this childish conversation."

"There would have been no conversation if you had not left me alone in your mind."

"I apologize, again." John was exasperated.

Chapter Three

Sunday morning came. Nicholas and Peggy were having their morning meal. Their daughter, Mary, had risen early and set off to Marlborough Mills to begin the day cooking at the canteen. Even as wealth had now come to the Higgins household, Mary enjoyed cooking and the attention she received.

"Nicholas, I know you sent a note to Margaret, but I would feel better if we just rode by her home. It worries me, what you have told me."

"Yes, it does as well for me. John doesn't realize it yet, but his feelings for her are surfacing again. He will be talking to himself before long. He could realize it and is hiding the fact, or he could repress it and erupt any day. I would like to be one step ahead of him for his sake as well as Margaret's. I'll rig the buggy, and we'll take a spin near her flat."

"Perhaps you can be ahead of him enough so that he's not asking you to mind the mills while he's finding his fate." Peggy laughed. "Have you met this Elaine Hawkins?"

"Yes, I have. She has been to the office several times to wait for John's return from somewhere. She's like every other woman he's taken time with. I know he loved Margaret more, but I think he's getting ready to settle. He is a loving man. He wants someone to share his life and raise a family. Most men want that at heart. John is badgered by women when they know he is not seeing anyone on a regular basis. Sometimes I think he stays with one just to put off the others. I never thought to be tall, handsome, dark-headed and wealthy would cause so much upheaval in one's life. He is an unhappy man at his core. I would hate to think what his mother is saying to him. I'm sure he tires of her suggestions."

"John, you have been rather moody of late. What is bothering you? Are there issues with Miss Hawkins?"

"No, mother," John said from behind his newspaper.

"Well something is wrong. It shows on your face and in your silence. You are introspective. Is it the mills?"

"Mother, I am worried about Miss Hale. Please do not say anything to make me walk out of here." John kept pretending to read, not fully prepared to engage his mother in a conversation about Miss Hale.

Flustered by his answer, Hannah Thornton was taken aback. She had not heard her son utter Miss Hale's name for a very long time. Memories quickly sprang to mind involving her interference, which broke her son's heart when he was rejected as a husband. She had never seen him so depressed. His demeanor took many forms. He hated that people were feeling sorry for him. His pride was hurt, his heart broken.

"May I ask any questions?"

"I wish you wouldn't."

"Could you at least tell me if she is well?"

"No, I cannot."

"Do you mean you won't or you don't know?"

John threw the paper to the floor and stood. "I saw her briefly a few days ago. I felt she looked pale." Shoving his hands in his pockets, John walked to the window that overlooked the mill yard, leaving his back to his mother.

"Did you see her passing on the street or visit her?"

"Neither. She walked here and asked about employment. Before I could answer her, she said she was in error seeking me out. She fled the house. May I leave the witness box, now?"

"Do you remember me telling you how her dying mother asked me to look after her when she was gone?"

"Mother, you are not going over there under any circumstances. It would be my place to inquire about her, not yours."

"And will you?"

"No."

"I see. So you will spend your days moping around here and the office, wondering why she looks pale. I thought you finally laid that ghost to rest."

John seethed, hearing those words. He turned quickly, grabbed his coat and left the house, uncharacteristically slamming the door. Nicholas was off today and John decided to calm down before heading into the weaving sheds. He stormed over to his office.

"Mother?" Fanny called as she came from the hall. "What's my brother done now? Are you two fighting?"

"Fanny, you know we never fight. It seems Miss Hale stopped by the other day. John said she looked pale. Now he worries about her."

"Miss Hale? What business does she have with John? This family can't go through John's moods as we did a year ago."

"Fanny, don't you have compassion for anyone?"

"Not Margaret Hale. And I should think you would not have patience or compassion for that woman, either."

"We interfered before, and you see what happened to your brother," Hannah reminded her daughter.

"We? I don't recall having a hand in that. You were the one who pushed John into a proposal that he wasn't ready to make. She brought it on herself—standing between John and the rioters as if she was shielding him. That was an insult to him, and you know it. In order to rescue Miss Hale from her own mistake, you convinced my brother to ask for her hand. She's smart. I'll have to give her that. Margaret Hale saw through that. John, as a gentleman, had an obligation to save her reputation by marrying her."

"He did love her, you knew that, didn't you?"

"As it turned out, John did not feel she was ready to be proposed to by a northern man, who differed much from the southern gentleman. But ask he did, mother, and she rejected him. I am not ready for another bout of Miss Hale."

"You will not speak in that tone of voice, young lady."

Fanny turned and left the room, heading back upstairs.

Hannah pulled herself slowly to her feet. She walked to the mill yard window and looked over at John's office. He was pacing the room. It seemed as if Miss Hale was going to split the family again. *Why can't she leave us alone?*

Dixon found the one egg and hard bread for their breakfast. She brewed a nice cup of tea and wondered how to cheer up her mistress.

"Good morning, Dixon. Did you sleep well?"

"Good morning, mum. The room has a smell to it, but it didn't bother my sleep."

"Dixon, I don't think it is your room with the smell, it's the area. We are only a few streets over from the Princeton district. I am not sure if you have ever been there, but scraps and human waste can be seen along the streets. It's a terrible and disease-ridden place, too. Thankfully, we are spared from living within those boundaries, but we are close. If we both work, we shall be able to make ends meet, here."

"Miss, my sister would take us in before we have to go lower than we are now. I could manage it, but I wouldn't want you to have a life like that."

"Dixon, misfortunes touch everyone at some time in their life. This is mine and yours. It is not of our making, and we are not giving up. We are not people who need charity. I believe one will eventually adapt to their surroundings and make the best of it. They have no other choice. We should not pine over the situation we have left behind. The flat has changed considerably, but there are still many friendly people in the area, I suppose."

"Well mum, you will not live lower than this. Where is your aunt? Does she not know of your plight?"

"She too is somewhere on the continent, traveling. I wish never to have her involved in my life. She would help. Indeed, she would, but I want to make it on my own. Could you pass the bread and my tea cup?"

Nicholas and Peggy arrived close to Margaret's former flat. They had to walk a bit to get to her home, as the street was crowded with vendors.

"Nicholas, look! There are no drapes on the windows. That is very odd."

"Yes, it is, love."

Nicholas knocked on the door. He rapped several times and then again. No answer. "I don't think they're home, Peggy. If fact, it looks like no one lives here."

Nicholas turned to talk with one or two of the vendors near Margaret's doorway.

"You, sir."

The scruffy man pulled his cap from his head, courtesy to the gentleman before him. "Me, sir?"

"Yes. Do you know anything about the tenants living here?" Nicholas pointed to the door.

"Aye, sir. Yesterday, a wagon and two men moved their furniture and boxes out of there."

"Where did they go?"

"They never said. Only told us that the flat was too large for them and they were going to a smaller one."

"When they left, were they in a carriage?"

"No, sir. They rode on the wagon with the men."

"I see. Is that all you can tell me?"

"'Tis all I know, sir."

Nicholas handed him some silver. "If you find out anything further, come to Marlborough Mills and ask for Higgins, that's me. You will be paid. Do you understand?"

"Aye, sir. Yes, sir. Thank you, sir. I surely will." The man backed away, bowed and replaced his hat.

Peggy overheard the conversation "I'm not sure I like this. It is most unlike Margaret to move without telling us."

"I don't like this either, and coupled with the fact that John thought she looked pale makes it much worse. We should probably ride over and tell him."

"Yes. He might become upset if he knew you held something back for a day."

"He is trying to act disinterested in the whole affair, but I know different."

Two brothers, James and Jeremy Wishaw, sat at their morning table having tea. James was a higher-lever mill worker than Jeremy. However, Jeremy was being trained for more responsibility at a different mill.

James, forty-four years of age, had two years on Jeremy. Many folks thought they were twins, as both had yellow hair and brown eyes.

"You weren't here yesterday, were you? It seems we have new neighbors across the street. One is a sweet little thing. The other must be her mother. The young one was dressed real nice. I wonder if they need any help settling in."

"Well, I guess we could ask them. Maybe they need furniture moved around. Did they bring any?"

"Actually, quite a lot. I don't know where they put it all. It was nice stuff, too. They must have moved from a larger flat. I bet they've fallen on hard times," suggested Jeremy. "I think I'll sit out on the front stoop later today."

"Suit yourself, brother."

John was still pacing in his office when Nicholas and Peggy's coach rolled into the yard. Seeing Peggy, John immediately assumed they had word about Margaret. He went to the office door and opened it before they got there.

"Good morning, you two. You are out early for a Sunday. Church, was it?"

"No, John. We took a ride over to Margaret's flat."

John tried to look uninterested. "And how did you find her?"

"She wasn't home," Nicholas added.

"Oh. Perhaps another time." John turned his back, not showing his disappointment

"She's moved, John. A vendor near her door said she left yesterday."

"Moved, did you say?" John replied, turning and facing Nicholas.

"Apparently so. He said a wagon came and picked up their furniture and boxes. They told someone, I don't know who, they were moving to smaller quarters. The flat was too big for just the two of them."

"It is probably a good idea."

"Maybe so," Peggy remarked. "The vendor said they rode on the wagon when it pulled away."

"Hmmm… I hope she received your note before they left. I am sure she will write soon and let you know their new situation."

Peggy looked at Nicholas and knew he doubted John's uninterested demeanor.

"John, Peggy and I agree that we have some concern. You did say she looked pale, did you not?"

"I did. Thin, too," added John.

"That doesn't bother you, just as a former friend to her?"

"Yes, it troubles me. She was here and quickly left. I would like to know that she is well. I believe two women think my life is about to change with Miss Hale's reappearance, and are separately mounting defensive stances."

"Such as…? Of course—your mother and Miss Hawkins," Nicholas intimated. "And that scares you, does it? Peggy and I will continue to investigate where she has moved and anything about her health. I will keep you abreast of any news."

John ignored the condescension. "Please, do. Let me know if there is anything I can do."

They said their goodbyes to John, and departed.

John slammed his fist on the desk after they left. He had lost hope long ago. This was going to be a nightmare, if he became optimistic. At the moment, he felt like a coward. He was stuck. He couldn't move towards her or away from her. Towards her could mean another broken heart. He would never survive it. Away from her was impossible to contemplate. John wondered if she was in need of something and if he helped, could he stop there. How would Miss Hawkins react, and even his mother?

John argued with himself. Why did he feel obligated to his mother or Elaine and not himself? Whose life was it? From her note, it sounded as if Miss Hale could have had doubts about her rejection. If she had moved to smaller quarters, it would be unlikely that she had married. That thought brought bile to his throat. Where in this Godforsaken city were there smaller quarters?

Financial worries were starting to sound plausible. Smaller flat, pale, thin, employment … it was adding up.

John walked back towards his stable and asked Branson to harness the carriage. Leaving Branson, he strode to his sheds and spoke with the weekend foremen about expectations. He was departing to look for Adam Bell.

Margaret stood in the middle of the sitting room, with her hands on her hips. "Dixon, what can we do about this furniture? It looked beautiful in mother and father's home, but it seems very out of place now."

"Remember, miss. This is just temporary."

"Yes, I must learn to believe that. We've got to shift a few pieces to allow a path for ourselves. We have to purchase some food today, too. It would seem that is the most urgent task. I will have to find a clean frock for work tomorrow, as well. Let us find a grocer first."

"Yes, miss."

Dixon and Margaret donned their shawls, bonnets, and baskets. Margaret slipped some coin into her pocket before leaving the house. Both were accosted with the smell as they stepped outside. Margaret tried to wave it away from her nose, but gave up. Both women had their heads down and were seen grimacing as they strolled the walkway.

Jeremy watched them and noticed they spoke to several people on their way, with one pointing in a direction. Margaret and Dixon turned left at the next block. Having nothing better to do, he took up behind them, but at a distance. He looked down at himself to see if he was presentable to introduce himself to the young lady. He wasn't.

Margaret and Dixon walked slowly, looking over the shop names and into the windows. Dixon heard Margaret sigh.

"Here we are, Dixon. I will look at the meat and you collect the rest."

It was a small room with only ones and twos of various foods. Dixon looked at the fresh vegetable crates outside, finding satisfaction with those. Margaret saw no meat.

"Excuse me, sir, are you the proprietor?"

"I am, miss. How can I help you? I haven't seen your face before."

"My mai–friend and I moved here yesterday. We have to stock our larder."

"Your larder? I didn't know anyone around here had one of those."

"You are right. That's a word I picked up from my last employer." Margaret lied. "I do not see any meat for sale."

"No, miss. Not here. No one can afford it, so the butcher moved his shop nearer the high-rent area long ago. You would have to take several more streets and a few turns before you come to him."

"I see. I guess we'll make a special day to visit, but not today. Thank you. We shall finish selecting our needs."

Although healthy, Margaret envisioned their meals being vegetables and bread. Finding some eggs and butter, she placed them in her basket.

"You may find a man with a donkey and cart selling fish. Once a week, he travels the streets. Just check it good, mind you, and smell it before you buy. The fish may be a week old."

"Thank you for that information. I see we are ready to purchase our goods." Margaret wondered how they would get that weight home. There was a sack of potatoes, heads of cabbage, carrots and other items. At her other flat, those would have been delivered, but now they must be carried home.

Jeremy was watching when they departed the grocer with their cumbersome packages. Both women had heavy baskets. In addition, the pretty little one carried a sack of flour, while the other seemed to be struggling with a cloth pouch of potatoes. They had traveled to the end of the street by weaving around groups of people and merchandise which was displayed outside. Arriving at the corner, they set their bundles down and rested. As he approached them, they were having a conversation about how long it would take them to reach home with all the resting.

"Excuse me, ladies. My name is Jeremy Wishaw. I believe I saw the two of you moving into the flat across the street from me. I am headed home, and I would very much like to assist with your items." Jeremy doffed his cap.

"Mr. Wishaw," said Margaret, "you are most kind, but I believe we can manage."

"Pardon me, but I don't believe you can. I watched you struggling, and you have several streets to negotiate. I am not going to take off and run with your food. As poor as this area is, there is very little stealing. I promise, I only want to carry some of that weight for you."

"Sir, I cannot pay you."

"Pay me?" Jeremy looked insulted. "You really are new to this part of town, aren't you? It seemed so, as I watched all that furniture go into that small flat yesterday. No one around here pays for anything. We just help each other."

"Mr. Wishaw, we will kindly accept your offer."

Jeremy took the two heavy sacks and left the women with the baskets. He led the way so they could keep an eye on him.

"I don't mean to pry, but may I ask your names?"

"Yes. Of course. My name is Margaret Hale and this is Dixon."

"And Dixon, are you her mother?"

Before Dixon could blurt out the word maid or housekeeper, Margaret replied, "Dixon is my guardian. She has been with me since my birth. My parents recently passed away leaving her and me."

"I take it you are still in your bereavement stage, wearing that black frock as you are."

"Yes."

"I am mighty sorry about that. I live with my brother, across from you. He is becoming a foreman at Christianson Mills, and I work at another."

The one-sided conversation continued until they reached home. Jeremy was shown through to the kitchen when they arrived. Setting the heavy sacks on the kitchen work table, he remarked, "You seem cramped in here. My brother and I would be very glad to help you arrange your furniture. Today would be best, as we are both home."

Margaret looked at Dixon's expression, which said no. "I am sorry. We have taken up your time today. Perhaps next week. I am not sure where I want things to go as yet."

"Well, you just let us know. Usually, we are home in the evenings, too."

"Thank you. You have been most obliging."

"Very well, ladies, if that will be all, I will take me leave."

Margaret walked him to the door, thanking him once again. Through the curtains, she watched him cross the street and enter his flat.

John Thornton arrived at the Milton Grand Hotel, where Adam Bell always stayed, entered, and asked for the owner.

He waited a few minutes for the man to be located.

"Ah. Mr. Thornton. This is early for you. Can I help you with a reservation for dinner?"

"Not this time. I am looking for information about my friend, Adam Bell."

"Oh yes. Mr. Bell, a college professor. What can I do to help?"

"Has he been here recently?"

"I don't believe so, Mr. Thornton. He informed us that he was headed for the Americas for several months. Let me check our guest register for the last time he was here."

"I would appreciate that."

The registration book was thumbed looking for his signature while a clerk was looking for his guest card. "Excuse me, sir," the man said, handing the card to the owner.

"Mr. Thornton, it says he was here a little over four months ago. If he were to be gone several months, I should expect him any time now. Would you care to leave a note for him?"

"Yes, I would." John was handed a folded note card and a pen.

Adam,
Please contact me immediately upon arrival. Urgent.
John Thornton.

John folded the note and returned it where it would lay in wait for Adam Bell. He hoped Adam had not succumbed to his illness while abroad, which could begin to look likely now. If Margaret were to inherit some financial security from him, it could take months before reaching her.

"Thank you, sir."

"Our pleasure as always, Mr. Thornton."

John rode quietly home. What more could he do? There had to be some simple explanation for this mystery. In his mind, John went back to where it began for him.

Margaret had arrived on foot. It must be assumed she walked from her flat, as there was no sign of even a hackney coach waiting on her. That in itself signaled limited means. She seemed to hesitate to enter his home, apparently because of his mother's previous attitude toward her. She said she might falter. "With great humility" she spoke in reference to asking about employment. Those words had taken his attention away from studying her gaunt appearance. Being startled by her words and thrown off balance, John had stared at her in disbelief. It was then that she made her excuses and fled the house.

What happened at that moment? Did she look into his face and feel remorse for the past? Had he inadvertently shown his once great love for her in his eyes? Everything turned on those few seconds, it seemed to him. She was in a humble mood at the time. What was left to make her shy away?

Chapter Four

American States: Somewhere in Georgia

The Hale family's closest friend and dearest to Margaret, Adam Bell, was lying in bed struggling to breathe. Fearing he would never again return to London or Milton, he thought it time to post a letter to John Thornton, whom he knew quite well.

To my dear friend, John Thornton,

By the time this letter reaches you, I am sure I will have passed from this life. The warm and moist climate here in the southern states has taken its toll on me, leaving very little time to put everything in order.

I am most upset that I had no time to return home and visit with Margaret for the last time. Death: it is not a gentleman.

I write to you because I still believe Margaret is in your soul and always will be. I think you will always have her best interest in your heart. I am asking a great favor–that you be the one to tell her of my demise. She is going to need comforting and someone to oversee my holdings that have been left to her until she is ready to take her own control.

I have written to my solicitor and my college. Aside from clothing and books, my personal items will be sent to you for your own choice of disposal. There are very few. Letters confirming my demise will follow very shortly after my death. I will be buried here, as it makes no matter to me, and I do not care to have Margaret crying over another grave. She has had far too many, for such a young woman.

My solicitor will contact you when the time comes, as I know you will still be at Marlborough Mills. I assume Margaret will have returned to her Aunt Shaw's by now.

I know you are aware of my very fond regard for the Hale's and Margaret, especially. If I could trust her to anyone other than myself, it would be you. John, I know she loves you. Whether she knows it or not or is too proud to renew your affections, you are the only man she will ever love. Being as close as I have been to her, I could see it wilting inside of her. Yes, she made a grave mistake a year back, but it was her naïveté that trapped her. I will always believe your proposal was sincere and not one of duty. Margaret, of course, felt differently at that time. We have spoken little of it since it happened, but a sadness came upon her, the likes of which I have never seen. Richard and I were at a loss to help her. She didn't know how to speak of love to anyone. Being raised as a clergyman's daughter, has built walls around her—ones over which she is only now trying to climb.

I write these final words, as she will be my last thoughts on this earth. You are not mentioned in my will, but I leave my most precious possession to you, Margaret Hale. Please watch over her as I wished I could have done. She became my world.

John, don't change. Keep your pride, your ethics, manners and gentlemanly deportment. I feel certain a happy life is still ahead of you. Keep Margaret safe.

A friend for all times,
Adam Bell

Monday came, with Margaret beginning her walk to work at 6:30 a.m. It was barely light, as the grey overcast smoky sky could not be seen. She hadn't walked far when she fell into crowds of workers headed in the same direction. She kept her head down, and many people were giving her a brief stare. *It must be my frock.* Tomorrow she would look for a different one to wear—nothing with lace or fancy stitching. A man bumped into her, nearly knocking her over. He never realized it and continued walking. Margaret had caught her step before she fell.

"Nice manners, these here men," a female voice said from behind. "Ye all right, deary? Ye is a little one. If ye fall, they'll just walk over top of ye." The well-worn woman of advanced age stayed with Margaret until she was fit to carry on.

"Thank you. I am much obliged. Is it always like this?" Margaret asked.

"At this time of day, it is. 'Bout the same going home. If ye can leave a little earlier or later, ye might avoid it. Those mill horns blare at 7:00 a.m."

"I am early, I suppose."

"Your first day, miss?"

"Yes. I was told to report at 8:00 a.m."

"Lucky you. What kind of work you be doin'?"

"I will only work for two weeks. I will assist a Master in setting up his bookkeeping area."

"Educated, are ye?"

"Yes, somewhat." Margaret felt horrible, as if she were taking away a poorer person's mill job. "I recently lost my mother and father and the income he provided" she thought she should add.

"No man, deary?"

"No man." Margaret immediately saw John's eyes piercing her own, as they did several days ago.

"What mill ye at?"

"A…a…Griffin, I believe. I'll know it when I see it."

"That one there is Marlborough Mills." The lady mentioned as they walked passed it. "Too bad ye can't get work there. Everyone wants to work for Thornton."

"Why is that?" Margaret asked with real interest.

"He's fair. Pays fair. Cares about his people. He heads up all the Mill Masters in some organization. I don't pay no attention to politics 'round here, but they like him."

"I see."

"What's ye name, lass?"

"Margaret. And yours?"

"They call me Sally. My real name is Samantha, but they've gone and started callin' me, Sally. Anyone called ye Maggie?"

"No, not yet," Margaret laughed. It had been a long time since she had smiled.

"I don't know nothing about Griffin. He's new, I think. That's 'bout all we talk about anymore—is our masters. I hope you got a good one. I work further down at Christianson's. I work in the carding room."

"What is that?"

"Deary, how long you been in Milton?"

"Two years."

"Two years, is it? Seems more liken two weeks. The carding room is where we takes the raw cotton and untangle and clean it. We gets it ready to be woven on a shuttle for the weavers."

"I see. I've been at home since school taking care of my aging parents. I never got around the mills very often."

"Well, deary, there's your mill up there. See it?"

"Yes. Thank you for the enjoyable talk on the way this morning. I hope to see you again."

"Fare thee well, m'dear. Good luck to ye."

Margaret watched Sally walk on, when she stopped in front of the Griffin mill entrance. With Sally, it was almost like having Bessy beside her. How their lives had changed.

Margaret realized that she and Bessy had changed places. How fast the world can turn on you, she thought–from Prince to pauper, and from pauper to Prince. Margaret opened the office door and entered.

"Miss Hale, lovely to see you this day. I have spent the weekend gathering supplies for you, creating a desk area and piling the invoices in date order. Please hang up your shawl and bonnet here. I want to give you a tour."

Margaret did as she was asked, and followed Mr. Griffin up a flight of stairs. She was beginning to feel weakness in her legs.

"Miss Hale, this is where I live. This floor and the one above it. I have a housekeeper, Mrs. Brom, who will bring you coffee or tea several times a day. I bring you up here because you will use my personal facilities and not the mills. It's right down that hall," he pointed.

"Thank you, Mr. Griffin. It is not necessary."

"I think it is, and I wish you to see it that way. I would rather you not be out in the yard."

"I am obliged."

"Now, let's go back down and I will show you through the mill."

"Is that really essential, Master Griffin?"

"I would like you to become familiar with a few of the faces that may be coming and going from the office. I thought you might like it this way, rather than having them all come to a meeting to meet you."

"Yes, yes, I believe so. Carry on."

"Carry on?" he laughed. "All right, I shall. Several men have permission to purchase for the company, and you will see where I am most of the day, should I be needed."

"I shall follow."

"Nonsense. Walk beside me. You are being paid as a foreman and will be accorded the same courtesy."

"But, I shan't be here very long."

"We shall see. My budget may tell me how invaluable you are to this factory."

Just as her first meeting of John Thornton, Mr. Griffin rolled the big door open to a room cascading with white fluff. As loud and as dangerous as that room could be, it was still beautiful seeing it for the first time.

Master Griffin took her up on the walk to oversee the looms and workers. He shouted sharply into her ear when he was pointing out something in particular. From that room, she was shown the carding room, a canteen, the warehouses for incoming and outgoing material—raw and processed. She met the foremen of each area. They would be in and out of the office several times a day with papers, bills of laden, manifests, and other assorted expenses.

Next came the factory facilities area, the stables and a small meeting room, which brought them back to the office next door.

"Do you have any immediate questions thus far, Miss Hale?"

"What do you do when a worker is injured?"

"Most of the time, we have someone who can patch them up, but otherwise they are carried to a doctor."

"And the company pays for that?"

"Yes, of course, unless we find gross negligence or some type of sabotage. We have never had a negligence case. No one can afford to lose their jobs."

"And the other?"

"Disgruntled workers can cause a lot of damage. I cannot say that hasn't happened to any Master."

"Do you feel your workers respect you and your ways of treating them?"

"I do. You have some rather interesting questions. Also, I am very careful in selecting anyone in a leadership position. Are you ready to begin your day in the office?"

"Yes. I am eager."

Master Griffin showed Margaret where her desk was and his. They both were in the same room, but it was the second room in from the front office door. The wall separating the two rooms was half wood and half glass. She would be able to see anyone that entered, yet it afforded the Master some semblance of privacy to speak of matters not for the waiting public.

"Miss Hale, you will see that I have purchased a second set of journals. I am sure what I have done is cocked up, and I wish you to organize everything by date and pen it a second time. When I am satisfied that your accounts have included everything in my initial work, I will dispose of them. Do you understand the principle of debit and credit—bills and income?"

"Yes, I do, sir. I was schooled in clerking. That was a high level of achievement if a woman held the position of such responsibility."

"I see that bothers you, why?"

"I do not think you would be interested in my opinion."

"But, I would, Miss Hale. It will give me an insight into your ability."

"If educated, I believe a woman can hold any position that a man can, unless it involves strength."

Mr. Griffin smiled. "I see. Have I hired a loose cannon?" he laughed.

Margaret couldn't help it. She laughed as well.

"Mr. Griffin, I should tell you this before I start. I will not, even under your order, falsify any bookkeeping. I will not hide sales; I will not inflate purchases. If you ask me to do that, I shall leave your employ. If one of your men ask me to do that, I will come to you."

"Fair enough, Miss Hale. I am glad to hear you say that on your own. I hope you will always speak your mind in regards to any part of the business. Another set of eyes is always preferred."

"I do speak my mind and I hope you don't come to regret hiring me," she smiled.

"Today, I will be in and out of here as I expect you to have questions as you begin. You will come to our 'end of shift' meeting in the room next door at 5:00 p.m."

"Yes, sir."

"I believe you met Andrew, my chief foreman?"

"No, I believe he left the room, and I was never introduced."

"Very well. When I see him, I will send him to meet you. Make a list of any supplies you can use. Do not try to scrape by on what's here. I want it done right."

"Yes, I will."

"Then I shall leave you to your pile of papers."

"Thank you for giving me this chance," Master Griffin.

"I have a feeling I will be thanking you for wandering in here. Good morning, Miss Hale," Mr. Griffin said, leaving the office.

Margaret was finally alone. She began to walk the room and familiarize herself with where supplies were stored, sales records kept, bills of lading were matched with the purchase orders and the billing of the items. As she pulled out the drawers, she collected the papers inside. No doubt these would be matched to the work Mr. Griffin had entered. She wanted to see the full accounting. She wondered who handled the payroll and the hours worked by each worker. Margaret went to her desk and wrote down her first question.

In early afternoon, Peggy pulled her small buggy into Marlborough Mill's yard. She went to the office, but neither John nor Nicholas was there. She walked to the canteen and found them.

John and Nicholas were sitting together talking with the workers while her daughter was serving the incoming shift.

Seeing his wife come through the door, Nicholas stood and waved, hailing her attention.

"She's heard from Miss Hale," John said aloud.

"Are you psychic now, John?" Nicholas laughed.

Sitting next to her husband, Peggy handed Nicholas the post. He looked at the sender and then sternly at John.

"I knew it."

Nicholas read it aloud. There was quiet among the three of them when he finished.

"Is that all? Was there no return address?" John asked stoically.

"She may not have remembered her new address when she wrote this. Apparently she was in a hurry," suggested Peggy.

"Or she doesn't want us to know where she lives," John scoffed.

"John, what makes you think such a thing? Yes, it is a mystery, but you seem to have some worry over it."

"Add it up, Nicholas."

"What am I to add, John? Tell me."

"I am sorry. I guess I haven't mentioned all that I have learned."

"What the devil are you talking about? What have you added together?"

"She walked into Marlborough Mills inquiring about employment. She *walked*, mind you. From there, she was seen continuing further into the mills. Why would she be asking about work in the first place? I doubt she was looking for work for someone other than herself or Dixon. If the work had been for someone else, I do not think she would have said that she made an error in seeking us out. I have inquired at the Grand about Adam Bell. He has been in the Americas for many months. He never came to her father's funeral. If she were in financial difficulty, he would not allow it. We talked about this long ago. If he thinks her father is still alive, he has assumed they are thriving well enough. Now, she writes to you and, I believe, deliberately does not disclose her whereabouts. What does that tell you?" John questioned.

"I hope you're wrong, John."

"As do I. As do I," he repeated, looking off towards the window.

"John, let's go back to the office. There are some things I would like to get straight in my mind."

"Very well."

"You two go ahead. I want to speak to Mary," Peggy proposed.

John and Nicholas carried their dishes to the washing area and left the building. Peggy went to find her daughter.

"Mother, what are you doing here," Mary brightened.

"I've had a note from Margaret which is somewhat upsetting. I wanted John and your father to see it. Mary, have you heard anything about Margaret or Miss Hale? Any rumors? Anything?"

"No, should I have?"

"I hope not. She may be in very reduced circumstances and looking for work. She and Dixon have recently moved from their flat. We have no idea where."

"That is so very sad to hear. I remember when we were that way. What can I do?"

"You don't need to do anything, except listen for any word of her. Someone may see her and speak to another."

"You don't think she could be in the Princeton area, do you?"

"I don't know what to think. Just be on the watch. That's all."

"I will, mother. I will."

Entering the office, "John, I want to know about any feelings you still have for Margaret Hale."

Chapter Five

"Nicholas, I can't see how that is of much concern to you, now, a year after my… my failed efforts."

"As your partner and most of all, your friend, I would like to know how deeply you feel you will be involved in this."

"This what, exactly?"

"This concern of Margaret."

"I will be very concerned until I know she is not suffering in any way. I cannot stand by when a friend is in dire need."

"Friend, is she then?"

John fell into his office chair with a thud. Placing his elbows on the desktop and holding his head in his hands, "How can I give you a word for what she is to me? She will always mean a lot, but I think it ends there. Even though I thought she was back in London until I saw her at her father's funeral, she knew I was here. There had been no attempt to contact me, if her feelings for me had changed."

"And Miss Hawkins?"

John became angered. He stood rigidly. "Nicholas, I think this stops now. I have told you of my unease over Miss Hale. I cannot see where Miss Hawkins enters into this."

"And you can't foretell the future either," Nicholas said in a cocky tone."

"Spit it out, Higgins," John said. "If you have something to say, say it. Are you waiting for me to speak the words that Miss Hale will not bring me down again?"

"You can't say it, can you? No, you cannot. Above all, I don't want to hear or see what happened to you before, ever in my life. If there is nothing there, then allow Peggy and me to solve this and you stay away from it. You don't know it, but I see how affected you are by it. I see the pain in your face now. I can't let that happen to you."

"Nicholas, your worry for me is heartfelt. I learned more than you know, a year ago. I have built a wall around my emotions so I will never bear that again. Do not worry about me. Is it the mill? You're not worried about the mill, are you? We have men in place. If I am not front and center of these mills, it doesn't mean you will have to take time from your family much more than you do now."

Nicholas hung his head. "It's not the mills at all, and you know it. I know they will survive. It's you for who I worry. I cannot stand by and watch my best friend disintegrate before my eyes. I'm not sure you'll make it."

John sat down again and swiveled his chair so his back was to Nicholas. "I won't make it through another time," John finally admitted. "But her note to me gave the tiniest bit of hope."

"There. There is the real answer I was looking for."

"Well … now you have it." John tore out of the room and headed towards Mill 2.

Nicholas knew John was upset with himself. His feelings for her now made him feel weak, and he didn't like being a slave to them. Love had thrown down the gauntlet for John, and he knew he must pick it up.

Cecil came into the office on his way upstairs for his dinner. Margaret was busy with papers in little piles everywhere.

"I see you have jumped into the deep end, Miss Hale. Are you swimming?" Cecil laughed.

"Quite well, actually, sir. I do have two questions thus far. First, I will say that I have pulled all of the invoices from the drawers for everything. I want to go over what you entered and also match purchase orders with goods received and goods paid for. I hope that meets with your approval."

"Miss Hale, you have gone past my expectations. Continue."

"Would I assume that you, Andrew and the two foreman in the sheds have purchasing approval?"

"That would be correct. No one else. Next?"

"Are any personal or household items included among the business expenses?"

"That is a bit different. No, my home and expenses are separate, unless I am entertaining for business purposes. You can set those aside and I will take a look at them. My … that is thorough. Anything else?"

"Who is in charge of wages? Who accounts for the time spent by each worker?"

"Each worker is paid full hours, and we only track those who worked more or less. The two foreman take care of their own, and we discuss it every day at our meeting."

"Even though you did not hire me for that accounting, do you wish that I remain uninvolved?"

"Miss Hale, are you trying to become indispensable already?" Cecil laughed.

"No sir. Accounting is just that. I feel accountable for every pound and pence spent. I can see that part of it will be left to others."

"Miss Hale, you are clerking for me, not being an accountant. I have a team that oversees my work once a month. Thank you for the offer. I only want you to book money going and coming for goods, and company expenses."

"Thank you, sir. I am clear on your scope of work expected."

"Good. Now, take a break and have your lunch."

"Yes, sir."

Cecil climbed the steps. Margaret pulled out an apple that she had bought two days ago. She walked outside to eat it as she sat on the bench in front of the office. The workers were coming and going. Dust was wafting up as a horse and full wagon were leaving the mill.

"Good day, Miss Hale."

Startled, Margaret turned around, looking into the brightness, saying, "And good day to you." She weaved back and forth until the face fell into shadows. "Are you Andrew?"

"Yes, I am. Is this a bad time? It looks like you are having part of your lunch."

"This is a good time."

"I came to introduce myself. I am the overseer of the two foremen and all the mill workers. I am Mr. Griffin's eyes and ears."

"Do you have many disgruntled workers?"

"A few. It wouldn't be a mill if it didn't. Mills do not pay decent wages, but it's not the mill master's fault. It's a business. Can you understand that?"

"I am sure I can. It will definitely show itself to me as I put Master Griffin's books in order. How does your wage compare to the other masters? Are all the mills the same?"

"Mostly. There are a few masters with a lot of experience who have found a way to pay a bit more, but not all that much."

"I must be getting back to my work, Andrew. Thank you for coming by to meet me."

As Margaret stood, Andrew was still sitting down on the bench. Looking up at her, he remembered. "I knew I had seen you before."

"I'm sorry?"

"You were the woman at Marlborough Mills the day of the riot. Wasn't that you?"

"Margaret looked embarrassed. Yes, it was I. I was there to see Mrs. Thornton when the crowd gathered. I must get back to work. Please excuse me."

Looking quite content with himself, Andrew rose to his feet. "Yes, Miss Hale. I must return myself. I shall see you at the shift-end meeting. Will I not?"

"That is correct. Good day for now, Andrew." Margaret rushed into the sanctity of the inner office.

She sat at her desk and stared at the piles of paper. It had been a shock, but she remembered, all to well, why. She thought of it for a few minutes before she recollected how that one day had changed her life. Unfamiliar with northern ways, she had tried to protect a man from harm … a respected mill master. It was of great detriment to his character that a female tried to intervene on his behalf. Margaret knew her intentions had been good, but the result was that Mr. Thornton would lose face in his own community and to his workers. He had to establish a reason for her actions. Being his intended wife could be viewed as an act of love, which would not injure his pride or standing.

And then I rejected his proposal. And I used hateful words.

Until now, most of her memory had focused on John's departing words. She had never given much thought to what other problems he may have encountered after that. How was his character seen the following days and weeks? Did people talk behind his back? Whatever he suffered was all on her account, yet he had to carry the burden of it. He would never have defended himself at a cost to her. He had to take whatever was said about him. How chivalrous he'd been.

Margaret felt sick. She wanted to talk more with Andrew and see where John Thornton stood in the community today. She was afraid to know. Very little could be done now. She had briefly apologized in her note to him—but it wasn't enough. Over the months after the rejection, as she came to know the way of the north, feelings for him began to surface. Her opinion of him had slowly changed, as she learned more about him, the mills, and the north. She eventually quelled those rising thoughts until he appeared at her father's funeral.

Although it was a sad time of bereavement, she had felt something seeing him there—still caring, still supportive. Margaret was falling into a deep consciousness of him staring into her eyes, only days ago. Mr. Griffin came down the steps. She roused out of her state.

"I hope you had something to eat, Miss Hale."

"I did. Andrew came by and introduced himself. He never gave me his surname. How should I address him?"

"I don't think he'd answer to anything other than Andrew. Leave it at that."

"Yes, sir."

"I will see you next door in about three hours."

"Yes, sir. I can see I will have some questions to the foremen about their notes. They are quite illegible."

"Very good. Until later then …."

Margaret set aside her study into her own reactions as John had gazed into her eyes. She returned to her tasks.

John Thornton took lunch at his home that day. He ignored his mother, and she did not challenge him on that, nor even expect an apology.

He had barely buttered his bread, when his sister swished into the room and sat at the table. John was looking at the daily paper folded beside his plate. Fanny stared at her mother, who shook her head, as if to say "Be quiet."

Fanny, never one to see the obvious, asked John, "How is Miss Hawkins, John? I have not seen much of her these days?"

"I believe her to be as she has always been," John flipped his paper over, never looking at his sister.

"Have you asked her to the ball, yet? Mr. Watson has asked me. You did know the Master's Ball is in a few weeks?"

"Yes. I do know."

Hannah Thornton was vigorously shaking her head at her daughter.

"You are going to invite her, are you not?"

"Fanny, I will tell you what I believe mother now understands: I do not want to discuss my personal affairs with the ladies in my family, and if harassed, I will be forced to move into my office."

"Seems I have struck a nerve," Fanny gloated.

"I would say you have struck them all, as is your customary behavior." John rose from the table, leaving most of his lunch uneaten. He grabbed his coat and left.

John walked around to the stable and called out for Branson.

"Yes, guv?" Branson said, coming down the outside steps from his rooms over the stable.

"When the horns blare at 5:00 p.m. for the shift's end, I want you to walk out in the roadway and watch the workers as they pass our mill. Let me know if you see Miss Hale."

"Miss Hale, sir? Walking with the workers?"

"However unlikely that sounds, you may spot her. I want to find out where she is living now. If fact, rather than coming and telling me, follow her to her home, then return and let me know."

"Yes, guv. I hope this doesn't mean what it could mean. She cannot be a mill worker."

"I am not sure what is going on with her, but something isn't right. I only want to find out if she is in need."

"Aye, guv. How long do you want me to wait?"

"Until the crowd has died down. That includes those leaving from the first shift and a few going to the second shift. I would imagine about thirty minutes."

"Aye guv."

John walked back to the office. Nicholas was not there. He sat in his chair, propping his feet on his desk. As he gazed out the window, he picked up a pencil and began tapping it on his knee. For the life of him, he could not shake the image of her when he looked into her face. It was like Margaret had been struck. Some unexpected realization had halted her. He saw fear before she fled. That vision churned in his stomach over and over.

Pulling out of his reverie, he remembered Fanny's talking about the Master's Ball. Miss Hawkins had been in Milton long enough to know what and when that was. John was sure she would be expecting an offer to attend with him.

The 5 o'clock whistle blew, spurring Margaret to pick up her small pile of papers and walk next door. As she entered, there were not enough seats. Andrew gave her his.

"Thank you."

The three men and Margaret sat and listened to Master Griffin speak to the issues of that day. Before each foreman began his shift talk, Margaret was introduced once again and asked what she needed to report.

"I only wish to say that I will be visiting with all of you over the next few days, so that you may decipher your handwriting for me. I cannot make out some words or distinguish fives from eights. That is all I have to say."

The men were excited about having a pretty face in their meeting every day. The woman was worth the burden of having to watch their words in her presence. Master Griffin called on each man for his reports. Next was a discussion on events for the following day. The men were then excused.

"Miss Hale, how did your first day go?"

"Quite well, sir. As for the procedures, there have been no problems, only the handwriting."

"So, I can expect you tomorrow?" Cecil laughed.

"Yes. Yes, of course."

Cecil stood indicating the end of the meeting. "Miss Hale, I am going into town. May I take you home?"

"Thank you, sir. I will take a short ride, and then walk when I am near home." Margaret didn't want him to see where she lived, but knew she was silly. She was what she was.

"Very well. I'll only be a moment getting my buggy."

"I will return these papers to the office and wait there for you."

Branson left his lookout at quarter to the hour. Knocking on the office door, he was invited in.

"I am sorry, boss. I did not see her."

"Thank you, Branson. I had actually hoped you wouldn't. Would you mind trying that again at 7:00 a.m.?"

"Yes, guv. You can count on it."

"Good night, Branson. I don't think I'll need you this evening. Wait a minute. Saddle Arkwright for me."

"Very good, sir."

Less than an hour later, John found himself at his "reflecting" place. It was a small open spot in a wooded area several miles out of town. He had always wanted to share it with Margaret. John had a place to sit and could see all the mill chimneys puffing their smoke into the dimming rays of the sun. All the grey funnels were blowing eastward and looked as if they all had been sheared. The smoke had reached some invisible layer of air causing it to stop rising, like trees bending in the wind. Above that layer was the true color of the sky—a sight rarely seen in any industrial area.

Sitting on a log, he understood that something had to be done so he could return to his normal life.

My normal life. What is it, now?

Above all, he didn't want this ordinary life. Elaine Hawkins had made little difference in his existence. Where once he felt he could possibly settle for her, now it was impossible. This past year's feelings that he had gotten over Margaret Hale had been nothing more than vanity and pride. She would never be over. He knew that now.

He knew, Nicholas knew and perhaps his mother knew that his world now hinged on which direction he took. He stood at the crossroads with the knowledge that he would try to win her once more. If she had never shown up at his mill that day…

"Mr. Griffin, if you would stop the carriage at the next corner, I would be obliged."

"Are you sure? Is this your area, Princeton?"

"No, but only a few streets away from it."

"Well, let me take you there."

"I would rather you didn't, sir."

"Don't be embarrassed where you live, Miss Hale. It does not lower you in my eyes. Anyone can tell that you have fallen on hard times. You won't find any educated people around here. I know something must have happened in your life. I give you credit for doing your best to rise above it."

Flush in her face, Margaret couldn't look at him. "I am heartened that you understand, but I would rather walk from here."

"Very well." Cecil brought the buggy to a stop. Margaret hopped out before he could assist her.

"Good evening. I shall see you in the morning."

"Thank you for a good day, Miss Hale."

Margaret turned and walked away. Cecil watched her for a moment, and then went on. He didn't like leaving her there, although he felt she was safe.

She walked home feeling a small bit of pride in her day's achievements, but thinking of John, more and more.

Chapter Six

Nicholas had gone home for the evening. John was working, but dreading what waited for him at home. There was a knock on his office door.

"Enter," John shouted.

A strange scruffy man entered, pulling off his cap. "Pardon me, sir. I am looking for a Mr. Higgins, sir."

"Mr. Higgins has retired to his home for the evening."

"I guess I'll sees him in the mornin'."

"Is there anything I can do for you? I will be the first to see him tomorrow."

"Well… he told me to come tell him if I found out any information about them two women that moved the other day."

John rose and gave the man his full attention. "What is it that you have come to tell him? He is my partner."

"Pardon, sir, but he says he would pay me for any information. I am one of the vendors that works outside her old flat."

"I will pay you … and handsomely. What do you have to say?"

"One of the other vendors knew the men with the wagon and told me who they were. I met one at a rundown pub, as I was told he always goes there. I bought him a pint and he tells me where they took the furniture and the two ladies."

"Well … where is it, man?"

"First the ..." he said, holding out his hand.

John reached into his pocket and was very generous with a piece of silver.

"Thank you, sir. Thank you."

"Where?" John shouted.

"I can'st read, but here's a piece of paper. I think it says 12 Dwyer Street."

"Yes. That isn't in the Princeton district, is it?"

"Close, sir. I think it's about two or three streets from that area, but really not in it."

"Thank you, I will find it. I will tell Mr. Higgins in the morning. Good evening." John turned his back, looking at the note. The old vendor pulled on his cap and left.

John sat at his desk. It was several moments before he started to weep. It was worse than he could have imagined. He recovered himself and sought out Brandon.

"Have the carriage out front in ten minutes."

"Aye, guv."

John rushed up the back stairs from the kitchen. He passed his mother and sister eating their dinner at the table. There was a place set for him, but he continued on to his room to change clothes. Rifling through his drawers, he found some old work clothing and slipped into them. Once again passing the dining table without saying a word, he met Branson out front and gave him instructions.

Branson reined the carriage as close to Margaret Hale's neighborhood as he could without drawing attention.

John slipped out, and within one block he blended in with the locals. He ruffled his hair. Reaching down, he scraped some dirt from the ground and tapped it to his face in a few places. Thinking how he looked, he changed the gait of his walk and his staunch straight posture.

Along the way, he saw people eating their sandwich dinner on their front stoops. The smell of the area was only modestly less foul than Princeton. Finding Margaret's street, he turned down it. He realized he was on the same side as her living quarters; he crossed to the other side.

John wasn't sure how he could watch the place without being noticed. He happened to spot a man sitting outside, directly across from Margaret's place.

He slowed to watch what that man was looking at. He felt uneasy.

"Hey mate, is that where the new women moved in? Someone was talking about new neighbors."

"Yep. That's the place. You're new around here?"

"No. Just out for a walk tonight. My name is John."

Jeremy reached out his hand to shake John's. "I'm Jeremy. Have a seat."

John couldn't believe his luck. He prayed Margaret or Dixon would not come outside and recognize him.

"Do I know you?" asked Jeremy.

"You may. Been here my whole life," responded John. "Have you met them?" John asked, nodding towards Margaret's house.

"Yes. I helped them carry food from the grocer a couple days ago. I feel sorry for them."

"Why's that?"

"One's such a little thing, and the other, her guardian I'm told, looks like that long walk will take its toll on her. Both will struggle unless they buy food every two days."

"They working in the mills?"

"I think the little one is. Her name is Margaret. I saw her leave just before me this morning; about 6:30 a.m. She just got back a bit ago. She wasn't dressed like she worked a loom, though. Say, what's your interest in her?"

"I think I know her."

"Yeah, me too. She was that woman that was hit with a rock, during that riot at Marlborough Mills last year."

"Aye, she's the one. I wondered what happened to her."

"Why don't you go across and say hello."

"I won't this time. I will surprise her soon. I think she is embarrassed as it looks like her circumstances have been reduced."

"That's likely. They sure had too much furniture for that place. My brother and I are going to help them move it around one of these evenings."

Not if I can help it. By God, John thought, he couldn't let this continue.

"I guess I'll continue my walk. Glad for the company and talk. I've been worried about her. I want to surprise her real soon," John said, in hopes that Jeremy would keep quiet about a John asking questions about them.

Arriving back at the carriage, Branson was surprised to see his master looking disheveled.

"Did you find her, guv?"

"Yes. It's pitiful to see. I don't know how I am going to do it, but I am going to help. If Margaret Hale is the same woman, she will be too proud to allow me to give her money or pay for another flat."

"You could always send the grocer around tomorrow with some food. They don't have to know it's from you," Branson offered, standing with his boss beside the carriage.

"Guv, may I say something else?"

"Yes, Branson. What is it?"

"I've seen this Master Thornton once before, and it came to an unhappy ending."

"Branson, you know I cannot walk away from this," John climbed into the coach.

"If you would let me finish, sir. You said I could speak."

"Well then …."

"Let Miss Hawkins go, now. I know you will not give up your quest this time."

"Home, Branson."

When he arrived home, his mother stared at him, but was not about to question his absurd appearance. She knew it had to do with Margaret Hale. No one else could drive him to act so foolishly.

"John," she raised her voice. "Do you want your dinner now? Cook has kept it warm."

Before walking into the bath area, John responded, "Is Fanny out?"

"Yes, she is out with Mr. Watson, and I promise not to ask."

"Very well, I'll eat. Be there in a moment." John washed himself and changed into his regular clothes. His mind was everywhere but home. He hoped his mother kept her word.

He came to the table and seated himself in front of a full plate of food. Hannah sat in her regular place, sipping her second cup of tea. John began eating to avoid talking. As food went into his mouth, guilt overcame him.

Did Margaret and Dixon have enough to eat tonight?

He put down his fork and pushed away from the table. "She's in a bad way, Mother. I can't be certain they had a meal tonight," John said as he stared at his plate.

"John, are you sure it is as bad as you say?"

"Very certain. I don't know about the meal, but she is in a very low place. I believe Miss Hale deliberately left out of her note to Peggy and Nicholas where she was moving to."

"And you know where that is?"

"I do. Mother if you remember our hardest days after father died, and I brought home little, you'll have a sense of Miss Hale's situation."

"How could this happen to her, do you think? I guess her faithless clergyman father left nothing for them to live on."

"And where is her shame in that?" John said, getting angered. "Mr. Hale tried his best to earn a wage when they came here, at Adam Bell's suggestion. Mrs. Hale's long illness and then his own must have taken up most of their finances. If I understood correctly from Mr. Hale, Adam Bell was to leave his inheritance to see Margaret through her life."

"Well … where is he?" Hannah asked, trying to keep her haughty attitude under control.

"Mother, I have had all I can take from the women in this house and their disregard of Miss Hale. I am ashamed of my family. For the first time in my life, I am sorry for you. The woman has done nothing–*nothing*–to you or Fanny. She's educated herself, kept her family together through her parents' deaths, lost her brother to God knows where, and now her benefactor cannot be found. It seems she is keeping Dixon. They are trying to keep body and soul together around the corner from the Princeton area. Mother, I am seriously thinking of finding a flat for you and Fanny to move to. I must stay here, but I cannot do what I want to do or even what I should do with the constant innuendos about Miss Hale. It is clear to me now that there will never be anyone for me but her. I wish you to go to your room or I will."

"You will not dismiss me as a child, John Thornton. I will have my say, too. You cannot imagine the worry you put us through the last time you were in love with Miss Hale. I've never seen anyone so depressed. Nicholas saw it, too. Ask him."

"Mother, there was no 'last time' I loved Miss Hale. I *still* love her. Yes, Nicholas and I have talked about this, and he told me his concerns, but he knows me, mother, whereas you, apparently, do not. I know your worries are for me, but I will not be divided in my affections. I am sorry to say, but she now comes first in my life and has been for a very long time. If you cannot accept that or hold your tongue, I will find a place for you to live."

"Then do it, John. I cannot watch this again."

He was surprised to hear that, but he was not backing down. He had meant everything he said. He had taken care of his family when his father died. He continued to shelter his family as a good son would, and he had taken care of his workers. It was time to take care of himself.

"Mother, I will start looking for a flat for you and Fanny tomorrow. I will move you into town, which is more befitting of your attitudes. You can explain to my sister how I feel. I am going to look after myself for the first time in my life. I've done well by you and will continue to do so, but I will have Margaret Hale in my life however I can. Please begin pulling your things together tomorrow. I will have men here in two days to move your belongings and keepsakes. You will not have to move furniture with you."

John was livid and stormed out of the house. Hannah stood there, mouth agape. She didn't want this. Anything but this.

John went to find Branson. "Branson, take me to a nice pub. I want you to come inside with me, so make sure it is somewhere you, too, will be welcomed. Is there a driver's pub or tavern?"

"Aye, but sir …."

"Just do it." John climbed inside his coach.

Branson didn't even have the horses harnessed, but made quick work of his duty. His master had never acted in such haste. Miss Hale must be at the center of this. There was trouble at home. The poor woman didn't even know what was happening around her.

John had removed his top hat and coat before he entered the tavern with his driver. "Can we get something to eat in here, Branson?"

Branson walked to the bartender and ordered a scotch, a pint, and some sandwiches, as he pointed to the table where they were to be delivered.

"Thank you. I am sure you are wondering what has happened to me. You probably think I am going half mad."

"Sir, I have known you long enough, and I think I know more of your personal details than your mother. I do not believe you are mad. I think you are creating a path to a resolution."

"Where'd you learn to talk like that?" John smiled.

"From you, sir."

John felt himself smile more broadly. It felt good for a change. Branson was right. Somewhere deep inside, a gate had opened, and he was preparing to walk through it, no matter what lay beyond.

"I'm not sure which of you knows me best, you or Nicholas."

"It is me, sir."

Chuckling, "Why do you say it's you?"

"I know the intimate side of your life—remember, I wait with the coach while you … do what you do. I doubt Mr. Higgins is in that much of your confidence." Branson smiled. "You're a better gentleman than I'd ever be."

"I doubt you would be much different if you had someone that meant to you what Miss Hale does to me. Having her in my thoughts keeps most of the women in my life–safe." John laughed.

"I'm sure that's not entirely accurate. You are a gentleman in all aspects of your life. Why are we here, sir?"

John prefaced his opening with a sigh. “I will need a coach and driver for my mother and sister, who I am moving into town, off mill property, within a few days.”

John saw Branson’s stunned face. “Are you sure this is the right path?”

“I have never been surer of anything in my life.”

Chapter Seven

The following morning, there was no discussion at the breakfast table. John left the house, talked a long time with Nicholas about his plans, then set to work on them. Branson felt he knew a suitable driver, but wondered about the carriage and horse. Branson had an idea he would inquire about.

John began to think about a cook and maid for his mother. He would give Cook her choice, and then ask Mary Higgins if she were interested in the other opening. Jane would stay with his mother, as he knew there were several suitable women in the mills that had once been in service. Nicholas would take care of that for him. If Mary liked where she was, she could recommend someone who worked with her. John set out looking for a flat.

Margaret was in distress. She ran into the street and started shouting for help. Several women came running.

"What is it, miss?"

"Yes, how can we help?" asked another woman.

"Please help me. I believe my guardian is having a heart attack. Can someone fetch a doctor?"

"I'll get my son. He can run fast."

"Oh, thank you." Margaret dashed back into the house and three women followed her. They were offering advice about situating her. One lady pulled a pillow from the bed nearby and another pulled off the blanket to wrap her warm.

"Oh my—I don't know what to do for her," Margaret cried in worried sobs. She's been with me all my life."

The women quickly looked at each other and wondered who this woman was to have a lifelong guardian, but went back to their caregiving.

Margaret thought it felt like an hour before the doctor arrived. It had only been twenty minutes.

"Out of the way, ladies. Let me see the patient."

As they parted, Dr. Donaldson said, "Miss Hale!" Looking down, he continued, "What's wrong with Dixon?"

"I don't know. She was trying to push a heavy cabinet across the floor. She grabbed at her chest and then went down. She is going to be all right, isn't she?"

"Miss Hale, we need to get her to the hospital so she can be evaluated. With her age and weight, it could be serious. Would someone fetch my driver? I believe he and I can get her to the coach."

Dixon opened her eyes. "Miss, miss? She asked, looking at Margaret.

"Shhh Dixon, no talking just now. You have had an accident, and Dr. Donaldson and I are taking you to the hospital. Shhh … don't try to get up."

Dixon managed to help the two men who assisted her into the carriage. Margaret thanked the women and climbed into the coach. One of the ladies closed her front door.

Donaldson was quite concerned for his patient, but was sure he had a second one riding along with him. Miss Hale looked pale and malnourished.

As they day turned to evening, Margaret sat beside Dixon's bed. She had been given some sedative to keep her quiet and sleeping. Margaret's head was a whirlwind of thoughts. The bill would take the rest of their money, but that was of little consequence. She always had Nicholas and Peggy to turn to for a bed.

Dr. Donaldson came in and pulled a chair next to Margaret.

"How is she, doctor?"

"Miss Hale, she will pull through. But she is going to need rest and care for many months. She will look and feel fine by tomorrow, but she will not be inside. Is there any family she could stay with while she recovers?"

"She has talked about a sister. I do not know her circumstances, though." Turning red in the face and looking at her hands, Margaret went on. "Dixon said we could live with her sister if things became worse than they are. I am sure you were surprised to see me there."

"Can you tell me what happened?"

Margaret took a deep breath and began her tale of woe. She told him everything, including her working at a mill and even visiting Marlborough Mills. "Dixon has been taking in ironing, too. We were going to make it until our situation changed. I am sure of it. With the bills for her care and her not working, I am no long confident. I know I can ask help from Peggy and Nicholas. They have the bed that Bessie used. I can stay there while Dixon mends."

"Dixon will mend to a point, Miss Hale. She can still be helpful, but there will be restrictions on her activity for the rest of her life."

"I don't care what her restrictions are. I will … and want to take care of her until I cannot."

"Tell me about this mill work you're doing."

"I probably won't have the work when I go back. I only started yesterday. I am not there and the master will most likely dismiss me for failing to show." Margaret went on with the little she knew of where she was working."

"Do not worry about that. I shall see that master this evening and explain. Meanwhile, I need to examine you. I can see you are not eating. I am having a meal brought to you, now. If your pallor is not from malnutrition, then you have a problem, too. How long have you lived where you do now?"

"It's only been four or five days. I'm fine, really I am."

"You are not fine, Miss Hale, but I don't think you have caught any infection from where you are living. Not in that short of time. I want to offer you a bed here tonight. No charge. It's just for observation."

"I will take a chair here by Dixon."

"If that's the way you must have it in order to get you to stay, so be it. I will return shortly. Then I will examine you, too. There will be two meals brought, one for you and one for Dixon, if she is awake."

"All right, Dr. Donaldson."

Margaret walked to the window and watched the twilight begin to fall. It was the only time during the day that you could catch a glimpse of the sun setting between the horizon and the smoke layers above. It seemed that Dixon would not be with her for some months. Approaching the Higgins seemed inevitable. How was she to tell them?

John had secured nice living quarters for his family. It was a two-bedroom, smallish flat, but Fanny would soon marry and be gone. His mother's housekeeper could move in with her if she allowed her. He had arranged for three men and a wagon. Nicholas was finding the other two staff ladies.

Branson knocked on his office door.

"Enter."

"I think we're in luck, guv. An independent I know will be glad to stop at the flat and see if there are fares for that day or for a known day in the future. He will only charge by the drive. You will not have to hire him fulltime."

"Branson, excellent! I have an address, but do not have a date just yet. Higgins is working on a cook and housekeeper. Here he comes now."

"Hello Branson," Higgins offered, as he sat in his chair. "Mary would like to continue where she is, but she says she has a brilliant cook to offer your mother–or you. I have talked with the woman. Her name is Charlene, and she is mature, clean, and punctual. She is ready when you are. I can have the housemaid by tonight if the pay is more than millwork, which I assume it will be."

"Yes, by all means. Offer her what you think is fair. I guess I will talk with my cook next. I didn't think this would resolve itself in one day. Before you ask, I have thought, and thought again, about what I am doing. I guess I should go home and take my medicine."

"John, before you go, Peggy and I would like to go see Margaret this evening. She is our friend, too."

"Nicholas, I know she is your friend, and I know she values your friendship far more than mine. Please find out what you can and how we can help. I wish it weren't known to her about my mother. She doesn't need any more perceived guilt."

"If it isn't too late, I'll call on you at home tonight."

"Thank you. I am anxious to know."

"As we all are." Higgins left the office. Branson and John strolled across the yard, and then Branson went around back to his quarters and John willingly walked in to face his mother.

Jeremy was sitting on his stoop, looking to see if an oil lamp had been lit across the street. The house was totally dark. He thought that quite strange. One of the neighboring men crossed over to sit and chat.

"Why do you keep watching that house, Jeremy?"

"They're our new neighbors. You just finding out about that?" he said to Will.

"I didn't know they were new, but the wife says the older woman was taken to hospital today. Could be serious. Heart, I think."

"So, that's why there are no lamps. That's too bad. I hope she recovers soon. I liked looking at that young woman she stays with."

John walked into the parlor. Fanny was out, but his mother sounded like she was packing. He didn't call out to her, just sat and picked up his newspaper. John remembered Cook, closed his paper, and went downstairs.

"How are you this evening, Cook?"

"I've had better days. Never did I think I'd see the likes of what's going on in this house. You're making me choose, sir."

"I am at that. I hope someday for you to understand why I feel I have to do this."

"Oh, I don't need no explanation, sir. I love your mother, but I do see why you are doing this. This time in your life should be spent with another type of woman. You cannot miss out on a family to love, children to raise and a wife to adore. I don't think she realizes it, but she has made herself dependent on you. You're a good son. You couldn't see that happening. I can see the love you have always had for Miss Hale. Why your mother cannot or chooses not to see it, I will not say. This is a hard lesson for her to learn, but she must set you loose. With your mill here, it makes sense for her to find another place to live."

"I don't suppose you had this conversation with her today?"

"Oh, yes. Indeed I did. How long I have wanted to do so! I wasn't mean about it. She may have even begun to see it, since the words were coming from someone else that knew her."

"That was very bold for you to do, Cook. I am grateful, too. You are going to have a choice of for whom you would rather work. Has that been discussed?"

"It has. I am staying here. I will help if she needs someone to get her cook started, but this is my home. I live close by. I feel safe working here. And I might not mind *not* having someone looking over my back all the time," she smiled.

"Thank you, Cook. I may be hard to put up with, as you will cook and I may unexpectedly not come home. You have seen me do that for years, but before, you had someone to eat what you prepared."

"Doesn't matter, sir. I will miss the old days, but I need to grow you."

"Grow me?" John smiled.

"Yes, sir. You haven't quite made it to grown."

"I haven't? Well, you must explain that to me at our first opportunity."

"You bet I will."

"Thank you, again. I am sorry for what this day put you through."

"Get on up there and talk with your mother."

John bowed to her. "Yes, Your Majesty." They both laughed.

John slowed his pace ascending the stairs when he saw his mother pass into the parlor. He could tell her mood was poor because she jutted her chin up and out—always a sign of unpleasant things to come.

"Mother, I have found a flat for you and Fanny today. A driver will be provided when you need a ride. He will not live on the premises, but come by daily to see if you need to be anywhere. I understand that a brilliant cook has been found for you, and the housemaid is being selected now. She used to be in-service, so she is most likely far better than Jane. But you may have Jane if you wish, and if she agrees. I have spoken with Cook, so that is settled. You will be moved the day after tomorrow. Are there any questions?"

"Will there be any type of allowance or stipend?"

"You will put your grocery items on my account. You can use my accounts wherever they are, as long as they do not exceed the way you live now. Fanny will not be afforded the same privilege. She must come to me when she needs something other than personal items."

"She'll love to hear that."

"Perhaps she will move up her wedding."

"John, I had a rather serious conversation with Cook today. And …."

"I know. She told me."

"Was I a bad mother?"

"No, mother you were not. You are just too much of one for a man of my age. For a decade, I have listened and acquiesced to you. I don't know if I did so out of a sense of duty and respect for you or because of a lack of confidence in myself. It has gone on long enough. I allowed it to happen, and you saw no difference. I still and will always love you. I will see and visit you, but no longer live where your influence on me will greatly impact one of us. And yes, if you need an allowance after all of the accounts I have in this city, I will see to it."

Peggy and Nicholas were making their way to Margaret's flat. The sounds and smells haunted Nicholas as he drove through the streets, knowing the grim lives its inhabitants struggled to eke out. He was grateful that he never had to bring Peggy to this area where he once lived.

"Nicholas, I cannot believe Margaret lives anywhere near this. Can't we find a place in our home for her and Dixon?"

"I'm going to try like hell to get her out of here."

"You think she might refuse?" asked Peggy.

"Knowing Margaret, it is possible. There is also the fact that John will want to handle this. She will surely refuse him, at least for a while. She will be too embarrassed to face him."

"Perhaps a woman-to-woman talk is needed."

"You could be right."

"There are no lights back here to see where I am going. I'm glad I know where it is. There is only the light coming from the small windows. Here's the street," Nicholas exhaled loudly.

There were only a few flats that still had any type of number identifying them. Most numbers had worn off. Figuring generally which house was hers, he saw two men sitting on the front steps.

"Excuse me, gentlemen. Do you happen to know where a Miss Hale may live, or know of new neighbors that have moved in recently."

"Who wants to know?" asked Will.

"My wife and I are friends of Miss Hale. I am from Marlborough Mills. My name is Nicholas Higgins."

Jeremy stood. "I know you. You were the one who headed up the riot talks and negotiations. Miss Hale got hit by a rock that one day. I was there."

"We are quite concerned about Miss Hale. Do you know where she is or not?"

"She lives there, Jeremy said, pointing across the street. "She ain't there, though."

"Yes, it does look dark. Do you happen to know where she is?" Nicholas pulled a few coins from his pocket, but didn't hand anything over.

Jeremy noticed he had money.

"That older lady had a heart attack, they think, this morning. Both are at the hospital."

Nicholas flipped him a coin and climbed in his buggy, ruffling the reins.

"Miss Hale, will you follow me?" said the nurse. "Doctor wants to examine you."

Margaret rose and followed her, first checking on Dixon.

The nurse took her to a small room and helped her out of her dress and corset. Margaret was wrapped in a sheet and a thermometer was placed in her mouth. Dr. Donaldson entered the room.

"Well, Miss Hale, Dixon's heart doctor says she will be ready to go wherever she is going in a few days. But she must not carry anything."

"When she wakes, we shall settle that. I do not know where her sister lives."

"Now, let us see about you."

Margaret was instructed by the nurse to lie down on the exam table. She then stepped aside for the doctor.

Donaldson listened to her heart for longer than was usual. Next he checked her lungs and looked for swelling. When he pulled up her shift, his eyes went to her ribs, that were clearly defined. He went on to examine the remainder of her body.

"Miss Hale, you are utterly undernourished. You have been under a great deal of strain and stress, it appears, and now your housekeeper is down, which is going to cause you further anxiety. We cannot let this go on."

"But I have a job now. Things will get better. Mr. Bell should be here any day now," not believing her own words. Margaret started to cry. Suddenly, she felt so hopeless. Her world was caving in. She would be a beggar soon. She wanted to collapse from the weight of it all.

"Miss Hale, listen to me." Donaldson put his bent finger under her chin and lifted her face up. "This is not the end of the world. You seem to feel it is. There are people who want to help you, and they are friends. There are also groups that want to be involved in troubles such as you're having."

"I don't want charity."

"Whoever helps you, and I know two people who very much want to step in, will not think of it as charity. It makes them feel better when they can help someone. It's good for the soul. You of all people should know that feeling. You're a very giving person. Whatever comes your way, think of it as someone loaning you money for a business—just like a bank would. When you get on your feet, you will be an income-producing person. You will pay them back. If you and Dixon stay together while she and you get better, you will have to be under someone's care. She, as you say, could go to her sister's place for a spell, and you can heal yourself then. You cannot go back to where or the way you were. Not now, and I hope not ever. You cannot work and take care of her, so put that out of your mind. As for you alone, you cannot resume work for at least a week, perhaps two."

"But Dr...."

"But me no buts, as the saying goes. Until you have a caregiver, you will stay here in the hospital. That's final, Miss Hale. I will speak with your master. Who is he, by the way?"

"Master Griffin of Griffin Mill."

"I will speak with him tonight. Leave all the rest to me as well." Donaldson held up his finger to her. I will send the nurse in to help you dress. "No arguments. The nurse will escort you back to Dixon's room. I'll send some warm milk for you to drink. No arguments."

"Do we go see Margaret or John first?" asked Peggy.

"We'll see Margaret. That's what we told John, and that's what we'll do. I did tell you what he told me this morning about moving his mother and sister into their own flat in town, didn't I?"

"Yes, but I don't think it sunk in until just now. John will have an empty house. It will be suitable for two women to convalesce. He will be very tempted to insert himself into her care."

"I think you have that backwards, love. He will insert her into his care."

"And how do we feel about that?"

Nicholas laughed. "God, I wish I knew. I guess it can be boiled all the way down to … do we think they belong together? Do we?" Nicholas looked serious.

"Do you want my opinion?"

"I asked. I think I heard myself ask you that. Yes. I am sure I did." He chuckled.

"Don't be so flippant." Peggy was smiling. They were now on the gas-lit- streets of the town. Nicholas could see the woman he fell in love with.

"I believe they *do* belong together. And you?"

"I feel the same. John undoubtedly feels the same. How do we get Margaret to feel the same?"

"I think this needs to play out a little further. We cannot push Margaret into loving John, even though she does."

"What? Even though she does?"

"Yes, silly. Surely you knew that."

"I know no such thing," huffed Nicholas.

"Men! I guess it is better that you never realized that. You would have felt worse for John than you do now."

"How do you know she loves him and she does not know it?"

"A woman knows these things," Peggy admitted.

"Peggy … you have taught children their school lessons. You are a smart woman and educated. You don't seriously believe I am going to fall for that 'women know these things and men don't,' do you? I know. You're talking about that intuition thing, aren't you?"

"In some respects, but that isn't needed to see this."

"I give up. So why doesn't Margaret know she loves him and why doesn't John know?"

"Dear husband. I love you, but there are just some things a man shouldn't know, and this is one of them. God gave us this ability, along with a few other things, to be able to live with men."

"Yes, and I do love those other things very much."

Peggy and Nicholas arrived at the hospital desk and stood there with nothing to say.

"I don't know who to ask for. Do you know Dixon's last name?"

"No. How remiss of us."

The nurse was smiling at the two of them. "Please excuse me for asking, but are you two looking for Miss Dixon?" Then she laughed. So did Peggy and Nicholas.

"Of course, Miss Dixon," Peggy said.

They were being told how to get to her room when Donaldson spotted them at the desk.

Walking up behind them, he said, "Just the people I wanted to see."

"How is Dixon?"

"She's had a life-altering heart attack, but she will feel her old self in a day or two. She must take it easy for six months at least before she can resume her former duties. She will never be allowed to lift more than 2 stone."

"So, she is out of danger?"

"She is, for now. Margaret, however, is another story. That is what I wanted to talk with you about. It was either you or John. You came in first."

"What is it? How is she? How can we help?" The questions were coming from both of them.

"She is malnourished, dehydrated, and exhausted. Do you know where she is living?"

"We found out recently. We have not seen her since the funeral. Neither of us had any idea of what was going on. In fact, we still don't know. Margaret wrote us a note a couple of days ago, but did not mention where she was moving to. We have been there tonight."

"It is apparent that she has been in some financial crisis for a while. The worry has worn her down. She must be giving up her food so Dixon could eat."

Nicholas pinched his brow. "God, I wish I had known this. I feel awful that I never called on her. It's just like her to hide this from us."

"She said she is waiting on Adam Bell. I suspect she expected him to help her when he arrived. Do either of you know anything about him?"

"John inquired at the hotel. They said they had not heard from him, but he was to be expected about a month ago."

"Oh dear. That does not bode well for Miss Hale. He may have passed on."

"Regardless of that, John will take care of her for life, but what about right now?"

"According to Margaret, Dixon may have a sister where she can take her time recovering. They will have to decide on that. Much of that decision may be weighted by Margaret's caregiver. Someone has to take care of her. She needs to eat, rest and come to feel protected and safe from financial ruin."

"Whatever she decides, we will make a place for both or either of them."

"I was sure you would say that."

"Say what?" John asked loudly from behind them.

"John! You startled us," sighed Peggy. "How did you find out where we were?"

"I asked the man on the steps across from her place. Now, where is she?"

Chapter Eight

"I think we all have to talk before you go charging in there."

"I wasn't going to go charging in there, Nicholas."

"You three talk amongst yourselves. I told Margaret I would see her employer and tell him why she didn't come to work today. I want to save her job. It is crucial to her and offers some measure of self-respect, which she lacks in abundance," Donaldson said, in a hurried mood.

Both John and Nicholas asked at the same time, "Who is her employer?"

"She said a Master Griffin of Griffin Mill. Can you tell me where he is from your mill?" asked Donaldson.

"He's six mills down from us. He is relatively new here, but the mill isn't. He lives on his property."

"Very well. I will see you all on my return. I want to look in on my two patients before I go home tonight."

"Two?" questioned John.

"Higgins will tell you the story. I will take my leave now."

With that, Donaldson headed to the front door.

"John, let's go to the canteen for some tea. We have a decision to make."

"First, I want to hear why Miss Hale is a patient of Donaldson's."

"I'll tell you on the way."

Not knowing the new hospital, it took them many turns and several directions to arrive at it. By then, John was apprised of the entire situation regarding recoveries.

Pouring tea into three clean cups, Nicholas repeated, "John, as I said, Peggy and I will make room for both of them. It may not be a wise choice for you to offer shelter with you living alone soon."

John rubbed his brow … thinking. "You say Margaret needs a week of recovery?"

"No, we don't know how long her recovery is. Dixon needs a few days."

Peggy and Nicholas looked at John anxiously.

"I would hire someone to care for both of them. I know. I know. It is improbable that she would even accept my help. However, let her pick her choice. I know it won't be me, but I want her to know I care."

"John, you're a fool if you think she would miss that."

"What makes you say that?"

"Well, Peggy knows. Peggy knows what Margaret hasn't realized herself."

"Are you sure you are not the other patient of Donaldson's?"

"Peggy, explain it to him," Nicholas nodded toward John while looking at his wife.

"I will not explain anything. I told you, it's not for men to know."

"You both are driving me mad," John said, exasperated.

Peggy got up and fetched the milk and sugar. She was enjoying this.

"Here's how I understand part of this from my wife." Nicholas sighed and began. "Peggy says that Margaret is still in love with you."

John interrupted in excitement. "Has she spoken to you, Peggy?"

Peggy looked at her husband.

"John, hang on."

"You said *still.* You used the word *still* as in *all along.*"

"According to Peggy, Margaret doesn't know she is in love with you. There, I said it."

"What?" John asked, as he slammed his palm on the tabletop. Not comprehending, John's frustration increased.

"Peggy, see what you started."

"Me? I would say it was John Thornton who started all this–about a year ago."

"Peggy, may I ask a question?" John let out a heavy sigh.

She smiled.

"You think, but are not sure, that Miss Hale harbors some regard for me?"

"It was plainly spelled out in the note she wrote to you when she apologized for bothering you."

John had carried the note since he received it. He pulled it out and began reading it aloud.

Please forgive my behavior that I displayed yesterday. It is unlikely for you to believe me, but I wanted to apologize for the way I rejected your proposal, almost a year ago. I have come to learn the ways of a northern gentleman. I know I came to feel your proposal was sincere, and not one of duty as a gentleman, to protect my reputation from my own actions. I know the hurt that I have caused us.

That difficult time has passed, and I hope happiness can be found in moving forward with your life. I shall never forgive myself. I can only hope that God will.

All of the words that were left unspoken came to me suddenly, as we spoke. I was not prepared for that, therefore, causing my hasty departure.

"Plainly spelled out, is it?" John looked at Nicholas, hoping he understood what his wife meant. "I think I felt and still do, that perhaps there is some hope in the future ...."

"John, you're as much of an idiot as Nicholas is. Or maybe it's all men, or even perhaps living under a mother who persuaded you to doubt yourself. I hate to say that, but you are at a crossroads now, with your mother. It's time to open your eyes and your heart. You're afraid of the pain, aren't you? Your mother is afraid of your pain. Your partner is afraid of your pain. Everyone loves you but you."

John was pacing the room by now, and Nicholas was watching him carefully. "This must be a 'women only' thing. God help me, I hope I never understand them."

Nicholas chuckled.

"How sure do you feel about this, Peggy?"

"If you are asking me if you can go into her room and declare yourself to her, you cannot. Remember, she isn't sure of her love for you yet, but her fleeing from you when you looked into her face says it all."

"It does? I thought I knew women," John remarked, sitting back down."

"Cheer up, John. Men will never know us completely."

"Is this something handed down from mother to daughter?" John laughed.

"No, it is instilled in us from birth and nurtured through example as we grow. It's nothing taught or talked about—because we just know. I can't explain it any better than that. Perhaps, Margaret will be able to someday."

"So, where do I start?" John suddenly felt exhilarated and defeated in understanding anything Peggy said.

"John, you know Margaret is going to be terribly embarrassed by her situation. You remember that from before and see what happened," advised Nicholas. "This is much greater now. She is further reduced, destitute, and you have become wealthier. She will confuse your regard with charity. You are going to have to approach this differently, though I cannot say I know how that would be."

John looked to Peggy. There was quiet.

"Wait."

John and Nicholas looked around the room as if something was happening.

"No, silly. Wait. You must wait on Margaret to show you a sign. Her pride is crushed. She is ill. She will have to work for a living. She will think she cannot offer herself as a wife as she is now. Margaret has to get on her two feet and find her own dignity before she can offer herself for your approval."

John shook his head in disbelief. "Approval," he uttered to himself.

"John, Peggy and I will go in to see her first. We will offer her shelter while she recovers."

"What about after she recovers?" John snapped.

"Let me finish. We may have to get firm with her. I am not sure you will be involved, but we will not allow her to go back to that place."

"I will see to that," said John. "The men who will move mother and Fanny can pack up Margaret's furniture. I will find a place to store it."

"She must accept our help for now."

"I agree. I will help with any finances."

"John, how much could she cost us? She's our friend above anything else."

"You're right. I'm sorry."

"I believe you should show your face to her tonight. Offer your home as we will do. She won't know your mother won't be there."

"She will surely turn me down if she thinks she is."

"Just don't drop to your knees and start weeping," Nicholas laughed.

"You're laughing," John said. "I probably would have."

"I know."

Before they could complete their discussion relating to after her recovery, Donaldson was back.

"Have either of you talked with her?"

"No," said Peggy. "We have been resolving John and Margaret's life together."

"That far, are you?" Donaldson laughed. "Mr. Griffin is in seeing her now."

"What?" John heard himself say again. He immediately left the room.

"What's John think he's going to do?" Donaldson asked.

"I believe he's protecting his future."

"Thank you, Mr. Griffin," John heard as he walked to just inside the door. He couldn't see Margaret with Cecil standing in front of her.

"Miss Hale, I have no problem waiting on your recovery. You started my books with great precision and accuracy. I could tell by the column headers that you had put more thought into the details of accounting."

Cecil took a step closer to Margaret. "I …."

John cleared his throat with apparent intent.

John, get hold of yourself, he thought.

Cecil Griffin turned to face the person clearing his throat. He was now blocking Margaret's view of who just came in.

"John … John Thornton. I wouldn't have expected to see you here." Cecil walked across the room to shake his hand.

Margaret watched the glass of warm milk in her hand begin to shake. She clutched at her shawl, wishing to hide herself.

"Good evening, Griffin. He shook Cecil's hand, trying to keep his attention off of Margaret.

"My foreman informed me the other day about that riot you had in your mill yard. I understand Miss Hale was visiting your mother that day. I can see how you two know each other."

John caught a glimpse of Margaret. Both seemed relieved by Cecil's understanding. Each had tried to put that behind them, they thought. Cecil was unknowingly bringing the core of their past issues to the forefront before they could have spoken about it to each other.

"I guess I will let you two talk," he said turning to Margaret. "Miss Hale, return when you can. The papers will still be there. I am sorry for your friend. Return when she is situated, and you are well."

"Thank you again, Mr. Griffin, for being patient."

"Miss Hale, do not give it another thought. It is my pleasure. Good evening. And good evening to you, Thornton."

John's posturing was in full force. Through his body language, he was telling Cecil that she was his property. His back was erect, his head held high, holding his top hat in front of him. He became aware of himself suddenly and smiled. He had just talked with Nicholas about something being a woman's thing. Here he was establishing boundaries around his woman through his look and movements. That was definitely a man's primal territorial dance. He finally laughed after Cecil left. He walked towards Miss Hale.

"Good evening, Miss Hale. Please pardon me for smiling. This is not a moment to be doing that. There seemed to be some unspoken words crossing between Mr. Griffin and myself. I guess it's something men do."

"It looked like a snarl. Do you know him?" Margaret asked.

"Slightly. He comes to our meetings, but he's new. I have had very little reason to contact him. Let's not talk about him. Peggy and Nicholas are waiting their turn to see you, too."

Margaret stood and walked to Dixon's side. She was still asleep. "You've come to offer charity, haven't you?"

"I've come to offer friendship. I want to understand why you fled from me the other day, I want to discuss your note, but now is not the time. However, we shall make time in the future. I want to scold you for not letting your friends know of your difficulties, but I will not do that. I know you, Miss Hale. You are not to be pitied, but admired for doing your very best before you inconvenienced your friends. I hope I can be seen as a friend after all this time. I would like you to know that I thought you had returned to London with your aunt. I was just recently informed that you had stayed in Milton. We, as your friends, have been discussing your situation, and that includes Donaldson. Not one of us will let you return to where you were under any circumstances. Perhaps I could convince you to walk with me to the canteen so that we may all speak together, away from Dixon."

"Thank you."

John saw Margaret was slow moving towards the doorway. He offered his arm. She took it.

John's pulse went through the roof at that moment. He could see weakness beginning to overcome her. There was an empty rolling chair sitting in the hall, and he guided her to it.

"I would sling you in my arms and hold you to me, if that were proper, but I am sure you would rather have the chair." John wondered if he had said that out loud.

"I feel I can walk, Mr. Thornton, although that is a rather amusing offer."

He *had* said it out loud. Peggy was right: He was an idiot when it came to Margaret. "Do me the courtesy of letting me be your driver."

He thought he saw a smile trying to peep out. His pulse raced still higher.

"Are you committed to this?"

"I am."

"I will oblige you, then." Margaret's heart was lifted. She felt heady. Being so low for so long, in an instant, this small act of kindness seemed to drain away the weight she had been under. She was lightheaded.

John took her arms and gently rested her in the chair. He was bent down on one knee situating her. Then he looked into her eyes again. John didn't realize when he returned to the back of the chair that Margaret had swooned.

He wheeled her into the canteen with a smile. Nicholas and Peggy ran to her.

"John, what have you done to her?" Nicholas asked.

Peggy smiled. John, puzzled—frowned at Nicholas.

"What do you mean, what have I done to her?" John repeated as he moved to see her the way Nicholas did.

"John! She's unconscious."

"She can't be. We just talked." John knelt down to see her face, which was now moving towards her lap. He caught her.

"John let me do that," Peggy requested.

"Peggy, I think I can handle this, but thank you."

"John, you can handle it, but apparently she can't." Peggy pushed John aside.

"Can I help?" asked Nicholas.

"Yes, you can. Just hold her up and I'll get a cool cloth for her forehead. John, you stand behind her."

John stood by, bewildered and speechless.

With the soothing cloth administered by Peggy, Margaret soon came around.

"Where am I? Oh, Nicholas … and Peggy, hello."

"You are in the canteen at the hospital."

"How is Dixon?"

"She's the same … still sleeping," came a voice from behind her.

"Oh, Mr. Thornton–yes. Now I remember. Where are we sitting?" Margaret started to rise out of the chair.

Peggy put her hand on Margaret's shoulder. "You stay there. We will all have a cup of tea over here." She pointed to a table.

Nicholas began to push her chair. Peggy caught John by the cuff to stop him. "John, sit beside her, not in front of her," she mentioned through a giggle.

Another frown from John, but he listened.

Once Margaret was situated, John did the honors of fixing the teacups. Margaret's was first, and he didn't need to ask how she took hers.

"How are you feeling, Margaret?" asked Nicholas. "Never mind, I think we can see that. We're only going to ask this once, and then we'll move on. What didn't you let your friends know of your situation?"

Finished serving the tea, John sat next to Margaret. Everyone saw the tremor in her hand when she raised her cup. As she returned it, the china clinked several times against the saucer before coming to rest.

Margaret took a deep breath. "Thank you for letting me say the words that I knew you would hear one day." Margaret saw her hands shaking on the tabletop, and pulled them into her lap. "I never thought things would go this far. I never knew how much Father was relying on Mr. Bell to see me through life. After Father passed away, expenses were coming to the house. Ones, I suppose, he was repaying with his teaching instead of coin. He was still paying for mother's burial costs when he met his end. I settled all of the family's debts, but there was little left. I was expecting Mr. Bell to arrive two months ago, after hearing of my father. I fear for him, but it is possible that he never received my note. I eventually started selling pieces and parts of the household so that we could eat and keep the flat. Dixon started taking in ironing, and I prepared to look for work."

Everyone was quietly listening to her struggle to say the words. Margaret sipped her tea, this time holding it with two hands.

"It was a few weeks ago when it became evident that Mr. Bell might not ever come back and that we were at the end of our finances. I had to find another residence for the two of us–the flat you know of. Dixon offered to write to her sister, asking for shelter. I told her I thought we could make it if I could find work. I did not want to suddenly appear on your doorstep as a beggar. I wanted to keep as much of my dignity as I was able. I did find work, and I believe we might have been all right soon. But now Dixon is very ill and needs care. It seems I am at your mercy. I am ashamed to admit we are in need until she recovers."

"Miss Hale, Dixon may never return to an earning person," John said quietly.

"Perhaps she can live with her sister, although I know she does not want to. I may be able to support myself in a week or two. Margaret looked up and saw tears in Peggy's eyes, Nicholas's head down, and she knew John was looking at her again. She avoided his eyes.

"Miss Hale, we are going to talk about your choices, but let me say that within two days, your furniture which remains in that–that residence will be moved to storage." John looked at Nicholas to continue.

"Margaret, both Peggy and I, and John, here, are insisting you stay with one of us for as long as you want. We have room, and John now has room." Nicholas looked at John.

"Miss Hale, for reasons of our own, my mother and sister are taking a flat towards the center of town. My house will be empty. Both you and Dixon can recover there. You each will have a room."

"Margaret, I am not trying to sway you on your decision, but coming to our house, you and Dixon would share a room. If Dixon wanted her sister to tend to her recovery, you would have your own room. Peggy and I would love to have you. We would hope you would not feel compelled to work, either. You won't need that money."

Margaret started weeping and sniffling. "You can't know what this means to us, me … particularly. You both are very kind and generous." Margaret sniffled.

"Margaret, we are not kind and generous. We are your friends. You are almost like family to us," Nicholas offered.

"Miss Hale, I may not be like family, but I have great care for what happens to you. I believe Nicholas said that you were spending the night here as per Donaldson's request."

"Yes, I am."

"You don't intend to sleep in that chair near Dixon, do you?"

Margaret hesitated only a moment and John left the table and the room.

"Where's he going?"

"I would think he's insuring you have a bed for the night."

"But I can't pay for that."

"He knows, Margaret."

"Why is he so nice to me? It's been a year and we parted under the worst possible circumstances."

"Have your feelings changed at all for the man?" asked Peggy.

"Quite a lot, actually. I wish I could take back some of things I said that day. Many understandings are now clear that were not so at the time. But that doesn't explain his behavior."

"When you are restored to the person you were, you will understand," Peggy finished. "Here he comes."

John sat in his chair. "Now, where were we? Miss Hale, you will have a choice to make before you leave the hospital. I have now found a caregiver to be in the house with you and Dixon, should you choose my home."

"I cannot thank you, my friends, enough. Dixon and I will discuss this as soon as she is able. How will I contact one of you?"

"Nicholas, myself, or Branson will be in and out of here most of tomorrow. It is not rushing your decision; it will be to see how the two of you are faring."

"How is Branson?"

"Doing quite well, Miss Hale. He sends you his regards."

"When I am a bit stronger, I would like to complete the work I had started for Mr. Griffin. I was only going to be employed for two weeks. At first glance, I am not sure it can be completed in two weeks, but surely it can in three. I have promised the gentleman that."

"Margaret, wherever you stay, our drivers will see you to and from work."

Margaret looked at Nicholas. "How is Bessy?"

"From her letters, she is taking pride in her education. I believe she really loves her school."

"Mr. Thornton, how are your mother and sister? Well, I hope."

John cleared his throat. "Mother is as well as she can be for a woman of her age. Fanny is Fanny, and she is now engaged to Master Watson. I believe you met him at the dinner."

"Oh yes. Yes, I do remember him. I remember a lot about that night."

There was silence in the room. John remembered that night too. Margaret was politely chastised for siding with the poor and starving workers during the strike.

"I am tiring. I would like to go back to Dixon, if you don't mind."

"It will be our pleasure," Nicholas said as he reached for the chair she was in. Perhaps she will be awake and we can say hello."

Nicholas rolled her down the hall. John and Peggy lagged behind.

"Peggy, what was all that 'stand behind her' and 'sit beside her' talk? Am I offending her in some way?"

"John, you are so wrapped up in her that you don't see her. You are blinded by her."

"I cannot argue much there. All my feelings, which I have been repressing for a year, are rushing at me."

"You are not hiding that very well, you know?"

"Should I be?"

"Yes, at least for a time. Margaret has to get on her feet, feel safe from what's she's been through, and she needs her pride restored. Her working at the job should help with that a lot. Keep your distance. Be a good friend, not a lover in waiting."

"How do I do that?"

"Being a woman, I am not really sure. I can see when it is too obvious too quickly."

"I do not mean to present myself as a lover, but a man who loves her. Do you still feel there is a regard for me from her, though?"

"John, when did women suddenly become unknown to you? There must have been plenty of females who had a genuine regard for you."

"I don't really know. I never really cared. Now, I do. This is a turning point in my life–again."

"Yes, John, she has a regard for you. How deep it is, I don't know. Does she know it? I think she feels something she doesn't understand."

"How can you see this and I not?"

"It's in your eyes. Can you see your eyes?"

"You mean I am blinded by her?"

Peggy sighed. "John, has no woman told you that you have penetrating eyes?"

"What!"

"Don't you see?" Peggy giggled at her own remark.

"Is that supposed to be a joke?" he asked.

"No, but it sounded like one. I would say that Margaret fled from you that day at the mill because you were standing close and stared at her."

"I am—"

"And I would say that you helped her into the chair and maybe stared into her eyes a bit too long for comfort. You made her swoon."

"Now, you're ridiculous."

"Have it your way. Just know that you weaken her when you look at her. That means she loves you. Watch how she avoids looking at you when you are close."

Chapter Nine

John thought it was all nonsense. He dismissed Peggy's observations as unrealistic. She saw something in Margaret that perhaps she wanted to see.

Reaching Dixon's room, Margaret went to her side. She was waking. Margaret turned to the others waiting behind her.

"It seems she is coming awake. I think she and I need to talk about her condition. If you will excuse us for the rest of the night."

"Margaret, we will be around to see you sometime tomorrow. I hope we find Dixon feeling better. Goodnight."

Peggy followed up, "Goodnight Margaret. I will collect your clothes in the morning."

"Thank you all, ever so much," Margaret responded in fervent sincerity.

John remained for a moment. *Be a friend*, he remembered.

"Miss Hale, I want to offer my services in any way possible. Will you be offended by that? After our last conversation a year ago, I am unsure of your tolerance of me. Do you have a moment to help me understand? Perhaps you don't know how you feel."

John started to close the gap between them.

"Mr. Thornton, please stay where you are."

John stopped.

"Soon, I want to talk with you about that day. I want to make clear my feelings that have kept me swirling for a year. I am exhausted from the worry of it. Let me say that I invite your company into my presence. I appreciate the help that you offer. Also, I am pleased to see that you have somehow forgiven me for the words I spoke that day. I think that is all I can say for this brief encounter."

"Thank you, Miss Hale. I am most pleased to hear those words and look forward to the others. I will see you tomorrow and say goodnight at this time." John bowed his head slightly and placed his top hat on, turned, and left.

"Miss Margaret, where am I?"

"Dixon, you have overworked and caused yourself a heart attack. We are at the hospital."

"What does that mean?"

"A heart attack? The doctor explained it as damage to a muscle in your heart. The heart is all muscle, and you have impaired a part of it."

"Will I live?"

"The doctors say yes, but your life will change in some respects. You will need rest for many months, so it can begin to repair and strengthen again. As you go through life, your heart will remain weak. You can no longer do heavy lifting or long hours of labor. And you must not do a lot of worrying, about yourself or me. Apparently, continued stressful situations are harmful, too."

Dixon began to rise. "We must leave here. I will rest, but we have no money for this here place."

"Calm down Dixon. We have mercifully been given some options by our friends. We must discuss it. Do you feel like doing that now or tomorrow?"

"Miss, how are you?" You still look pale."

"The doctor has given me a few restrictions too. Now …."

Before John left the hospital, he found the accounts department. He asked that all medical expenses for Miss

Dixon and Miss Hale be billed to him. He walked to his carriage.

"Sir, how are the ladies?"

"Dixon has a long recovery ahead of her. Miss Hale should gather her strength and color in due course. They've had a difficult ordeal."

"Where to, guv?"

Seeing that night had fallen, "Home, Branson."

Arriving home, John found his sister talking with their mother as she worked on her needlepoint. John quietly came up the back steps from the stable and heard a conversation in progress. He stopped to listen.

"I for one will be glad to be out of here and in town," said Fanny. "You know I have always thought this was a dirty place to live."

"Fanny, you should be grateful to your brother. We would have had a much different life without him. You have taken him for granted. You will never truly understand the sacrifices that he and I have made because you will never be in that position."

"Well, I cannot help that, Mother."

"You know you will have to ask him for anything you need. No more going off shopping for bonnets and dressmaking."

"He said that because he was mad at you. He won't hold us to that. That Miss Hale has become a thorn in our side. John's been far away for a year. He's buried himself in work or comes home to sulk. I'll be glad when I am married and have another man to rely on."

John tiptoed back down the stairs and closed the back door with a loud sound. He made sure they did not mistake that he was home.

Coming to the top of stairs, he said, "Good evening. I am making myself a drink. Can I pour for either of you?"

"I'll have a brandy, John," said Fanny.

"Nothing for me," answered Hannah.

John poured the two drinks and handed Fanny her glass. On the way to his usual chair, he grabbed the newspaper. He turned up the gas lamp and sat down.

"John, before you get into your paper, may we talk?"

"Yes, mother, what is it?"

"Fanny and I are nearly done our packing. Are you sure this flat is fully furnished?"

"I believe it is. You may return here whenever you like, if you need to take something away with you. You could have the entire contents except for my room if you want it. I imagine I will eventually have all the trinkets of china, brass and crystal packed away and placed upstairs. You know how I keep my own room. That is the way I will keep this house, so take all of those things you've collected over the years with you."

"So this is all settled and final. You aren't just punishing us for our attitudes."

"Oh, that is a big part of it, I grant you. I am a twenty-eight-year-old man. I need to be on my own. I want the freedom of making my own decisions without arguments, advice, or consultations. I believe I have a good head on my shoulders or my mills wouldn't be profitable. I want to use that same head in making my life happy. I have goals I want to reach, people I want to be close to, and I want to make friends with whomever I like. I don't want to have others to consider before I do such things. Have you decided on Jane or the other new housekeeper?"

"I will take Jane."

"Very well.

"John before you throw mother and me out on our ear, I will need a dress for the ball that is coming up."

"Fine."

"I can have one made?"

"Do whatever you want. You will have to pay for it, of course."

"John! You cannot do that to me." Fanny said, breathing fire.

"I think I can. I will tell you something I can do for you and your dress."

"As you should, dear brother." Her tone was demanding. "What can you do?"

"I can find work for you at the mill, and you can earn the money to procure it."

"You wouldn't do that to me."

"Yes, I can–and I will."

"I'll get Watson to buy it for me."

"I would be greatly relieved if you did."

"John, you cannot be serious," remarked Hannah.

"Mother, I am most assuredly serious."

Fanny stamped her foot and went off to her room, mumbling unintelligibly.

"John, as much as this hurts me, I think somewhere in my mind I am proud of you. I've been giving your life a lot of thought since your depression onset. I am not blameless. I know that. I am not sure I can ever come to totally accept Miss Hale, and I don't know why. But if you want her in your life, I will be happy that you are happy."

"Mother, I know why you don't want to or chose not to take her into our family. You originally began with the conceited attitude that her family was lower than we. You thought Miss Hale scandalous for attempting to save my life, which embarrassed you. You never took the time to know her and her Southern ways. She reacted that day as she would have most of her life before moving here. She felt sorry for the poor and wanted to help them. You never could see that we, this northern mill town, are the outsiders of the world. This burgeoning industry is bitter, but we must go forward. Then came the shame when she rejected my proposal–one I had considered, but at a distant time. She needed to know this northern industrial town and our culture here. Because of your embarrassment, I proposed, and she rightly refused. It has taken a while for me to see that. I don't think you ever did. Mother, I hold nothing of that against you. You acted yourself rightly. You never wanted to know her, though. Even though I was showing an interest, you were blinded by her genuine naiveté of our area. You once talked about *airs and graces.* To her, I am sure we were the ones displaying them."

"Have you seen Miss Hale again?"

"Yes. She is in hospital under Donaldson's orders. The worst news is that her lifelong housekeeper had a heart attack this morning."

"Oh. John. I don't like hearing that. You must believe me."

"I do, mother."

"What is Dixon's condition?"

"Mother, I have answered all I am going to. If you wish to know more, you know where to find them. "

John swallowed his drink in one gulp, threw his paper in the fire and turned off his gas lamp.

"Goodnight, mother."

"Goodnight, son."

John had rarely talked to his mother so harshly. It wasn't his tone, it was his words. His voice was even, but resolute. As much as he loved his mother and sister, they were making it difficult for him to begin a journey to capture Margaret's heart. He would not stand up under another rejection, so this time had to be perfect. He wanted no one to give him opinions on his actions. Somehow, he felt his mother understood.

John went to his room and disrobed. He had a strange sensation once he settled into his bed. Hope lifted his body up, and he felt light. Many different things were about to change in his life, and he still must maintain the old in regards to the mills. He was confident that Margaret would select the Higgins to stay with, and that was fine too. Being close to her was dangerous for a fresh new relationship. Suddenly, Miss Hawkins came into his mind. He hadn't thought about her since their dinner engagement several nights before. He never committed himself to her, but John was sure that she was expecting it. Had not Miss Hale come to his mill that day, he could be in a very grave position. How would he handle it now?

The Master's ball was coming soon, and she would expect to be invited. He would have to see that through. Eventually, Miss Hawkins would have to fade into the background, and Miss Hale would become more prevalent.

Margaret and Dixon talked well into the night, as Dixon had been sedated for a long time. The good, the bad, and propriety were discussed. Margaret was eventually shown to a room and fed warm milk again.

Margaret opened her eyes to Dr. Donaldson early the next morning.

"Good morning, Miss Hale. Time for a nice, healthy meal. I know you will start to object, but let me stop you before you start. I will be keeping you one more night. You may keep company with Dixon, but you will have your meals and one more night of rest."

"I dare not refuse, alas, I cannot refuse. I believe my flat is disappearing today, or perhaps tomorrow."

"Have the two of you come to some new temporary arrangement?"

"Yes. Dixon will reside with her sister for several months, and then she shall return."

"And you?"

"I haven't decided. Nicholas and Peggy still have many in the house. Marlborough Mills is very close to where I will work, but I would have to see who is in the house. Who stays overnight?"

"I know that is purely propriety speaking, as you know John is a total gentleman."

"Yes, I have come to understand that more than I once knew. I have no fear of him or my own reputation, as I know no one who would care; however, I would not care to have perceived aspersions heaped on his character."

"Miss Hale, if it will help make a decision in either direction, I should tell you that he is seeing a lady. There have been rumors of a pending betrothal. I would also say that many falsehoods are put about as to whom he is going to settle down with. It has been never-ending for the poor man."

"Has he spoken of this with you?"

"No. He would not confide information like that with anyone. If there may be a medical condition that should be examined before a nuptial, then I would know."

"With Mr. Bell still out of town, you are the only unbiased person I can talk to."

"I would be honored in all but your spiritual well-being."

"Doctor, how do I hold my head high?"

"I wish I had a potion to concoct for you. That must come from within, my dear. You are no less a person than you ever were. It is only your circumstances that have changed. You are making an effort that shows that you are doing the best you can. No shame in that. I am sure, in fact, I know, among those many thousand millworkers, there are people performing tasks well below their ability. For your education, there are not many positions available that meet your qualifications. Seems like you have decent work now."

"Work ... work! That's just it. I have to work to earn my keep and although worthy, I should be helping the poor. I can hardly look into the faces of my friends. I think I see pity. I don't want that."

"Yes, there is much compassion for you and guilt."

"Guilt?"

"Your friends feel sad for not knowing about your situation. It would cost them little to make a great change in your life. They feel guilty about what you have been going through, as they should have inquired and known. I believe John was under the impression that you went to London after your father left us. Nicholas and Peggy too may have thought you left, but they were busy with Bessy and her school at the time."

"I certainly do not blame them, and they should feel no guilt. I would have refused it."

"Miss Hale, you are a caring and giving person to all but yourself. You have a high, almost exacting, intolerance for your own actions. Why is that?"

"I never really thought about it."

"Well, you should."

"You think I should have accepted Mr. Thornton's proposal?"

"I cannot answer that. Only you can. Have your feelings changed?"

"Considerably, but in many ways. I believe I have burned my bridge with Mr. Thornton."

"I cannot say much to that. I have my opinion, but I will keep it to myself. I shall leave you now. Don't forget to eat well today. I will drop in on Dixon later. Good morning, Miss Hale." Donaldson left the room.

"Miss Margaret, what are you going to do? I will worry about you if I don't think you are being cared for. I will return from Sister's as soon as I can."

"Dixon, knowing you're being nursed properly will give me peace of mind. I will only have to take care of myself. I have quite a tangled web to cross."

"What do you mean, tangled web?"

"Ahead of me, I see a multitude of decisions to make. Where each one branches off to will require another change my life. Somewhere there is a spider that stalks me as I run hither and yon." Margaret was looking off as if she were in a dream.

"Miss Margaret … Miss Margaret! Are you having nightmares again?"

"Not last night."

"Did you tell the doctor about them?"

"No. I am sure it is the stress causing too many negative thoughts while I sleep. Things are about to change for the better," Margaret said in a cheery tone, one which she did not feel.

Peggy and Nicholas had stopped at Margaret's flat and collected all their clothes, packing them in carpetbags.

Jeremy, from across the street, was watching them load the bundles into their cart. He ran out to inquire.

"Excuse me, I think we spoke before. Are you removing some of Miss Hale's belongings? How is her guardian?"

"Your name is Jeremy, correct?"

"Aye sir."

"My wife and I are taking their clothing to another location. Miss Hale is going to be moved from here since her guardian will be away for several months. Her name is Dixon. We are offering a place for her to stay until they both are well."

"Is Miss Hale ill?"

"Run down, I would say. She was not reared to live and work the way she has been trying to lately. It has taken a toll on her."

"Her furniture?"

"Will be gathered later today and stored."

"Tell her that Jeremy sends his best. I hope they are both well, quick as you like."

Chapter Ten

Margaret was still pacing Dixon's room when John entered.

"How are the patients this early morning?"

"I believe you will see a small improvement in both of us. Thank you for the room."

"Any time, Miss Hale."

"May I ask a question about your home staff?"

"Of course."

"Is there anyone who stays overnight?"

"Do you mean if you elect to recover at my home, will we be alone at night?"

"Yes."

"I will have someone to chaperone you while you stay. Jane is going with my mother, and Nicholas has found a former in-service housekeeper to take Jane's place. I believe I will ask her to stay at the house. Does that put your mind at ease?"

"Yes, I am sure it does."

"Can I assume you will recover at Marlborough Mills?"

"What's this?" asked Nicholas when he and Peggy entered the room.

Peggy walked over to Dixon to express her regards. Nicholas echoed her with his own.

"Nicholas, what is the news about a housekeeper for my home?"

"The mature woman I spoke of first does not feel she is at a good age to go back into that type of work. But I have found someone else. A bit younger and less experienced, but anxious to return to housekeeping. She is in Milton only because her father came here to work."

"Do you think she will take quarters at the house?"

"Yes. I did not give her that information specifically, because I didn't know who she would go with or if they wanted her overnight. She would like a day off each week to visit her father."

"I see no problem with that." John replied.

Nicholas pulled up a chair next to Margaret. John stood.

"Have you come to any decisions?"

"I will have that answer by the end of the day. Dixon will travel to her sister's home. I will accompany her and return. That will take place as soon as the doctor says she may get on a train."

"Margaret, we have yours and Dixon's clothing in some carpet bags. She could leave straight from the hospital if she wants." Peggy looked at Dixon sitting up in bed.

"And you are still making up your mind on staying at Marlborough Mills or our home?"

"That is correct. Thank you both for offering, and I would feel comfortable and safe in either home. I do have one or two other issues to resolve in my mind first."

"We shall leave your clothing in the buggy until you decide. Peggy and I shall visit again after dinner."

"I will be seeing to my mother and sister's situation and will be arranging for your furniture to go into storage. Is there anything else you want done?"

"I believe all the perishable food should not be stored."

"Of course, Miss Hale. That will be set aside for the home you will occupy."

"Peggy and I will leave now and catch you up after dinner."

"Thank you both. Until then–."

"Miss Hale, would you take a walk with me down the hall for a few moments? I will not exhaust you."

"If you wish."

"Dixon, I shall return." Margaret followed John to the doorway and passed through it before him. She stopped, not knowing which way. She was nervous.

"This way, Miss Hale." John pointed in a direction with his hat. "There is some seating down this way."

They sat after John pulled his chair closer to Margaret's.

Margaret was avoiding looking into his face.

"Margaret, Miss Hale, am I to conclude from your note that there is much to be said between us since a year ago? You do not have to answer that. Whatever it is that you propose to say, I will honor. I wish I could avoid pressing you to discuss this, but I have longed for words from you."

John noticed she wouldn't look at him. "I only bring this up," he continued, "because you have a choice as to where to recover and live until Dixon's return. This opportunity, for me, may never come again. If you decide on Marlborough Mills and are uncomfortable, the Higgins would gladly have you to their home." John was nervous trying to get the right words out without sounding too emotional.

"Mr. Thornton …."

"Please call me John, as you did once before."

Margaret cleared her throat and looked toward him quickly, and then away.

"Do you not feel that my presence in your home would cause some disruption with your 'intended'?"

"My 'intended'? I do not have an 'intended.'" There are rumors, but there is no substance to them. Yes, I am seeing a lady. Your being there will have no effect on our acquaintanceship, though I cannot know the future."

"So my being in residence in your home will not prevent you from seeing her as you are doing now?"

John swallowed hard and looked away from Margaret. There was a moment before he began his answer.

"It seems you question your own answer to that. I will not come into a place, even as desperate as I seem to be, and spoil anyone's relationship," Margaret added.

"I will promise you, Miss Hale–"

"Margaret, please. Call me 'Margaret.'"

"As I said before, she is not my 'intended.' No words have been spoken in that regard. I cannot exactly know her expectations, but I believe mine have differed from hers all along. She is like any other woman whom I have spent time with, except—I do not wish to pursue this discussion about someone else. I will act as my emotions dictate. Perhaps there will come a time when we can speak more freely, but nothing can be said until we speak the words we have held inside for so long."

"I've become quite destitute and am weak in spirit. I am afraid I will react to a kindness too quickly and without thought. Can you promise not to take advantage of my fragility?"

"I promise. But you must be truthful and allow me to help you, even if it is not financial."

"In what regard?"

"If you have doubts or worries, I would like to discuss them so you have the benefit of another opinion. If you wish to attend church, or walk in the evening, or shop in town, consider me your friend, and permit me to accompany you, as Adam Bell would. If you are worried beyond that, be assured I will act as a friend, nothing more unless you–" He caught himself again.

"John, I think you have said enough. I must return to Dixon, and I am sure you have a big day ahead of you. Thank you for answering the questions that were in my mind. I can now make a more satisfying choice." Margaret stood.

John stood in front of her. Margaret wouldn't look up. She just stared at his chest. He took one knuckle and gently lifted her face to his. He heard an audible sigh as Margaret ran down the hall.

When John returned home, the packing of the wagon was underway. Nicholas was standing outside directing the workers handling some fragile items, and beside him stood a young lady. John remembered seeing her working the line. Everyone called her "Benny." John left the coach and walked over.

"John, this is Benny, your new housekeeper."

"Hello Benny. I've always wondered why they called you Benny."

"My mother named me Benevolent. Caring and generous, she expected me to be. She is no longer here to see how I'll turn out, sir."

"Have you met Jane, the current housekeeper?"

"No, sir."

"Let me take you to her. I want her to explain her duties." John walked her to the front door and picked up what he assumed was her satchel of clothes.

"Your room will be off of the kitchen, since Cook goes home after evening meal and does not stay here."

"Very good, sir. How do I address you?"

"You can continue with 'Master' or perhaps better, 'Mr. Thornton.' Benny, there is a small chance that this position is temporary. The housekeeper of a friend is recovering. Her recovery will take about six months. Should she return to Milton, which is likely, I will reinstate her as a housekeeper. Depending on her condition, your job may change. You might have to return to the mills or maybe work part time here, but she would need your room. Are you still willing to accept this position?"

"Yes, sir. Should it only be a few months, I will enjoy being away from the machines."

"Good. Now, let's go find Jane. She will give you instructions, and then there is always Cook, who knows the entire house routine. Oh, one last thing. Unless there is an occasion when I am entertaining and you are needed to serve, most of your evenings will be your own. You will have one day a week off. But upstairs is off limits after dinner."

"Yes, sir. Thank you, sir."

John went to find his mother and sister. They were upstairs directing men as to what and what not to take to the wagon.

"How is everything going, Mother?"

"It was a rough start but seems to be going more smoothly. I did pack most of the china and crystal items. I just hope they don't steal them."

"I have one of my foremen coming to watch them."

"I am carrying my jewelry in my handbag. Other than that and Fanny's constant whining, I think we're all right."

"Mother, I might as well tell you that both Higgins and I are offering Miss Hale a room while she recovers."

"I see," Hannah said folding her arms. "Well, the best to you."

"Mother, it isn't *like* that."

"Don't lie to me, son. Would this moving day have happened if Miss Hale hadn't come to the mill a few days ago?"

"Probably not. And I would have continued on in my dreary life. It was not because of her directly, though. I finally had heard enough from my family about what I want in my life. I made the decision based solely on that. I have no idea if Miss Hale would wish to recover here. I am not even sure that she would consider me a friend. I could not foresee Dixon's heart attack, which presented the freedom to make such an offer."

"No, I guess not. I'm sorry. This is just not a good day."

"I am aware of that. Perhaps you and Fanny would care to have dinner with me tonight. I've always wanted you to dine out with me."

"Some other evening, John. We will be too exhausted. Cook is over instructing my new cook on our favorites, and they will order from the grocer."

"Very well, then. I will go and secure one of the foremen and send him over. Once they have moved your belongings, which will not have much furniture, I take it, they will collect Miss Hale's furniture for storage."

"You are lending her a helping hand, aren't you?"

"Mother, must I repeat myself? The tone in your voice provokes me to say this. I will always see to your needs. Fanny will soon be Watson's responsibility. What I do with my money is up to me. Should I die without an heir or wife, it will all go to Miss Hale. That is how much she means to me. Now, if you want to see me rarely, continue with your snide remarks and expressing disappointment about my decisions. You are driving a wedge between us. Think about that."

John turned and left. He was seething. His mother seemed determined to not understand him. Even if he lived alone forever, he would not miss that. The older she got, the more set in her opinions she became. *No one will ever be good enough for me, he silently reflected.*

John went to the mill. He found the foreman and sent him to the house. He continued on through the mill with his daily routine.

Benny was enjoying her walk-through with Jane, and both overheard John's conversation with his mother.

"Benny you will hear things, but you are trusted not to repeat them. I am sure you understand that."

"Oh, yes, Jane. It has always been like that. I still have a few uniforms from my last job as a housemaid on an estate near London."

"So you aren't exactly a housekeeper?"

"No, but I will have no problem becoming one in a house this size. I know that Cook and I are equal in staff ranking."

"If you say so. It wasn't like that for me. I liked Cook, and she didn't interfere with me unless I was stepping out of line."

"And how is it working for handsome Mr. Thornton?"

"Handsome? I guess he is in a way."

"In a way? You don't see it?"

"Perhaps I have been here too long to notice it anymore. I hope he is not the reason you put yourself forward for this position."

"Oh, no."

"Did he tell you not to go upstairs until 6:00 a.m.?"

"No. What happens at that time?"

"By that time, you know he is dressed. Make sure there is water in the pitcher so he can shave in the morning. He doesn't do it every day, but make sure the pitcher is clean and the water is fresh daily."

"I will."

"Dixon, I have made up my mind."

"I know what it is," Dixon responded quietly, "or what it should be."

"What or which one?" asked Margaret.

"I think you need to go to Marlborough Mills," Dixon continued.

"Yes, I am. I feel assured that John will be the gentleman I have always known him to be. There is much I wish to talk about with him, regarding our past. I've always wondered if he proposed out of obligation rather than love, and if I ever really did love him. As time has passed, I have come to believe that I did, indeed, although I did not know it at the time. What estrangement has done to my feelings, I will never know unless I try. He does have a lady friend who believes he may ask for her hand. He has promised me that having me there will not alter any plans he might have–though he doesn't even sound as if he has plans. John is going to let his emotions tell him what to do."

"How will you get along with Mrs. Thornton?"

"John is having her moved out today. She going in town and Fanny with her."

"Have they had a falling out?"

"I am not certain of the reason, but John feels he's at a point where he needs to be his own man and make his own decisions without the interference from Mrs. Thornton and Fanny. I cannot imagine what this is costing him."

"Costing?"

"Not only financially, mentally, but also personally."

"Do you think it is because of you, miss?"

"How could it be?"

"You said you went to the mill. He speaks of it with his mother, and they argue again."

"Oh, no. I mean yes, it could be so, but he has another lady. And I believe his decision was made before your accident. He couldn't know I was coming there. He still doesn't know."

"I suppose."

"What would you have me do, Dixon?"

"I do not know about now, but I think you need to marry that man. I like him better than Mr. Lenox and the young man before him. I like the shy but confident man I see in him."

"I like that, too. He is mature and wise. Working and supporting the family has molded him into a man early in life. He has never faced many of the temptations that corrupt more wealthy young men.

"And you know your mother, father and Mr. Bell respected and liked him. He is a good man. It all depends on if he can make you happy. I hadn't seen you happy since long before we moved here. I think you have forgotten what it is like."

"I believe it to be the same for you too. Let's hope we both achieve that in the future."

John returned to his office after his midday meal, which consisted of a sandwich Cook had made that morning. The wagon had gone. Soon, he would accompany his mother and sister to their new flat. He fell into thought, shuffling his post around on the desktop, but not reading it. Suddenly a note from E. Hawkins came into view. He opened it.

"You are invited to dine with me at my home ...."

John knew that the invitation was for tomorrow night, believing it to be Margaret's first night in his home. This was poor timing. But accepting the invitation should help ease Margaret's worry that she was interrupting his life. What an understatement that was. She could only recover it. She *was* his life.

John decided to stop by Miss Hawkins's home, after taking his mother and sister to town. He heard Branson bringing the carriage.

John left his office and went inside to see if they were ready. Fanny had a handful of things, and John took them from her and carried them outside. Hannah stood back and looked around the yard and the house before she entered the coach. John felt guilty suddenly, then wondered if guilt was the emotion his mother intended him to feel.

Branson ruffled the reins, and they were off.

"Fanny, have you decided what work you would like to do?" John smiled.

"I will be working on my wedding. Mr. Watson has suggested we move it up. I think he is grateful to you for this. It will be nice having a spending account and not have to ask when I want something."

"I am happy for you, Fanny."

Hannah snorted in disgust of her daughter. She never wanted for anything.

"Mother, I shall be around tomorrow morning to see if you need anything. Also, the coachman will start then."

"Jane is there now, seeing to the arrangements of boxes we are to unpack."

"I have an account at a local book store near your flat. I have used it on occasion. You may want to take advantage of that."

The rest of the ride was subdued. It was a strange feeling all around. John did, indeed, feel some guilt, but not as much as he anticipated. That was mainly because Fanny seemed happy about it all, and it looked as if his mother just might come to terms with his being an aging young man. Branson pulled the coach to a stop, and John exited and helped the ladies out. Once again, he looked over where he was leaving them and assured himself they were in a safe flat.

They all walked together inside and saw people coming and going. Jane was directing the carriers to different rooms and Cook was in the kitchen.

"No, put that over here, please," Hannah said. She unpinned her hat, removed her shawl, and began barking orders. Fanny went directly upstairs to see which room was hers.

"Mother, I am going to leave you to this. We shall talk soon. I am having dinner at Miss Hawkins's home tomorrow night, but we'll make plans for a dinner out." He walked to his mother and kissed her forehead. "Good-bye, mother."

As John stepped into his coach, a sense of freedom enveloped his countenance.

"Miss Hawkins, Branson," he shouted from inside.

"Aye guv."

Chapter Eleven

"Nicholas will be awhile before arriving, but I thought I would come ahead and bring you a change of clothes, Margaret," Peggy greeted them. "I also brought your books. I didn't think you would like those stored."

"How thoughtful, and you are very much correct. Do you have any idea where my furnishings will be going?"

"Nicholas says there is a small shed that isn't used for much on the mill property. He thinks John will most likely choose that. They shall be close by, I would think.

"Dixon, you look more cheery. You gave us all a right good scare. How are you feeling?"

"I am feeling like myself, but the doctor won't believe me."

"You must listen to him, or the next one might take you from us permanently."

"I know that now. I thought he was just saying that to make me mind, but Miss Margaret has explained it so that I can understand it."

Peggy looked at Margaret. "Do they know when she will be released?"

"I believe it may be three or four more days. She will get out of bed tomorrow. She will be asked to do something and they will listen to her heart. That goes on for several days. Dixon can leave after that," Margaret smiled, looking at Dixon.

"Did I tell you that Dixon will recover at her sister's home? They have kept in constant touch, but have not seen each other in several years. We wrote to her yesterday. I will look at train schedules tomorrow, so we can write her sister again as when to expect us."

"Yes, you mentioned about Dixon going to her sister's home, earlier today. But what is this *us?"*

"Yes, I will attend her on the trip. I will return late that day, if I can; however, there is a chance I will stay the one night. It seems I must get approval from a doctor to do this."

Two nurses came in with a wheelchair and told Dixon it was time for a bath. Dixon grumbled when they helped her out of the bed. Margaret laughed.

"To hear you Dixon, one would think you never had a bath before."

"I've never had anyone with me since I was a child."

Peggy and Margaret laughed.

The two women were quiet as they watched Dixon man-handled into the chair.

"Nurse, do you know that she can't swim?" Margaret got the giggles.

Peggy stared at her in wonderment. "It seems you are in good fare today. How long has it been since you laughed?"

"Quite a while. Recently, being surrounded by friends has lifted my spirits. John and I had a conversation this morning, and I am glad I can make an informed decision. I will be staying at his home. Is that wrong, do you think?"

"I think it is the best decision you could make. Should you feel uncomfortable, you will forever be welcome at our home."

"You really think it is the right choice for me."

"For both of you, my dear. I believe you both have things you want to say. This will give you plenty of opportunities to talk. I'd hate to see John regularly taking you away in a coach so you could discuss the errors of your ways from year ago."

"Yes, I know I was in error."

"And he was, too."

"You think so?"

"I know so. It probably never would have happened that way, if his mother hadn't felt embarrassed and obligated John to do the right thing by you."

"Don't say any more. I've had this on my mind a long time. I know what I need to say. I don't want to be swayed by your opinion. I have to satisfy myself."

"All right, Margaret. As much as I was looking forward to having someone to talk to, I think you are making the best choice. Do you know if you will be alone in the house?"

"Yes, I know I will not be alone. John, as of today, has a live-in housekeeper."

"Then propriety is met."

"I care little for that these days. I have lost the status where that holds significant importance in my life. I have come so low."

"Margaret! Stop doing that. Stop putting yourself down."

A woman came into the room carrying clean bedding.

"Do you feel like a walk?"

"Yes, please, and some air."

Peggy and Margaret strolled a short distance to the entrance where benches waited outside. Margaret felt tired.

As Jeremy arrived home, he saw men filling a wagon with Miss Hale's belongings. He walked across the street to inquire.

"This Miss Hale wants her furniture moved again? It's been here a week, maybe."

"We were told to pack it all. It is going into storage. Apparently, she and whoever lives with her, got sick. They are recovering somewhere else," said one of the men.

"You look familiar. Aren't you a millworker?"

"We all are. For today, we are movers. We're at Marlborough Mills."

"Is Miss Hale staying there?"

"I don't know where either of them is staying. I only know where this furniture is going. Master Thornton may know her destination."

"Thank you. I will remember that. I might want to visit her."

Jeremy had enjoyed her company for the brief time they'd been neighbors and hated to lose sight of her. He wondered why her household was directed to Marlborough Mills' property. He thought it must be Mrs. Thornton's idea. He shrugged his shoulders and went home.

"Good afternoon, Elaine," John said, handing his top hat to the footman and following her into the parlor.

"It is good of you to come by. Is your visit to answer my invitation?"

"Indeed. I will be delighted to attend." John felt strange, as if he were lying to her. He thought her a nice woman a week ago. Nothing had changed, except him.

"Please sit. You do have a moment, do you not?"

"I do have some time. Tonight I have a short meeting to attend."

"Is it secret?" Elaine smiled coyly.

"No. I believe the last time we spoke, I mentioned a friend of mine might be in need."

"Yes, that was the one you proposed to a year ago."

"That is correct."

"Nicholas and I have come to find that her guardian has just had a heart attack, and the doctor has also hospitalized my friend as well. They have been under grave financial burdens since her father passed away. The story is too long to go into now, and it is her private business, anyway. Tonight, she will have a decision whether she is to recover at my home or my partner's."

"So, I am not to feel a bit intimated by a former lover who may move in with you?"

"You make it sound sordid. It was never like that, and will not be now. For heaven's sake, I said we were friends. I've never even kissed her."

"But you asked for her hand?"

John stood. "I will discuss this no further. I should never have brought it up. Do you still wish me to be a guest tomorrow evening?"

"Yes, of course, I do." Elaine walked over to John and placed her arms around his neck. Her sultry voice begged for a kiss. "Kiss me."

John untangled her arms from the back of his head. "I shall be here tomorrow night." John turned and walked into the hall. He grabbed his hat and left.

This woman is more than a friend, Elaine thought, as John walked away.

"Margaret, how has it really been for the two of you? As you may remember, I was a working woman when Nicholas found me. I was educated, too, but my father worked hard to send me to school. He was never considered a gentleman by society's standards as you know them. The family had a very common history. I was never quite in the position in which you find yourself, so I don't really know what you had to endure these last months. Your health is strikingly different from before."

"It came as a great surprise when I realized the financial situation after father died. There were debts from the illnesses and burials. Keeping up appearances was costly, as I look back on the records. I believe father was bartering in trade for some of his debts. He would teach in some situations as a means of payment. When he died, there was no longer even that income. I was led to believe

Mr. Bell would become my benefactor, but he seems to be missing. He was spending his last months of life traveling. He never wrote or came home for father's funeral, which we expected he would attend. I don't know what to think about that, and I am worried about him."

"You've written, of course?"

"Several times. As the days and weeks wore on, my bereavement turned into concern for our welfare. Within a month and a half, it was clear that Dixon and I would have to find employment to continue as we were. We were both brave and committed to keeping our heads high, but there were bills outstanding. I began to sell some heirlooms and jewelry. That paid all the remaining bills and saw us through the next month. Looking forward at that point, I had to give up the flat and take a place that I could afford to keep–if I could find decent work. That is not easy to do in Milton. And you know the rest."

"You left out the part where you gave up eating and worried yourself out of sleeping. Margaret, you cannot see yourself. Your health is poor."

"I know. My clothing has become loose on me. It's most unbecoming now. But thanks to your help, that will change in time."

"Was it embarrassment that kept you from coming to us?"

"Yes. I was a beggar, any way you look at it. I did not want John to see me either. I knew that if I turned to you for help, he would know. However, in the end, I was desperate for work and approached Marlborough Mills. John met with me, but when he looked into my eyes with his own, the past reared. He looked at me as he once did. I wanted to die of humiliation and lost chances. I ran. I still cannot look directly at him for longer than a moment."

"I thought that would be your reason. I've noticed how you cannot look at him. Is it love, do you think?"

"I will find out in quick order."

"He is seeing someone, you know."

"I am glad of it. That helped me make my decision. Whether he continues with her or not, I will know my real feelings. I was so confused the day that he proposed that I did not know if I had any regard for him. For a while, I felt I was heading that way. I felt different, but things changed. Nothing was left clear to me when he walked away that last day. I made accusations, and he made accusations. I don't believe any of these were actually true, but it ended all that had started. And it's been that way ever since."

Peggy put her arms around Margaret. "You poor dear. What you have suffered."

"I will go back to work and get on my feet. I am thankful that Dixon has a place to recover and I will have no flat expense. That should allow me to save. Master Griffin is holding my position, but that is only temporary until I can set his new books in order. He is paying me the salary of a foreman."

"That is brave of him. He must have great confidence in you."

Margaret started to smile. "I set my own price. He was taken aback, but I think he liked my taking a stance on my value."

Peggy laughed. '"Good on you."

"I should be returning to my room. My dinner must be there, waiting for me. Come with me."

They parted company for a few moments, and Margaret entered the hospital door. She was breathing hard by the time she arrived. She sat heavily on the side of her bed, more exhausted than she had anticipated. Her woman's week was under way, and Margaret decided that this was the cause of her mounting fatigue. If she could be strong, get through her bleeding time and get Dixon home, she would be well on her way to recovery.

Peggy noticed Margaret sitting still on the side of her bed contemplatively. She had brought Margaret's clean clothes from Dixon's room.

"I see your meal is waiting. What kind of fare do they feed you here?"

Margaret perked up, noticing the tray by her bed. "Oh, I missed seeing the tray." She slipped off her shoes and sat back against her pillow.

"Peggy, would you do the honors?" she smiled.

"*Oui*." She laughed. "Would you prefer white or red wine with your–your–what *is* that?"

"I think it's a different type of porridge. I seem to be getting fattening foods since coming here. I probably should have told them I have very little appetite for porridge. A nice potato and a small piece of meat would suit me."

Peggy smiled weakly as she watched Margaret pour her tea from the little teapot. Her hand wasn't steady, and a small amount flowed into her saucer.

"Can I help you, Margaret?"

"No, I will be fine. I have to find my muscles. Please don't mention this to anyone. Sometimes I feel like a child having to learn all over again. I know it is only this weakened state that I am recovering from. It shall soon be in the past."

"I am not making any promises when it comes to hiding your health issues, but you must let the doctor know if it does not improve."

"Naturally, Peggy."

"Don't say *naturally*, Margaret. You tried to be too brave through the worst ordeal in your life, and you see where you are now." Peggy didn't want to scold her as a good friend would, but she knew Margaret's pride matched John's. If they loved each other and both had too much pride, each might recognize in the other the problems caused by pride

"I know. I see that waiting this long time has been foolish. I am probably the cause of Dixon's heart attack. She was as worried and anxious for me as I was for both of us. She was doing more because she is a servant. She's been doing work usually done by a male. I should have seen it coming."

"Margaret, I am going to ask John to put you over his knee and paddle your backside if you keep this up. You are still worrying or berating yourself for this. That must stop. You made the decisions that you felt were correct. Most people would have done the same, I suppose. But it is in the past now. You must learn from it and begin anew."

"Yes, mother." Margaret giggled.

John was in his coach, being driven to the mill, when his thoughts turned to Elaine, whom he had left only moments before. He wondered how much at fault he was for that conversation. He never should have told her about asking for Margaret's hand long ago. Of course, that would upset her. It would upset any man or woman to know a former love was so close again. Elaine had an irritating way of speaking about it. She made unwarranted assumptions about Margaret and himself. His personal relationship with Elaine had passed propriety, at her urging, long ago. Aside from Elaine's feelings about him, where was her sense of charity? She came from wealth. Did her family not subscribe to helping their fellow man?

John knew he was looking for ways out of his arrangement. He was unfair. Perhaps tomorrow's dinner would see her in the light he once had.

Branson pulled around to the far back shed, where the delivery of Margaret Hale's furnishings was taking place. Exiting the coach and seeing the furnishings being prepared to be moved inside, he noticed very few boxes.

"James, are more boxes in the shed, there?"

"No, master."

And you've packed everything from that flat?"

"We have, sir."

"What did you pack in these few boxes," John asked, surprised there were not more.

"All but two of those is for the kitchen pantry. We didn't feel that was to go in here."

"Quite right." John strolled over to the two boxes not holding pantry foods and opened the first one. It wasn't food, but kitchen plates, bowls and cookware. A horrid realization came over him, as he realized that a lot of fine china and some family heirlooms and decorations were missing. He opened the other box and found incidentals in the form of desk items, a woman's face paints, perfumes and feminine things. There were other odd lots of necessary things, but nothing of real value. Where were her books and her father's large collection of books?

"James, were there no books in the house?"

"There were a few, but Mrs. Higgins collected those."

"Was there any jewelry?"

"We never saw any, and I watched the men real close. You will find a small brass jewelry case in the bottom of that box, but there was no jewelry in it when we opened it."

John was sick. He looked back up at the furnishings. For a three-floor flat, there were only about ten pieces of wood. If only Adam Bell could see what he was looking at now.

Nicholas closed out the second shift and headed for the hospital. He heard a whistle as he started up the concrete steps to the entrance. Turning around, he saw John exiting his coach. He waited.

"Did you whistle?"

John smiled. "No, Branson did that for me. He's much louder." John smiled.

Both men walked towards Dixon's room together.

Chapter Twelve

Nicholas and John entered Dixon's room, expecting to find Margaret there, too. Both men inquired as to Dixon's condition.

"Is Miss Hale in her own room?" asked John.

"I do not know, Mr. Thornton. I was taken away for a bath, and Mrs. Higgins and Miss Margaret left for a walk."

Nicholas heard his wife and Margaret coming up the hall. "I think they're on their way here," he said.

"As they came through the door, Peggy was sure John had a twinkle in his eye. He was wearing a slightly suppressed smile.

"Good evening, ladies," John greeted them.

"Good evening."

"Dixon, would you mind if we found a place where we could all sit?" John inquired.

"No, I don't mind. I would like to sleep a bit."

Nicholas looked at the others. "Canteen or front foyer?"

"Let's go to the canteen. Margaret hardly ate her dinner. Perhaps there is something else to eat there."

John instantly looked at Margaret.

"I am fine, Peggy. But a biscuit sounds nice."

John looked for a wheelchair. There didn't seem to be any around. "Miss Hale, please take my arm. I do not think you are really steady on your legs."

Nicholas noticed the same thing and briefly looked at Peggy, who frowned at him. "I'll take your other side, Margaret."

"I am fine, really I am."

"Miss Hale, please take my arm," John insisted.

Margaret did not want to look into his face and argue.

"If you insist," she said with an exaggerated sigh.

John took one side and Nicholas the other. It wasn't too many paces before the men realized she was using their arms quite firmly. Nicholas glanced over Margaret's head and noticed John was all too aware and worried about her. When they arrived in the canteen, Peggy made the cups of tea and found some biscuits to eat.

Margaret began to speak before everyone was settled. "I wish to thank you all again. I believe I have learned my lesson, and I apologize for any guilt you may feel for not knowing what I was enduring. That was all my doing. I tried to hide it, and save my reputation until the last minute. It appears I don't do very well when it comes to my reputation." John knew she must be thinking of the riot, too.

Placing the cups in front of everyone, Peggy mentioned, "She continues to beat up on herself. I told her she had to stop that. Begin life anew. She will never see her recent past life again."

"Peggy is right, Margaret," John added.

"She quite convinced me today of my lapse in judgment. This shall be the last apology. I would be comfortable in either household, but I am choosing Marlborough Mills."

Peggy smiled at Margaret, and she looked at John. He was visibly exhaling.

"Should I feel I am in the way or find my presence to be a disadvantage in John's life, I know I am welcome in your home," she said, looking at Nicholas.

"Any time, Margaret," Nicholas said.

"I am selecting John's home because I think we have unresolved words to say, and living in your home, John, will save Branson a lot of trips."

Everyone laughed. Margaret was honest with what they all knew should be done.

"Thank you, Margaret. And just so you know you will not be interrupting my life, I have a dinner engagement tomorrow night, which I am not canceling."

"I am heartened to hear that. I will enjoy having a meal with Cook and whoever is your new housekeeper. What is her name?"

John was chagrined. "I've actually forgotten."

The moment was light and enjoyable. John was keeping himself in perfect control, showing no signs of his heart thudding heavily within his chest.

"I will stay with Dixon in the morning. She will have some medical testing in the afternoon. I hope I will be able to visit her every day until she is released. I will accompany her to her sister's home from the hospital. We should hear something from her sister in another day or two. If I can, I will return the same day. Otherwise, I will spend one night."

John nodded, but he knew he would go with them. Margaret was still very ill, and he wouldn't let her ride the train alone. They would talk about that soon.

"Margaret, I will be most anxious to have you at my home. The timing of a new housekeeper coming in, and you with your knowledge of such training will benefit me greatly."

"I'm glad I can be of some value to you. When I am well enough, I shall return to complete the work I started at Griffin's Mill."

"If you wish," John said, knowing immediately that was the wrong thing to say.

"Mr. Thornton–John, I hope not to live off of your kindness if I can work."

John lowered his head, knowing Nicholas and Peggy were waiting for his answer to that.

"I am sorry. I misspoke. I did not mean to indicate that you would do other than what you feel you must do. What time can I pick you up tomorrow?"

"Would noon be suitable? I have no idea what kind of schedule you keep for the mills. You could send Branson on his own, too."

"Margaret, I will bring your other clothes and books to John's home sometime tomorrow," interjected Peggy.

"Where are my furnishings?"

"They are in a shed on the grounds of Marlborough Mills. Everything will be close at hand."

"Do you think there would be room for my writing desk in the bedchamber?"

"I believe so. There is always room in my study, too, or in the sitting room. Please do not worry about anything. I would like to see Dixon and you settled in comfortable quarters, so your lives can return to what they were."

"I am looking forward to that as well. Thank you all for heading me in that direction. I think I am done with this discussion."

They had barely finished their tea when Margaret asked to be left alone. Fatigue was beginning to exhaust her. She wanted to bathe and get into bed early. Everyone thought that was a good idea, but didn't mention it. John decided to see Donaldson after leaving the hospital. There was a wheelchair outside the door and no one in the canteen other than a cleaning lady. John pushed it towards Margaret.

"Margaret, I will most likely see you tomorrow," said Peggy. Get a good night's sleep. You really need to rest."

The two said goodnight and went on their way. John enjoyed having her to himself for a moment, although he had nothing to say.

"Margaret, is there anything you desire before you arrive tomorrow? What foods can you eat?"

"Please don't bother yourself. I will talk with Cook."

"Would you permit me to take you out for dinner now and again?"

"I'm not sure that would be appropriate for you."

"Let me be the judge of that. I am my own man."

"I am sure you are."

"Is that a yes, then?"

"If you wish," Margaret laughed. "Perhaps you could invite Miss Lady Friend over for dinner, so she can meet me. If she knows what you are doing, she will probably give you a hard time. I can help her understand that I am no threat to her. You and I are friends."

John reached around and placed the back of his hand on her brow.

"What are you doing?"

"I was checking for fever."

"I have no fever."

"I thought you must have one. You are either ill or quite mistaken, if you think I could do what you suggest." He laughed.

"Is it not true?"

"Is what not true?" he asked.

"Is she not the lady you see tomorrow evening?"

"Yes."

"Are we not friends?"

"Yes, we are friends, very good friends, I hope."

"I will invite her over when I am feeling well. I shall let you know what you should be doing to win her hand."

John stopped pushing the chair. He walked around in front of Margaret and knelt so he could see her eyes.

"Margaret Hale, hear me when I say this. I do not want to win her hand."

"That might change, John." Margaret was starting to get the giggles. She was playing a game, at least she thought so, but his answers were no game.

"Margaret, you know very little about me. You didn't like me, if I remember correctly. Your residency will change that if I am lucky. At least that is my wish."

"And mine."

There was silence for the rest of the way.

"Will you be all right, or would you care for a nurse to prepare you for bed?"

"I need no help, but thank you for the push. If you will just leave the chair outside the door for someone else. I shall see you near noon tomorrow."

"I will be here. Goodnight, Margaret."

"Goodnight, John."

John was almost exhausted from the stress of not showing his emotions. Margaret's misfortune might be his salvation, he was thinking on the way to Donaldson's. Many wondrous thoughts were rushing through his mind.

There was still light burning in Donaldson's office as he approached.

"Branson, I shan't be long."

John entered the office. The nurse was absent, probably had gone home for the day. John shouted for Donaldson.

"It that you, Thornton?"

"Yes. If you could spare a moment, I wish to speak to you."

"C'mon back. I'm just having a bite to eat."

John found him in his office. A basket with a meal wrapped in it was sitting on his desk.

"Do you ever eat at home?" John asked, setting his hat down on a small table.

"I don't really have a cook. I have a woman who will bring small meals to me and some patients who are staying. Otherwise, I eat out somewhere. I see you out there with your ladies, on occasion."

"I'm here to ask about Miss Hale."

"You know I should not discuss that with you."

"But you will. You've always known how I feel about her. She is pale and weak. She does not know it yet, but I will accompany her and Dixon to wherever Dixon's family resides. Mr. and Mrs. Higgins and I took her for a walk to the hospital canteen tonight. Nicholas and I had to support her on each side when she tried to walk. She could hardly stand up."

"You see this book I am reading?"

John nodded. "What of it?"

"About forty years ago, a condition—let's call it—was discovered. I haven't had any cases that I have treated. It is called anemia."

"And what is that exactly?"

"It is a problem with the red blood cells. Margaret seems to fit the symptoms. She is malnourished. And when she does eat, she hasn't consumed food rich in iron. Since she seemed to have been in good health originally, I will wager this is temporary, meaning she was not born with abnormal blood cells. The healthy red blood cells carry oxygen to the organs that keep them strong. When little oxygen is getting to the organs, great fatigue can take place. Her body cannot recover its strength."

"So what is done about this? There must be something."

"Calm down, John. There is one other cause, too."

"What is that?"

"This is a bit personal, but she is a young woman in her child-bearing years, and her menstruation week could be causing a loss of more blood than is usual. If we combine that with her diet and stress issues, I believe that is what I need to treat her for."

"And what are the treatments?"

"Not as bad as you may think. She will need rest, complete rest, and I will make out a diet she must eat, at least for a few weeks. It takes a while for the red blood to regenerate. The book says the condition is rarely fatal, and that it is found more among people born with certain characteristics."

John audibly sighed. "What about this woman's week condition. Can anything be done about that?"

"No. But if we treat the rest of the body, she will be able to get through those weeks with only moderate weakness and discomfort."

"Discomfort? Something more than the terrible inconvenience for them?"

"Yes. I tend to think she suffers from pains or cramps, as we call them. These can last one to three days. Women have learned how to hide them. They are embarrassed when it is life itself carrying on its intended purpose. I find it hard to get women to open up to me about it."

John stood and walked to the window with his back to Donaldson. "I intend to marry her, you know."

"Oh, she has accepted your suit?" Donaldson laughed. "I dare say the lady I saw you with last week will have something to say about that."

"Let her. I will marry Margaret under any circumstances, even if she cannot carry a child. Should I know anything beforehand? I mean, there will come a time when we are intimate. And I believe she is still chaste."

"John, what is happening to her now will not alter anything with childbearing or intimacy. She possibly could feel discomfort for a day or two a month. If you two had to hold her up tonight, I would think she is in that week. I will examine her fully tomorrow. And you had better make other plans for delivering Dixon to her family. Margaret must not go."

"You will explain this to her?"

"Yes. I am sure she would wish you not to know. Information this personal can be shared between a husband and wife, but not with friends or acquaintances."

"Yes. Yes, of course. It may be easier to pay for train fares to have Dixon's sister come and take her home."

"I will leave that up to you and Dixon. After I speak with Margaret and examine her tomorrow, the full picture should show itself. I hope there are no other irregularities with her."

"Such as?"

"She could be pregnant, John."

John was stunned. In his heart, he knew it would not be true, but she had been out of contact for a year. She could have been assaulted.

"Tell me, could it happen to any woman that she is assaulted or raped and not know it or report it?"

"Not reporting it is a significant problem. There again, the embarrassment, as if she is at fault, rises and prevents her from reporting the crime. Many will consider an innocent woman degraded for the rest of her life, as "damaged goods" in the eyes of proper men. As for not knowing it has happened—if she were unconscious, she would not know it. If she was chaste, she might see remnants of the assault. Young women in comas have been victims of this. They have no idea they are pregnant. If–and I say, "If" that had happened to Margaret, she could be miscarrying the child. I am sure that is not the case. Let's not search for rare problems where they do not exist."

"Should the worst ever happen to her, she will still be my life forever."

"You're a decent chap, John. Any woman would be lucky to have you."

John didn't smile. He was not interested in comments about his appearance or character.

The next morning Donaldson walked into Dixon's room to check on her. She spotted Margaret asleep in the chair.

"When did Miss Hale come in here?" Donaldson inquired because of the worried look on Dixon's face.

"I don't know. I woke up an hour ago, and she was there. I don't know how long. I hated to wake her because I know she hasn't been sleeping well."

Donaldson walked over to look at Margaret more closely. He immediately left the room and came back with two men in white and a rolling bed.

"Dixon, she is not sleeping, she is unconscious. I don't want you to worry. I am fairly certain what it is, which is nothing too serious."

"Oh, my God. Look!" Dixon pointed to the chair that Margaret was just lifted from. "There's blood on the chair, and she has stained her frock."

"Dixon, calm yourself. I expected that. Stress has brought on an abnormal flow of her menstrual week. She just needs bed rest. As I was telling Mr. Thornton last night, she will not accompany you to your sister's. She will be in bed. I am sure he will have figured something out by now, or soon will. I shall get her settled and be back to see you."

"Are you sure Miss Margaret will be all right?"

"As certain as I can be, for someone who's never treated such a case. I will question one of the woman's doctors this morning and have him look at her."

Not finding Margaret in her room, John walked towards Dixon's room. Coming towards him, he saw Donaldson and two male hospital men rolling a bed. He began to greet Donaldson until he saw Margaret on the cot.

"Good God, what is happening to her?" He grabbed her hand to hold. Noticing the stained frock, tears welled in his eyes.

"Donaldson!! Do something!"

Chapter Thirteen

"I am getting her into her room to examine her. She is unconscious, but I want you to remain calm. I still have no worries beyond what we discussed last night. I have sent for a woman's doctor. It's going to be a while. Don't wait outside the door."

"Then I will be inside the door and stay behind the screen. I cannot walk away from her, not now, not ever."

"John, you will do no such thing. You are not her husband. Please be calm. Find someplace else to pace. I don't want you to make me worry about you. Go see Dixon and discuss her way home."

"I will, but not yet."

John continued to hold her hand. She looked so white, and her clothing was darkened by her blood.

"She can't bleed to death, can she?" John said, belligerently.

"If she were pregnant, which we both seem assured that she is not, that could happen if she is miscarrying."

Donaldson turned when he heard footsteps trotting down the hall.

"Dr. Price. Thank you for coming so fast. This is John Thornton, Master of Marlborough Mills. Miss Hale is an especially good friend of his, and he is quite concerned."

"Good morning, Dr. Price," John said without looking away from Margaret. "Save her, please," he lamented.

Donaldson pulled John's hand away as they turned into her room. "Go."

John stood there while they lifted her into her bed. The cot was bloody. As they began to cut her clothes away, John was pushed backward out of the room.

"Donaldson, I want to hear from you within a few minutes, or I will enter the room. If she is near death, I must be with her, no matter what you say."

"Calm yourself before you have a stroke. She is not going to die. John, the exam is going to be internal and is not over in a hurry. As soon as I know something, good or bad, I will open the door and tell you." Donaldson saw John's glassy eyes and worried face as he nudged him back. Never had he seen John Thornton so vulnerable.

John was in a fog, unable to grasp this turn of events. He wasn't able to wrap his mind around it. He leaned against the hall wall and slid down, holding his head in his hands. God could not have her.

John, pull yourself together. Donaldson doesn't seem worried.

John listened to his feeble attempt to quell his anguish and stood upright.

"I thought that was you, Thornton," greeted Cecil Griffin. "Is this Miss Hale's room?"

"Yes. You cannot go in there. She has taken a turn for the worse."

"I daresay. I am sorry to hear that, old man. Is it very serious? You looked quite worried a moment ago."

"I came here today expecting to take her to my home to recover and found her unconscious."

"Unconscious? Your home? "

John couldn't hold a conversation.

"Yes. If you will excuse me–." John popped on his top hat and walked away. He knew his face would tell Griffin something that he wanted no one to know.

Griffin caught up with him. "Care for a cup of coffee in the canteen? You look like you could use one."

"I–I believe you are right. Yes, lead the way."

As they walked, little was said. Arriving in the canteen, they found the room quite full, but a small table was empty. A serving girl came to the table. "May I get you gentlemen something?"

"Two coffees, please, Griffin ordered. He could see John's mind was barely on him. "You said 'unconscious.' Do you know the cause?"

"He is examining her now for something called anemia."

"Anemia. Yes, I have heard of that. I have a niece that suffered from it about two years ago."

"Is she well today?"

"Yes, quite well. She needed plenty of rest, and I think she had to eat foods rich in something."

"Iron?"

"Yes, that was it. I take it Miss Hale will be recuperating longer than she estimated."

"She wants to complete her assignment on your books. Will this prevent her from returning to that work?"

"No," he chuckled. "She will just have a bit more than we anticipated. When she is feeling well enough, I would like to speak with her. I can see how she was setting it up. Perhaps I could continue, but there are questions."

"Thank you."

"Don't thank me. Regardless of when she returns, she will still be doing me a service. May I ask why she is recovering at your place? Oh, I suspect your mother is there to tend to her."

"Nicholas, my partner, and I have known her and her family for almost two years. We are her only friends, but that's a story for her to tell. Nicholas and I were horrified to discover her plight. When she was brought to the hospital, he, his wife, and I agreed that she would never return to where she was living."

"And you are taking on the responsibility."

"I'm not sure that seeing a friend through a difficult time is a responsibility. I do not see it as such."

"Of course, of course. Do you think there is anything I can do?"

"I would not think so at this time, but I am sure she will want to speak with you. I shall notify you when she can see people if you wish."

"I do wish. Thank you. I wish you could have seen her when she came looking for a position. When we began to negotiate for a salary, I offered her a fair wage. She turned to leave. She argued she offered a much greater value of service and named her own price. Would you believe I am paying her a foreman's wage?"

John finally chuckled. "That is Miss Hale for you. She does know her mind. At least I remember her that way. Stubborn, too. I feel she would not be where she is right now, if she weren't. She does not want charity."

"Indeed. An admirable quality in anyone. It's not that she is so pretty, but I, for one, will enjoy having her in my office. I like a high-spirited woman."

John rose, hearing that. He wanted no more of Margaret's praise being sung from another single gentleman. "I need to go back. The doctor may be looking for me. I will send you a note when the time is right for her. I am happy to hear of your niece's successful recovery."

The men shook hands, and John hurried back to the closed door of Margaret's room. He felt Dixon would be overwrought with worry, as he had been. He walked down the hall to her room.

"Donaldson, what do you know of this woman?" Price asked as he began his internal examination.

"Recent death of her last parent, which has put her in financial difficulties. Her stress level has been high for many weeks, perhaps months, I believe. She is accompanied by a servant who raised her, and who is hospitalized, too. From what the housekeeper says, Miss Hale was eating very little. Knowing her the little I do, I am sure she was seeing to her servant's health, and allowing her own to falter. Her life-long guardian recently had a heart attack, which brought on severe depression. I was coming in this morning to begin treating her for anemia when I found her like this."

"She has anemia, all right. See this," Price pointed. "She is not clotting well. Nothing is stemming this flow properly. That is from a lack of iron. It is a shame that her menstrual week and her housekeeper's heart attack came at the same time. Together with her rundown condition, it has caused this."

"What would you prescribe?"

"I have a list of foods rich in iron that I give all my pregnant patients. A steady diet of that and rest should have her well within a few weeks."

"Is that bed rest?"

"Bed rest for a couple of days. Once her woman's week is over, she can move around, but no exertion. You just have to monitor this flow to ensure it slowly recedes. I suspect she is not married. Her maidenhead is still intact. Who will watch over her?"

"The man you just met."

"He will see her through this?"

"John Thornton will demand to, and no one will know it, except his partner and his wife. I know John is deeply in love with her. He proposed a year ago and was rejected under a misunderstanding by her. They have just recently found each other and are becoming friends again. That is, except John Thornton. She is his life. He will do whatever it takes to win her hand and heart."

"All that? I see. I would suggest two days in this hospital before turning her over to his care. You should see her every couple of days after that. I will look in on her again before she leaves. I'll put in an order for the food and leave a list with Mr. Thornton. It seems she is coming around."

"Oh, Mr. Thornton, how is Miss Margaret?"

"Donaldson and a woman's doctor are seeing to her now. I am being told she will recover without issue."

"But all that bl…." Dixon looked over at the still uncleansed chair.

John silently gasped. "I know. It is very alarming. That is what they are examining now." John paced the room, not wanting to embarrass himself or Dixon if the conversation continued down this path.

"I am only here to tell you that and to discuss your travel to your sister's. Miss Hale will not be able to go. She will have to stay off of her feet for few days and have plenty of rest. Sounds like your remedy, too."

"Yes, but they are certainly different."

"Would you be opposed to allowing Branson, my driver, I think you know him, to escort you to your family's home?"

"I can go myself, Mr. Thornton."

"I am afraid I cannot allow that. And think of how upset Miss Hale would be if she knew you were alone. No, you will have someone with you from this door to theirs. Where does she live, your sister?"

"In Oldam."

"Oldam? Why that's only a two-hour train ride, if that."

"I wouldn't know, Mr. Thornton."

"Let me know when you receive word from her, and I will schedule your train."

"Thank you. I can't leave Miss Margaret until I know she will get better."

"I am sure Dr. Donaldson will tell you so. I want to return to her. The exam must be completed by now. I will have Donaldson come and talk to you about her."

"Thank you. You will take good care of her?"

"As if she were my own."

John Thornton was a striking figure as his tall, trim physique paced the hall outside Margaret's door. Some of the people in the hospital that knew of him wondered who was in that room to make him act uncharacteristically agitated.

John finally knocked lightly on the door.

"Will you excuse me? I must speak with Thornton. He is painfully in need of information," said Donaldson.

"Yes, see to him before you have another patient. I will begin to speak with Miss Hale."

Donaldson opened the door slightly, and John was right there trying to see her. The small scene he could see upset him further.

"Tell me something. I am going mad," John said, rubbing his brow. "Is she going to make it?"

"Let's take a walk, John."

"Don't give me that. If it is bad news, tell me now."

"It is not bad news. There's a seating area around the corner. This is going to take a bit of time to explain and if you are going to be her nursemaid, you will be in a delicate position."

As they walked, Donaldson quietly began to tell John of her condition—everything from the rundown health to her woman's week and even the blood not clotting as it should.

"I only explain these personal facts fully because you are the only one she has and I know what she means to you. You are a mature man, and I believe you to understand most of the medical facts of women that I am giving you."

Still hanging his head as they sat, John nodded.

"She is going to remain in the hospital until this time of her month has stopped. You must ensure that she eats and rest properly when she is in your home, so we don't see a repeat of this next month. John, we are mere men and cannot find a way to understand what they have to live with. It rarely touches us in our day-to-day lives. We forget about it, and they don't speak of it, of course. Are you sure you can cope with this? I can have a nurse with her when she leaves."

"I want to talk with her and convince her to allow me to be part of this recovery. I want her to know that I understand it all. I have to put her embarrassment at ease. Tell me, could she have died with all the blood loss?"

"Yes, could have. Had she never had her friends intercede when they did, and all this was happening to her alone, it possibly could have been fatal. We still have a dangerous situation until her time passes, but she is here getting the best attention she can. She should be able to regain a lot of strength with an iron-rich diet in this coming month. Just to regenerate the red blood cells in the volume she has lost will take over two months. I will have to monitor her through the next month and that week."

"Does she understand this?"

"She was waking up when you knocked. Dr. Price is speaking with her now. She may not be fully cognizant of what he is saying, just yet. I will go over it with her. Mrs. Higgins should be close by to talk with her, too. She might want to discuss things that she will not talk to you or me about. To her, you are a friend who is seeing other women, and she does not know of your feelings for her. Margaret will be terribly ashamed to discuss this freely with you."

"Ashamed?" John hung his head again. A look of incredulity came to his face.

"John, we cannot put ourselves in their place. Our only hope is to understand that's the way they were brought up. I find it quite heartbreaking that one of life's greatest gifts is so readily pushed into the dark mystery for us men. We are quite the opposite."

"I will ease her awkwardness. I don't know the words yet, but I will find them."

"I knew you would John," Donaldson said, patting him on the back. "I need to get back. Give her an hour. We have to talk, and clean her up. It will be good for her if you have Dixon sorted by then. At least plans."

"How long will she remain here?"

"They both should be able to leave in two days. Tomorrow Dixon can come to her and visit. I don't want Margaret out of her bed today, at all. Not even for a ride in that chair."

John nodded.

"Now, go find something to do. You do work, don't you?" Donaldson chuckled.

"I think I will go see mother," John said, still with a serious look to him.

Donaldson knew he would lose that worry when he could see Margaret.

What a strange feeling, John Thornton thought, to be knocking on his mother's door. Jane answered.

"Mr. Thornton, come in. I will get Mrs. Thornton for you."

Jane took his hat and John sat in a chair by the window. He rose when his mother walked into the room. He walked to her and kissed her forehead.

"How is it going, Mother?"

"Aside from not having you near every day and the noiseless surroundings, I am fine." Hannah sat. "I have met one neighbor, and I think she will be a nice, decent widowed woman."

"Not unlike yourself."

"I cannot say that as yet. She kindly brought us a pie on our first day here. Her husband was a Master long ago."

"What is her name?"

"Mrs. MacMullen.

"Oh yes. I have never met her, but knew her husband. I was just becoming profitable then."

"She knows of you well enough. She reads the papers daily. Did you know there are many articles about the mills in there and you are often mentioned?"

John laughed. "Yes, mother, I knew. I read, too, in case you have forgotten."

"So how is Dixon?"

"Coming along well."

"And Miss Hawkins?"

"I have a dinner engagement tonight."

"Then that is going well?"

"Not as you would hope it to be, I'm afraid. I know she is not the woman I want to spend my life with, as you well know."

"And Miss Hale, is she recovering?"

"I am sorry to say, she has had a grave setback. Donaldson just told me if it had not been for her coming to the mill that day, we may have never discovered her difficulties. If she were alone right now, she would be dying."

"Dying? Oh John, I *am* sorry to hear that. I had no idea it was that serious."

"Neither did anyone."

"What has happened?"

"It is a bit difficult for me to explain to you. I will be taking care of her."

"Does it happen to be a woman's problem?"

"Very much so. To put it bluntly, in her reduced health, she had nearly bled to death. Mother, I saw her paleness, the stains to her clothes, bed and chair. I wanted to die in her place."

"John. John," Hannah went to her son and put her arms around him."

He cried on her shoulder.

"Let it out, son."

Chapter Fourteen

"And you say John Thornton knows all of this?"

"Yes, he had to know it all, Margaret. You need not upset yourself over this. I think the biggest part of our conversation is why women hide these things and seem to be ashamed. Do not underestimate John. He understands all things, perhaps better than you do just now."

"Oh, how can I face him? Rejecting him wasn't this distressing."

"You do know he cares greatly for you, don't you?"

"I'm not at all sure of anything. I need to be forgiven first."

"Forgiven? You are a strange bird, Margaret. I cannot believe you have been under that thinking all this time."

"What thinking?"

"That you need forgiveness. Well, all I can say is, you two have a lot to discuss."

"I thought so too. That is why I am recovering at his home. But … but now, recovering is much different."

"That is preposterous, and you better know that now. He will demand to be the one to care for you. He's been practically fighting his way into your room. John is most distraught." Donaldson chuckled.

"I won't even have Dixon."

"No, but I understand there is another female in the house all the time. I am sure Mrs. Higgins will want to help you. I can always send a nurse, too."

Wringing her hands, she uttered, "I suppose I have little choice."

"Remember, you do have a choice. You seem to have made one for good reasons. You will recover as you have always been if you eat properly. I want to consult with you on your next … what do you ladies call them … woman's week. I want to ensure that problem is a result of your unhealthy condition and nothing more serious. Dr. Price does not foresee any issues going forward. Intimacy and childbearing should come naturally to you. And yes, John knows that too."

Donaldson chuckled. "Except for the vision of your nakedness, I believe the man knows everything about you."

"Oh dear, oh dear. I am in quite a predicament, aren't I?"

"I would say you are in good hands. Now, I have talked to him and I have talked to you. Would you like me to be here, or perhaps Mrs. Higgins, when you two discuss this with each other?"

Margaret put her hands to her face. "I don't think I can do that. I don't know anything anymore. I cannot believe what has happened to me in this past week alone. I feel like I am on a runaway horse and can't reach the reins. John's in charge of me, I'm in charge of Dixon, two of us are in the hospital, one is leaving town, our flat is now gone, I–." Margaret broke down crying. "Everything is converging, and I do not feel I have any control anymore."

"You don't, and that is a good thing. Your questionable control, although heroic, is what placed you here. I am going to give you a medication that will help you calm down and cope with all that is around you. Have you ever had too much wine?"

"Why do you ask? I think I did at school once."

"Do you remember giggling and enjoying yourself?"

"It's coming back to me."

"This medication won't be that potent, but it will take away your anxiousness. I will go get in now. The nurses are coming to bathe you."

Margaret noticed her torn frock thrown across a chair in the room. She lifted the sheets.

"Yes, Margaret, you are in a serious state. How many more days of your menstrual week do you have?"

"What day is this? How long has Dixon been here?"

"Counting the day she was admitted, this is the third day."

"This is also my third day."

"That is good. I believe the worst is behind us. The nurses will be in here quite soon. They will have to bathe you while you are lying in that bed. They will change the sheets, give you a cotton hospital frock, and tend to your bleeding. I cannot keep John away for much longer. He is liable to break the door down any moment now. Do expect him within an hour. I shall return after I see the chemist."

While waiting for the nurses, Margaret stretched to see what happened to her clothing. She had nothing on at all. Margaret pulled the sheet back again to see just how bad her condition had or still was. The bed was stained, but she had nothing to protect herself. Suddenly the door opened. Expecting to see the nurses, Margaret was surprised to see John walk in.

"John!" she gasped, grabbing for the sheet to get it to her shoulders. "You should knock."

"I know I should. I've been waiting to see you for some time, and this time I was going to do it," he stated resolutely.

"You can't stay here, I have nothing on."

"I can stay here if I wish it … I wish it."

"But …."

"Yes, tell me how improper it is. You see before you a man at his wits end. Propriety be damned. I feared you were dying. You can't know how that feels."

"Sir," came a firm voice from the doorway, "please remove yourself from this room." Two nurses had just arrived.

"We are here to clean and care for Miss Hale. She can see you in half an hour from now."

John couldn't take his eyes off of her, so he backed out of the room. One of the nurses followed him to close the door.

John found himself pacing again with relief. She was well enough to scold him. That gave him peace to some extent.

Peggy and Nicholas were rushing towards him.

"We just talked to Dixon. What is going on? Dixon thought she was bleeding to death."

"I believe she might have been. Can we talk in the canteen?"

"How did you sleep last night, Benny?" asked Cook.

"It was nice. Much nicer than where I have been living. The master was gone when I woke. Have I done something wrong?"

"I doubt it, deary. He often does that. As long as you remain in the routine that Jane explained, you are not accountable if he goes without shaving or eating. He knows the hours. He sets them. There is never any problem with that. He is a good master."

"And handsome, too."

"I suppose he is, but don't you go getting' no ideas there, deary."

"Does he see many women?"

"I don't know how many is many and I don't go prying into his affairs. I suggest you do the same if you want to work here. He is not even supposed to know you are here if you are doing your work correctly."

"Yes, miss. Are we even in staff seniority?"

"I doubt it. You will have to ask the master."

"Do I take orders from you or just him?"

"Ask that of the master. If you were hired to replace Jane, she took orders from both of us. I have been with the family since the master was a young boy."

"Who is that nice young man with the yellow hair pulled back with a bow?"

"There are hundreds of young men on this property every day. I do not know any of them, except Branson, the master's driver."

"Is he the one around back by the stables?"

"That's usually where drivers stay."

"Does he have a lady?"

"Mind you girl. You'd better get these foolish notions out of your head. Have you made the master's bed and brought down his wash?"

"No, I will do that now."

Benny went upstairs. Mr. Thornton's door was open, so she walked in without knocking. She walked the room, touching and feeling everything. Benny sat on the bed and bounced, listening for noises. She picked up his shirt that was thrown over a chair and held his scent to her nose. A thrill ran through her as she inhaled his manly essence. Dropping the shirt momentarily, she made his bed, but breathed in the pillow's smell. *Was he a man like any other?*

Finishing the bed, she cleaned and filled the pitcher and bowl, grabbed up all his clothes and went downstairs. She slipped his handkerchief into her apron.

"Set the lunch table for two, deary."

"Two?"

"Yes. A close friend of his will be convalescing here for the near future. I believe she will be released today. Let's just be prepared if that should happen."

"A close lady friend is going to be staying here?"

"Yes."

"So, which of the other two bedchambers should I prepare?"

"Are you sure you were an in-service maid? They are both to be prepared and kept in readiness all the time."

"Yes, of course. Should I put flowers in one of the rooms?"

"No, we don't have a garden here anyway. This is a mill yard with a house on it. We're not like where you must have come from."

"It certainly isn't. Where I came from had grand affairs and balls with handsome men in their finery and ladies with frocks made of yards and yards of lace." Benny twirled in a circle holding her apron out as if it were a dress hem."

"Did you come from one of the master's mills?"

"Yes. Hard to believe, I know. Me, of all people, working a loom. My, how life changes in short order."

"Miss Benny, without an education this is about as good of a job that you will ever have in Milton. So many are starving to death out there. Be grateful you are here."

"Oh, but I am."

"And don't go flirtin' with the men of this house."

"I wouldn't dare," Benny said, turning with a smile on her face.

John had difficulty explaining Margaret's condition with Peggy there. Surely he was going to say the wrong word. Peggy eventually helped him with the words that he tended to mull over. It would have been easy if it had been just Nicholas and himself. He had no embarrassment of his knowledge, but with Peggy there it was like a teacher sitting in your classroom. Disturbing.

Peggy said. "Aren't we glad that she came to our mill that day?"

"I cannot begin to imagine how we would feel if she hadn't."

"Do you think it is better for her to come and stay with Peggy and myself now?"

"I want to care for her, no matter the condition, but she can make up her own mind. However, I had a long talk with Donaldson about her embarrassment or awkwardness, and I resolved to speak with her about it. At least let me do that before we ask her again of her preference."

"John, we will do anything we can. Don't try to hide behind her health as a reason for your interest. The fact is that you still love her. You don't need any excuses with us," Nicholas admonished.

"I'm only hiding it from her. At least I hope I am."

"John you are kidding yourself if you think she won't suspect that in short order. You had better try harder. When she finds out you are seeing Miss Hawkins while showing the interest of a man for a woman to her, it all may blow up in your face. Believe me, we are on your side. You are blinded by her, which is a good thing, but this has a timing issue, like before."

"You're right. I cannot take the chance of doing that again. And I just nearly broke the door down to her room moments ago. It has been an unpleasant morning for me."

"Would you like Peggy and me to visit her before you? We can ease some of the initial difficulties in others knowing about her." Nicholas asked.

"If Peggy wouldn't mind talking with her alone."

"I would be glad to. Then I'll call in Nicholas and also tell her you are waiting. Impatiently, I might add."

"I am that. But don't upset her with that fact."

Nicholas had stopped outside her door when Peggy entered. A nurse came out with a bundle of stained and ripped clothing. Nicholas felt faint for a moment.

"Peggy! How did you get past John?" Margaret asked.

She laughed. "I am afraid we didn't. We went to find you in Dixon's room, all prepared for you to leave today. Of course, Dixon was in a dither and John was pacing outside your door. He has worn a path with his boots."

Margaret smiled weakly.

"John said that he could not see you yet or we neither, so he took us for coffee and explained your current condition. You poor dear."

"I don't know how to talk about it with anyone but you. I believe the doctor is confident of a good recovery, so I am not too worried about myself. I picked John last night, but he didn't know what he was in for, nor I."

"Margaret believe me when I tell you, he understands everything completely. He has full knowledge and no reluctance to care for you. His own concern is that you will feel mortified."

"I am."

"Do him the courtesy to hear him out before perhaps changing your mind about being there. As for your woman's week, which is what bothers you most in discussing with him, it will be over when you are ready to leave. There will be little concern, I should think, over that issue—according to him that is.

"Now Dixon, John, Nicholas and I know what's happened to you. Nicholas, being a husband, will take this in his stride since you are no longer in danger, so don't worry about him. He is waiting outside. I'll get him."

"Ah… ah … all right. I have to move forward, I suppose."

When Peggy came out of the door, Nicholas was sliding to the floor in a faint. John was running down the hall towards him.

"I saw him flop back against the wall and slide down. I think he's fainted," said John with incredulity. "I wonder why."

"We both saw Margaret's clothing being carried out. I guess he cannot stand the sight of blood. Will you call for a doctor? I've never seen a man faint."

"Neither have I," chuckled John. He went off looking for anyone that looked like a doctor.

Margaret could hear the commotion outside of her room. "Did Nicholas faint?" she shouted.

"Yes, Margaret. It is rather hysterical. He will be fine. Here comes a nurse now."

Nicholas was rolling his head when the nurse put something under his nose that snapped him out of it.

"What happened?"

"Honey, can you not stand the sight of blood? Many people can't."

"I thought I could. I've been through two childbirths."

Smiling, John helped him up.

"Thornton, I don't want to hear about this."

"Peggy take him home for a while. I am going in to see Margaret."

Chapter Fifteen

As John walked into her room, Donaldson was right behind him.

"Thornton, give me a moment. I want Margaret to take some medication."

Margaret was shaking with John in the room. She noticed he watched everything carefully that Donaldson was doing.

Donaldson handed her a half glass of water in which a powder had been mixed into it.

"What is that you are giving her?" John tried to sound calm.

"It's a potion to ease her nerves. As she said, much has happened to her in the last week or so. She is having difficulty coping with all the changes. This will help her deal with her life and bring her out of depression. Don't be surprised if she seems to change. In a few minutes, she will be mentally feeling relieved." Donaldson smiled.

John was not so sure what he meant. But it didn't matter. If Margaret could feel better in any way right now, he wanted it for her.

Donaldson propped a second pillow under her head. "I don't want you to sit up just yet. The extra pillow will help you see who comes into your room, which shall be limited after John leaves."

"I'm not so sure I am leaving." He looked Donaldson sternly in the eye.

"We cannot exhaust her."

"I am acutely aware of that."

"Margaret, I will see you in a couple of hours. Rest and eat."

"Yes, doctor." Margaret knew the time had come to face her hardest obstacle, but hopefully the last one.

John set his hat on a nearby bureau. He took off his coat and rolled up his sleeves. Margaret watched him pull a chair close to her bed.

"You look like you are setting in for a siege," she remarked.

"That I am. I am ready for a fight."

"A fight?"

"Are you going to dance around words, trying not to say what is evident? Will you try not to embarrass yourself or me? You feel you need to explain the goings on with you, but don't know how to broach the subject with a man?"

"Well..."

"Is this not a subject that only women discuss with each other? This is better locked away in a closet where no man dare set foot, isn't it? Do you think coming to my home will cause situations that you dare not speak with me about? Yes, Margaret, I am ready to fight all those issues with you. Right now. Right here." John spoke firmly.

Unexpectedly, Margaret broke out in laughter. She was amazed at how he could make her feel.

John's heart melted. A huge weight just lifted from his shoulders. "That giggle is not at all what I expected. But it is most welcome."

"John, yes, I have worried over all of that, but your determination to put me in my place, and quickly I might add, has lifted my spirits. I was dreading this."

"Do you have faith that I can take care of you and watch over your health, including your womanly needs?"

"It seems I have been bluntly persuaded." Margaret smiled.

"Is that the end of this discussion, or need I continue my campaign to make Margaret Hale believe that I am knowledgeable and eager to participate in her recovery—in every way?"

"Yes, John. I do believe you can send the brass band home." Margaret could feel light gushes of blood every time she laughed. "Please try not to make me laugh. Every time you do, I leak!"

It took John a second or two to understand what she meant. He smiled, but felt stung at the same time. He found it hard to believe she was playful. It was another reminder of what he loved about her.

"See … you thought you knew it all, but you don't, do you?"

"I believe I have been deceptively and purposefully humiliated. I see this is a struggle for who is boss."

"I'm the sick one."

"I'm the healer."

Margaret contemplated.

"I'm the pitiful one."

"I am your champion."

"Yes, but I am a female person endowed with certain rites."

"I am a male person who towers over you enabling those rites."

"I'm feeling good."

"I rest my case. I am the boss."

"Are you still a magistrate?"

"Are you changing the subject?"

"I'm trying to."

"Is the past conversation accepted as read? You will have to sign the document."

"Accepted."

"Fine. I will have the papers drawn and ready for you to sign tomorrow."

"If you don't stop this, I will need a nurse."

"Why do you do that to me?" asked John.

"Do what?"

"You make remarks in which I have to draw a conclusion as to what you mean before I can respond."

"What's the matter? Johnny can't keep up?"

John laughed to himself. She was getting funny as Donaldson had said. This was going to be amusing.

"I think I can. I was not expecting riddles from you. It made me pause. Now I know what you are up to."

"And how tall is 'up to'?"

John laughed. He couldn't help it. "So, you will be coming home with me when you are released from the hospital?"

"Is your mother there?"

"No."

"Will I be alone with you?"

"No. There is a live-in housekeeper."

"Oh … I guess I will accept anyway."

John rolled his hand into a fist and covered his smile with it.

"Good morning, Mr. Thornton," came the voice of Dr. Price from the doorway. "I am glad you are here. This paper is a list of her dietary needs."

"I will see to it," John said, standing, folding the paper and shoving it in his pocket.

"Could you excuse us for a few moments? Please wait outside."

"Good luck with her."

"Why do you say that?"

"Donaldson gave her some medicine to calm her worries. She is making me laugh."

Dr. Price laughed. "All right. I am forewarned."

John left, leaving his hat and coat in the room. He decided to speak with Branson, telling him to take off for a while and pick him up at noon.

"How is she, guv?"

"Her condition has been quite serious over the last twenty-four hours, but improvement is being seen. She will not come home today or tomorrow. Tonight I will need to speak with you about a trip I wish you to make."

"Aye guv. You look strange without your coat and hat, sleeves rolled up and all that. Is she a lot of work? About tonight, I believe you have a dinner engagement."

"I thought she was going to take a lot of convincing to recover at Marlborough mills, but I told her how it was going to be and that was that." John did not hear or didn't want to hear about his dinner with Miss Hawkins.

"Good on ya, guv."

"Find me at noon."

John walked back to Margaret's room, slightly embarrassed at his own appearance. That had all been for her sake. He was rarely seen in such an unkempt state.

He waited outside of the closed door. He was beginning to hate that door. It made him think. That door separated them. If she were his wife, he could be in there. By giving that door some type of meaning bothered his fragile hopes?

The door suddenly opened. John looked at Price expectantly.

"Miss Hale has given me permission to speak with you about her condition."

"And?"

"There was nothing new in the last hour. But you were right about her being funny. I guess she does not remember our first meeting as she was just coming around. She told me I was rude and ungentlemanly when I lifted her gown. Just don't let her up and keep her happy. That is her best medicine right now. That and eating well."

"You have my word, Dr. Price."

John strolled to Margaret's side. "Are you expecting any more guests?"

"Peggy and Nicholas?"

"I guess you have forgotten. Peggy was here while Nicholas was fainting outside of your door. Oh, and Cecil Griffin came by. He knows your recovery will be at least two weeks, perhaps more. When you are feeling better, he would like to stop by and speak with you about how you began to set up his books. He assured me that your job would be there when you were ready. So, there is nothing to worry about with that."

"He's a nice, polite man, isn't he?"

"I have no reason to doubt it."

"I think his foreman likes me."

"Anyone that meets you will instantly like you."

"Your mother didn't."

"Miss Hale, I believe you were mistaken about me," came a voice from the hallway door.

John stood immediately and spun around. "Mother! What are you doing here?"

"After you telling me of her serious condition, I wanted to pay my respects. I want to make amends."

"Mother, now is not a good time," John said.

"Now, is not a good time," Margaret repeated with a slur.

John walked his mother out into the hall, out of sight.

"Mother, I am comforted that you take an interest. But she is under medication to calm her nerves. She is saying strange things. She just told the doctor that he was rude when he tried to examine her. It is nothing. Don't take offence."

"Now is not a good time," Margaret shouted. John wanted to laugh, but couldn't.

"John even if she were not mimicking you and meant what she said, I would not be offended. I deserve that and a lot more. Like I said, I want to begin to make amends to the woman who will please my son for the rest of his life."

"Mother, I think we've been through this before. I am encouraged that you will want to atone for your treatment of her, but now *really* isn't a good time. She will remember little of the next few days. Can I walk you to the door?"

"Where is your coat and what are your cuffs doing rolled up?"

"That is my business. Do you wish me to escort you to your carriage or not? Otherwise, I am returning to Miss Hale."

"You go to her. I will be all right."

"Thank you, Mother, for being brave enough to come for a visit." John kissed her on her forehead. "Good day, Mother."

"It's not a good time, is it, John?" Margaret repeated as he entered the room.

"No, it isn't a good time. I think I will close the door. The doctor said your visitors were to be limited after me."

"Are you leaving?"

"No. I will be here with you for a while longer. Is that all right?"

"Is it a good time, now?"

John was going to laugh out loud any moment.

"Margaret?"

"Yes," she said as she studied her nails.

"Do you have a hard time looking into my face?"

"Yesss."

"Do I disgust you?"

"I don't know how any woman can look at you."

John sat back, folded his arms and pondered the complexity of her answer.

Margaret continued to study her nails.

"I need to scrub these?"

"Your nails?"

"Yesss."

"Are you listening to me or studying your fingernails?"

"Yesss."

"Why can't any woman look at me? I don't know of anyone who would rather run away than face me."

"Do you have a mirror?"

"I do. I see myself daily."

"Then you know why."

"What do I know from looking at myself in the mirror?"

"You have eyes."

"I do not believe I am unique in that situation." John smiled.

"Those eyes."

"Yes, these eyes. And?"

"They draw me to you?"

"Is that a good thing?" John was aroused. Margaret was the only woman on earth for whom his appearance meant something to him.

"It's too good. Do my fingernails look nice?"

John took her hand and placed one of her fingers in his mouth. He suckled it. It was out of character for him and he knew it. It was pure intimacy of which he had never shared with anyone.

Margaret closed her eyes and smiled. Her lips parted.

John put down her hand and walked away from the bedside. He should have known what his own reaction would have been.

"Do it with this one." Margaret held up another finger for his attention.

"I think they are bringing your lunch."

"Is tonight when you have dinner with Miss Lady Friend?"

"Ahem." John cleared his throat and returned to her side. "Yes, it is."

"Will you bring her flowers?"

"No. Do you like flowers?"

"Yes. I have missed them since moving north."

"I shall remember that. So you like my eyes, do you?" John couldn't get enough of this. Were these her inner most thoughts? Was it possible that she would accept him into her heart, somewhere?"

"No."

John forgot what he had asked. "No, what?"

"No, I don't like your eyes. I love them." Margaret giggled.

John pulled in his breath and pulled out his pocket watch and found it was nearing half past eleven. He rolled down his sleeves and donned his coat.

"I must be going so you can rest. I think your new medicine is making you sleepy."

John leaned over the bed. "Close your eyes."

"What?"

"Just close your eyes for a moment."

Margaret did as asked, and John kissed her on her forehead.

"I will return later." He turned, picked up his hat and left the room. He felt his control slipping. Words wanted to spring from his mouth. He wanted to say, "I still love you, Margaret."

Margaret slid down in the bed and rested her eyes, falling asleep until lunch came through the door. The nurse set her tray to the side and inspected Margaret's condition.

It seemed to be lessening, which she noted on the chart. The nurse sat beside Margaret and fed her beans and liver.

"Miss Margaret," she heard Dixon call.

"Dixon. Come sit by me."

The nurse moved away and made a place for the other patient to visit with her friend.

"Miss Margaret, how are you feeling?"

"Oh, fine. Simply fine. Mr. Thornton has been visiting me."

"Yes, miss. I know. Are you sleepy?"

"No. Why?"

"You're acting silly, Miss Margaret. After all we've been through, you have a grin on your face."

"I know. I feel fine."

The nurse interrupted. "Miss Dixon, Miss Hale is on a medication that makes her act like that. It is to keep her anxiety away so her body can return to normal."

"She don't look normal?"

"I'm afraid we're not there yet, with her. It will take a couple of days. The two of you have been through some very hard times."

"Yes, hard times, Dixon. This isn't a good time."

"What is she talking about?"

"I doubt anyone knows." The nurse laughed.

"She is going to be all right, isn't she?"

"Yes, she will. If she listens to the doctors, rests and eats good meals, she will return to her old self. Mr. Thornton seems determined to see that she follows orders."

"Oh, Mr. Thornton," Margaret cooed.

"Does she have a fancy for Mr. Thornton?"

"She wouldn't tell me if she did. They weren't friends until a couple days ago. A lot seems to have happened to both of us. She's going to recover at his house. I'm going to Oldam to be with my sister. I think I will go back to my room. I had to see her."

"She is going to be fine, Miss Dixon."

Before John dressed for dinner, he had a talk with Branson about escorting Dixon to her sisters.

"When will I be doing that, sir?"

"Perhaps as early as the day after tomorrow. Dixon is waiting to hear from the woman. We will rent you a coach to ride in to the hospital and train station. You won't have to drive it."

"Can I choose the driver?"

"Yes. In fact, I prefer that."

"What will you do while I'm gone?"

"I should be home with Miss Hale by then. You will only be gone the day. I think I can stay home for one day."

"What time do you want to leave tonight, guv?"

"I'm going to get ready now. Give me an hour. Then I will visit Miss Hale one more time. From there to Miss Hawkins."

"Right you are, guv."

John said, "Hello," as he passed Benny and Cook downstairs. He stopped on the stairs.

"How is your first day going … ah …?"

"Benny."

"Yes, Benny. I am sorry I forgot."

"That is quite all right, Mr. Thornton. Everything is fine. If you see something I haven't done or haven't done properly, please let me know."

"I certainly will. Cook, you remembered I am having dinner out tonight?"

"Yes, sir."

"I'm going to get ready." John continued up the steps.

"Cook, do I have any duties now that dinner time is near?"

"Not tonight. Normally, you would make the table, serve and clean the table. After the master has gone, you can set the breakfast table. Remember to turn the plates upside down. I don't know if that's the way it was done where you came from, but it's how we do it here. With Mr. Thornton running the house, things may change. You can set our table now."

"Yes, mum."

John found his evening clothes and began to dress. He couldn't help smiling and chuckling to himself about Margaret and her medicine. His smile began to fade as he thought of the night ahead. He really wasn't looking forward to this dinner at Elaine's home.

Benny completed the staff table, then tiptoed upstairs.

Chapter Sixteen

Benny turned right in the hall which led to other rooms. She stood far back into the darkened corners. From there, she could look across the parlor to the small hallway which led to John's room. She saw him slip off his bracers and pull his shirt over his head. If he undressed any further, she thought she might be forced to turn her head. She watched as he washed his face and under his arms. Benny assumed it was a wardrobe that he walked to when he disappeared from sight. She took that moment to slip back downstairs. Her heart was racing.

"Where have you been girl?"

"I was in there," she said, pointing. "I was in the privy."

"Well, sit down and eat before your tea goes cold."

"Who launders Mr. Thornton's clothes?"

"He employs a local woman who does a fine job of removing the cotton fluff from his coat and trousers. She cleans and irons everything. Why?"

"Oh, I don't know. I don't think I am clear on all my duties. Someone like me would have helped with the linens where I came from."

John returned to Margaret's room, but she was dozing. He set a small bouquet of flowers on her bedside and went looking for either of her doctors. After traipsing through several halls, he spotted Dr. Donaldson. He was forced to trot to catch up with him as he was going away from him.

"John! Well, I can hardly say this is a surprise. I left Margaret about thirty minutes ago. She has done well today, and Dixon too. Dixon received a note from someone. I thought you would be interested to hear about that."

"Yes, I am. I will see her before I leave."

"You look like you have an engagement out tonight."

"I do. I now see what you meant about Miss Hale being mentally relieved. I'm afraid she had me laughing. I was quite embarrassed."

"Did she say something embarrassing?"

"No. Not really. It was the way she was saying things and then would repeat them later. She did have a few things to say that were of interest to me. Should I dismiss these ramblings as false?"

"Quite the opposite, John. Margaret could declare all manner of secrets. She is relieved of any inhibition and worry with this powder. That is the nature of it. Her pulse and blood pressure are returning to normal ranges and her metabolism is stabilizing. That will allow her to eat. Now, that isn't to say that she will repeat them when off the medication. She may even deny saying it, even if she knows it to be true. It would be something she wants to keep to herself. Margaret couldn't possibly have any hidden negative admissions, could she?"

"No, I wouldn't think so."

"But you are smiling, John."

"She did have something positive to say which I liked hearing."

"Hmm … I see. Well, my boy, I wouldn't tell her what she said. She may worry about that and refuse the medication."

"No one will hear it from me."

"I will release her and Dixon the day after tomorrow. Can you have arrangements made for both women by then?"

"Yes. Branson will escort Dixon to her family, which is only a two-hour train ride. Depending on her note, she can stay at my house as well, if the timing doesn't suit."

"I or Dr. Price will be giving you instructions. Did you get the food list?"

"Yes. I will see that Cook collects those tomorrow."

"John, I know you are paying for their stay here. I want to help contribute too, so I am waving my fee for both of them."

"That isn't necessary."

"I know it isn't because I know you. But please let me do this. My heart has broken knowing what has happened to them. Miss Hale sold nearly all of her family heirlooms just to eat, or just to let Dixon eat. I can picture them arguing over who got the potato on any given night."

John hung his head and twirled his hat by the brim. "I never felt welcomed after last year. Mr. Hale and I would exchange a post now and then, but I never went for a visit. I, of all people, should have sensed that some tragedy could befall them when Bell didn't come to the funeral. Higgins and I agree that we let that family down. It was the worst of all possible misfortunes."

"John, you cannot blame yourself. Margaret need not have kept this hardship to herself until the last minute. She holds most of this on her shoulders. That's why she's in the state she is in now."

"Donaldson, she's a woman … a lady. It would never occur to her to ask. She would feel like she was begging. Margaret is so tenderhearted that insinuating herself into someone else's life is a behavior abhorred in her upbringing. I know how you see it being mostly her fault. I cannot quite see it that way. It is no excuse that I assumed she went to London after her father passed. Nicholas was busy getting Bessy ready and into a fine school. He feels bad, too."

"Well, at any case, she is at the end of that for a while."

"What do you mean?"

"John, as you just said, she won't want to insinuate herself into your life longer than she has to. Once she is completely well, I bet she will start looking for somewhere she can afford to rent with a job which she will need to get."

"I hadn't thought that far ahead. I am going to see that that does not happen. You may have to delay her certification that she is well." John looked at Donaldson in a strange way."

"Let's talk about that when it becomes necessary."

John said goodbye and began walking towards Dixon's room. Donaldson had been right. Margaret would never agree to live on in his home when she felt able to tend to herself or Adam Bell returned. What kind of strategy would be needed? There was some hope that she could understand that neither Nicholas nor he would let her return to that life, even if he had to turn that shed, with her furniture, into a small cottage. She was not leaving his life.

"Good evening, Dixon," John greeted.

"Oh, Mr. Thornton, it's nice to see you. I have some news for you and Miss Margaret."

"I heard you received some post today. Was it from your sister?"

"Yes, she is anxious to have me there to recover and has invited Miss Hale, too. She has plenty of room."

"I am very happy for you. It will work out nicely. I understand you have not seen her in a long time."

"I think it's been about five years. I can't wait to ask Miss Margaret to go with me."

John pulled a chair over to her bedside.

"I will not ask you to do anything, especially withhold anything from Miss Hale, but I want her to stay with me if she will. She has agreed to it, but that was when she only had two options. Dixon, to be honest, I need her in my life. I want her in my life forever. I see her recovery as giving us a chance that was thrown away last year. I don't know how much of the story she has told you, or how much she even knows herself—we haven't spoken. There was a lot of misunderstanding. I loved her then and I love her still. This … this reconciliation may never come again. Can you understand what I am saying?"

"Yes, I do. We have discussed very little since you left the house that day. It wasn't until she saw you recently that your name has been mentioned. I have felt for a long time that she knew she made a mistake and believed she must live with it. She became wistful that day, even when her father was well. Her spirits have been low and then came our problems. She got worse. I will not tell her about the invitation if you don't want me to."

"No, I am not saying that. I believe she should know. If she accepts, then I will have to live with that, but if she hesitates it would mean a lot to me if you did not earnestly encourage her to come with you. That is all that I am asking."

"I love Miss Margaret and I want to see her happy more than anything. I think she will find that with you."

"Thank you, Dixon."

"I am not saying this because you are a fine gentleman with wealth and can take care of her. I am saying what I think is in her heart. I do think she is on the edge of knowing that herself."

"Again, thank you. Dr. Donaldson said he thinks you and Miss Hale will be all right to leave here on Wednesday. Tomorrow, I shall see to your passage to Oldham and Branson will attend you all the way to her home. Peggy Higgins has your clothes collected and ready to travel. She will bring in some for you to wear by tomorrow. The only unknown is how many tickets are to be purchased for Oldam. Do you want me to discuss it with her since I am going to see her next?"

"No, I will see her later tonight. You shall have our answer in the morning."

"Very good, then. I will leave you to your dinner and be on my way. Dixon, you're a woman with a heart of gold."

It took two minutes for John to reach Margaret's room. She was holding the small bouquet in her hands, twirling and smelling the assortment of flowers.

John knocked lightly. "May I come in?"

"These are lovely John, but haven't you given them to the wrong lady this evening?"

"I did not bring you those."

"Yes, you did."

"I came here, spoke with Donaldson. I heard that Dixon received a post today, so I went to visit with her before coming to you."

"Really?"

"Really what? Really I didn't give them to you or really I went to see Dixon?"

"Never mind. I will find out."

John couldn't tell if she was on her medicine or not. She seemed normal. "Have you had your dinner?" he asked while pulling over a chair. "Dixon was just getting hers a moment ago."

"I think it will be soon for me, too. Was Dixon's note from her sister?"

"I believe it was. She said she would be by later to discuss it with you."

"I hope it is before they give me my medicine. I lost the whole morning."

"Actually, you entertained me this morning."

"I did?"

"Yes, just for a little while."

"Did I embarrass myself?"

"Now, how could you possibly do that? You were ever the lady."

"I didn't say anything that was private?"

"I shall never repeat it. I promise," John smiled.

"Are you sincere?"

"You once knew me. What do you think?"

Margaret looked at John quizzically. He was smirking. She never saw him smirk before. "I think I want to know you again, more than before." Margaret wasn't sure if her mouth said that or her mind. John did not change his expression.

"Forget I said that."

"Said what?"

"Didn't I just say something to you?"

"Yes, you asked me if I was sincere."

"After that. Did I speak any other words?"

"No." John struck his normal stoic pose, but his heart was slamming against his chest wall."

"How did I entertain you this morning?"

"You kept looking at your nails and telling me how nice they were. Then you wanted me to see them."

"I did not."

"You are having a difficult time believing me tonight. What have I done to draw this out of you?"

"Could be the way you look … all fancy."

"Miss Hale, those are words of jealousy. Surely that is not you."

"Tsk." Margaret looked away before she blushed.

"Tsk? What does that mean exactly? I am unfamiliar with the term."

"It means you're daft, you're nonsensical."

"I am sure you are correct," John said. There is no reason for you to be jealous that I am dining with another woman tonight."

"That's right!" Margaret expounded loudly as she slammed the bouquet to the bed.

"I see I am upsetting you. Perhaps, I should leave." John rose from his chair hoping for the words she said next.

Leave me? How those words stuck in her mind.

"Must you?"

The nurse arrived with a tray of food and asked to borrow the chair that John was just occupying.

"Here." John held it for her to sit. "I was just leaving."

"Mr. Thornton?"

"Yes?"

"Have a nice time tonight."

"It will be an effort. I shall see you tomorrow."

"Thank you for coming by."

John left the room.

On his way to Miss Hawkins, John stopped at the street flower vendor again and ordered three deliveries of flowers for tomorrow and one for early Wednesday. He did not give his name and left no card.

The nurse was feeding Margaret because she was in a nearly prone position, when Master Griffin knocked on the door.

"Come in." Margaret didn't recognize the voice until his face came into view.

"Master Griffin! This is quite unexpected. I am all at odds at the moment."

"Nonsense. You are in hospital. How are you feeling, Miss Hale?"

"They say I am doing better. I will be released the day after tomorrow, but I am afraid I will still be ordered to rest."

"I have come to relieve any worries that you may have in that regard. Your health is most important. I was muddling along before you walked into my office. I believe I can continue muddling until you return."

"You are very kind, Mr. Griffin. It's not many employers or Masters who would grant a worker such a privilege."

"Your job will be there for you when you return. Do you have an estimate on your recovery?"

"For complete recovery, I think the doctor is looking at two months. But I will feel much better and able to perform many tasks in a couple of weeks. I cannot be strenuous and must watch my food intake. Mr. Thornton is going to see that I have a carriage to your mill every day. He will not allow me to walk."

"He is a gracious host. Might I inquire if I would be permitted to visit you at his home? I liked the way you began to set up the books. Perhaps, I could come to ask you a few questions about it. I may be able to keep my paperwork in some order for your return."

"I shouldn't think Mr. Thornton would mind that. In a week or so, I will send you a note as to when would be a convenient time to see me."

"That is most agreeable. I won't take any more of your time. It appears your nurse has some medicine for you to take. Again, relieve yourself of any doubts regarding your job. Good day, Miss Hale."

"Thank you for coming by."

Cecil left the room.

"I don't know how he got in here. Your visitors are limited to a select few," said the nurse.

"Must I take that medicine?"

"Yes. Here. Drink it all. Let me check you while I am here. How is your bleeding doing?"

"I don't know. I have been afraid to move for fear someone will shame me." Margaret replied with a tinge of sarcasm.

"My … aren't we feeling better?" The nurse pulled down the sheet and lifted her rough cotton gown. "I will need to clean you. Let me get my supplies. I shall only be a moment," the nurse said, as she pulled the sheet back up.

Margaret reached for her small bouquet while she waited. It wasn't like Mr. Thornton to play a game with the flowers. It must be someone else. Perhaps the missing signature was just that … missing … lost in the delivery, not some admirer.

"I see someone sent you flowers. Would you like me to put them in a glass of water?" asked the nurse on her return.

"Do you know who brought them here? There was no calling card attached."

"I'm sorry, I do not." She closed the door. "My name is Gemma, by the way. I'll have you all cleaned up in a wink. Would it be unheard of for Mr. Thornton to have brought them?"

"I asked him. He seemed emphatic that they were not sent by him. I don't believe he thinks much about flowers. Few in Milton probably do."

"Maybe you have a secret admirer."

"If you knew how my life has been, you could understand how improbable that is."

"Well, I hope you find out. I would like to know, too. There. You are ready for the night. I'll remove your food tray. Are you sure you cannot eat a bit more?"

"I am quite full, thank you." Margaret handed her the bouquet."

Margaret closed her eyes for a moment when she heard some movement in the room. As she opened them, she saw Dixon leaning over her.

"Dixon! You look like you are recovering. Your cheeks have color."

"I don't see much in yours, miss. What does the doctor say?"

"I haven't see either one for a while. Mr. Thornton said you have a note from your sister today. What does she say?"

"She is happy that I am coming to stay for some months. Would you like to read it?"

"No. You told me what I wanted to know."

"There was more."

"Oh, yes?" Margaret looked expectant.

"She said that she would be glad to have both of us, if you wanted to get well at her home."

"How very kind of her to offer. Please thank her for me, but I will decline. As you may know, there are matters I wish to resolve with Mr. Thornton. Also, Cecil wants to see me."

"Cecil? Who is Cecil?"

"You know, my new boss."

"I know no such thing. I thought it was a Mr. Griffin that you spoke about your first night after work."

"Oh, yes. He is Cecil Mr. Griffin."

"Cecil Mr. Griffin?"

"Yes. Like I said, Mr. Cecil Griffin."

"Do you call him Cecil?"

"No silly. He is my boss. We are not yet acquainted. He left a short time ago."

"Your boss came to see you … here?"

"Dixon, I think you should have Dr. Donaldson check your hearing. Do you know who brought me flowers?" Margaret said, pointing to the glass with gaily colored bloom clusters in it.

Dixon looked where she was directed to look. "Oh, miss. Aren't they nice? We haven't seen flowers since Helstone."

"Yes, we haven't seen flowers since Helstone."

Dixon finally surmised that Miss Margaret had taken her medicine, which seemed to cheer her.

"We get to leave here after tomorrow. I think they will let me sit up soon. How are you traveling to your sister's home? I think I have enough money for that."

"Mr. Thornton is paying my way and Branson's too. He will stay with me until I reach her."

"You will be alone with a man, Dixon." Margaret grinned sheepishly.

"And so will you."

"What do you mean, alone?"

"When you go to Mr. Thornton's home."

"No. No. There will be a housekeeper there."

"Does she stay overnight?"

"I think so. He said so. She won't be as pleasant as you are. I will be counting the days until you are truly well again."

"What will we do when I come back?"

"What do you mean?"

"Where will we live? I may have to turn into your guardian or chaperone. The doctor says I can never do any heavy work. I think I will become just a burden to you."

"You will never be a burden. You are my family. We will always be together, come what may."

Dixon dabbed her eyes.

"Dixon, don't be sad. I am sure Mr. Bell will return any day and all of our troubles will be over."

"If you say so, miss."

"I say so, miss."

"I think Mr. Thornton is happy that you will remain with him."

"I am happy too."

"You look happy about that. Will you try to make him fall in love with you?"

"I don't think he will ever do anything that he wishes not to do. He is having dinner with Miss Lady Friend tonight. That means there is someone that he fancies."

"Are you sad about that?" Dixon remembered how Mr. Thornton hoped she would stay with him.

"Yes, I am sad. Well … no, I am not sad. It is right that he went on with his life. I wish him happiness. I did want to talk about my misgivings a year ago. I was wrong, and I want him to know that so we can be friends."

"Friends?" Dixon was stunned.

"Well, yes. He is so generous to us that I should make friends with him. I don't know how long he will have to care for me."

"I think you are talking rubbish. Can't you see he still has some feelings for you?"

"Yes, but they are friend feelings."

"All right. Have it your way. You are silly, so I will go back to my room. Have a nice sleep, Miss Margaret. We will see each other tomorrow. Mrs. Higgins should be bringing us some clothes."

"Goodnight, Dixon."

Jeremy had finished washing the dishes from dinner. His brother James was reading the paper. He walked outside and looked at the empty flat across the street, wondering about Margaret and her guardian. He decided to visit the hospital tomorrow. If she wasn't there, they should know where she went when leaving.

Peggy had sorted the clothing that had been lumped together when she took them from the flat. She packed all of Dixon's into one large bag. She didn't have many pieces, but there was a lot of material to the ones she did have. She thought Dixon could choose what she wanted to wear when traveling to her sisters.

Margaret still had some lovely frocks, some of which would hardly ever have been seen in Milton. She selected a simple frock to be worn home. She found one corset and the other undergarments that were needed. They were set aside … the rest were packed in a carpetbag. Searching her home, she found the few pieces of jewelry that she had removed from Margaret's velvet jewel case.

"Whew, I am done, dear husband. Will you have someone fetch those bags tomorrow?"

"Yes, of course. I've been sitting here thinking about this whole situation with Margaret. It is a mess, isn't it?"

"I think so, but in what regard are you talking?"

"Do you think we have different feelings about this?"

"We could," she smiled. "You first."

"These two women have been together since Margaret's birth. Now they will be separated for months. You know Margaret will not accept John's charity if she can survive on her own. We will all have to work on her then. She will want to be stubborn and proud."

"I think she has learned her lesson there. What else?"

"She will seek work. Dixon will be of little use as a housekeeper, I should think. That means she will have to hire someone else, pay them and keep Dixon fed and housed. I know she would not have that any other way, as she shouldn't. But it is still an obstacle for her. I have been wondering if we can turn that building where her furniture is being stored into a small cottage for them. What do you think of that idea?"

"I am proud of you Nicholas. I think that is a brilliant plan. Will you suggest it to John?"

"I'm afraid I know what his answer will be."

"What is that?"

"He will want to see her in something finer. What are your thoughts on this mess?"

"Are you blind, dear husband?"

"Are you talking about John still having feelings for her?"

"Yes!"

"I don't see that as a problem."

"Men!" Peggy said with her hands on her hips.

Nicholas chuckled. "You women worry too much. Things will work out."

"Suppose Margaret does not return his affections? What then?"

"Do you think that is possible? It is written on their faces." Nicholas smiled.

"I tend to think it will eventually work out, but until that time, it will be a mess. He has Miss Hawkins, who he has been seeing steadily for several months. She's not going to give in so easily. She has money, so I don't think she is looking for that. She may genuinely love him. How does John extract himself from that after giving her impressions that he may be near to a proposal?"

"I know for a fact, John does not do that. If he is the John I've come to know, he has made no commitments. He has left himself a way out. He's had plenty of practice."

"Do men love in that fashion … leaving an 'out' for themselves?"

"No, men do not. Not men in love anyway. But John is not in love with Miss Hawkins."

"And you know this how?"

"I just know. I know John. He hardly mentions her name."

"Where is Mr. Bell? That is a mess. He is Margaret's future if John isn't."

"John will be."

"Are you sure? Oh yes, you just know. You know John," Peggy smarmed.

Peggy was getting exasperated and Nicholas was chuckling.

"Don't you know that we men know how to get what we want and we take it."

"Yes, so it is rumored."

"Not that, silly. A man in love will win or die trying. There is no way he will lose her twice."

"That is if he ever gets her a second time. Margaret could easily mistake his closeness and protection as charity. Then we're back where we were a year ago."

"You may have a point. She could be that proud, but I doubt it after this."

"She has joined the work force, she has lived in a new area. Men are seeing her now. Someone could come along and take her favors before John unravels himself from Miss Hawkins and plans his pursuit of Margaret."

"You women really do think like this?" Nicholas inquired.

Peggy laughed. "Like I said, I think it will eventually work, but it may be a mess getting there. I think you should really give the cottage idea some real thought."

"I will. It wouldn't take long. It has running water. I will look into it."

As John Thornton was being driven to the home of Elaine Hawkins, he couldn't help but smile at Margaret and her flowers. He didn't know why he led her to think they were from someone else, but it seemed like fun. They were on the verge of having enjoyable times when the riot broke out. Everything went downhill after that. John couldn't ever remember teasing anyone before. And best of all, he sensed a bit of jealousy, even with her denial.

His smile faded as Branson brought the coach to a halt at the front door of his Lady Friend.

Chapter Seventeen

"Good evening, John," Elaine said as he handed his hat and coat to the doorman. "Before we start this evening, I wanted to apologize for my behavior the other day. It was jealousy, which I am not very familiar with. I couldn't hold my tongue. I believe you when you say she is only a friend. May I be forgiven?"

"There is no forgiveness needed. I am glad you voice your mind, whether I like it or not. I only want understanding. I will not build a future on secrets, doubts or devious scheming."

"That doesn't sound like I am forgiven, and I don't believe you can accuse me of any of those traits."

"Did you not doubt my words about Miss Hale? I told you she would recover at my home. I cannot say with all certainty that we are friends or will be. I do think there were words left unsaid the past year."

"What kind of unsaid words?"

"Elaine, this is my business. Are you pushing me to engage in a conversation about another person and their personal life? I will not do that."

"Even if you are involved in it?"

"Even then."

The footman brought in the customary refreshments that the two usually drank. Elaine lifted her brandy glass and John, his scotch.

"Please sit, John." John sat in a single chair this time, and not on the sofa with Elaine.

"You sit far away this evening. I have upset you."

"I'm sorry. I find my mood and mind are weary. The last few days have been somewhat chaotic for me."

"Speaking in general terms and not about anyone specific, has a woman ever proposed to you?"

John was taken aback, but did not show it. "Not directly. There have been hints."

"And when those hints start becoming stronger, what do you do about that?"

"Elaine I don't have a written plan of action. I do not subscribe to one way of living me life. My actions or words would revolve around that particular person and our relationship. I never speak words of committal until I am sure. I have only been sure of that once, and it didn't work."

"Indeed. What do you think you are looking for in a marriage partner?"

"I cannot say, but I will know when it is there."

"I take it that I do not have whatever that is?"

"Excuse me. Dinner is served," said the footman, who would attend the table, as well.

John felt a relief to be interrupted, but he was ready and always willing to tell her the truth. No, he thought, he has not yet seen his spark of life in her.

John escorted Elaine to the table. He hoped she was not expecting an intimate night.

"Good evening, Margaret," Donaldson said as he came through the door.

"Do you have to pull the sheet down and my gown up?" Margaret asked in her sing-song voice.

Donaldson said, "No. I just talked with your nurse. Tomorrow we will get you sitting up and walking around a few steps. When you leave here you should be able to walk to the privy. That is my goal before you can be allowed to stay at Thornton's house. He has steps, but I shouldn't think you will need to use them. I don't want you trying that until you feel steady walking around."

"Steady walking. Yes sir."

"May I ask a personal question?" Donaldson inquired.

"If you can lift this sheet, I don't think what you ask can be more personal than that."

Donaldson laughed out loud. "John said you were making him laugh. Since you are recovering in John's home, I wondered if you have an affection for the man, which is stored away somewhere in the back of your emotional mind?"

"I don't know where that is. How am I supposed to see that?" Margaret asked with seriousness.

"Margaret, is there any love for John Thornton by you."

"I am not allowed."

"Not allowed what?"

"What you just asked."

Donaldson sighed. "Are you saying you are not allowed to have feelings for Thornton?"

"Yesss …."

"And who is giving you or prohibiting you from having feelings for Thornton?"

"Yesss …."

"Yes, who?"

"Yes, John Thornton."

"I see. So am I to conclude that John told you not to have feelings for him?"

"Yesss …."

"He said those words, did he?"

"Not exactly."

"What words did he use?"

"He is having dinner with Miss Lady Friend tonight. You know what that means."

"I'm afraid I don't. Tell me, Margaret. What does that mean to you?"

Tears broke through the medication and leaked from the corners of her eyes. "He has a fancy for her, and she has one for him."

"Why are you so sure she fancies him?"

"Wouldn't you?"

Donaldson laughed to himself. "No, John isn't my type of woman."

"We will be good friends though."

Donaldson was trying to gauge what she would come across when he stopped her medication. He felt sure that Margaret was the only woman for John, but could Margaret hold her stamina until that was realized by her? Yes, John was seeing Lady Friend, but that was normal social interaction for him.

"I think you will be good friends too."

"Do you?"

"Yes, I do. Now, it has been a long time since you lived with your brother. Do you remember how it was to live with a young man in the house?"

"Yes. I was not to be naked around him as I grew bigger up here," she pointed to her breast."

"That's right," he chuckled. "Will you weep when John goes out with other women?"

"I hope not. I would have to move away."

"I want you to come to me if you ever feel that you must get away from that."

"I will. Do you have a spare room?"

"No, but the Higgins do."

"Oh, yes."

It was after 10 p.m. when John and Elaine finally left the dinner table. She had put on a feast for him. Margaret was not mentioned any further that night. When they entered the sitting room, John remained standing and Elaine knew he was ready to announce his departure.

"John, I see you want to say goodnight, but would you join me in one last drink for the night? I really don't want to be alone so early."

"If you wish. Shall I pour?"

"Yes. Please. The staff is not serving at this hour."

As John handed Elaine her glass, she patted the sofa suggesting that he sit there. He did.

Elaine didn't feel she had the nerve to return to the question left unanswered before dinner. Did she have what he was looking for in a mate? She felt John would have taken the opportunity to speak up had the answer been positive. She slid closer to John and took his arm and laid it behind her shoulders. She nestled into his chest while holding her glass. She felt John maneuver at bit to accommodate her.

"What plans have you tomorrow, John?"

"Aside from being a Master of two mills?"

She smiled. "Well, yes."

"I shall visit my mother, I suppose. Until I feel easy that she likes where she is, my trips there will be frequent. Also, I will purchase train tickets for Miss Hale's guardian, the one who had the heart attack. She will be recuperating at her sister's home in Oldam. I may stop in to see Miss Hale and see that nothing has changed with her coming to my house the following day. I stopped in today, but she was highly medicated. Although she spoke, I don't believe she remembered anything she said. It was gibberish."

Elaine bit her tongue. John could feel her tensing, but she said nothing. She reached over and set her glass on the table, then turned in John's arms to be kissed. She felt a slight hesitation as he obliged her. The kiss was lacking with intensity that other men had shown her. John had never been a man lusting for her. He was forever the perfect gentleman.

Elaine slid herself onto his lap and kissed him deeply. She took one of his hands and placed it on her breast. His manly response was what she wanted, but he offered little.

She hoped for a wild passionate lustful kiss and embrace, but it never came. Elaine stood and put her hand out for John to take.

"Please, John."

John took her hand in his and was led the way upstairs.

Arriving in her darkened room, John let Elaine guide him. For the first time, he had no need of her. He wasn't even sure he could perform.

Elaine began disrobing John and encouraged him to do the same. There was very little romance to the action. Elaine was in a hurry.

John wondered if her motive was more to please him, ensuring his interest in her, than her own pleasure. Once naked, Elaine pushed him to the bed and straddled him. She pulled John's hands to her breasts and moaned for him while she worked the massaging. John finally joined in and her hands left his to tickle the hair on his chest.

John's impending erection was a slow process. He actually started to sweat that she would not find gratification. That had never happened to him before. His arousal never quite got there, but Elaine rocked against him long enough to pleasure herself. John had no words. He was humiliated.

Elaine laid down beside him, spent.

"I am sorry, Elaine. That was an indignity that I have never suffered. Perhaps I am overly tired."

"Perhaps it is someone else," she said getting out of bed.

John sat up. "What do you mean?"

Elaine was throwing a night robe around her. "Are you sure that little problem isn't because you were thinking about someone else?"

John walked over to where his clothes had fallen and began to dress.

"You have nothing to say to that?"

"What do you want me to say, Elaine?"

"I want to know the truth. Is there a chance for me in your life? Tonight would tell me no. There is no you and me and a happy future. You know I love you, don't you?"

"You have never spoken those words." John replied.

"You have never spoken them either. Do you think I just invite any man to my bed?"

"I don't think any such thing. I have always been of the opinion that a woman's desires have a place in this world as a man's does."

"That's charitable of you. John, do you have any love for me at all?"

"Elaine, I am very fond of you. You have a lot to offer a man and a husband."

"But I don't have whatever it is you're searching for in a mate."

"I don't believe so. I've been hoping to feel something different, something that tells me in no uncertain terms, that you are the one. I think I am asking for too much in a woman."

"I thought we had something. We saw each other a few times a week. I've enjoyed being in your company. I thought you enjoyed being in mine. The two other times in my bed were not like tonight. What is it about me that turns you from me now?"

"Your jealousy has been irritating."

"You should be flattered."

"I am not. I have never sought nor revel in flattery unless I have made a good stride forward in the millworks. Flattery for my personal sake is always there. That sounds more than cocky and brash, but it is a fact I have had to live with. On the surface, men admire the life they think I live, but inside I am not the man they see. I am a serious man. A man who has thrown his whole self into his work. Happiness is only a desire for me, never fulfilled."

"You never smile, either."

"I am quite aware of that, and that could be what I am looking for … someone to make me laugh or smile. I don't know. I do know that it is lacking in my life. It seems to bloom in others."

"Do you want to cancel my invitation to the Master's Ball?"

"No, I do not."

"Will we see each other between then and now?"

"Elaine, I cannot answer that. I would like to see you again, but after tonight you may wish I would not. Perhaps there is someone else in your life that has been waiting on the sidelines."

"As it is in yours, I suspect."

John pulled on his last boot. "I think that is all for tonight, Elaine. Apparently you did not believe me when I spoke of your jealousy. Goodnight."

Elaine protested and then apologized to John all the way to the front door.

John had to wake up Branson when he arrived at the coach. "Home, guv?"

"Yes." John hated these scenes. It seemed he was always the one leaving the relationship. And if he weren't seeing one young lady, the others were being thrown in his path. Margaret had been different. She walked into his path spouting thunder. He knew they got off on the wrong foot, but it was refreshing to see a woman of such innocence and self-assurance. She didn't chase him. She wasn't being promoted by her father or Adam Bell to him. Her mystery was the initial allurement. Margaret's naïve knowledge of the northern ways was amusing at first, but soon it became the wedge that finally separated them. He wondered what she now thought. When she wrote the note, she mentioned unsaid words. He had to hear them. Always, too, in his mind was the slip she made when she said she wanted to know him.

Margaret had had a restless night. Nightmares of moving into the Princeton district plagued her through the moonless hours. She was given a sleeping draft that made her awake late in the morning.

Peggy was sitting by her bedside holding her clothing for tomorrow. Margaret was startled to see Dr. Price leaning over her when her eyes opened.

"Good morning, Miss Hale. I heard you had a disturbing night. Mind telling me what happened?"

"I barely remember, now. I believe it had something to do with where I was living."

"Near the Princeton area?"

"Yes. That was it. That's all I can tell you."

"You do understand that your friends will ensure you never go back there to live."

"I suppose. But I can't live on charity. I must do something to pay my way … and Dixon's."

"That is a long way off, Miss Hale.

Peggy was sitting there listening to the Margaret she knew. She hoped John would be open to a small cottage idea. That would solve a lot of worries for Margaret. John would be forced to take rent from her, but it would be minimal. She would be protected and driven where she needed to go.

"Oh, Peggy. I didn't see you there," Margaret said as Dr. Price helped her into an upright sitting position. "Have you been waiting long? What time is it?"

"It's going on near 10 a.m., sleepy head. I wish I had the luxury you do … sleeping all the time … being fed the best of foods."

Margaret smiled. "I bet you wouldn't like urinating into a pan when it is brought to you."

Dr. Price laughed. "How are you going to feel when your caregiver brings you the pan when you leave here?"

Margaret stopped for a moment, realizing he meant John Thornton. "I think I shall hold it until I am well."

Peggy and the doctor chuckled. "Miss Hale, the nurses will be in soon to help you stand and walk you around the room. You can sit in a chair for a few minutes off and on today."

The room looked smaller than Margaret had imagined, being relegated to look at the ceiling for two days. She looked around the room and spotted a new small bouquet of flowers. Peggy saw her looking and rose to hand them to her.

"A secret admirer?"

"Again, there is no calling card. Doctor, do you know where these came from?"

"Yes."

"Oh, do tell. I would be so grateful."

"If you insist. They came from the ground." He smiled.

Margaret couldn't help but giggle at his joke. "Peggy, you must know who's doing this?"

"Are you sure it's not Mr. Thornton?"

"He says no."

"Well, I haven't any idea. It may be your boss."

"You didn't bring them, did you?"

"Not I or Nicholas. I have your clothes for tomorrow. And I have Dixon's, too. Branson has them ready to go to the station tomorrow. I think he's looking forward to riding a train and riding inside a coach."

"I will spend some time with Dixon today. It will be sad tomorrow."

"Margaret whatever happens with you after your recovery, we will see that you always have Dixon, if she wants to be here."

"I will pay you all back someday," Margaret promised.

"Yes, you will pay us back with your friendship and pleasant company. I have written to Bessy. She will be coming home for a short break in a few weeks. She is anxious to see you."

"I too will be happy to see her. We can have long talks like we used to."

"If I may interrupt you ladies … ahem."

"Yes, Dr. Price?"

"I have spoken with Dr. Donaldson, and we want to continue your medication for another week. I believe I will have a sleeping draft made for you, too. You will only take that at night. The other medication you will take twice a day."

"Must I?"

"Yes. We want to get you on a solid path to recovery. You are gaining a small bit of color in your cheeks. In two weeks you will feel like your old self, except you will be weak. You will exhaust quickly, but that will subside as the weeks go one. I don't want you returning to work until I say so. Mr. Thornton will be advised of these instructions, so don't get mad at him should you not want to do something. He or his housekeeper will help you walk around for the first couple of days. Even though you were weak when you came in here, your legs have grown even weaker. That was expected, but now it has to be corrected."

"Can I bathe?"

"If you have a copper tub. No standing at the pitcher and bowl or at the kitchen sink. Also, and this is important, Dr. Donaldson will examine you during your menstruation week next time. We just have to ensure that has returned to normal."

"Does Mr. Thornton have to know that?"

"He already does. He even has the dates. So there." Price laughed. "He is your selected nurse, am I right?"

Margaret looked at Peggy and she was covering her laugh.

"I suppose."

"Fine. I think that should do it. I will see the nurses this evening and know of your progress today. Until tomorrow then, Miss Hale." Dr. Price tipped his invisible cap and left the room.

"Peggy, what am I going to do about that week?"

"You just go up to John, tap him on the shoulder and tell him it's here."

"Then he'll ask what's here."

Peggy burst out laughing. "I think John is smart enough to know what's there. He lived with two women you remember. You are no different."

"Yes, but they were family. He had no choice."

"Margaret you are making it sound like the curse that women want to make of it. You are educated, and so is John. Don't be ashamed, for God's sake."

"Perhaps I will come stay with you during that time."

"You will not. John will attend you."

Margaret threw her hands over her ears. That was never discussed openly in her upbringing. She always thought it was because her brother and father were around. It stayed hidden. "Thank heavens there will be little if anything for him to do in that regard."

"Margaret, you are too funny."

"Yes, but it's John Thornton!"

"Did I hear my name? To what am I being accused of doing?"

Chapter Eighteen

Margaret turned red for the first time in months. Peggy was bent over laughing.

"Miss Hale, I see your color is returning. May I ask about the discussion that included my name?"

"No."

"Have I done anything? Have I embarrassed myself?"

"Not yet," Margaret said, watching Peggy choke from laughing.

"If it weren't for Mrs. Higgins' amusement, I might worry."

"No, I am the one to worry."

"I shall see that you don't," John replied.

"And that's the dilemma."

"You are going to be secretive?"

"For as long as I can."

"But I shall know eventually?"

"Against my better judgment, but yes."

"Is this that woman thing?"

Margaret grew red again. She was speechless.

"I see. There is no worry there."

"How do you know that?"

"I just do."

Margaret peeked up at Peggy, who was staring out the window trying to keep a straight face.

I have come for a short visit this morning to speak with Dixon about her tickets and travel. Branson is in there now, ensuring she will be comfortable on their journey.

Margaret saw John spot the small bouquet.

"Those don't look like the flowers you had yesterday. Have you found who they are from?" John said, turning his hat around by the brim.

Margaret wondered if he could be a wee bit jealous. "These were delivered before I woke. No card was attached."

"They could be from my mother. She wants to make amends, you know."

"Oh. Yes, I guess they could be. If so, why would she not sign her name?"

"Perhaps she is not ready to enter your life, yet. She believes she has a lot of forgiveness to ask for."

"Oh, no. I don't want that. Thank her for the flowers, but don't let her take any blame. I was …."

"Please speak no more about that. That discussion can wait. I hope to return later. Cook has your food ready to go. Benny has your room all tidy and bright."

"Benny?"

"My new housekeeper."

"Oh."

"Good morning, ladies." John turned and left as he popped on his hat.

"Margaret," Peggy added, "you are hysterical, and you haven't even had your medicine."

Benny had been given instructions in regards to Miss Hale coming to the house. Mr. Thornton seem pleased to be telling her that, she thought. She would be weak. She needed special food. She needed this and she needed that. Benny already did not like the fact of another woman arriving. She was also aware of the hour that her master returned home last night. He must have lain with his lady.

Margaret was sitting in a chair looking out the window when Dixon entered. They were glad but sad to see each other. They spoke for more than an hour until their dinners arrived in their rooms. Dixon left promising to see her tomorrow before Branson escorted her away. Margaret was going to return to her bed, but she pulled a chair next to the bedside table. She was going to eat sitting in a chair. She felt at ease. There was no stiffness or weakness. Another bouquet of flowers arrived, but this time she met the person delivering them.

"Excuse me, young man. Who is sending these to me?"

"Ma'am, I do not know. The owner gives them to me to deliver to you. I deliver to other places and pay no attention to who is sending them."

"Thank you."

The lad left the room. Margaret was twirling and smelling them again. She wondered where some of them came from at this time of year. Some were in season and some were not. John may be right when he suggested his mother. Margaret would send her a note of thanks tomorrow. Gemma came in carrying her dinner tray. "Here we go. This is your last dinner here."

Margaret looked down and saw liver once again. If it hadn't been for recent weeks when she only had half a potato, she wouldn't have eaten the liver at all. She did not much care for the meat. Margaret was anxious to look at that food list she had heard about. What was it going to be like at the Thornton's?

While chewing the meat, which didn't seem to want to go down her throat, she heard a light knock at her door. Turning, she was surprised to see Jeremy standing there with a rather large vase of flowers.

"Jeremy! How nice of you to come and visit me."

He blushed and handed her the flowers. "These are for you. I see you have some, though."

"Yes, but these are lovely and you've come a long way. There is a chair over there. Please sit."

"Only for a moment. How is your guardian?"

"She is doing very well. We will both leave the hospital tomorrow. Dixon will convalesce at her sister's home."

"And you? Your flat is empty now."

"I will be at Master Thornton's home for a while."

"I see." Jeremy didn't know what to say next. "I've never been in a hospital before. This is some place."

"I haven't seen much of it to know."

"You are doing well, then?"

"Yes. I will be fine in no time."

"Here. May I put the flowers over here for you?"

"Yes. Thank you."

John was walking down the hallway when he heard a strange man's voice coming from Margaret's room. He waited outside the door.

"How is your brother? James, isn't it?"

"He is himself. All he does is read. I am not much of a reader for pleasure. Are you?"

"Yes, I love to read, but I have no books anymore. Do you know if Milton has a library? I thought I heard of one, but never was able to find it."

"Yes, it does. I could find out from my brother where it is and bring you something to read."

"Thank you, but I prefer to select my own. I shall be busy with Master Griffin in another week. He will visit me at Mr. Thornton's home to help him with his books."

John had heard all he wanted. He entered.

"Good evening, Miss Hale. Oh, hello."

Jeremy stood to shake hands. "We have met. I am Jeremy, Mr. Thornton … a former neighbor of Margaret's."

"Yes … from the stoop across the street. Yes, I remember. I am sure Miss Hale," he said with emphasis, "is glad to see you again."

"She is looking better than she did. I guess I will go now. I hope to see you again, Margaret."

"Thank you for the flowers."

"My pleasure. Good evening to you both."

Before John could get a word out, the evening bouquet arrived.

John was embarrassed seeing the large vase of flowers next to his small bunch.

"More flowers!"

"I visited with my mother before coming here. They are not from her."

"I asked the boy who delivered the flowers at lunch time where they were coming from. He didn't know."

John breathed a sigh of relief and sat down on the edge of her bed.

"Look, there are now five bunches of flowers."

"Yes, I see. And Jeremy brought a nice large vase of them."

"I like the little ones so much more, though."

"You do? Why is that?"

"Oh, I don't know. They are from someone unknown. They are brightly arranged, and some of these flowers are from very far away, I believe. The small ones look like love bouquets, more personal. The large vase is pretty, but it is a centerpiece, more for show. The small ones have a message being conveyed through the petals. I wish I knew who to thank."

Margaret started to lean. "Did you take your medicine recently," John asked.

"Yes, with my meal."

"I think you had better sit on your bed before you fall on the floor."

John helped her over. She put her arm around his neck and he looked into her eyes while moving her. She closed them.

Her eyes did not open, "Miss Hale! Miss Hale!" John started rubbing her hands.

She opened her eyes and looked away.

"Should I call the nurse?" John asked anxiously.

"No, she cannot help me."

"Are you sure?"

"Yesss …."

John felt a grin starting to spread on his face. His cheeks ached. He was so elated and wanted to laugh at the same time.

"Are you sure you want to tender me?"

"Tender?"

"Tend … tend me?"

"I am sure."

"You know there are worries ahead for me?"

"Such as?" He assumed the situation she must be referring to...

"I can't say."

"Should I know what to expect?"

"No, you shouldn't be expecting anything."

"I am prepared for whatever happens."

"You are prepared?"

"I am."

"You are prepared for my worries?"

John covered his smile. "I am a grown man. I am prepared for anything that you, a woman seem embarrassed about."

Margaret pulled in a large breath and her eyes widened. "You really *do* know!"

John couldn't hold it. He chuckled loudly at seeing her stunned face. "Yes, I am quite familiar with the process. Book learned and not rumored." He smiled.

"But not experienced. I don't want to talk about it."

"As you wish, but I am."

"Did you have a nice meal last night?"

"It was a feast."

"A feast?"

"Yes."

"Did you enjoy yourself?"

"For a while."

"You enjoyed yourself for a while?"

"Must you repeat everything I say?"

"Am I?"

"You were sitting when I came in. Did you do any walking today?"

"Yes, I went from here to there," Margaret said, using her finger to point. "I did that many times. I am not weak as they say."

"Very good to hear."

"Are you sure you want to tender me."

"I very much want to tender you."

"Will I meet Miss Lady Friend?"

"It's possible. Would you like to?"

"Yesss…."

"I shall invite her by some evening in a few days. I believe she is interested in you too."

"Not me! You. She is interested in you."

"Is she?"

"And you are interested in her?"

"Am I, now?"

"Yesss … She fixes you feasts."

"Nicholas sends his regards. He will be glad to see you tomorrow."

"And Bessy is coming home soon," Margaret said, excitedly.

"I didn't know that. I am sure you are pleased about that."

"About what?" Margaret was squinting, as if in thought.

"Miss Hale. You are making me laugh again."

"You are laughing at me?" Margaret's lips pouted.

"Margaret, you shouldn't do that!"

"Do what?"

"Pout your lips that way."

"Are they making you laugh at me?" Margaret took her finger and pushed the pout inward. "There."

"There is only about twelve hours before you will be out of here."

"Really?"

"Are you looking forward to that?"

"I am. It will just be you and me?"

"And Cook and the housekeeper."

"Oh."

"Do you prefer to be alone?"

"If you will be there."

Again, John's heart started hammering.

"I will always be there for you." John felt strange. He was able to woo her, a practice he had never engaged in. She would never remember it, but he loved the joy it gave him.

"I am tired."

"I am sure it is from all the walking you did today from here to there." He smiled to himself as he laid her back on her pillow.

"Would you mind if I stayed here until you fell asleep?"

"You will protect me? I had bad dreams last night. Where were you, anyway?" she frowned.

John snickered. "If I had known you had bad dreams, I would have been here. That won't happen at my house."

"Good … good … good night." Margaret rolled on her side and closed her eyes.

John sat there for a while studying everything he remembered loving about her. Perhaps Elaine meeting her would help her understand why he would be returning to Margaret.

John rose early, shaved and dressed smartly. He had a short meeting with Cook and Benny to clarify any questions and establish that all preparations were complete. Benny served him breakfast after that.

Benny noticed how John sat with his newspaper beside him, reading while he ate. Tomorrow she would have that waiting for him. He finished his meal, grabbed his coat and hat and left. Benny went to the window to watch. She saw a coach roll into the yard and wondered who that was for. It was a few minutes, but Branson entered the carriage while the coachman saw to a carpetbag. Benny didn't know what that was about. She went down to Cook.

"Cook, why is Branson riding in a coach today?"

"He will be away all day seeing to Dixon, Miss Hale's housekeeper. Branson is escorting her to her sister's home. She will be there for a couple of months."

"And then what?"

"I have no idea?"

"What about Miss Hale? What will she do when she recovers?"

"It will be something that she and the Master decide. It's their business, not yours or mine."

Cook, never having experienced it when Jane was here, was leery of Benny's interest in her Master's movements. If it continued, Cook better have words with the lass about her place. She was beginning to doubt that she had much experience at all.

Margaret woke early. She was anxious for the day. The nurse came in to clean her and give her the powdered medication.

"Good morning, Gemma. Could you ask the doctor if I can take this medicine later? I want to see Dixon before I feel light-headed."

"I will ask. I should think that will be fine. Give me a moment."

While Gemma was out of the room, Margaret stood and looked for the clothing that Peggy had brought. There, next to her bed, was a small bouquet of flowers. Another one. Margaret hated to leave the hospital and miss receiving those or the chance to find the sender. She picked them up, smelled them and held them to her breast. Someone had thought of her to send her flowers all the time. No one had treated her that special. It was like a fairy tale, and she wished she could take it home with her.

Home … she had no home. She was a ship without a port. The gentle tide would allow her to anchor in the harbor or rock in the birth, but she had nowhere to live if she left the ship. Somehow she had grown accustomed to the safe haven of the hospital. Friends came to visit her. People waited on her and someone was sending her bunches of blossoms. Margaret noticed on this new bouquet that many of the petals were still coiled closed as if waiting for a new day, the sun, a beginning. She wondered if the sender realized in this handful of nature's beauty, there was a message of hope. She was lifted up to think someone cared that much.

"Miss Hale?" Gemma's return interrupted her speculation. "Miss Hale. It looks like you were in deep thought."

"I was, I believe."

"More flowers, again! You are one fortunate woman. I know no one who would do that and not want to be known. Dr. Price, who will be here shortly, said you can hold off on your medication until your home-nurse feels you need it."

"I am not sure how to take that. What does he mean?"

"He will explain to you and Mr. Thornton when he arrives."

"Very well."

John went to his office to see Nicholas, who was letting his driver escort John to fetch Margaret.

"Top of the morning, John. Are you ready for your big day? I imagine a day such as today has been in your mind a long time."

"It's not quite how I envisioned it, but I think it will be one of my best days. I am ashamed to admit it, but I am a bit nervous," John said, standing and looking out the window. "Aside from you or Peggy and even Branson, I hope no one comes to pay their good wishes today. I guess I will have to get used to that."

"Yes, I think you will for a while, unless you are holding her prisoner. You know it's going to be very hard on you?"

"I know that right enough. In my mind, I have pictured her in my home … our home, under much different circumstances. Treating her as a friend will be a painful challenge."

"And you will succeed."

"I *will* succeed. I must succeed."

"How went your evening with Miss Hawkins the other night, if you don't mind telling me what you can."

"It's difficult to see it without bias. I was honest. To me, it seemed the beginning of the end as all others have been. How she understands it, I am not sure. I will still escort her to the ball as I had promised. Would you believe, Margaret has asked to meet her?"

"Was she being kind, or do you think she really meant it?" Nicholas asked.

"In Margaret's mind, she and I are trying to become friends once again. She will say she is happy that I will continue my life as I have been, but yet the tone in her voice and the look in her eyes says something much different. I have seen this many times in women, but I have never allowed that to affect me as it does now. I may be striving too hard to read something in her countenance that isn't really there."

"You are a bundle of nerves. Give this some thought. If she has feelings for you, they are being revived from a time long ago. She thinks of you as a stalwart gentleman, stoic to the point of annoyance, but caring for people, including those that work for you."

"I haven't changed, have I?"

"If you could see yourself like I do, you remind me of a scared rabbit. You will jump this way and that way depending on her mood at any given time. You never showed weakness of purpose until now. Control that, and she should return to you."

"Am I really doing that?"

"I can see it. Peggy can see it, and I imagine Branson can see it. I believe your move with your mother came at a good time. She would shame you for condescending to Margaret. Only you and I know how much the women we love dominate us. It can't be helped.

Nicholas chuckled, "We know when we were created to be protectors and providers, and given much strength and power, our creator made us weak to the allures of the female. We are nothing without them. We would have little purpose in life. They sustain us. I am sure they have their need for us, too, but I am done trying to figure them out. They have a language we will never understand. They are lovingly complicated."

John laughed. "You settled into married life easily, I believe. Most of these feelings are new to me if you can believe that. For the first time, I want, I need, I obsess, and I dream and plan. Life is tossing me about in the wind. I don't know where to grab a hold."

"You will find your way. It will come naturally." Nicholas advised. "When are you leaving to collect her?"

"Very soon. Her doctor wants to speak to us both. If the time permits, we may ride along to the station with Dixon and Branson. She doesn't know that yet."

"Has she figured out the flowers?"

"How did you know about that?"

"John," Nicholas sighed. "The signs are there for those that know you well. Friends wouldn't have sent that many bunches. That is the sign of a true romantic. I grant you, that has not been you in the past, but maybe it's time."

Chapter Nineteen

Branson entered Dixon's room and found her and Margaret hugging each other. The tears were prevalent. Apparently the doctor had just left, as Dixon had papers in her hand. It looked like instructions.

Dixon handed them to him, and he took a look. Yes, it was information for her sister to follow. He stood back as they said their goodbyes. Parting was sad, yes, but he never understood the crying. It's not like they would never see each other.

"Miss Dixon," Branson called out. "We have half an hour before the train, and I want to take time and care getting you there. Is there anything I need to carry?"

She pointed to a small cloth bag, which had the clothes she was admitted with.

"Miss Hale, it is great indeed that you will be staying with us. I am looking forward to some reading lessons again. I hope you are feeling well."

"I am good, Branson … not well, but on my way."

The two women looked at each other and hugged one last time. Branson extended his arm for Dixon to take. And she did.

Margaret plodded along behind them at a slow pace, watching as they grew further apart from her. Unexpectedly, she became winded. Seeing no help in the hall, she sat on the floor. She felt foolish. They said she would have limitations for a while, but she thought herself stronger.

A nurse came running towards her as she heard heavy boot steps hurrying in her direction.

"Margaret, all you all right?" John asked in a panic-stricken voice.

The nurse took one side and John the other in picking her up.

"I don't think I can stand. That is why I am down here." Margaret tried to laugh it away so no one worried.

John couldn't help but chuckle at her foolishness in the face of bravery.

"Wait. I saw a rolling chair back there. I will get it."

"Yes, John, get it. I will wait here." Margaret heard the nurse laugh.

"Did you fall on your bum or hit your head as you fell? Does anything hurt?"

"Fine. I am fine. Nothing hurts. I was winded. I sat down on purpose. I did not fall."

John came with the chair. He asked the nurse to stand aside and he lifted Margaret into his arms and set her in the chair. He smiled when she looked away from him.

"Are you hurt?"

"No. As I told this nice nurse, I felt winded and sat down. I did not see a chair in the area, so the floor was my second choice."

"Jokes! Jokes so early in the morning," John smiled. "What are you doing so far from your room?"

"I was saying goodbye to Dixon."

"Had you planned to do that at the train depot?"

Margaret burst out with a giggle, which made John grin, behind her. Even the nurse laughed.

John knew he had found heaven and she was coming home with him.

"What did you say about jokes? I thought you didn't know what they were."

John began pushing her back to her room. The nurse went another way.

"Tell me. How long has it been since you laughed?" John asked.

"I fear it's been many months. I will ask you the same since I have never known you to laugh."

"You have been quite amusing since beginning that medication."

"I mean before that."

"I do not know."

"Miss Lady Friend doesn't make you laugh?"

"Not like you do. Here we are. When is your doctor due to release you? He wants to talk with us together, you know?"

"Are you in a hurry?" Margaret asked, looking at him with a side glance.

"Miss Margaret Hale, we are going to have a difficult time if you don't learn to look at me once in a while. You must get over your infatuation with my eyes," John grinned at her.

"How do you know that?"

"You told me."

"I couldn't have. I wouldn't have. That's … that's too …."

"Intimate?"

"No! Improper," Margaret blustered.

"Well, you told me you didn't like my eyes. You said you loved them. What is it exactly that you love about them?"

John held firm to Margaret's shoulder as the doctor walked in. He wanted to laugh as Margaret seemed like she wanted to run away.

"Good morning. Miss Hale, I would bet you thought this day would never arrive."

"I must admit that I have been treated so nicely, I am sorry to leave."

"I have watched as those flowers pile up on your table. He is a lucky man." The doctor looked at John briefly.

"John, could you pull that chair over here?" Dr. Price sat on the bed, flipping papers while Margaret wiggled in the rolling chair.

"Miss Hale. I will ask you once again if you wish to recover at this gentleman's home."

John hadn't expected that, and a sweat came over him.

"I can change my mind?" Margaret was getting even with John for his last remark about his eyes.

"You can change your mind at any time. Dr. Donaldson said you could speak with him, and I know Higgins's have offered."

"I am sure Mr. Thornton has gone to a lot of trouble for me."

"Miss Hale, don't let that be your reason for going there. Gratitude is not a good reason."

John thought he was going to be sick. He wanted the doctor to shut up.

"I wish to go to Mr. Thornton's home. He has room for me. As friends, he will care for me to his best ability, I am sure. And there are past issues that need to be resolved. This should force that issue. Should he not want me or I change my mind at that time, I will contact Dr. Donaldson."

"Fine. I'm sorry, Mr. Thornton. I had to ask her."

"I understand. I am relieved to hear her answer."

"Miss Hale, as I understand you found out just moments ago, you are not as strong as you think you feel. Is that not correct?"

"Yes."

"You will walk no further than you did in your room yesterday for a couple more days. If you need something at a distance, Mr. Thornton or his housekeeper will aid you. Do not try using the steps for another week, and do not attempt them alone for the first few times." Price could see John nodding.

"If the employment that you have allows you to sit, you may return in two weeks, but I will see you before that happens. When you have your next woman's cycle, have Mr. Thornton contact Dr. Donaldson. We are sure this concern was due to your anemia condition, although we need to monitor you through the next one."

Margaret prayed for the floor to open up and swallow her.

Sitting behind her, John could see her cheeks redden.

"Your cook has a list of items you should eat. Please try to stick to those as best you can. You can start to taper off to a more traditional dietary routine after your next visit with me. So … plenty of rest, eat, moderate to light walking until I see you in two weeks. In three weeks you will bleed again. Mr. Thornton, do you foresee any problems in helping Miss Hale, help herself?"

"None whatsoever. I will contact Donaldson, as well."

Margaret finally put her head in her hands. Two men were discussing *her* woman's week … *hers* …not some other flustered woman. Well, it was out now. Tomorrow it may be headlines in the newspaper. No sense trying to hide it, she sighed inwardly.

"If for any reason, bleeding, fainting, weakness not improving, vomiting or swooning, contact myself or Dr. Donaldson immediately."

Margaret covered up a giggle with a cough when he mentioned swooning. John would have to stay at a distance.

"I believe that is all I have. Are there any questions from either of you?"

There was silence, and then John and Margaret both spoke at once.

"You first, Miss Hale," John offered.

"Thank you. I have no questions."

"Mr. Thornton?" Price asked, looking his way.

"Can I know more about this medication she is taking?"

"Oh yes. Of course. I think I wrote that down on this paper for you, but we should discuss it."

"Please," John remarked.

"Miss Hale has suffered from a bout of anxiety and stress at a prolonged period which caused her anemia. This has interfered with her daily life, including eating disorders, relationships, sleep, job performance and other effects that we have seen with her. Knowing what we know about her recent history, I feel safe in saying this is not a chronic problem."

"Chronic?" John asked.

"On going. A little anxiety and stress are normal, sometimes necessary, but not to the detriment of your physical well-being."

"The medication?" John interjected, afraid he was going to hear the medical history of the condition.

"I am going to leave that at an 'as needed' rate of intake. She is not returning to the problems that brought her here. If you see that she is melancholy, anxious, or becoming over-wrought easily, encourage her to take it. Today, I would like to see her take another dose as soon as you get her settled. It is another change in her life. It will last about six hours. We know she says whatever she wants to—giving no thought, but she may be sleepy as well. It will bring her contentment, nothing more."

"Very good, Dr. Price." John held his hand out to shake the doctor's hand, who stood up.

"Thank you so much, Dr. Price, for all you have done for me."

"I will see you in two weeks Miss Hale. I hope to know the sender of those flowers by then. Please use that rolling chair to get to your coach. Good day to you both."

John walked around and sat on the bed before her. "Is there anything in this room that you need or want to take home?"

"Yes. My flowers."

"All of them?"

"Just the small ones."

"Can I put them in your lap until we reach the coach?"

"Yes."

"Are you ready to go home?"

"Your home, yes."

John sensed the melancholy that Price alluded to. A new reality was now facing her. To Margaret's general way of looking at things, it was another step further into charity.

As John pushed her chair toward the entrance, he asked, "Are you tired, Margaret?"

"No. Did you have something you wanted to discuss now?"

"I was wondering if you wanted a short ride before being settled into another residence."

"Would you mind?"

"Of course not. That is why I asked. Where to?"

"Griffin Mills? Could I stop there?"

"If that's what you wish, we shall go there."

When the rolling chair was pushed outside the door, John picked up Margaret and carried her to the coach. She wrapped her arms around his neck, giving him a warm and close sensation. He didn't think she feared him in any way.

"Margaret, do you feel uncomfortable around me in any regard? You do know you are safe in my presence. I hope I never do anything to scare you."

"I am far from having any worries when I am with you. I feel quite protected and safe from harm."

"I am glad to hear that. I will always be a safe shelter in your life. That is for any reason and forever. I know we have some words to say at a later time, but you impacted my life in the greatest possible way, and I will always cherish the good days. I want to see that you have everything you want or need."

"John that is lovely to hear, but I don't want to start crying so early. Let us just go home. I can see Mr. Griffin at another time."

"Very well. I will warn you I know this new housekeeper, Benny, very little. Please do not hesitate to correct her or give her orders. I will make sure she understands that you are to be treated as the woman of the house. If you don't mind, you may fill in for what mother would be doing with the staff. I will be working most of the time, and I really don't know what all their chores should be. I only know how they are to interact with me, mostly."

"I will be glad to get her started. It will lift my spirits to be of some help to you."

"Margaret, I don't expect you to sing for your supper," he laughed. You are a guest at the very least. Never think you are in the way or that I would be better without you. That just won't be true."

As the coach rolled into the mill yard, Margaret saw a face at the parlor window. "Is your housekeeper a young woman?"

"Yes. She was not Nicholas's first choice, but he felt from her former work that she may be good enough to replace Jane. I think Cook is watching over her. I sense something strange between them, but I am sure that is because she is new to the home."

Margaret had heard many rumors over the years about the Master of the house and the housekeeper or lady's maid. In large staffed homes, the servants above stairs were always under the roving eye of a greedy Master. John was not of that ilk. He was forever the gentleman with high standards, but Margaret knew he could be an innocent drawn into the game of scheming women. These she learned during her schooling from the other females.

Higgins was walking the weaving shed when he caught sight of his coach returning. John was home with his prize. Nicholas scurried down the catwalk and headed out to welcome Margaret. As he was walking towards the coach, he saw an arm handing out bunches of flowers and John was piling them up in his arms.

"Nicholas. Just in time, as always. Would you mind taking these from me? Margaret will need some help."

Looking at John, Higgins smiled. "You carry them. Let me do the honors."

Nicholas took her hand as she began to exit the coach. Not knowing her excessive weakness, Margaret went down on one knee.

"Margaret, I am so sorry. I hadn't realized." Nicholas looked over his shoulder, while helping Margaret up, and saw a smirk on John's face. It was one of those "That'll teach you" looks.

"Nicholas, I am fine. Don't fuss. I just wasn't ready for my own weight coming off that step. I do believe I can make it over to the door, but will need help from there."

Nicholas took her arm and watched her carefully as they walked to the front stoop. Arriving at the front steps, they stopped. Margaret lifted her arm expecting Nicholas to lift her and she cling to his neck. Nicholas hesitated, wondering if John would mind him continuing with the honor. John was standing there with an armful of flowers, looking at the clouds. That was a signal to Nicholas that "You started this, you finish it."

John knew Margaret was in safe strong hands to be carried up the steps, so he took his time. He let Nicholas know he was looking over his shoulder. Nicholas was now tasked with carrying the king's jewel into the castle. John smiled.

Nicholas easily carried Margaret up the steps. Benny was on the top step waiting to take the flowers from her Master. Margaret bid her a brief hello, but expected a formal introduction later.

"Mr. Thornton, let me takes those." Benny saw that he couldn't take his eyes off of Miss Hale while handing her the bundle in his arms.

"Put these in water and set them in Miss Hale's room."

"Yes, sir." She curtsied.

As Benny took them to the kitchen, she crushed a few of the blooms here and there. The woman didn't even know there was a new delivery waiting in her room. She felt an act of war had been declared.

Nicholas rested Margaret on the sofa, John put up his hat and Cook brought a tray of hot tea.

"Miss Hale. How lovely to see you return to this house. I have never forgotten that you have been the only person to find your way to the kitchen and compliment my dinner to me personally."

"And I meant every word of that. I am afraid Dixon is only a modest cook. She was originally hired as a nanny, then housekeeper. After moving to Milton, she became a cook as well. It has been several years since having a nicely prepared meal. I am looking forward to it. And if your Master knew the whole truth, your cooking was a reason I selected Marlborough Mills as a place to get well."

John smiled at Cook. He had taken her for granted since he'd grown. Margaret was shining a light on her he had never considered–another reason for loving Margaret.

"Miss Hale, please don't lay all that at my door. You will not think of me so magnanimously when you see what I must serve you. I'll have you know that master has insisted he will eat the same meals."

Margaret looked at John, who looked embarrassed. He was caught in the act of being sympathetic.

"Nicholas, sit, will you?" John walked over to his own chair.

"Are you comfortable Margaret? Do you care to change into something less restrictive? You can lie down if you wish?"

"I am quite fine for the moment. I've always loved this room. It seems a bit sparse now, but it is still beautiful. Oh, thank you, Cook." Margaret took the cup and saucer from her.

"Margaret, Peggy will be over to visit in a day or two. She wants you to settle in and she will visit when John is working."

"How nice. Peggy and a book to read is all I need just now."

"Margaret, I visited the book seller several days ago and inquired about novels of interest to women. He quickly mentioned two titles, but I made an assumption that the first two he thought of, you may have read. I selected two others. They are in your room."

"I am not sure I can take much more attention, but I will try," she smiled. She sipped her tea, but wouldn't look up.

"Nicholas, are my eyes any different than anyone else's?"

Everyone one heard Margaret sputter her tea back into the cup. She wiped the drops running down her chin. John chuckled.

"John, are you seriously asking me that question, or is it for Margaret's entertainment?"

"I would say a bit of both. As you see, she cannot look directly at me. All I can get from her is that it has something to do with my eyes."

Nicholas caught on. "Well … now that you ask …."

"Stop it! Just stop it, you two!"

John and Nicholas broke out in a laugh. Margaret was forced to smile, too.

Margaret suddenly felt like she had come home. Sitting there with best friends and laughing. There was no greater gift except being married to one of them.

The room quieted and Margaret realized all eyes were on her. "Must you stare my way, the pair of you? If you supply me with three balls, I shall juggle for you."

Still silence.

"Margaret," Nicholas said, "I believe your settlement into this house will come easier than you thought. I must get back to work. One of us must see to our 600 workers."

John stood and thanked him for the coach and the visit. "I dare say I will carry the eggs next time." John slapped him on the back.

"Margaret, I shall see you tomorrow."

"I hope so."

John walked Nicholas to the door. Margaret set down her cup and attempted to stand. Using the arm of the sofa, she rose with little problem. She tried to remember where the privy was.

"May I help you, mum? My name is Benny. How should I address you?"

"You may call me Miss Margaret or Miss Hale. Can you direct me to the privy? It is on this floor, is it not?"

"Yes, mum. And there is one downstairs with the copper wash tub."

"This one upstairs will be fine."

"Can I help you to it? It's down the hallway, just outside of the Master's bedchamber."

"I will try on my own, but if you could follow and await me, I would be grateful."

"Of course, mum."

John returned and saw the procession to the washroom. He started to take Benny's place, but she waved him away. His thoughts were that Margaret wanted a woman alone, so he went to his chair.

Benny watched her slow progress. Her weakness was apparent, which heartened Benny. Any number of things could befall someone in such pitiful health.

Chapter Twenty

John found that his papers had been piling up for several days. He pulled one free, but couldn't read it. As he sat there, he decided that Margaret would have his chair. She would have good light, comfortably large seating and a view out of the window and over to the office. He would be able to see her from the office, too. John quickly moved his pile of papers and tea cup to the other matching chair away from the window.

As Benny and Margaret came down the hall, John interceded, and Benny was replaced.

"This is your first exercise for the day. Are you ready for your medication?"

John led her to his large chair.

"Oh no. This is your chair."

"Benny, you are excused," John said.

"I have one just like it over there, see? I am putting you here so you have light to read. You can watch the people working in the yard. It even looks into the office. I will find something that you can set in the window if you wish to call me home."

"You have thought of everything."

"This was only now thought to be an idea. It wasn't planned. What about your medicine?'

"I am feeling quite happy right now. I don't need to be carried away to wonderland just yet. I would like to rest and then see my room."

John carried over her cup of tea once she was seated. "Don't hesitate to ask for anything."

"I am so appreciative of using your home. I do not wish to impose myself on your personal time if I can help it."

The words that John wanted to spill right then were being held back with great effort. He wanted her to use him. Use him up until there was nothing left.

"Did you mind about Nicholas and I having a laugh over your impossible adoration of my eyes," he smiled.

"I think you have taken a comment I made under an abnormal state of mind and fitted it to your own self-esteem." Margaret grinned, knowing that to be a good retort.

John stoically mulled that around in his mind. She had launched the first salvo. He felt lovingly ambushed.

"Oh, so it isn't true, then?" John had never heard of this eye thing, never aware of anything different about himself, but apparently Margaret thought otherwise, and he was intrigued. At least it was a place to redeem a friendship for a start.

Margaret tried to reach for her tea cup, but it was out of reach. John jumped up and moved the table closer to her.

"Thank you."

John waited for an answer to his earlier question. None was forthcoming.

"I shall take your silence to mean that it is true." *Touché'*, he inwardly said to himself.

"I'm sorry. Was that a question?" *Victory,* she inwardly said to herself. Margaret wanted to laugh at his confused face. She knew her education was far better than his, but she was handed hers while he had to work for his. It seemed one of the few weapons she had against the famous John Thornton.

First round to Margaret, John conceded to himself. At that very moment, he realized he was living his dream. He was willing to take these small snatches of heaven when he could. There was much to resolve on several levels before he reached paradise. She was near him at least, and she loved his eyes.

John left Margaret after a while. She seemed tired from holding a conversation. He went down to speak with Cook about lunch.

"Cook, you know, Miss Hale is right."

"I do? What is she right about?"

"About your fine culinary expertise," he laughed, folding his arms as he leaned against the back door.

"Oh shoo … get out of my kitchen. I don't need those words from you. I'm still here, so I have assumed it is good enough for Mrs. Thornton."

"Did she ever compliment you?"

"On those big yearly dinners. It wasn't exactly about my cooking, but handling the whole affair."

"Well, she just didn't know how well you cook."

"And you do, I suppose?" she teased.

"You know I eat out often. Most of your meals could stand tall to many of those chefs working out there."

Cook waved him away as if he were joking.

"Cook, you have never known me to compliment very often. And you certainly know I don't say it if I don't mean it. You do a great job for this family, and I want to appreciate you for it."

"Do I have a new Mrs. Thornton in-waiting upstairs?"

"I think that is my business, don't you?"

"I don't know what your mother would say, but you have my approval and blessing."

"I have your approval, do I? Well, that's good enough for the Queen, indeed. Thank you. She is far from that, though. She may not want to be mine. I have my work cut out for me."

"Oh, I think you are misjudging her feelings."

"What makes you say that?"

"I see in her now what I once saw in her. There was a time she loved you. If she was aware of it, I don't know. But she did. Her demeanor and her eyes spoke the words. Your rush to marriage took her by surprise, as I think it did you. She could do nothing else but refuse you and still retain her values as a proper woman. And you–you silly goose–let it lie there and wither."

"What choice did I have?"

"How many times in your life did you feel you didn't have a choice? You are not John Thornton, mill master, if you had many. You allowed it to fall into ruin. You feared her after that. We all knew the rejection was devastating to you. Forgive me for saying this, but your mother made a mistake in not seeing you clearly. Perhaps, no woman is good for a son. Your mother was jealous of her. She's learned her lesson now, though."

John hung his head.

"Don't look down. You have done the right thing for both of you by setting her up in town. It will be hard on her at first, but she will come to find enjoyment eventually. She never had women her age to talk and visit with. She will find it there."

"If Miss Hale is agreeable, I would like to have mother over for dinner in a few days."

"Excellent idea."

"And what wonderful dish have we to eat today?" John asked with a frown.

Cook laughed. "Today you are in luck. It will be fish."

"I think I will find the red wine for that."

"When do you want to eat? It will be your big meal today. I can serve tea and cakes soon, though."

"Can I see that list again?"

Cook shuffled some papers in a nearby drawer and handed the list to John.

"Yes, that will be fine. Say … in about half an hour?"

"Aye."

He'd never had a talk like that with Cook. It felt good.

John returned to the sitting room and found Margaret in a ball, sleeping with her head on the upholstered arm. There was a portrait he would love to have in his study. He burned the image in his mind, and then carried her to her bedchamber.

Margaret whispered, "Thank you," and stretched her legs out. John slipped off her shoes. On the chair across the room was a coverlet he used to throw over her. After tucking it under her neck, he backed out of the room.

John decided to leave her door open so he could hear if she left the bed. They would have to discuss that as she should be attended for one or two more days. She wouldn't know the house in the dark.

Several hours later, John walked to his study for the first time in several days. Personal postal mail had piled up. He quietly sat thumbing through papers on his desktop. There were a few ideas that he was working on about the mills, which he had brought home from the office. He relaxed back in his chair, hands behind his head, wondering where to start. Looking out of his door, he could see past the sitting room, down the short hall and into Margaret's room. Only from her knees to her toes were visible but it was enough to know if she was trying to get out of bed.

Sitting back upright, there was movement in his peripheral vision. He started to rise, happy to think Margaret was waking, but instead saw Benny standing at her doorway looking in. He didn't think that strange, but then she entered the room. John knew that wasn't proper even if the door was open.

It took John only a second to walk around his desk to leave the room, but Margaret was out of sight for that moment. He kept his eye steady on her door, but Benny never exited the room that he saw. She was not in there when he arrived. John noticed that Margaret had thrown off her coverlet, and he replaced it. He looked around the room and saw nothing out of place. He assumed that what he really did see was Margaret removing her cover.

John went back to his desk and noticed among the scattered mail was a note with odd stamps on it. He knew it was foreign, but not from where. It must belong in the office, but he looked into it anyway. It was from Adam Bell. John flopped down in his chair and opened it immediately.

To my dear friend, John Thornton,

By the time this letter reaches you, I am sure I will have passed from this life. The warm and moist climate here in the southern states has taken its toll on me, leaving very little time to put everything in order.

I am most upset that I had no time to return home and visit with Margaret for the last time. Death: it is not a gentleman.

I write to you because I still believe Margaret is in your soul and always will be. I know you have her best interest in your heart. I am asking a great favor that you be the one to tell her of my demise. She is going to need comforting and someone to oversee my holdings that have been left to her, until she is ready to take her own control.

I have written to my solicitor and my college. Aside from clothing and books, my personal items will be sent to you for your own choice of disposal. There are very few. Letters confirming my demise will follow very shortly after my death. I will be buried here, as it makes no matter to me, and I do not care to have Margaret crying over another grave. She has had far too many for such a young woman.

My solicitor will contact you when the time comes as I know you will still be at Marlborough Mills. I assume Margaret will have returned to her Aunt Shaw's by now.

I know you are aware of my very fond regard for the Hale's and Margaret, especially. If I could trust her to anyone other than myself, it would be you. John, I know she loves you. Whether she knows it or not or she is too proud to renew your affections, you are the only man she will ever love. Being as close as I have been to her, I could see it wilting inside of her. Yes, she made a grave mistake a year back, but it was her naivety that trapped her. I will always believe your proposal was sincere and not one of duty. Margaret, of course, felt differently at that time. We have spoken little of it since it happened, but a sadness came upon her, the likes of which I have never seen. Richard and I were at a loss to help her. She didn't know how to speak of love to anyone. Being raised as a clergyman's daughter, has built walls around her—ones from which she is only now trying to climb.

I write these final words, as she will be my last thoughts on this earth. You are not mentioned in my will, but I leave my most-precious possession to you, Margaret Hale. Please watch over her as I wished I could have done. She became my world.

John, don't change. Keep your pride, your ethics, manners and gentlemanly deportment. I feel certain a happy life is still ahead of you. Keep Margaret safe.

A friend for all times,

Before he could read it a second time, there was movement from Margaret's room. He quickly slipped the note into his pocket. John took long strides to get to Margaret before she could stand on the floor.

"Margaret. You slept well."

"I am sorry to have fallen asleep like I did," she said as she rubbed her eyes.

"Do you wish to get up?"

"Yes, please. Can you take me to the privy?"

"Do you want me to carry you," John quickly checked the bed for any sign of bleeding."

"No, I don't need to be carried," she laughed.

"Has anything unexpected happened?"

"No. Stop your worrying."

John helped her stand, gave her a moment and the offered his arm.

"Thank you. I will try on my own. I only need you near."

As I do you, Margaret.

"Did you say something?"

"No," John replied.

John waited outside the door with his arms folded, thinking of the note he had received. He was not about to tell Margaret anything until a note from the solicitor arrived. As sorry for Adam as he felt, he knew this was Margaret's path away from his home. He wanted it to be her home.

Margaret opened the door.

"Are you ready for some fish this evening?"

"You mean there is no liver in the house?" she smiled.

"For tonight we have fish, but I will talk to the chef and see what we can do in the future." John waited until she walked ahead of him. There seemed no issues with her making it to the couch.

"The doctor advised medication today. Do you feel you need it?"

"I shall try not to take it, but if you think I need it, I will oblige you and the doctor. Did you know there were was a small bouquet waiting for me in my room? Did you put it there?"

"No."

"Are you sure?

"I think I would know if I had done that. I will ask Cook and Benny what they know about it. I must admit, it is starting to make me anxious."

"Do you want some powders?"

John laughed. "I will just have to find a way to not worry about it."

"Why would you worry?"

"I cannot have some unknown man stalking my guest."

"I am sure that bouquet should be the last of them. Perhaps I will receive secret love notes in the future. I have never received a love letter. That would be quite thrilling, especially not knowing who it is. It's like a valentine. You don't look as if you approve. Have you ever written a love letter?"

"Yes."

"Who to?" John's reply had stung her.

"I never sent it."

"But who was it to?"

"A gentleman doesn't tell."

"Is it to Miss Lady Friend?"

"A gentleman never tells."

"You said that before."

"And I will keep on saying it until you stop asking it." John grinned at her.

Margaret turned when she heard the rattle of plates and cutlery being laid out on the table. The young woman did not seem to have a care if she was loud or not.

John noticed Margaret's interest, which had also caught his attention. "Benny, would you come over here for a minute?"

"Yes, sir."

"I wish to say this in front of both of you at the same time so there is no misunderstanding."

Both women nodded. Benny went to sit down. "Benevolent, you will remain standing until asked to sit."

She curtsied and hung her head.

"As you know Miss Hale is a guest of this house for as long as she cares to stay. She is acquainted with the assignments and manners of staff servants. She would say servant, we tend to say staff here in the Milton. It is rare to find even a very wealthy Master with a house full of servants. We have shunned an upper-society mentality. Miss Hale will have my full authority to change or command your duties as she sees fit. I am asking her to do that for me. She will be treated as the 'woman of the house.' Miss Hale will teach if she can, but she must be obeyed. If you have any problems with that, come speak to me. Anything you see or hear in this house is confidential, is that clear?"

"Yes, sir."

"Mr. Higgins was never able to locate the employer you used as a reference for this job, so we have no testament as to your character, your allegiance or your loyalty. You are on a trial basis."

"I understand, sir and miss."

"Margaret have you anything to add?"

"Nothing that I wish to say in front of you, just yet."

John wondered what Margaret had seen in Benny.

"I trust whatever you decide, Miss Hale. Benny, you may complete the table with far less noise."

"Yes, sir. Forgive me, sir." She turned, picked up her tray and went downstairs.

The meal was eaten to everyone's satisfaction. The dishes were removed, and Cook had gone home. John assumed that Benny was in her room, or the larger staff dining room which served as a sitting room for them. It was a large room which measured the length and width of the parlor and John's study above. It was meant to have another staff bed area, but with Cook going home, the separating walls were never constructed.

Benny turned out the kitchen gas lights and sat on the bottom stair, listening.

John saw Margaret notice something outside. He rose to look out the window. A coach had arrived.

Chapter Twenty One

"I see Branson has returned. He should be here shortly for a full report."

The back door opened suddenly and Benevolent was spotted by Branson, sitting on the step in the dark, listening. She quickly moved out of the way. Branson scampered up.

Branson removed his cap and bowed slightly. "Good evening, Miss Hale, guv."

"Well, sit, Branson, and tell us of your day," John encouraged.

Branson almost smiled seeing his master seated differently in the room. "All went very well. The train ride was enjoyable, at least for me. Dixon just looked out the window. Her sister had a carriage waiting for us, and the driver took us directly to her home, even though it was just outside of the main town. I paid him, of course, but he did wait while they insisted on feeding me." Branson grinned.

"I've never seen so much hugging and pampering goings on. It seemed a very pleasant reunion. Miss Hale, I will urge you not to worry about Dixon, she is in good hands."

"Thank you, Branson. That does comfort me to hear your words. And thank you for taking your time to travel with her. I am sure our letters will cross in the mail, each wanting to tell the other of our initial situations."

Branson would tell his master about the new housekeeper, but not where he could be overheard. It would have to wait. "Sir, here is the coin I did not use. May I be excused?"

John stood as did Branson and accepted the money. "Thank you, Branson. I am unsure of plans tomorrow, but sleep in if you can. Good night."

"Good night, Branson," Margaret added.

"Good evening to you both," Branson replied. As he went downstairs, the housekeeper was not there, but the room was dark.

"John, I would like to go down that hall again, but by myself this time. Don't even follow me. I need the sense of accomplishment."

"Are you sure?"

"Yes. I may look unsteady, but I will shout if I need you."

"Let me go ahead of you and turn on the gas light." John entered the privy and turned up the gas. He looked around to see if Margaret would need anything and realized he really didn't have any idea about what she may need in there. He had been so adamant that he would care for her in every way and he may already be failing.

"Margaret you can come ahead. I must admit that I am not sure of any necessary supplies are in here. Mother and Fanny had this closet, but it is now empty."

Margaret looked quickly about the room, but had been in it several times today. It didn't lack anything she needed that she knew of. "I have all that I need, thank you."

John closed the door for her and went back to the sitting room. Without thinking, he went to his own chair and sat. They would now be alone, and he puzzled what kind of conversation they would have. If he treated her as a guest, naturally she may tend to think herself to be imposing. He would be happy with her reading a book while he studied her all night. It was too soon to approach all of the unsaid words. Anything could go wrong there, and she could wish to leave. The door opened.

"John, should I turn out this light?"

"I believe I will leave it on until you become used to the house in the night."

She slowly walked down the small hall, holding the wall, and from there balanced herself to walk across the room to the sofa.

"There I made it. From here to there," she laughed.

"You remember telling me that in the hospital?"

"I remember the words, but I thought it was to one of the nurses. It was you, was it?"

"You may have told the nurses. You repeated yourself many times."

"I did?"

John started smiling, thinking back. "Do you remember my mother coming into your room?"

"No. Oh, how terrible to not remember what must have been a big concession for her."

"She will return. I persuaded her it wasn't a good time to see you because of you being on that medicine. She understood and left, but you kept repeating "It isn't a good time."" John laughed.

"Margaret, do you wish to have a brandy or port?"

"I believe wine is good for me. Yes, thank you."

"Oh … I am sorry. I was sitting in your chair, wasn't I?"

"Please don't apologize. I am going to try not to feel like a visitor."

"I do hope you succeed in that. Having you here is a benefit for me, too."

"Oh?" Margaret accepted the wine glass.

"May I sit next to you?" he asked.

"Please sit wherever you wish. I think we just went over that, didn't we?"

"Yes, we did. I am sorry."

"There you go again." Margaret smiled.

"I'm nervous, Margaret, if you must know."

"Yes, I must know. Is it because of me? I can make other arrangements."

"That is what makes me nervous. I am afraid I will do something to scare you away, to make you feel uncomfortable."

"John, before I would change my mind about staying here, we will have a talk about it. I have reasons I wish to be here. I am not going to run off. However, I don't want you to cease inviting friends while I am residing here."

"The only ones that ever come here are Nicholas and Peggy. Once in a while a few masters will come for a discussion."

"Miss Lady Friend doesn't ever visit?"

"She has been here once to meet Mother."

"John, it wasn't because of me that your mother lives elsewhere, is it?"

"No, Margaret. It was time to be my own man. I no longer wanted to live the life my mother expected. Times have changed, and I am changing. She will not change."

"I'm not sure I understand all you are saying, but that is your family affair." Margaret sipped her wine.

"Can I ask why you didn't come to your friends when your situation became desperate?"

"I am not sure how you measure *desperate*. Yes, hard times were upon us, but I feel we could sustain ourselves. I had assumed it would be temporary until Mr. Bell returned. If it had grown any worse, I would have contacted Nicholas and Peggy."

"Margaret, do you realize if Dixon wasn't with you or had her heart problem, you may have died?"

Margaret started tearing up. "I wish to not talk about it. That is in the past."

"Yes, but the past is where you and I must go to one of these evenings. Isn't that how you feel as well?"

"Yes, but not tonight."

"Margaret, any time. Any time you are ready, I will be too. So many words want to voice themselves, but they are being ruled by the moment. My mind and mouth are far ahead of where they should be." John stood and walked back to fill his glass.

"I have some steps I must take before I can be completely open to you," he said.

Margaret dabbed her tears.

"I should get you some medication. Do you want the nerve calming powder or the sleeping powder? I am upsetting you, and that is the worst thing I could be doing."

"John, I am not that fragile."

"I disagree. Right now, you are fragile and vulnerable to all manner of conflicting emotions and thoughts. Think of where you were and what you were doing three months ago before your father was taken from you. Compare that to what you have been through to be here. With my greatest hope, I have wanted you here, but not at what it has cost you. You've lost your mother and father, your brother by all accounts, and now Mr. Bell is not to be found. Bessy, once a very good friend to you is away. There is one person above them all that wants you more than anyone else in this world. I'm talking too much. Which medicine?"

Margaret could feel the love that he couldn't speak. She hitched her breath at John's spoken words. "I don't want anything that will make me forget what you just said." Margaret was looking away. She rose to walk to the window. John rose, too.

John watched as the scotch in his glass shimmered.

God, we are right there and nothing can be said or done.

"Can I get you anything or do anything for you?"

"Not at the moment." Margaret looked upon a shift change apparently in action. People were leaving in large numbers and few were coming into the yard. "You have a night shift?"

John walked up and stood beside her looking out. "Yes, a small one. They will be noiseless. They make ready for the morning shift. Raw cotton is moved into the sheds, bolts are moved out and boxed to fill orders. They will load the train tomorrow."

"I wish I had understood your responsibilities better two years ago."

"I was a different person two years ago."

"In what regard?"

"A woman came into my life about then and slowly began to change my way of thinking about my workers." John sipped his scotch as they both stood quietly still looking out the window.

"I must sit," Margaret said.

"Yes, surely you must by now. Here, do you need help?"

"No, and don't apologize. It seems to be dangling from your tongue." She looked at John and watched a smile come over him. Margaret almost went to the floor.

"I think I had better retire for the evening." Margaret could feel a flush coming to her face. "However, I will need your help undressing," she giggled.

"And you are prepared to let me help you?"

"Are you or are you not my nurse?"

"I am assuredly that. I have papers to prove it. How can I assist you in undressing? I don't have to close my eyes, do I?"

"No, but there will be no light on."

"I can do many things in the dark."

"First come with me to my room."

John set down his scotch and followed behind her. He stayed several paces away, so she couldn't see his excitement.

"Please, just sit for a moment until I find my night shift. I need to have everything ready."

"I will pull down your bed."

Margaret found her night clothing and sat on the edge of the bed. "I am ready. Please turn out the gas light."

John did as asked. There was only a sliver of light coming from the sitting room.

Margaret unbuttoned her frock. "I do not think I have enough strength in my fingers to unhook this corset. Dixon always did this for me, and I haven't needed one since the hospital. That is all I will need."

John ran his hand lightly down her ankle and removed her shoes.

"Thank you."

"Margaret, take my hands and put them where you want me to start."

Margaret lifted his two hands to the lowest hook. She would stop him at the last few and get them herself.

"Are you ready? I can scarcely see what I am doing."

"I believe that is the point of no lighting in here."

John began unhooking the hooks and eyes. He had done this in his life once or twice, but he never counted how many there would be. He thought of them as a means to an end, but not this time. He took it slowly.

"John, God didn't take this long to make the earth." Margaret laughed.

John dropped his hands as laughter overtook him.

"I can finish the rest."

"Which one of us is the nurse?" John protested, reaching again for where he left off. "I will hurry it. I think I have it sorted now."

"I believe you had it sorted before ever meeting me." Margaret felt the whisper touch of his fingertips across the top of her breasts. Goosebumps came up.

John had to react to his crouched position. He stood and turned his back to Margaret. "Can I be of any further assistance?"

"I trust I can manage the rest. I will sit on the bed and finish."

"Very well. I will be up a while longer. Would you mind if we leave your door open? I want to listen for you in the night. Should you need to call out, I will hear it."

"Are you leaving your door open, too?"

"Yes, but we can't see into each other's rooms if you are worried about that."

"I suppose for this first night, it may be a good idea."

"I may come in and check on you. So cover yourself."

"I will be properly dressed."

"I will leave you then. Do you want the light on and the door closed while you finish?"

"No. You can leave it as it is. Just don't go peeking in here for a few minutes."

"Miss Hale, I am a gentleman."

"You know … when you call me Miss Hale, I feel you are up to no good."

"I wish that were the case. Excuse me." John left the room.

Benny thought what an interesting night she had ahead of her. Her master was going to sleep with his door open. She decided to nap and wait for the middle of the night.

John purposely went to his study in order to see movement in Margaret's room. She had opened the door a bit more but not fully. It wasn't very long before her movement stopped, whereupon he retrieved Bell's sorrowful note and read it once again. He did not know what Bell was worth in pound sterling, but knew of several holdings he had in land. To his reckoning, they would be quite valuable with Milton expanding rapidly and factories going up around his vacant parcels.

Tomorrow, he would bring up the subject of converting the shed into a small cottage. If good strides were made in their relationship, Margaret might consider a move into it before moving away. Safety from the world outside could be the deciding factor to keep her here once she began work again, or even if she were starting to receive her inheritance. John dared not rely upon himself as a draw to keep her there.

It was 3:00 a.m. when Benny sensed upstairs was fast asleep. She crept upstairs and hesitated, finding it not totally dark. There was a light coming from the privy. After waiting long moments, she was assured it wasn't in use.

At the top of the stairs, she was closest to the miss. She peeked through the door opening, seeing that the miss was sleeping. Benny took her time tiptoeing and circumventing the room to stay out of the light being thrown from the washroom as she traveled to another room. She knew she was going to have to pass into full light to reach near the master's bedchamber.

Benny waited what seemed an eternity and quietly dashed past under full exposure from the gas lantern. Before she knew it, she was standing in John's doorway frame. Very little of the privy lantern shone into his room, being slightly around the corner, but there was a spot of moonlight. She was disappointed to find him mostly dressed. His trousers were still on, but his shirt was pulled free. That was good enough for the fantasy she had of being in that bed next to him.

Standing there, her eyes grew accustomed to the dark. Draped over a chair back, she could make out a cravat that had been tossed there. She wanted it. It was only a few steps into the room, but the floor creaked on her step and she stopped. The master moved in his bed. Was he wakened or just changing position? Again she waited. Finally, reaching hard, she snatched the cravat and fled on tip toes.

As she reached the top of the steps, a thought came to her. What if she left the cravat on the floor in Miss Hale's room? Would some doubt ensue by her as to his intentions? Or should she keep it? What a nice piece to have under her pillow. Ultimately, she settled on saving it for herself. There would be other opportunities to start driving a wedge between them. However, Benny still had to find a way for him to take an interest in her. But a plan was forming.

Margaret slept restful in the nice bed. She woke earlier than usual, most likely from the late nap she had yesterday. She couldn't dress herself until Benny or Cook came, but she had to visit the lavatory. Rising in her night shift, Margaret felt the steadiness in her legs and struck out on her own. It was the distance of a "from here to there," but all in one direction. She could rest in there before she walked back.

Her woman's week was totally over, and she was glad of that. Now all that liver may do its work in building her red blood cells. Feeling stronger than yesterday, she reached for the light and turned down the gas as she left. Opening the door, with the room dark now, she could see into John's bedchamber if she turned to her left. She really could see nothing from where she was and felt bad for looking. In her path back to her room, the darkness prevented her from seeing a small table which held her wine glass. Over it went with a sound. Thankfully the glass landed on carpet and didn't break. The surprise of knocking it over caused her to reel back, landing on her bum.

She wasn't too sure how she would raise herself to a standing pose with nothing to hold onto. Suddenly she felt two hands slide under her arms and lift her.

Chapter Twenty Two

No words were said. John placed his one arm under her knees, sweeping her up and carried her back to bed. Laying her down gently, he covered her and left the room.

Margaret wondered if he thought she had been sleepwalking since he uttered no words. Her door was left opened, but he disappeared into the night.

John went to his room, closed his door, lit his lantern and prepared for the day. It was only an hour ahead of his usual time, but it meant he would have no warm water. It didn't matter. Nothing else mattered but Margaret.

Margaret rolled over and managed to sleep another two hours, waking at 7:00 a.m.

John, finished dressing, went to his study to compose his first real love letter. This one he would send.

Cook arrived at 6:00 a.m. She put on the big kettle for washing and the smaller kettle for tea. She was surprised hearing footsteps above. Her master was up early. Cook knocked on Benny's door and told her it was time to get up. Hearing no response, she entered her room and shook her awake. Benny had a familiar-looking piece of material in her hands, which she attempted to hide when she opened her eyes.

"Cook, its only 6:00. I have another half an hour."

"Not today you don't. The master is awake. C'mon you lazy lass … up ya get."

John came down to the kitchen and told Cook that Miss Hale was still sleeping. He was going over to the office for a few minutes. "Should you hear her moving about, please send Benny to her immediately. She's already fallen once through the night."

"Oh no, Master. Was she all right?"

"I simply laid her back in bed. She spoke no words of injury, so I didn't want to wake her further with a discussion."

"You know she wouldn't say anything, anyway if she were hurt."

"We must get her out of that thinking. I will only be gone for a few minutes."

John threw on his coat and walked across the yard. The first shift was coming through the gates, and soon the looms would be splitting the air with their noise. There would be no sleeping for anyone at this end of town.

He was surprised to find Nicholas there working on a drawing. John glanced at it quickly, but didn't know what it was.

"Good morning, Nicholas. You are here early."

"And so are you! Miss Hale sleep well?"

"She is still sleeping. She had a fall through the night. I think she used the lavatory and then turned down the gas light I had left lit for her. She must have bumped into something trying to return to her room."

"Perhaps you two should change beds for a couple of nights. Just until she is stronger, that is."

"That is a good idea. Why didn't I think of that?"

"You have other things on your mind." Nicholas grinned.

"Yes, her comfort and safety," John said, disregarding Nicholas' veiled innuendo.

"So what happened?"

"I didn't speak to her. I just put her back to bed."

"You didn't speak with her?"

"No, I didn't want to wake her more fully."

"John! She could have hit her head. She could be lying over there unconscious."

John bolted from the office and up the stairs. Benny was speaking with Margaret. He listened to some of the conversation. Relieved, he returned to the office.

"I assume all is well?"

"Yes. I wanted to take care of her, and I am failing."

"John, that's not possible."

"I went ahead of her to the privy last night to turn on the light and see if it looked as it should. I suddenly realized I had no idea what she specifically needed. The cupboard that mother and Fanny used was empty. I've never bothered to look in it."

"John, I raised two girls, two wives and a couple of other young girls. If you need a man's point of view, I'm your man." Nicholas chuckled.

"And as you just pointed out, I didn't take time to ensure she was not hurt last night. I am watching my words, my hovering, I'm even eating that horrible menu of foods. There are times of silence that drive me mad."

"How is your manly control?"

"Oh, well controlled. I am fearful of losing her again, Nicholas."

"I may have a solution."

"Whatever it is, I want to hear it."

"What do you think of turning that shed where her furniture is stored into a small cottage for her and Dixon?"

"How so like you to think like me. I have had the same thoughts myself. Look into it, will you? I want it nice enough to even satisfy my mother. That day may still be ahead of me—Margaret as my wife, and Mother in the cottage with a caregiving nurse or a housekeeper."

"If that may be the case, I will pay special attention to the details. Give me a week. I should have something to show you by then. That is what I have been drawing here."

Nicholas turned the paper around for John to see it, but he didn't look.

"I should be getting back. I will see you later today. Oh, don't ask why, just knock on the front door in an hour. Then you can leave."

"Why?"

"Didn't I just say don't ask why? I'd rather not say as yet."

"Very well."

Benny had set the morning table, and Cook was bringing the tray.

"Benny, has Miss Hale asked for any help this morning?"

"Oh yes, sir. She needed help dressing."

"Thank you."

"Sir, I am unsure how to tidy the house when you are in it. Jane said that you usually were at work."

"Miss Hale shall be out directly, and she can give you instructions."

"Very good, sir."

John spotted his newspaper on the dining room table. He took it to the sofa where he could see when Margaret opened the door. He scanned the headlines and flipped to the mill sections, but never read a word.

Margaret's door opened. He quickly walked to it.

"Good morning. You had a fall last night. How are you doing?"

"I am a bit bruised on my knee, but that could have happened getting out of the coach yesterday. There really is no need to concern yourself."

"I think there is, and we shall talk about it tonight."

Margaret saw that John was upset with himself. "John, I am not delicate, you know."

"Well, put on some weight. You look like kindling. I am afraid you will break." John rubbed his forehead nervously. "I'm sorry. That was an awful thing to say. I just want to … want to … protect you."

"Are there any suits of armor anymore? I would be glad to put your mind to rest if we found one I could wear." Margaret grinned. "Should we give someone else the worry of me?"

"No!" John nearly shouted. "No," he repeated more softly. "I think I am upset that I didn't see to you last night. I just put you back in bed. Nicholas pointed out I could have put an unconscious person in bed. I never spoke to you."

John seated Margaret at the table.

"John Thornton?"

"Yes. I can hear it in your voice. I have a tongue lashing coming, and it is well deserved. Carry on."

"I can understand how you feel because I am responsible for Dixon's condition."

"Margaret, you can't say that."

"Perhaps I won't say it, but I feel it. My pride kept us from seeking better circumstances. Dixon wasn't eating well either, and she worried about me constantly. Then I decide to move, and she winds up moving heavy furniture. That is my fault. Now she is sent away from me. You shouldn't feel responsible for any of this."

"I don't."

"Well, what is it, then?"

"We will take a ride in the carriage later. I feel I can talk with you better away from here. Do you feel up to it? I will insist on carrying you up and down the stairs, today, though."

"I would like that. I haven't been in a carriage very often in many months. I will look forward to it. Is there any way to take liver on a picnic?" She giggled.

John smiled. The day Margaret's small giggle didn't make him smile, he would be dead.

"If there is a way, Cook will find it?"

Benny came upstairs with a tray in her hands. She quietly set each food plate in front of John and Margaret and they waited for her to leave before picking up their fork.

"Margaret, Benny asked me about what chores she should be doing while I am at home. Normally I will be at work as I was with Jane, and Jane didn't give her any specific instructions. I told her that possibly you could give her ideas of what to do when the house is occupied. "

"Yes, I will be glad to do that for you. There is a type of schedule where they move behind the rooms you have just left. After she serves this meal, she would be tidying the bedchambers. At some point of the day, the dining room and sitting room would normally be empty and she would work in those rooms. Do you have any special instructions for your study, or do you call it a library? "

"I believe I have called it many things. *Library* seems to be the most used word, but *study* is also in use. I plan to grow my collection of books, so I tend to call it a library."

"Do you think you have anything in there that I would care to read, perhaps a history book?"

"Have you forgotten that I said I had picked up two books for you?"

Margaret picked up her fork as she looked down into her plate. "Yes, I had forgotten that you said that. I will be anxious to see what you selected. If I am not mistaken, you declined the first two suggestions because you felt that I had read them. It seems you remembered that I liked to read."

"I remember many things."

Margaret wondered if her paleness was disappearing and a blush was able to be seen. "You haven't answered my question, John."

"I'm sorry. Was it the library?"

"Yes. Do you have any special instructions for that room?" Margaret leaned forward and whispered, "With her being new here, I am not sure I would trust her with any papers that she should not see."

"I firmly agree and will look into that later today."

There was a knock at the door, and John shouted to Benny that he would get it. When he got to the bottom of the stairs and opened the door, John spoke a few low, mumbled words and closed the door. He pulled the love note from his pocket and carried it upstairs.

"It seems this is for you. I wouldn't think many people would know you were here." John handed her the letter.

Margaret slowly took it from him, looking into his face with confusion. "Perhaps it's from Dr. Price with some additional instructions." Margaret hurriedly broke the seal and looked for a signature. She gasped.

Miss Hale,

I fear sending you flowers at Marlborough Mills may cause questions to arise, for which you will have no answers. Therefore, a note I hope will be acceptable.

I hope the flowers did convey words that I will eventually speak. For a long time and far from you, I have thought of you every day.

A Milton Man

"Margaret, you are smiling. I cannot imagine what Dr. Price has said to make you brighten the way you have. May I read it? "

Margaret started to stutter. "John, I am not sure that this letter should be read by anyone other than myself. It appears to be quite personal from someone unknown to me."

"Someone unknown to you? Is that note from the previous flower man? I want to see it. You very well may have a stalker."

"Would you mind terribly if I didn't show it to you right away?" Margaret responded. "I have never received such a letter, and I would like to enjoy it for a bit longer before you do something drastic. I don't believe I am in any danger."

"So, it *is* from the flower man. He has taken to sending you what, a love letter?"

Margaret folded the note and slipped it into her pocket, to John's consternation.

"If I receive another one, I will let you have them both. Perhaps this game has gone on long enough. I cannot say that I don't like it, though. Are you sure it isn't you that is writing me?"

"Margaret, you are sitting right in front of me. If you remember anything of me at all, you should know I say what I mean and never hide behind words."

"I remember that quite well from your mother's dinner party."

John looked down and pretended to straighten the dinner napkin in his lap. "I have forever wanted to explain that to you. I am sure you do not know that I was doing that for your own good. We will discuss such things in our carriage ride, if that is agreeable to you?"

"Yes, that is agreeable to me. I feel like we are walking on hot coals around each other. Since we will be sharing this home, your home, it is best that we have cleared the air. It is quite possible I will need my medication on return." Margaret didn't smile. She wanted John to know that she was prepared for a serious conversation that had to take place.

"Would you care to read your newspaper while I ready myself to go out the door? I am quite looking forward to a ride in the country. We will travel out of town, will we not?"

"Yes, I have a special place that I call my own. I visit there when I need to think. It is quiet, on a hill, and overlooks Milton. I have never been interrupted while there. I have never taken anyone there. Most of the time I saddle a horse to ride there."

"Does Branson not know where this is?"

"No. He will be seeing it for the first time himself today. Perhaps in the future I will come upon him and his lady friend visiting there."

"John, let's go to a different area, so that you can keep this place to yourself. I know I shall never know of it again, but Branson will certainly remember it. I would hate for it not to be your private place."

"I will do that only if you ride with me someday when you are fully recovered. I would like to share it with you."

"John, some of your statements are not suitable from a man who is engaged to another woman. Should someone overhear you, your words could very well be misinterpreted."

"Margaret, we shall talk about that today. I do not care if I am overheard. I have no secrets, but one. Now go ready yourself, and I will finish what I need to do. I will take a few moments to speak with Nicholas before we leave. I guess it would be a good idea if I spoke with Branson, especially after telling him he could sleep late." John smiled.

As Margaret returned to her room, John noticed that her legs seemed to be carrying her with little difficulty. He closed his paper and went out to ready Branson, but first stopped by to speak to his partner again.

"Nicholas, I am taking Margaret out for a ride in the carriage. She recognized that we were struggling to avoid saying certain things. I am not sure we would ever feel really comfortable if we didn't get this talk out of our way. I believe I will not confess fully my feelings for her, but I will make her understand that Miss Hawkins is not the woman to be in my life."

"John, I did not expect it quite this soon, and I am not sure this is the right time. You still have the obligation to Miss Hawkins for the Master's Ball."

"I think I can make Margaret understand that. She knows that, as a gentleman, I would never back out of an invitation that I have extended. I do plan to have Miss Hawkins for dinner at my home in the near future. I would like them to meet, so as time goes on, there won't be the fear of running into each other. Any words of advice?"

"Don't pour all of the water out of the bucket."

"No, I had not planned on those words this quickly. I have to remember that it is only I who have been waiting for her for a year, never thinking I would see this day. I cannot expect her to have any feelings of that depth. Before I go, is there anything at either mill that we need to discuss?"

"Will I see you at all today?"

"I will be here when Margaret lays down later this afternoon."

"Well, be off with you and good luck."

Chapter Twenty Three

John entered his sitting room and found Margaret waiting patiently. Her clothing hung from her bones.

"I have spoken with Benny on ways to go about cleaning and tidying the rooms. I asked her to leave your study alone today. You may now call my chair bearers. They may lift me high and carry me through my horde of admirers." Margaret smiled.

John laughed as he saw Margaret stand and walk towards him. He picked her up gently, cradled her in his arms and took her out the back door.

Branson was waiting, and he walked over to his master and said, "Perhaps you don't need me today," as he looked at his guv, smiling.

"Branson, I have made assumptions that your master only lifts newspapers and invoices and occasionally raises his voice. He may have strong legs from walking all the time, but I doubt his arms will carry me very long. I think it fitting that you should drive us."

"I believe today he may lift his spirits. They have weighed him down a long time."

"Branson!"

"Yes Branson, just how much does a spirit weigh?" Margaret played with Branson, while John had to stand there and hold her longer.

"They must weigh many stones, as he has been unable to lift his own. This might be your day that he will lift your spirits"

"Does he appear to be tiring to you?"

"Here, let me get the door."

"If you children are done with your game I would like to be on our way."

John set her beside the window and seated himself on the same bench, leaving a space separating them. Joy was in his heart as Margaret felt at ease to play games while he held her to his chest.

"Are you comfortable?"

"I am quite content. Where are you taking me today?"

"I have given instructions to Branson to drive into the country. It will be his destination. He knows that we wish to talk in private, so he will leave us alone and return at my whistle. I imagine it will be somewhere near a lake. He has talked about a lake where he takes his lady friend."

They traveled in silence for more than 20 minutes, each rehearsing the words they had waited a year to speak. As time had drawn on, Margaret came to know the northern gentleman and now believed much of what happened between them had been her doing. The question uppermost in her mind was if she not interceded in the riot that day, embarrassing him in front of his peers and workers, would he have eventually asked for her hand?

John wanted to explain to her why he had acted as he had. She had brought up the subject of being scolded at the yearly dinner about helping the poor. He prayed to know on the day of her rejection, when she said she hated him, whether she was in earnest or just in anger, eager to employ whatever words would most hurt him.

"John, I feel I should be the first to speak. I would appreciate it if you would not interrupt. I know you will want to, and I do wish to hear what you say. But let me exhaust all the words that have haunted me for so long."

"That will be difficult for me to not interrupt, but I will try with all due respect."

"I have gone over in my mind, many times, what I would say if this moment ever came. I can hardly count the apologies that I owe you. In treating you as I did, I also owe an apology to your mother as well, because I elicited a certain behavior in you that she did not care for.

"I believe that most of my inappropriate behavior was due to my lack of understanding of your northern culture. I remember how my father chastised me when you'd left that evening. When you extended your hand to say goodbye, I turned from you. After you left, father told me that that was a traditional greeting coming and going between men and women. He said that I insulted you when I did not reciprocate. Quite frankly, I think it hurt you more than insulted you. You must have thought me impolite. I told my father that I was sorry for hurting his friend."

Margaret took a deep breath. John was ready to speak, but she shushed him.

"There are two areas in which I find my biggest mistakes. The first, of course, was running out between you and the rioters, believing I could protect you. I know now that it was gravely embarrassing to you to have people assume you would allow a woman to speak on your behalf. It made you look weak, for allowing me to say what I did, and that, once my words were spoken, you could do nothing to salvage your dignity in front of your peers and workers. I have often wondered how that day impacted your life after that. I couldn't help feeling that I damaged some of the respect you earned and commanded. For anything that may have resulted in others treating you without the respect you deserve because of my actions on that day, I am most humbly sorry. You are a man of good standing in the community, and I know I disgraced you."

Margaret could see out of the corner of her eye that John was shaking his head. She felt she'd better continue before he burst in.

"I may not get to all that remains unspoken before you want your say, but I must address the day you asked for my hand and received my rejection. I felt your offer was prompted because of my actions. You, as a gentleman, felt obliged to save my reputation. Looking back, that is the most chivalrous act that I have ever known. When I declared hatred for you, my intent was to hurt you. I didn't hate you, but I was trying to avoid facing my own embarrassment. My words were not true, and from the moment you left, I regretted having spoken them. As you left, you said that you knew me. Indeed, you knew me far better than I knew myself then. I have lived in anguish for almost a year that I left that impression with you. Many times I wanted to write to you and tell you it wasn't true. As my knowledge of your culture grew, I could see the hole that I had dug was becoming deeper. I felt there was no salvation for me in your eyes, and have hoped your life would continue and you would find happiness and all the respect you once had. The question whose answer I have yearned to know, was would you have proposed at another time when you were free to do so? You may answer–or not. I have lived with the thought that I have burned all my bridges with you, until you looked at me in the mill yard that recent day. It wasn't until I came to see you about employment and looked into those eyes that I remembered so well, wondering whether I might be forgiven.

Margaret looked over at John and noticed his eyes were glassy. It appeared he had struggled to hold his composure and not be embarrassed by any tears. The silence grew heavy as the moments wore on. Margaret found the courage to continue.

"The man who visited our house, the same man you saw me with at the train station late in the evening, was my brother."

"I know, Margaret. I remember how I treated you after that evening. You seemed to have no regard for your reputation. I admonished you. I was beginning to feel that there was no hope for us. You may have thought me mad at you for that, but I was experiencing tremendous heartbreak. I felt there was another man in your life and that there was no room for me. Months later, when Nicholas could see that I was not returning to the man I once was, he told me that story to relieve me of the thought that you were in love with another.

"Bloody hell … I am sorry. Forgive me for saying that," John added. "I've waited nearly a year to speak the words I should be saying, and find myself failing miserably. Under no circumstances did I expect the words you have said. I never aniticipated you to understand or embrace our culture. Many of my words were going to be explanations as to my actions, but mercifully you understood my situation regarding the riot and the obligation which I was made to see. To answer your question, I had for a long time been aware that you were the woman I wanted in my life. I must admit you did make it difficult at times, but I should have understood more about your naïve way of looking at the differences between the North and the South.

"I am sorry for my reaction to your being at the station with your brother. I did come to believe, or perhaps hope, that you never truly hated me, only felt determined to hurt me because you thought I was asking for your hand out of duty. That was the most difficult experience I have ever had in my life. I loved you beyond anyone I had ever known and wanted you for my wife, but I knew when I asked you that the timing was all wrong.

"I lived hoping to receive a note from you, any attempt to communicate with me, but none ever came. As a gentleman, I was obliged to take you at your word – to accept that you hated me and that you felt I wanted to own you–and, if I were to conduct myself as a gentlemen, I could no longer insinuate myself into your life. It seems within a month that both of us felt we had ruined each other's lives and our own. There didn't seem to be a way back. Did you feel the same?"

"Almost immediately. As a woman, I felt I had very little that I could say. My own propriety prevented me from doing what I should have. I still feel I faltered at the most important step of my life. My father came to know of my change of heart, but could offer no solutions. Since we both are determined to bare our souls and find the bottom of this year of pain, may I ask about Miss Hawkins?"

"Although previously I extended to her an invitation to the Master's Ball and feel indebted to keep my promise, I am certain that I do not love her. She has been like many of the women I've seen socially–none of whom I cared for beyond escorting for a pleasant evening out. I will admit that I eventually hoped I could meet another woman like you. I should have known that was impossible. Elaine Hawkins knows that I am not interested in marrying her. I told her I was looking for something in a woman that I had never found. I lied to her, for I had seen it you."

There was a pause of silence.

"At this point I wonder what your feelings tell you as we live on from today."

Margaret had pulled a handkerchief from her bag. John saw her dabbing her eyes and wiping her nose.

"John, may we exit the coach for some fresh air?"

"Yes, of course. Would you care to try and walk a short distance?"

"Yes, I need to clear a few points in my mind. Like you, I didn't expect this unprecedented surrender."

John exited the coach, and allowed Margaret to walk to the edge of the door where he lifted her out. They walked toward a small clearing and found a nice shade tree to sit under. With both of them leaning their backs against the large tree trunk, John bent forward and picked up a leaf and began to tear it in silence.

Margaret could see that they both had much to dwell on. The unspoken words seemed to have surpassed one's expectations, leaving them questioning what–if any–future they might share.

"John, my mind is quite occupied with what I have heard from you today. I have many more words that I would say, but the time is not yet here. Perhaps those words will never be welcomed."

"Margaret, no matter where the fates may lead us, I will always welcome your words. I too have other words for you. We have both been taken by surprise, and much thought should be given to what we have learned. I would tell you I need nothing else from you to know my path in this life. However, I believe we need to step back and reflect about what we've learned before we step forward. I hope I am right in believing you still hold me in some regard. We have definitely reestablished a friendship in a most agreeable way."

"I feel the same, John. Branson was right: You have lifted my spirits. I do feel they want to take flight, but I will keep them firmly on the ground for now."

"You know, I am going to invite Elaine over to my home to share a meal with you and me. Perhaps I will invite my mother at the same time or maybe on a different night. I want Elaine to see in you why I am turning away from her. She knows that is about to happen. She knows she is not the woman or type of woman I would want to marry. But I think it best that you two meet each other to avoid embarrassing situations in the future."

"John, I don't understand why you feel it necessary that we should meet. Are you jumping far ahead? Are you making any assumptions that I should know about?"

John smiled. There was the Margaret he always loved, the one who made him smile and whom he would protect with his life.

"Miss Hale, would you care to make a wager with me?"

"It all depends on the bet and the winnings."

"Let me see ... the winnings ...hmm.. I should probably tell you that Nicholas and I are making plans to turn the furniture shed into a small nice cottage. We both agree that, knowing you, you may wish to leave Thornton house once you are completely well. Neither of us will let you return to your previous living area, but I cannot stop you from working–at least for now. So, here are your winnings. If I win, you will consider staying there, rather than leaving the property. It would be a safe place and near to me. If you win, you can have whatever you want. I think that sounds fair, don't you?"

"It sounds like I cannot lose. I think you have a trick up your sleeve. What is the wager?"

"We have cleared most of the air today. Whatever remains has been most likely covered under our larger faults. I want to bet you that you will kiss me before I kiss you." John smiled.

"What constitutes a kiss?"

"Must I teach you everything?" John replied.

"It seems that you must, since you are the one with the experience. If I kissed your hand or your forehead, would that be considered a kiss for the purpose of this wager?"

John thought for a moment. "No. It must be a romantic kiss–nothing that could be mistaken for politeness. It must be passionate."

"Oh, well, then ... Since I do not know how to do that, I will accept your wager."

Margaret turned towards John and looked at his mouth. She knew he was seeing her desire, but she remained in place. She closed her eyes and puckered her lips.

It felt like forever before John … amused the heavens with his groaning roar of laughter. “Oh that was tempting! I think that should be considered ungentlemanly. That, I admit, will be very difficult for me to resist, but you must play fair.”

Margaret frowned as if a thought had occurred to her. “Wait a minute … if you lose by kissing me, you get the kiss and I live safely on your property. There is something rather unfair about your bet. I must think further on this. We both seem to win either way.”

“And what could possibly be wrong with that?”

“I want to hold any wagers or words until after the Master’s Ball. That should be time enough for us to know our own hearts. How far away is the ball?”

“Miss Hale ….”

“Uh-oh ….”

“Miss Hale, kindly remember as we go forward, that our mistakes happened a year ago. I, your intended suitor at the time, had been waiting a long time before that. I must stress to you that my words and emotions are reaching a critical level.”

Margaret giggled and giggled. She had to hide her face in her handkerchief because she found in John a sense of humor that matched her own. Peeking over at John, she could see his shoulders moving up and down from silent laughter. She was sure he was laughing at her actions and not his own words.

With a smile that could not be contained, Margaret asked once again, “How long before the Master’s Ball?”

“Three weeks. Three weeks tomorrow.”

“John, are you sure you are ready to set aside all misgivings and misunderstandings from our pasts?”

“For a very long time I have been sure of that. Do you feel the same, Margaret?”

"I am a woman. You should know that at some point in the future I will have questions which I have not spoken today. I have that right. Never trust a woman not to fling something back at you," Margaret said with a smile.

"I am a man. You should know that I have nothing to hide from you. Being a gentlemanly man, I shall never fling anything back at you."

"You are not one of those man who believes that women should be seen and not heard, are you?"

"If I were, you would never have had an interest in me, nor I in you. You regard me because I differ from other men in that way. Admit it."

John heard Margaret gasp at his boldness. He was trying to keep a straight face–and succeeding.

"I will admit no such thing," Margaret replied.

"Also, you are mystified but proud that I have taken on all responsibilities for your recovery, including issues about which you dare not speak. Is that not so?"

Margaret grew red.

"I thought so. Go ahead. Ask me anything?"

"That's cheating. You just said that I would dare not speak of such things, so you know I will ask you nothing."

"I even have a chart. My own personal chart for Margaret. You are charted out for the next year … long past being well."

Margaret inhaled loudly and stared at him. "You can't. I mean you can, but you wouldn't!"

"I would and I have." He was only teasing her, but she didn't know that.

Margaret was speechless. She hid the redness of her face, not wanting to believe him. "I need a powder," she mumbled through her hands, still hiding.

John chuckled. "Then it is time to get your home," he insisted, and whistled loudly for Branson.

Just as John set her inside, Branson appeared across the open clearing.

On the way home, Margaret asked, “So, do we have a bargain until after the Master’s Ball?”

“Certainly, we do *not* have a bargain. I will always be a gentleman, but you may be as forward as you’d like.”

Chapter Twenty Four

Margaret sat where she had on the way there. As she looked out the window, in her dreamy state, she contemplated how John Thornton could put her at ease. He seemed to have a mesmerizing power which overcame her inhibitions. Was it the eyes, or was it John himself? His subtle, yet take-charge behavior always gave her the sense of feeling protected, yet he balanced this by treating her with respect, as his equal. Margaret was hoping for a truce with earnest apologies, explanations, and cordial words. Instead, she was assailed with impassioned responses, redemption and the anticipation of being loved by him. John surrendered himself in cloaked phrases and words, thereby surpassing anything Margaret could have expected.

John couldn't help but stare at Margaret's profile. How long he had waited for this! His dreams that died at dawn every day now seemed attainable. It would only be three weeks which he promised to restrain his words and actions. He wondered if doing so would be hard for her as well after their words of atonement today.

"Margaret, have you given any further thought to our wager?"

"I'm sorry, John. What did you say?"

Smiling, John asked again. "Have you given any more thought to my wager with you?" I really don't believe that you can keep your distance from me for three weeks."

"It has only been minutes since we spoke of this. You know, I learned the word 'smug' in school. It was hard, I remember, the teacher having to explain what that word meant." Margaret said turning to John.

"Do I detect an accusation pointing towards me?" He asked.

"Yes, you do. I think you have most efficiently shown me a smug look. You seem to have a contented confidence in yourself. I only ask one thing of you."

"You wish me to live in the office?"

"Hardly that. Don't be foolish. Just don't change your socks for three weeks."

John laughed so loud that Branson was stunned at the noise coming from his carriage. That had never happened before while driving his master.

Margaret folded her arms and watched the display of John laughing to the point where no sound was coming out. She thought her little quip would entertain him, but not to the point of tears in his eyes. "John, can you breathe? I hear a lot of air going out, but I don't hear much going in."

Margaret started slowly, but her own giggles grew and connected one to another, as she continued to watch John. It seemed he would look at her, and his laughing continued, which incited more giggles and tears in her own eyes. Before they knew it, Branson was even chuckling up front, even though he could hear nothing but laughter.

Finally coming to his senses and gaining control of himself, John pulled out his handkerchief and dabbed at the tears that had run down his cheek. He looked over at Margaret with a smile that wanted to burst, but he noticed a beautiful pink color to her face. He stared at her as he smiled. He leaned closer to her and closer again."

Margaret turned her face from him and said, "Oh, no, you don't. You are not going to draw me in. In our conversation under the tree, you somehow managed to weaken my shyness. In the past I've been told that it is rather unpleasant habit that I have, being shy, but you bring out a person in me whom I have never known. I don't know what it is about you, or perhaps I do and wish not to say, as it lowers my defenses. Bessie and I were and I hope still are very close friends. What you bring out in me is entirely different from that. You remember quite vividly how I ran out to the rioters. That also was a new me. You may be about to embark on a, let's say, 'friendship' with a total stranger. I suggest a three-week moratorium on any romantic inclinations. After the ball or after Elaine Hawkins has exited your life, I propose a whole new start for us. Do we have an accord?"

"Margaret that was an awfully long explanation when you could've said, 'Please, move away from me.' I didn't realize we had a lectern in the coach." John started smiling again because his mood filled the air with happiness.

They had a light bite to eat when returning, and Margaret lay down within the hour. John had been sleeping so lightly for fear of not hearing Margaret that he was tired himself. He was exhausted with her amusement most of the morning. Before Margaret rested, John said that he would be at the office. He also informed Benny and Cook.

"I take it that your long-awaited conversation went better than expected. You have a very uncommon smile on your face. Is there anything I should know?" asked Nicholas when John entered the office.

"There is nothing that you should know, but you are right–we cleared up most of our unpleasant history. Then she proceeded to make me laugh, and I lost control of myself. We made a bet that she could not keep her distance from me until after the Master's Ball."

"John, did you really?"

"Yes, believe it or not, I did. That is how well our conversation developed. When I asked her if she had given any further thought to our wager, she ambushed me by telling me I could not change my socks for three weeks."

Nicholas started laughing, as did John, again.

"She said I bring that out in her and that person is a stranger. And then I find myself doing the same thing. The silliness is intoxicating."

"John, I couldn't be happier for you. Did you kiss her?"

"No. We are taking the three weeks to get to know ourselves again and reaffirm the direction that each of us wishes our lives to take. There will be no romance, no words of love, and certainly no actions. In good propriety, we both feel that Elaine Hawkins should be out of my life before we are seen together."

"I think that's an excellent idea. Did you happen to mention about the cottage?"

"I did. That will be part of the wager. Should I win, she would live in the cottage rent-free. And should I lose, she could have anything she wanted. Somehow we got off of that subject because she couldn't decide whether the wager seemed fair to me."

"I wish I had been a little bird in the tree, listening to this. When you speak of such subject matter I find it difficult to believe it came from you. Say, what was that business about knocking on the door this morning?"

"I don't know how long I will keep that going. I started sending her anonymous small bouquets at the hospital three times a day, as you guessed. I think I have her believing that they are not from me, but from some secret admirer. Now, being here at the house I have switched the deliveries from flowers to love notes, which she says she has never before had. And I must admit I'd never written one before the one I sent her. When you knocked on the door this morning and I opened it, that was a pretense of a post being delivered. I had the note in my pocket, and I handed it to her when I returned. I did claim a guess that it was from the flower man, but she wouldn't let me read it."

"I can't imagine any woman allowing a man to read a love letter that she has received from another. John, this is so unlike you. I can't help sitting here chuckling once in a while when I think of how you have behaved in the last, well, almost two weeks. You are a different man, my friend, and I really like what I'm seeing."

"I will admit to feeling different. A year ago I was living in endless hope. Now, unless I make a mess of things, I feel we are both moving toward lives fulfilled."

"I've been out there looking at the shed, and I've come up with a few drawings, if you care to look. Keeping in mind that either of the two possible Mrs. Thorntons could live there, I know you will find some additional changes." Nicholas handed them to John.

John carried the sheaves of paper to his desk and sat down, studying them. The first depicted what, more or less, stood there at present. On the second page were added several additional rooms, including one for a maid. The third page, which he seemed to be working on, included drainage areas and water pipes leading in. "Nicholas, this is brilliant. You have a very good start. I didn't know you could draw like this. I would have drawn this with boxes and straight lines. You seemed to have a way to make it look like it is lifting off the paper, as if you are looking down into the room. Have you done this before?"

"It seems you forget that I drew the revisions to the second mill," Nicholas laughed.

Still looking at the pages, John said, "So you did … hmm … so you did."

On another small piece of paper that Nicholas held up, he said "I have been keeping a running estimate of cost and labor, which I know you care nothing at all to know. But if we can decide on the basic fundamentals and get started, we could be nearly finished within two weeks."

"Two weeks?"

"I thought you'd be pleased to hear that. Oh, wait a minute, I see why you have that look on your face. You have a wager with Miss Margaret that will last three weeks, and she will be in your home for only two weeks. Is this where you pay Donaldson money to extend her recovery time?" Nicholas laughed.

John was smiling, even though Nicholas was not correct in his thinking. "Very good, my man. You are also wrong. I cannot lie and say that two weeks is disappointing for the reasons you suggest, but living on her own without Dixon may continue to reinforce her perceived level in Milton's society. We know how she despises London society and speaks of it quite earnestly, yet when it comes to Milton and her own place in it, she unconsciously includes herself either as one of the Masters or one of the workers. You do remember how she treated you and me back then. She respected us both equally, which reinforced her words about society. But when it comes to herself, propriety seems to be ingrained from birth. This whole issue regarding her woman's week and her complete denial of it is a sign of how she was raised. Saying this out loud had made me realize the disaster that she thought her life to be when she moved from their flat. I believe it was a much greater fall in her mind then we knew."

"John, you may be right, in fact, I am sure you are, but it seems when you two become engaged and married, all that should disappear. She will forget how it unconsciously reared its head in her mind, and yet she will be sympathetic to the workers forever."

"Yes … she may have pictured someone handing a piece of bread to her, as she had once done to a laborer during the strike. Her sympathy for the strikers might have made her feel so deeply conflicted that the stress drove her into depression. Well, maybe someday we can talk about it. Bringing it up now would cause her to deny it."

John shuffled the draft papers and handed them back to Nicholas. "Have you walked either of the mills today?"

"Yes, I went over to mill 2 after you left. I will do this mill if you wish, but I left it in case you wanted to spend some time away from Margaret today."

"Before I leave, are there any issues or posts that we need to take care of?"

"Nothing you need to take care of, but you should know that our international sales continue to increase. We are going to need to do some trending and ordering to be ahead of the other buyers. Another large storage shed for raw cotton may be on our horizon."

"Very good news, indeed. I wonder if Margaret has had any experience or learning in that function. I will ask her. It seemed like she was willing to do that for Cecil Griffin, but he didn't need that depth of clerking. Yes, we will take a close look at that in the next few days. I'm leaving now. I will do this mill and return to my home for the rest of the day."

"I will see you tomorrow. Do you want me to knock on the door again?" Nicholas asked, laughing.

John stood there for a moment. Today had been a very big day in his life, and he wondered if he should continue writing her love notes. It didn't matter. He wanted to.

"Yes, same thing tomorrow. I might have to let Cook or Branson in on this so, we have a knock at the back door or some change. I don't want Margaret to be waiting at certain times at certain doors. We will talk."

Margaret woke from her nap feeling well rested. The morning air and the incredible conversation had brought peace to her. She had fallen asleep too easily, as she had hoped to lie there daydreaming about all the words that had been said. Perhaps the night would bring them back and more. She sat up in bed and worked her way to the bottom, where she could grab the bedpost and pull herself into an upright position without trembling. Once she was standing, moving forward was not as hard as it had been yesterday. She heard a noise echoing through the parlor and assumed John was home, in his library. She slowly opened her door and could see that Benny was moving about in the room. She now believed the noise she heard was the slamming of a desk drawer. Margaret tiptoed into the center of the parlor and called her name.

"Benny!"

Benny looked up and saw Miss Margaret staring at her. She had been told specifically not to touch that room today, and now she was caught browsing through John's papers and letters. She hurried out to the parlor.

"Yes, Miss Margaret?"

"I believe you were told only a few hours ago not to touch that room. What were you doing in there?"

Before Benny could give her explanation, Mr. Thornton was at the top of the stairs.

"What's going on?" John could see that there was some type of unpleasant exchange in progress.

"Benny was just beginning to tell me why she was in your library looking through your desk, after she was told specifically not to go in that room today.

John looked at Benny, expecting an answer.

"I am sorry. I wasn't sure if you said study or library this morning. I am confused as to what that room is called."

Margaret looked at John to see if he seemed to be believing her or not.

"Benny," Margaret said, "please understand that that room is off-limits until Mr. Thornton can file away his business papers. I'm sure there is nothing in there that you cannot see, but there may be vital papers that cannot be lost or mislaid. You are excused from this floor."

"Thank you, miss." Benny walked quickly between them as she headed for the stairs to the kitchen.

Margaret walked towards the kitchen steps to ensure Benny was not listening. John understood what she was doing and walked over to her so she could speak softly "What is it, Margaret?"

"I cannot be sure of this, for I may have dreamed it, but yesterday after you came in and pulled up my coverlet, I vaguely remember her pulling it off of me. I have noticed several things which lead me to believe that she has intentionally misled us as to her former service. When she is unaware, I want to ask Cook what she may know."

"That is very strange behavior. You are not going to ask me how I know this, but I think she is trying to catch my attention. I treated it with indifference, but I am aware to watch for further evidence of her behavior."

"John, do you know of any restaurants or place to eat that are not fancy?" Some place where you don't have to dress in your fine clothes and shoes and wear jewelry and perfume?"

John had to smile at that. "I get the distinct impression that you wish not to have any liver this evening. Furthermore, we must patronize a place where Elaine Hawkins would never walk into. Am I close?"

"I would like nothing better than to have a beef sandwich and perhaps an ale, if you'll let me. Father seemed to enjoy that meal once in a while. Mother never could stand ale. She always said it was a man's drink, and a woman would never be caught drinking such a thing. Today feels like a day of celebration, and I want to do something different. Do you know of such a place?"

"I do. Only my closest friends know that I occasionally stop at such a pub. We Masters often feel we have a reputation to protect. We are supposed to separate ourselves from the workers. Quite honestly, I like their food better. Miss Hale, would you care to accompany me to a small tavern on the edge of Milton?"

"I would, indeed. May I try to walk down the steps this time?"

"No."

"I shall allow you to carry me another day or two, but past that I am going to think you have other motives."

"I will alert Branson and then change my cravat, and I would appreciate it if you would put your shoes on," John laughed.

Margaret looked down and realized she had left her room barefooted so as not to alert Benny to her presence. Margaret returned to her room and did not immediately see her shoes. She assumed that she had kicked them under the bed and bent down to look for them. Clutching the pair in one hand, she rose too quickly, causing her head to swim. Losing her balance, she fell to the floor. Margaret did not hurt herself, but was afraid that John may have heard her fall. And she was right.

John took one large stride into the room and pick Margaret up and set her on the bed. "What happened this time," he asked worriedly. "Are you injured anywhere?"

"It is nothing to worry about. I just tried to stand up too fast and became a little dizzy. I will be more cautious in the future, as I cannot have you running all over the house checking on me."

"Let us not forget who took the oath to be a caring nurse–although I would not be surprised if you planned that because you did not care for the distance between us."

"There goes that smug face, again. By the time the Master's Ball has taken place, you will have refined that smugness to an art form." Margaret stood almost toe-to-toe, looking up at John and feverishly trying not to smile.

"I see you have no denial as to your reason for falling. I thought so. My wager is as good as won." John clapped his hands once, turned and left the room.

Margaret stood there agape. *What has gotten into the man?*

"John," Margaret found herself asking a short time later, "why are we stopping at Dr. Donaldson's clinic? I told you I was fine."

"I am the one responsible for you, and I am taking no chances. If you get tipsy later on this evening I will want to be sure it is from the ale and not dizziness. I'm sure he is just going to tell us this is normal for your condition."

John lifted her out of the carriage, but extended his arm for her to assist until they got to the door.

Donaldson came from the back, surprised to see John and Margaret sitting there. "What have we here?"

"Margaret had a bit of dizziness," John responded, "and she fell to the floor. She did not hurt herself in the fall, but I just want to be sure that a lightheaded condition is acceptable with anemia."

"John, bring Margaret back were the bright light is. I need to take a look at her eyes. But to answer your question, yes, dizziness can be found. Her brain is getting less oxygen because of the fewer red blood cells. I have read where this is a common enough effect. I would not expect her to faint, though."

"Well, she has been acting strangely today."

Margaret frowned and stared at John as he lifted her onto the exam table. "Dr. Donaldson, please do not pay any attention to John's overprotective nature. Yes, we have cleared a lot of the misunderstanding, and I think we both are pleased with our progress. John has been acting quite silly today, himself. I think he is the one that you should be checking. He laughed so long and so loud today that he scared me. I didn't think he could catch his breath. Have you ever known him to do that?"

"I admit that is strange behavior for the John Thornton that Milton knows. I am glad he is no stranger to you."

"Ah … Dr. Donaldson, he is still a stranger to me in many ways. I want you to believe that."

John rolled his hand into a fist and once again held it in front of his mouth to keep quiet and watch her struggle. He knew Donaldson didn't need to know that.

"Margaret, please lie back and look at the ceiling," Donaldson said.

Donaldson spread her eyelids open wide and looked closely with some type of magnifying glass. "John, come look at this. Tell me what you see."

Margaret suddenly stiffened. There was John's beautiful slate blue eye, magnified, looking at her. In her mind, she pointed her two hands in front of her and dove into the depths of his soul. She swooned. Donaldson could no longer hold her eye open.

"Oh, God!" John exclaimed. "She does have something wrong with her. Why can I not seem to protect her?" She has fallen twice and now she has fainted, which you said is not common for anemia. Donaldson I want the best people you know to take a look at her. She is the rest of my life and I don't want to die."

If John hadn't been seriously worried, Donaldson would have laughed at this. He stretched across the room to a small drawer and pulled out a vial, which he waved under Margaret's nose.

Margaret's eyes fluttered open immediately.

"Miss Hale, you have given Thornton, here, a very big scare. I must take the blame, though, as I was going to play a small joke on you, but I had forgotten about your fascination with his eyes. John, she did not faint–she swooned. Basically, they are the same thing, but for different reasons."

John, feeling utterly embarrassed, turned his back to Donaldson and Margaret and rubbed the bridge of his nose with closed eyes. What was he going to do about his eyes?

"Miss Hale, there is nothing in this world that Thornton can do about his eyes. It is you who has to make the adjustment. I daresay in the future, should there be an intimacy, that problem may resolve itself."

"Dr. Donaldson, I wish you would not speak to me in that manner. I don't think you know me well enough to speak of future situations which may or may not arise."

"Oh, that situation will arise, believe me."

"I'm sorry, I don't understand that, and I wish to leave. Please assure John that what I experienced with my dizziness is nothing of great significance."

"I can do that. John, if you could turn around and look at us, I will tell you that Miss Hale could experience dizziness for several more weeks. As it was this time, it was brought on by fast movement of her head. She should not feel any dizziness if she is sitting still. And just try not to get too close to her face, if at all possible."

"I can't believe this is happening." He looked at Donaldson and chuckled. "Miss Hale, are you ready for your liver?"

"If I must."

John lifted her off the exam table and carried her to the coach. Setting her inside, he instructed Branson to take them to a particular pub.

Benny believed she would soon be fired, as her employer was about to discover that she was not who she pretended to be. But before she left, she had promised herself that she would seek pleasure with John Thornton. He was a man like any other–one who found it impossible to turn away from a woman's body. Just looking at the man inspired in Benny fantasies of erotic acts that she was sure he could perform.

In the dead of night, she thought, she might easily have her way with him. He might think he was dreaming, or that Miss Hale, with her boldness, had crept into his bed, naked. She just had to whisper to him.

"God help me to make it through three weeks," John said as he lifted Margaret into the coach.

"John, you're not planning any specific action with me at that time are you?"

"I'm going to have to if I want to save yours and my sanity. It's like you're allergic to me. I feel I cannot get close. No other woman has ever reacted to me in this way. I don't know what to do. My desires are strong for you, but they are worthless if you are unconscious." John smiled.

"John Thornton, I don't think it's very fair that you compare me to other women. You know, as women, we hate that and we fear that. Now, you readily admit that you do it."

"Margaret! You know that's not what I mean. If I am to be honest, I believe I have compared all women to you since I've known you, but I have never felt the need to compare you to anyone else in this world. I'm starting to think swooning is your way of winning the bet. I'm going to call off the bet. If you do not stay in my home then, you will stay in the cottage at Marlborough Mills. It's one place or the other, but you are not leaving me again."

"Is that the way you see it? That I left you the first time."

"Margaret, you are twisting my words. If you don't stop teasing me, it will be liver for you tonight. I can't win with you. I am damned either way. I want to be close to you but my eyes affect you. I say there has never been another woman like you and you accuse me of comparing women. Being around you is like being in a train wreck," he smiled.

"Yes, but you lo… like me anyway. I'll be good."

"Maybe we should practice."

"Practice what?"

"You looking at me. You looking at my eyes as they look at you. You're going to have to get used to that because I'm going to be doing it often."

Margaret looked down, ashamed that she was affected in this way and could but little control it. When he looked at her with his penetrating blue eyes, she felt her heart beating rapidly. She could only assume that she was holding her breath, causing herself to swoon.

"John, I may have an idea that we can try. If you stand at a distance and look into my eyes and continue slowly to walk forward, you need to instruct me to breathe. I don't think I can consciously alter my heart rate, but if you say breathe, I believe I can do that. Has no one ever spoken to you about your beautiful eyes?"

"Yes, although I wouldn't use the word 'beautiful.' Some women have mentioned them, but I've paid little attention. Up until having to take you to Donaldson, I've always thought it one of those compliments women give all men. You make me feel different. I can't help it, you understand that, I hope."

"John, it isn't just your eyes–it's those eyes with the rest of you."

"And you haven't even seen the rest of me," John smiled.

Chapter Twenty-Five

"Here we are. How rare can you eat your beef?"

"Are you saying there is more iron if it's cooked through or if it's red inside?"

"The redder the meat, the better for you right now."

Branson pulled the coach close to the tavern door, and his master lifted Margaret out.

"I don't have my bonnet," Margaret realized.

"I'm sure it doesn't matter in this place. I'm not going to wear my hat either. Ready?"

John took her arm and helped her steady herself going up the few steps to the pub entrance. They were seated right away, and Margaret remarked how loud the voices in the room were.

"Although I prefer the simple meals of a tavern, it is the boisterous sound that prevents my coming more often."

The maid came up to see what they preferred to drink, and John ordered for both of them. "I would like a glass and a pint of ale and two beef sandwiches. That will be all, thank you."

"John, I am sure I cannot eat a sandwich the size of the one I see over there," she said pointing.

"I felt sure of that myself, but I know I can eat what you do not. He watched as Margaret looked around the room. She seemed thoroughly fascinated by the tavern. Behind the bar with the stools in front of it was a long mirror, which had drinking glasses stacked in pyramids in front of it. She noticed the large barrels of ale and watched as the maids turned the tap and filled large pitchers until the foam spilled over. John occasionally heard profanity, but Margaret seemed oblivious to this. Apparently, she had found a way to shut out all the noise.

"What is that over there, John? It looks like a monkey inside of a glass case. How odd."

"Oh, that." John chuckled. "That monkey tells your fortune. You deposit a coin, and the monkey drops a small piece of paper down that hole which will slide out where you can take it. It's just a bit of foolishness for amusement. Would you like your fortune told?" John said, smiling.

"Yes, but only if you will do it as well."

"Well, let's go do it. Remember, I said it is for fun. You are not to take anything seriously."

John walked her over and found coins for the machine. He handed one to Margaret.

"You first." Margaret urged.

John dropped his coin into the slot, turned the little knob, and the monkey began to move. Although the device was quite unique, John found more fascination watching Margaret's bright eyes light up. The paper was collected from somewhere that John couldn't see, then deposited down the hole. He took it out and began to unfold it.

"What does it say? What does it say, John?" Margaret could not jump up and down, but she was showing her excitement the best she could.

"Let me look at this before I read it aloud." He was smiling. "Ready?"

"Yes, yes. Hurry!"

"I think I will wait until we sit down. I don't want you to faint or swoon. Your turn."

Margaret reached up and slid her coin into the slot. The sound it made as it dropped through the mechanism surprised her. The monkey dropped her fortune down the hole. John was going to hand it to her, but she grabbed for it quickly. He was surprised that she didn't unfold it and read it.

"Let's return to the table," Margaret said, excitedly.

Still not reading her own, she asked John what his said. Before he spoke a word, he took a long draw on his pint of ale.

"Now, let me see." John pretended it was hard to read in the lighting. "It says that I will meet a tall, dark, handsome stranger."

"It does not." Margaret pulled the paper from his hand to read it herself. "It says, your life will change because of her."

"It does not," John chuckled as he grabbed the paper back.

John looked at Margaret and she looked like her cheeks were going to burst from laughter. "Ahem … what it really says is 'You will experience great wonders.' I think I knew that myself. At least that's what I see ahead for you and me. Now, your turn."

Margaret slowly unfolded her paper. He laughed to himself, seeing the child that was still hiding inside. He couldn't wait for the Christmas holiday.

"I don't understand mine. It says 'She Awaits You.'" Margaret threw hers on the floor. John was taken aback by the way she seemed to be troubled by this prediction.

"Margaret, you know these pieces of paper are randomly chosen and are not true."

"I thought they were supposed to be telling you good things."

"Margaret, I find it hard to believe that you are placing any faith in what you just read. This being a tavern and mainly frequented by men, I would think the papers that fill the monkey cage would be more of interest to a male."

"Yes, of course, you are right. Here comes my beef sandwich, and it looks like the best meal I have seen in months."

On the ride home, John told Margaret that she was going to sleep in his bed tonight and he would sleep elsewhere.

"But why, John?"

"For one or two nights I'd like to keep you closer to the loo, which is only several steps from my room. I don't want you walking across the house in the dark again. There is nothing for you to trip over between my bed and the lavatory door.

"But I shall be lost in that big bed."

"Never fear. I will always be able to find you when you are in my bed."

Margaret blushed. "Will you stay in my bed? I don't think you will fit in it."

"Do not worry about me. I have slept about every place there is in that house. You may even wake up and find me sleeping on the floor beside you." John smiled, but told her he was teasing her.

"I do believe that is going to be you who cannot keep your distance from me." Margaret replied tossing her head in the air.

John snickered at her little joke, but he knew down deep it was true.

Cook had gone home by the time they arrived back, and Benny must've been in her own room because she was not to be found.

"John. I would like to ready myself for bed. I am worn out with enjoyment of the day."

"Can I assist you into your night shift, or would you prefer that I call Benny?"

"I think I shall try it myself tonight."

"Do you happen to have a night robe to place over your shift? You could feel comfortable and stay in the parlor with me. We could talk or you could read. I am only saying that because if your concern is for comfort, you need not go to bed this early."

"I do have a night robe, but I have not seen it yet. I will see if I can find it. Many times at home I would find comfort in the evenings in my night attire. I would occasionally read in front of the fire. Sometimes father and I talked, as mother was usually in bed. Do you ever get comfortable in your night attire?"

"I am a little embarrassed to admit that I do not sleep in any night attire. I sleep as God has made me. I always have my trousers laid at the foot of the bed in case an emergency arises. Until only a few days ago, there were women in the house, and my door was always closed. Actually, that hasn't changed much. I still have women, but two different ones. Do not worry that you might find me on the sofa undressed. Most evenings I remove my coat and vest and my cravat. At times, you will also find me without my boots or my three-week old socks."

Margaret giggled. "I think I will go and change now."

In a serious tone, John said, "Do not struggle. Call if you need help."

John went to his library and located the two novels that he had purchased for Margaret. He carried them over to the light by the chair he had given up for her, set them on the table by the chair, and returned to his study.

He pulled out a piece of paper and began his second love note to be delivered in the morning, smiling to himself as he put pen to paper and wondered what would please her. He knew he was wooing her in a way. Many words leapt to mind, but they were not words to be written by a stranger.

Margaret opened her door, causing John to quickly slide his paper into his top desk drawer. It would have to wait until later or tomorrow morning. He turned out the gas light in his library and walked back into the sitting room. Margaret was looking at the bindings of her two new books. She held them to her nose and took a deep breath to smell the freshness of the paper.

"Have you read those, Margaret?"

Margaret set one of the books back on the tabletop and rubbed the title surface of the other. "John, did you select these books yourself, or did you seek advice from the book seller?"

"Both, actually. I told the bookseller that I was looking for something a woman would enjoy reading. I said that you had read several novels, and would like to avoid the two most popular ones. He then ran his fingers down a small shelf of books that he thought would make appropriate gifts. Have I purchased something which you have read?"

"Amazingly, you have selected one that I believe I will enjoy a great deal. Somehow I feel like it will mirror my life in many ways."

"How is that?"

"It is about a young woman who spurns a man that she loved because her family did not feel him worthy. He was an officer in her Majesty's Navy. He went to sea and did not return for eight years. Although she had opportunities, she never married even though she never expected him to return. That's about all I know. I shall read this one first.

"Did their love last eight years while they were apart?"

"They parted on unhappy terms. Does that sound familiar?"

"Much of it. I think I should like to read this book. Shall we read it together?"

"How would we do that?"

"Perhaps in the evening we shall take turns reading it to each other. Does that interest you?"

"I think I would like to try."

"Margaret, do you remember earlier when you suggested that we practice?"

"You mean … looking into your eyes?"

"Yes."

"Do you want to try that now?"

"I want to try it and keep trying it until you can accept me. My God, I've got to do something, try anything, so I can be close to you. I can take care of you, if you swoon. I will tell you to keep breathing, but I will also tell you not to look away. You have beautiful eyes yourself, but I rarely get to see them. Do you understand what you are denying me? Do you know that your, whatever it is, inhibition to look at me, to look into my eyes, is robbing me of my own pleasure?"

"Aren't we going past our decision to wait until Elaine Hawkins is out of your life? We should wait on this until a later time. I have been giving it some thought since visiting the doctor tonight, and I think I know what the answer is. I think Dr. Donaldson was right."

"In what regard was he right?"

"Let us try it as you asked." Margaret replied, with an air of surrender that John could not see. "If it is what I think it is, I hope you won't be shocked at me. I believe I have discovered something new in my life and haven't been able to recognize it for what it is."

"Shall we start?" Tell me what I must do to help you get past this."

"I am not so sure that I want to get past this." Margaret could see the hurt in those eyes. His shoulders seemed to slump.

"I will remain in this chair. You will sit across from me. You will look at me in no specific way, no frowns, no smiles, and no brightened looks. I will then begin to look at you. I will look away and then look back. Pay no attention to the look that I give you."

John sat comfortably in the opposite chair. He crossed his legs and laid his hands in his lap, striking a natural pose. "Ready."

"I know this must seem silly to you, but it is the only way that I can prove or disprove my theory."

"Whatever it takes, Margaret."

"Please don't say a word, but just keep looking at me. I am going to get the answers to what is different about your eyes and why others do not see what I see."

The room was silent. Margaret slowly lifted her face to see John looking at her. From this distance she could feel only a slight flutter in her stomach, not enough to cause a swoon. Several minutes went by while John sat still, and Margaret continued her journey.

"John, please sit on the floor, and I will do the same. I wish to keep our eyes at equal levels. I believe it is much harder on me when you look down at my face."

With John and Margaret both sitting on the floor in front of their chairs, they were only six feet apart. John continued his silence and gave her his full attention.

When Margaret looked once again, the feeling was stronger. She knew what it was now. Yes, he did have beautiful eyes, but what she was seeing in them was his love for her. No one had looked at her that way in her entire life. It was weakening to feel that. She wasn't seeing his eyes–she was feeling his love.

"John, please move forward."

There was only about a hand's length before their knees touched. Margaret once again looked into his eyes, but this time was overwhelmed. Tears sprung to her eyes.

"Breathe, Margaret."

Margaret took a breath. It seemed to help. His eyes were penetrating. He was looking into her soul, a place she thought only belonged to her. The intruder made her heart beat rapidly; her breath came in short gasps.

"Breathe, Margaret. I can see it is beginning. Just hold yourself where you are now, calm yourself, and take deep breaths." John was fascinated at whatever this was that was happening to her. He was actually causing a reaction in her. When had he ever done so without using his voice to anyone? Inwardly, a huge smile was taking place. As he was feeling, so was she. It was the love of each other passing from soul to soul. He felt that there had never been nor would ever be a greater moment in his life than the present.

"Margaret, I know what it is. I feel it, too, and we should be joyful that this experience belongs to us alone. Although I am unable to look at you any other way, I believe you are seeing my love for you. It is not really my eyes, but the window to my heart."

The tears began to slip down Margaret's cheek, but she was still holding her gaze. "I will not swoon. I will not swoon. Breathe."

Unfortunately, John's endearing smile came out. It broke Margaret's intense experience. She closed her eyes and began to lean.

John was in such a state of euphoria that he barely caught her in time. He picked her up in his arms and sat down in his chair. He laid her across his lap and looked at her as the gas light fell, leaving her face in shadows. He didn't want to awaken her or shake her. He wanted to study her. John wanted to absorb her into his own body. He would never last three weeks. It may be that Margaret could not either.

Margaret's eyes fluttered open. She looked up at John and realized what had happened.

"Close your eyes again, Margaret."

She immediately did what he said. She felt him shifting her a bit and before she knew it his lips were on hers. It was a tender assault – one she allowed. Within a moment it was gone. Had she dreamt it? No, John had kissed her.

"Margaret, I think we have found a small bit of common ground."

"John, please let me up."

He stood with Margaret in his arms, turned towards the chair and placed her in it. He walked back to sit across from her.

"Thank you. I know now, as you said, I was seeing the love you have for me." She sniffled. "It is quite an intense emotion and most pleasant." She dabbed her eyes. "This is an overpowering, new experience for me."

"It is new for me as well. I cannot know that I am doing anything different, but I do know I feel the love I have for you. I am enchanted."

"Could you show me where I shall sleep?"

When he put Margaret to bed, he promised to thank the gods that she was finding her way to him. To think one could actually see love in someone else's eyes was, he thought, incredible. Love shines through all.

John tucked Margaret away, telling her he was going to leave the lavatory gas light on again. From his usual chair, he could see into his own bedchamber and he knew that she would consider this improper. He was going to miss taking care of her as she recovered.

John finished writing his love note and placed it in his pocket for tomorrow. He turned out the light in his library and quietly went to his bed chamber door. She was peaceful. He turned down all the gas lights in the sitting room and decided to try to lie corner to corner on her bed.

Shedding all but his trousers and shirt he lay across the bed and rested his head on her pillow. Her fragrant scent was there–the scent of a woman, his woman. He yearned for the time when he could reach for her in the night and find her there. For almost a year he fell asleep thinking of being with Margaret. It tended to continue into his dream state at night, but when he awoke they were gone. At one time he began to pen what he could remember about his nightly dream, but it was too short and fleeting. He realized he was only hurting himself if he lived within his dreams.

John fell into a sweet sleep. There was now hope in the last few dreams he'd had at night.

He was awakened by Margaret's scream.

Chapter Twenty Six

Margaret was dreaming that John was holding her around the waist as he had done in days past to assist her. It was comforting to feel his protection, and a slight movement on the bed awakened her further. Was John really lying beside her? Margaret thought of the day's conversation and her discovery of his soul. She felt eager for him to draw her body next to his. She knew John was not under the covers with her, but he did roll towards her, throwing his arm over her. She didn't know where her boldness came from, but she allowed him to hold her in the night. Once again she felt a light kiss to her lips. She heard him whisper.

"John, hold me here," Margaret thought she heard in his hushed tones. Not sure where he was going with this, she allowed her hand to be guided. He held her hand to his chest–but what her fingers touched was distinctly feminine. Startled, she was suddenly wide awake, discovering that the body next to hers was not John's, but Benny's.

She screamed, "John!" as Benny disappeared through the bedchamber door into the lavatory light. She was naked.

John passed a naked Benny as they crossed through the sitting room.

Margaret was crying. "John, I cannot live here with that girl. You don't know what she did."

John quickly turned up the gas light. He looked around the room and saw a night shift on the floor. "Margaret, as soon as I have you calmed down, I will find her and she will be dismissed. I won't wait until morning. She will be gone from this house immediately." John sat on the edge of the bed holding Margaret to his chest, patting her hair and kissing the top of her head.

"She made me touch her breast," Margaret tried to explain, "and she kissed me. I thought it was you."

"Shush, Margaret. You've been through a shocking assault. Whether it was accidental or not makes no difference. I am definitely giving you both medications to help you sleep for the rest of the night. And I will be by your side."

Branson came running up into the dark sitting room. "Guv, guv. What's going on? I heard a scream. Where are you?"

"I'm in my room, my bedchamber Branson."

"Can I come your way?"

"Come ahead. Margaret was attacked by Benny. It wasn't a vicious attack, but a sexual assault, with me her intended victim, as she thought I would be in this bed. But tonight I moved Miss Hale into my room so she might be nearer to the lavatory, and I slept in another room."

Branson could see that Miss Hale was clinging to his master with her head buried into his chest. She was embarrassed to show her face. "Do you want me to go find her, boss?"

"Branson, she was naked running out of this room, but you can go see where she is. She is dismissed immediately. If she attempts any argument, tell her I will bring charges against her."

"No, John. You can't do that. I don't want anybody to know," Margaret mumbled. "What kind of charges could you bring, anyway?" Margaret asked.

"I don't know. Trespassing." John said in all seriousness. "You are my property."

John felt her giggle into his chest. He pulled her away to see her face. He wouldn't have believed it, had he not felt it.

"I don't believe you. You surpass my expectations almost hourly. How can you laugh?"

"Trespassing?"

"Well …," John let his breath and anger out with a smiling gasp. He clasped his arms around her tightly.

"John, that could have been you," Margaret stared at him for an answer. "I think I championed your male pride."

"I doubt it. I've been waiting a long time to do to you what she did, and you let a woman get to your first. How shameful is that? Can you know how it feels to not be the first in your life?" John laughed, trying to lift her spirits.

"You wouldn't have liked a strange woman setting your hand on her bosom, would you?"

Branson snorted, as he returned to the doorway.

"No. Definitely not, Margaret. Now, you understand what we men have to put up with."

Resting against his chest, Margaret could hear the smile in that answer. She looked at Branson, and he was covering his mouth.

"You two think it's funny, now. How you would feel if her name was Benjamin?"

Both men stopped laughing. And Margaret started.

"Boss, that girl is gone. Her room is cleaned out. It looks like she was already packed to leave."

"Good. Sit with Miss Hale while I fetch her medicine. Not on the bed, Branson. Sit in that chair over there. Geesh! Heaven help me make it through until dawn." John left.

"Branson, I am making it very difficult on your boss," Margaret commented. "I am weak, I fall, I faint, I swoon, I complain about the liver. I need looking after, and I attract the women more than he does. I'm not sure which is hardest on the poor man. He's worried that I may leave. Now, I worry that he may kick me out."

Branson laughed loudly at that. "Miss, he wouldn't care if he had to carry you around on his back for life. You bring him more joy and happiness than he has ever known."

John returned with two glasses mixed with powder.

"Guv, Miss Margaret is afraid you will kick her out because she draws more women than you do. With that, I'll say goodnight."

"John … what if she knew it was me in the bed and not you? When she put her arm around me, she should have known I wasn't as big as you."

John thought for a moment. "I'm not sure what I should say to that."

"You mean you have an answer, and you just don't want to say it?"

"I mean I have no answer. From the little suggestions that I have picked up from her, I truly believe she thought it was me. But if you wish she thought it was you, that's all right with me. And I won't ever kick you out." John said, laughing. "So you attract the ladies, too, do you?"

Margaret belted him in the arm, but John only let out a laugh.

"You have been through an appalling situation tonight. I will not say why, but I will alert the Masters that I wish to speak with her. She is going to get a piece of my mind. I do have one or two questions, though."

"You do?"

"You said you thought it was me. You thought I was the one lying beside you and holding you. You thought I kissed you, yet you didn't fight me off. Why was that?" John handed her the sleeping draft, and Margaret took it without answering him.

"I think I will hold off on this other medication until you awaken, but you haven't answered my question."

"I don't have a proper answer for that. I was groggy with sleep, perhaps. I'm sure I was dreaming."

"I see. That is good to hear, too."

"Since I am awake I shall visit the lavatory before this powder takes effect."

Margaret threw her legs over the bed and stood. John remained sitting and watching as she walked toward the lighted hall. Her shift was thin, and the beauty of her figure was revealed to him. John suddenly realized his physical response would not easily go away, so he walked into the sitting room and sat in the dark. He would never make it, he realized. He had to end his relationship with Elaine Hawkins with all due haste. It was not a gentlemanly act, but his passion was propelling him forward. He did not lust for her body as much as he craved the freedom to express himself.

The lavatory door opened, spilling the light into the hall.

"John, I will turn this lamp down. I should think I will not wake until daylight."

"Margaret, I am sitting here in the parlor. Yes, turn out the light if you wish, but I warn you I will eventually come and lay by your side. I will remain dressed and on top of the covers. I'll even leave my socks on if you wish it, but I shall stay near you for my own sanity."

"Good night, John." Margaret went off to bed without denying John's sleeping arrangement.

Cook had been in the house for an hour and heard no movement anywhere. She finally knocked on Benny's door, which opened as she tapped it. Looking, in she could see that Benny had left their employ. She was relieved over that. Perhaps she and Miss Hale could interview the next housekeeper together.

Knowing it was past time, Cook set upon getting the breakfast to the dining table upstairs. There was no one about. She didn't know whether to call out or not. Finding Margaret's room was little help, as she only saw the Master's boots. As much as she felt intrusive, she went to the Master's room. There asleep was Miss Margaret, lying under the covers, and her Master lying on top with his arm across her waist.

"A most unusual night," she mumbled to herself. As she started to leave, she noticed Miss Margaret attempting to slide out from her Master's arm. Cook waited.

Margaret found her night robe and crept out of the room, closing the door behind her.

"Cook, we've had the most terrible night. John made me sleep in his room to be near the loo and its light, and I think he may have stayed in the room I was occupying. In the middle of the night, while I was sleeping, Benny slid into bed with me without her night attire. I believe she expected John would be interested in her merely because she was a woman. When I realized that there was a naked woman in my bed, I screamed. She ran out past John. Branson even came in to help. I was shaken by the experience, but not injured. John did his best to calm me, and he gave me a sleeping draft. When I fell asleep he was sitting here in the parlor, but he warned me that he might lie down beside me. The poor man has had very little sleep, staying up to protect me." Margaret smiled. "I believe my stay is wearing him out, both physically and emotionally. I'm sure he has no idea what time it is. He is just catching up on his sleep. If you'll excuse me, I will dress for the day. I may take a bath later today, but without a housekeeper, I may not. You and I will hire the next one."

"I can hardly believe such a thing happened in this house," Cook responded. "Even though I know the Master is a man, I am sure he was troubled about that happening, even if it had been him. I was beginning to feel that she was unskilled and just pretended the part to get into this house."

When Margaret exited her bedroom dressed for the day, John was sitting on the couch reading his paper. He had also dressed, with the exception of his boots, which he had left in her room. He looked up when she walked into the room and smiled at her, closing the newspaper.

"Are they clean socks?"

"No. You ask me not change them so you would find a reason to keep your distance from me. I do want to tell you that you need not go through such extreme efforts, as you did last night, for me to come to you. I am perfectly willing. I am at your beck and call. That was a rather elaborate plan to get me to sleep with you." John grinned.

Margaret smiled and blushed. "How do we go about hiring a new housekeeper?"

"I have an idea."

Before the day was over, John had found a service that trained housekeepers and cooks. It was a relatively new employment scheme which seemed to benefit the ever-growing Milton. John had Maddie, an older woman, come to his home and be interviewed by Margaret and Cook.

Both being satisfied with Maddie, she would begin the next day. Her husband would come to the Thornton home at the end of his shift from another mill and escort her home.

Margaret was pleased that John could satisfy the position without much work from her. She should've known, she realized, that John was likely to find a replacement because he did a lot of hiring.

While he was gone, Dr. Donaldson dropped in to see how Margaret was feeling. She confessed she was eating as she should, doing her exercises and felt she was growing stronger. Donaldson watched her walk back and forth across the room and asked her if she had tried the steps yet.

"I believe John has that planned for me tomorrow. I've been very good about following his directions. I did take a sleeping potion last night because there had been a disruption during the night, but aside from that I have not needed anything. John is making me quite happy, which relieves me of the need for medication."

"No doubt. And your monthly cycle?"

"It was over when I left. I shall be on my own when it comes next time. John will be fortunate not to deal with that. I am so thankful that I will not need his assistance."

"Well, we shall hope not. It may be that you will not have one this coming time. But I will see you by then."

"Did you know that Nicholas and John are planning on turning one of their small sheds into a cottage for me?" Neither man will allow me to return to where I was. I am so grateful for that. I am insisting on paying a small rent because I will be working. That reminds me, I should write Cecil Griffin and invite him to the house with his books."

"Margaret, just take care and do not overdo. You appear to be gaining a small amount of weight and color. If you should hear from Miss Dixon I would like to know how she is feeling. I shall leave you for the day and allow you to return to your book." Donaldson tipped his hat and left the house.

Before lying down for her nap, Margaret decided to make John's bed, since no one else was there that day to do it. As she walked around to the opposite side she found what appeared to be a note on the floor. She was tempted to read it, but took it to John's library and laid it on his desk. From there she went to her own room and closed the door to rest.

John had been out for most of the day, spending the early hours at the office and walking mill #2. From there he went looking for the housekeeping service and spoke with the manager about the sort of person they were looking for. He thought about Dixon returning at some point, but she would not be able to do the chores and use the steps as she once did. She could help in the kitchen and keep the washroom clean.

While out in his carriage, he made a decision to see Elaine. He called unannounced, but she received him.

"Come in, John. It's good to see you. How is your guest?"

John handed his hat to the footman. He followed Elaine into the sitting room and sat in a single chair. "Miss Hale is having quite a few difficulties, but we are dealing with them. In her weakened state, she has fallen twice. She fainted yesterday, but the doctor said it was lightheadedness from her anemia. One of the reasons I have stopped by today is that I would like to invite you to dinner at my home tomorrow night. I believe she is very interested in meeting you. I may go from here to visit my mother and perhaps she will come too. Do you have any objections to meeting Miss Hale?"

"No. Not at all. If she is the woman that I might be thrown over for, I would like to see the attraction."

"I guess I will take that as an affirmative answer," he responded, avoiding a direct response to Elaine's comment. "Shall we say eight, and would you prefer that I collect you?"

"Yes," Elaine responded with some chill in her tone, "I can give my driver the night off. Thank you."

"Very well then. I shall see you at eight. I am sorry to be on my way so quickly, but I must visit mother before Cook sets our table. We lost a housekeeper today, but hopefully we will have one tomorrow."

John wanted to be out of there. Elaine walked him to the door and said goodbye, and he felt lucky to get away with only five minutes alone with her. He told Branson to go to his mother's.

"Good afternoon, Mother," John greeted his mother when they arrived. "I am having a very small dinner party tomorrow night. It will just be Miss Hale, Miss Hawkins and, I hope, you. Would you care to visit with me?"

"I believe I would be happy to attend, if Cook is still there."

"She is still there and figuring out how to hide the taste of liver because Miss Hale must eat a lot of it. In order for her to accept the meat, I've taken to eating the same menu. I imagine we will have it tonight. I will tell Cook to fix something she knows that you like, and I shall pick you up at a quarter to eight. Then you and I will collect Miss Hawkins."

"I think I am going to enjoy watching you bringing Miss Hawkins and Miss Hale together. Are you doing it to compare them in your mind? Are you having difficulty deciding which woman to settle down with?"

"Mother I have never compared one woman to another, and I don't intend to start now. You know as well as I do who will eventually be my wife."

"I hope Miss Hawkins gives you up easily."

"I am keeping my promise to take Miss Hawkins to the Master's Ball, which is in two weeks. She and I have discussed what I am looking for in a wife, and she knows she does not have these qualities."

"And you seem to have found it in Miss Hale? What is it that has been lacking in all the other women in your life?"

"Mother, I don't feel the need to discuss this any further. If you can't see the difference between Miss Hale and the others, then you will never understand. Perhaps tomorrow evening you will see it. I shall pick you up.. Good afternoon."

Coming through the back door on his arrival, John told Cook about the dinner, then went looking for Margaret.

John found her looking out the window into the mill yard. It made him wonder how she would spend her time as a wife. He had never heard her speak of needlework, which his mother did. Perhaps she would be reading a book they had promised to read together. He didn't think he had been quiet entering the room, yet she seemed startled when he spoke.

"What have you done today, Margaret?"

Margaret turned toward him in surprise. "I have had a visit from Dr. Donaldson today. He only stopped by to ask about me and if I had heard anything from Dixon. He even thought I had put on a little weight and had more color. You know, it's hard …."

"What is?"

She looked out the window again. "It's hard being cared about so much."

John went to her immediately and knelt beside her chair. "What a strange thing to say. You seem pensive. Is there anything you're trying to tell me?"

"There were words I wish to speak and words I wish to hear. They will have to wait."

"Am I to worry? Has anything changed between us?"

"You take the fear away."

John pondered her words. They were perplexing.

Chapter Twenty Seven

"I wonder how they are doing, Nicholas?"

"I spoke with John this morning. It seems Margaret is coming along well. They both don't particularly seem to like liver, though they eat it often. But John told me about a frightening thing that happened last night to Margaret." Nicholas went on to explain how the housekeeper had crawled in bed with Margaret, thinking it was John.

"If it wasn't for Margaret's condition and having a great scare, it would almost be funny. She told John she thought it was him. Margaret was even kissed," Nicholas chuckled.

Peggy was astounded and gasped, throwing her hands over her mouth. "Oh my God, poor Margaret. I should visit her tomorrow."

"The other interesting fact is that when I last saw John he was intending to have Miss Hawkins and his mother over for dinner tomorrow night. Only John Thornton would do something like that, and I don't really understand it. I wonder if he has an ulterior motive."

"That is a bit of odd behavior. He must see some benefit in it. Perhaps it's to bring Margaret out of her depression."

"I think I could come up with some better way to do that than having Miss Hawkins and his mother for dinner. I couldn't even see that if Margaret wasn't there. Oh, by the way, today I started on plans to turn a small shed in the mill property into a cottage. If Margaret insists on leaving John's home when she is well, she will move there. In time I think John will marry Margaret, and as his mother ages she will be brought to that cottage."

"Brilliant. It sounds perfect. But John had better have a caretaker for his mother and not allow Margaret to spend her days nursing."

"What do you mean," John was saying, "I take the fear away? I am glad to hear you say that, but I wonder what you fear."

In her passive voice, Margaret continued. "As I look back over my life, I see how weak my parents were. Mother was always the proper lady, leaving my upbringing mostly to Dixon. Father at one time was devout, and he had the love of his family and his faith, but he was a weak man. When he lost his faith, my family changed. It was like we all escaped into our own direction to find comfort. There was love between us all, but the support we once had for each other was dying. Since I have been with you, I realize the fear that I lived with. With my brother gone, I endured the full weight of keeping my family together. As I lost one of my parents, the burden became heavier."

John took her hand in his, but didn't interrupt.

"As you know, my life continued to slip slowly from my grasp. There was fear around every corner. The fear of two women living alone. The fear of having missed my life with you. And the fear of no food. It was about to break my spirit. You have rescued me from *all* of that. You have taken the fear away."

"Margaret, I promise you, as long as you live, I will never let you fear for any reason. Even if you turn away. I'm sorry these words cannot wait, but you are my life and always will be. I will never let you go. You don't have to be brave anymore." John could see the tears flowing down her cheeks as she continued to gaze out of the window.

"I know that, John. I am discovering the depth of caring you have for me. You have not spoken the words that I believe you wish to, but I feel them. I see them in your eyes. If you never said another word to me, I would recognize your love through those eyes of yours. I understand now why women didn't remark about your eyes and that was because you didn't love any of them."

John couldn't believe the words that he knew were coming from within her. His own tears welled as he listened. She understood and believed his love was true.

"No one has cared for me as much as you. It is hard to accept that. Accept that as being real. Accept these innermost emotions. It is like my heart is trying to grow further still. It wants to take all that you can give. I feel strange sometimes, almost numb, as if nothing can ever hurt me again. I have been shielded by a knight's armor, and you are my knight. I remember once feeling that I was going to surrender myself to you. I have far surpassed that. You are living within me, now."

John embraced her and kissed her hair. She did not return any emotion, but allowed his touches to continue. Her eyes closed, and John gently kissed her lips.

"I am finished pouring out my new revelations," Margaret said softly.

"I hope not. I live to hear any words of love from you. You lift me up, you lift me up as a man."

With tears in her eyes, Margaret turned to John and said, "It appears that you cannot keep your distance." Margaret said with half a smile. "I think I win. I think I have won you and won a beautiful happy life. I had been sitting here dwelling on all that has happened recently. And then one thing led backward to another until I saw where I really became of age."

"Margaret, you are not quite there yet. The man you love and who loves you will carry you into your coming of age. So help me God, I will be the one." John stood and offered his handkerchief to Margaret and walked away. Her words had fallen on him like rain in the dessert, totally, blissfully and too quickly absorbed. Margaret's words were more binding than any physical love. They would last. He was being reborn. John went to his library to collect himself. The tears continued to shed, and he didn't want her to see that.

John walked straight to the window after closing his library door. For a year of loving and wanting Margaret, he never thought he would see this day. She had changed in a way that made him love her even more. She finally accepted her own value. Margaret realized she was a person worth caring about. Since he had known her, she had always done for others. Someone was doing for her, and her embarrassment about this was lifting. And now she was finding love: true and deep and beautiful. John wiped his eyes and went to his desk.

There was a note lying there, still folded. It looked like the love note he had written, but he remembered putting it in his pocket. He turned it over to discover that it was the note to Margaret, as he had written her name on it. With all the excitement through the night and the sleeping late, it went unread. With Margaret being the only person on this floor today, John wondered if she had found it and laid it on his desk. If so, had she read it? He thought this was a good time to confess to the note and the flowers. In just the past few hours, their commitment to each other had grown.

John heard a light tap on his door. A small voice called out, "Liver is ready." He laughed to himself. That little quip was needed to dispel the profound emotional bonding that was happening.

Margaret was standing at the door with her red puffy eyes. John looked down on her. "You look like a foundling standing there."

"I think that is because I was."

John put his hands on her shoulders and leaned down for a brief kiss. John knew this instance of kissing her was going to grow. He walked her to the table. Cook had set out their plates.

John seated her. "This looks good, doesn't it?" he said with a brief grin.

"John, you don't have to eat what I do. You don't need any more red blood cells."

"I do. Soon, I will be a very active intimate man."

"I am sure I knew that, but what does that have to do with eating liver?"

"It has more to do with the use of blood, but that is for another time." John chuckled lightly to himself.

"I see that smile. You are hiding something."

"Not for long, I am afraid."

"Will it be a surprise?"

John started to chuckle out loud as he cut through the liver on his plate. "Yes, I'm quite sure it will be. Oh, speaking of surprises, another note came for you today. I put it in my pocket and then a minute ago I found it on my desk. Did you put it there?" John withdrew the paper from his pocket.

"Oh. Yes that looks like the piece of paper I picked up beside your bed. I laid it on your desk where you would find it."

"But it has your name on it. Didn't you read it?"

"If you look carefully, Mr. Thornton you will notice that the seal is not broken. I didn't open it because I wanted you to know that I got another note. And I wanted you to hand it to me." Margaret sniffed the air.

"If you want me to know that you are desirable to other men, I know that. I'm thinking of hiding you."

Margaret giggled. "Sorry, I cannot be hidden until I finish my work for Mr. Griffin. Which reminds me, I wish to write him a note and invite him over along with his accounting books one evening or even an afternoon. Perhaps the daytime may be better. You wouldn't have to listen to us. You could be doing your own work."

"Although I don't want to leave you alone with anyone other than me, ever again, I believe our accounting books are private. I doubt that he would feel comfortable with me in the room. Any time you wish, except for tomorrow night."

"Is that when I'm going to get my surprise?"

Margaret watched as John's shoulders went up and down in his quiet laugh. He was smiling and laughing in silence.

"I have invited guests for dinner."

"Oh, you have? Is it Nicholas and Peggy?"

"No, but it might be a nice idea to invite them too. I have invited Miss Elaine Hawkins and Mrs. Hannah Thornton," John said with a grin on his face.

"You what!"

"I think you heard me."

"Is this the way my life is going to be? We don't even discuss things beforehand?"

"Miss Hale, I believe you mistake me for someone who has proposed to you … in recent weeks. I cannot know what your life is going to be like," John watched her expression carefully. Would she take offense or would she banter with him?

"Pardon me. You are correct. I believe there is another who would like to propose to me, perhaps two."

"Are any of them women?" John almost choked on that.

Margaret snapped a snarl at him.

John stood feigning anger. "How is that possible? You haven't met anyone."

"Sit down, John. I won't possibly accept any of them unless I get a better offer. So, have a care when you spring guests on me."

John was slightly confused. He knew that she wanted to be his wife, but were there really men out there looking her way? "I suppose one of them is the love letter and flower gentleman?"

"I wouldn't be surprised if one of these days there is a proposal written inside. Now this gentleman will know that I cannot possibly answer that without knowing him, but it will bring some joy to my life."

"Well, aren't you going to open it and read it?"

"Not until I know why we are having guests tomorrow night." Margaret purposely picked up the note and with flair, put it in her pocket.

"If I tell you the truth, you may become angry with me. I'm not sure I could take that from you just now."

"Let's just see how this works. You have something that you feel will anger me; therefore you will not tell me your reasoning behind this show you are putting on."

"It's something like that."

"If you wish not to go to the end of the line of the proposers, I think you must tell me what this something is all about."

John sat, folding his arms, and smiled at the woman he loved. This was the Margaret he hoped would appear for Elaine and his mother. Margaret could convince the Queen that she was different from the rest. "Do you think you can act like this tomorrow night?"

"Like what? What am I acting like? Am I to be set upon the stage for entertainment?"

John could see the frown starting, and he wanted to laugh so badly. "Something like that."

"You just said that. Something like what?"

"I want them to know what separates you from all of the others. I fell in love with your wit and humor and so much more. No one ever showed that to me, and I cannot help but love the way that you do. I have nothing planned. I just want you to be yourself. I especially want Elaine to see how she is lacking as a wife for me. There are many other reasons why I would never marry her, but perhaps she can see in you what I do."

Margaret put a piece of liver in her mouth, and it seemed like she would never swallow it. John could tell she was also chewing on what he just stated.

"Let me see if I understand you correctly. John Thornton, Master Bachelor …."

John rested his chin in his palm after placing his elbow on the table. He couldn't wait for what she was going to say. He was all smiles.

"John Thornton, Master of bachelors, the man who has launched a thousand sighs, a man to which songs are sung and pages written, the man voted 'Best Catch in Milton,' the one who is *the* man among men, admired for his body, mind, and eyes, noted for his prowess with women, yet *that* John Thornton is seeking help from a sickly little poor woman to extract himself from yet another conquest?"

John cackled loudly and clapped his hands. Even Margaret had to smile at his reaction.

"Yes, something like that," John merrily laughed.

"How did I get so lucky?" Margaret sighed.

Chapter Twenty Eight

Maddie, the new housekeeper, arrived by seven in the morning. Cook told her of the eventful evening that was to be had at Thornton house, and Maddie seemed to take it in stride.

"Is the family up yet?" Maddie asked Cook.

"Normally the master would be up by now, even having his breakfast. However, he has a guest, and I believe they have stayed up late talking. To answer your question, I have heard no footsteps, so I don't think anyone is awake."

"If you would show me where the supplies are, I will clean the foyer, sitting room and dining room immediately."

Cook was more than happy to help her.

"John, if you remember, today I start to try the steps. I don't anticipate any problems, but I know you want to stay with me while I try it. And, if you wouldn't mind, I will also walk across the mill yard with you and visit with Nicholas in the office. I have already informed Cook that Nicholas and Peggy may be with us this evening. So I would like to go over and extend an invitation for dinner tonight. I wonder what he would say if he knew your motive for inviting Miss Hawkins to meet me."

"He does know about the original plans for dinner and you are right. I think he questions what I am doing. Since he is my best friend and I care for you the most in the world, notice I didn't speak the words: You may tell him or not."

"When can we start? I'm sure Maddie would like us out of the way for a while."

"We have a couple hours before our midday meal and then your nap, so I guess there is no time like the present."

John and Margaret walked to the steps and he preceded her by walking backwards while facing her.

"We are now going to practice. We will see how you do on the steps. You will cross the yard and you will try to ascend a second set of stairs. You will also do the reverse in a few hours. I think that will be plenty of exercise on the stairs. Are you ready?"

"Yes, and I am eager. The sooner I can take care of myself, the sooner we can stop eating liver."

John could see that she was excited to try. If she accomplished the day without trouble, she could go where she wished. She could take the back steps and ask Branson to driver her somewhere. John would have a talk with Branson later.

Margaret started down the stairs with little trouble. She had air, she had energy and she had control of herself. John did not have to tell her to hold onto the banisters as she did that on her own. When they arrived on the porch top, John took her arm down those steps.

"Would you like my arm to cross the way?"

"I won't embarrass you?"

"No woman could ever embarrass the Master bachelor," John laughed. "I kind of like that. It's too bad it's coming to an end, just when I have been duly noted for my skills."

Margaret giggled, and before she knew it, she was across the yard. Once again, John stood behind her.

Margaret stopped at the first step. She looked up and the stairs seemed like they reached the sky. She was feeling slight twinges in her thighs, but regardless, was going to try.

By the second step, Nicholas had come out to watch the festivities. Margaret looked up at him and smiled.

"Nicholas! See. I am getting well. You'd better finish my cottage soon."

Nicholas chuckled. "May I come down to assist you even with John behind you?"

"That's not John. That is the Master Bachelor." She bubbled spittle from her lips as she laughed at that.

"I did not know that we had a celebrity with us. You should've sent a note ahead so I could've prepared." Nicholas just fell right in with the joke.

Halfway up the steps, Margaret faltered. Her thighs would lift her no more. John stepped up behind her, wrapped his arm around her waist and carried her to the top like a sack of wheat. For a moment Margaret was looking sideways at the world. He continued carrying her in that position until he could sit her in a chair inside.

"I am not sure if that constitutes going to the end of the line. You held me sideways like a long board, but yet you saved me from injury. I will have to think on this."

Nicholas was already laughing. Margaret cheered him whenever they were together. "What line is this," Nicholas asked.

"I think the Master Bachelor should tell you about the line."

Nicholas looked toward John who was already grinning and swiveling in his chair.

"Margaret Hale tells me she feels there may be one, two, or three men that wish to propose to her. She knows I am in that line as well. It now seems if I don't bow to her Majesty, I am sent to the end of the line. In my mind she has a clock over top of her. It is preset for a time that no one knows. When the time is right an alarm will sound, allowing the man at the head of the line to propose. I am not quite sure that she has to accept."

"Very good, bachelor. It is true I do not have to accept the person standing there proposing to me. But if I dismiss his proposal, he may not reenter the line. Apparently that's how Milton gentlemen handle their rejections."

Nicholas slipped a look at John and saw the stunned look on his face. It was apparent to everyone that she was referring to a year ago. Nicholas rubbed his hands in glee. He was ready for a war of wits. "It's WOW time."

"It's what?" asked John.

"WOW time. W – O – W. War of Wits," Nicholas laughed and so did Margaret and John.

"She's been doing this to me for days."

"Nicholas, would you believe he wishes me to display this to Elaine, so she knows why John doesn't love her."

"Is that true, John?"

"Something like that."

"Nicholas, I am here to cordially invite you and Peggy to dinner and this evening's performance."

"Miss Hale, let me make this perfectly clear. I am not expecting anything from you. You are to be yourself. Is that understood?"

Margaret wobbled but stood, saluting John. "Yes, Master Bachelor."

"You know how I can get you to stop calling me that, don't you?"

"But you said you liked being called that."

John grew a bit flushed.

Nicholas looked at him and laughed uproariously. "He said that? He's always told me different."

"I think his words were something like, it was … how'd it go … 'I kind of like that name. It's too bad it's coming to an end just when I have been duly noted for my skills.'"

Nicholas was bent over, holding his stomach and catching his breath.

"Miss Hale, I did not say you could tell everything to Nicholas."

"Well, it was something like that anyway."

Margaret stayed in the office for a while as the duo conducted business talk. John eventually got around to asking her what she knew about trending and forecasting sales.

"What is it you wish to know, Mr. Thornton? Is it something specific I may have learned in accountingl?"

"Well, I am not sure exactly. We once broached this issue with our accounting clerks, explaining what we were looking for. They said they would try. We then had no confidence in their ability to pin down what we wanted. I guess I am asking if you can see a trend in sales and expenses from several years back and going forward. We see movement in our product and feel expansion is needed to keep abreast of our current and new customers. Can you calculate something like that?"

"Yes."

"Can you forecast expected sales and inventory needed?"

"Yes."

"I'll keep going, then. It you can forecast sales and inventory purchases, can you determine if we need more space?"

"Yes, once I know the size of the raw cotton coming in and the finished cotton leaving, the size of your workforce and the square footage of your buildings. I can also anticipate wage increases by the workers' length of service and the rise of expenses to them and taxes everywhere. If they need more to live, you must pay it, or lose them. That cost will be passed on to your customer. I would need to know if you plan any new programs, such as higher wages for incoming educated, higher wages for third shift workers, free on-sight medical care, someone to watch children while parents work. Does that answer your question?"

"All but one," remarked Nicholas.

"What did I miss?"

"Will you come and work for us after Mr. Griffin?"

Margaret laughed. "What … and miss needlepointing?"

After their midday meal, Margaret had a bath prepared for her. Maddie assisted her during the whole procedure.

"If you don't mind me saying so mum, your ribs are showing. You need some meat on those bones."

"Yes, I have been ill, but I am on the mend, now. Are you ready to wait table this evening?"

"Yes, mum. Very acquainted with that, I am. And I am pleased to have this job."

"I know Mr. Thornton will be a good master to you. And Cook has been with the family for many years."

"Yes, she is a dear woman. She doesn't mind answering questions or showing me where items are."

"Once you've washed my hair, I believe I am done and ready to rest."

"Yes, miss."

As Margaret rested, John spent time with Cook. They talked about what his mother would like and how Maddie was doing.

"I think you got a good one there, sir."

"I think you are right, Cook. Did you tell Maddie about the housekeeper before her?"

"No I haven't sir. I don't think she's likely to tell her story, so maybe people won't know."

"From a man's point of view, Cook, that had to be a particularly funny sight."

"Sir, I'm going to have to shoo you out of my kitchen. Things are going to get busy now. It's only two hours until it's time to eat. Will you be serving drinks before you sit at the table?"

"Yes. Give us half an hour. And don't forget our little surprise."

"Guv, are you sure about what you're doing tonight?"

"I am only sure about Miss Hale."

John went upstairs and began to collect his various libations. He set them on one end of the buffet where Branson would serve from. Without his mother taking care of all of the details, it fell to him. He heard Margaret's door open.

She walked out and came into the dining room and looked over the table. "This looks lovely. Are you going to have a centerpiece?"

"What do you suggest?"

"Wait a minute." Margaret returned to her room and brought out the flowers that were still living. She set them on the table and picked through all of the wilting ones. She ended with the nice small centerpiece. "There. That should be enough. This isn't a formal dinner, so there should be no need for these tall candlesticks, do you think?"

"I thought it looked too fancy for what the evening was going to be, but I couldn't tell. What else do you see, Margaret?"

"It looks like you're getting to the drinks. I think you have special glasses for special orders. Are they to be used?"

"Yes. Branson should be up soon to set his bar. I just wanted to take a look at the stock and see if anything was needed before we left to pick up the ladies." John looked over the table again. "Aren't there supposed to be little papers telling people where they sit?"

"Yes, if you wish to seat people in a particular order."

"I do wish that."

"If you have some paper I will write the names for you and you can set them where you will."

"You can find some blank paper and pen in my desk. The paper should be in the top middle drawer. By the way, Margaret, you look beautiful."

"I shall put on some face paint later so I don't look so sickly."

"Can I ask you not to do that?"

"Can I ask you why?"

"When I first saw you two weeks ago, you were about as gaunt and sick as you could be. You were the brightest vision in my life. You could not have been more beautiful standing there looking up at me. I am going to have to take your natural beauty as it returns in small doses. My heart is so full, I wish nothing to spill out. If you should go and make yourself lovelier, I am not sure I could survive the shock."

"Thank you for the compliment, but I think you deceive to please me."

"I knew you would say that, but it is the truth."

"But the others …."

"The others will think what they like. You are sick. You are most likely about halfway through your initial recovery. There is no need to hide anything. There will be no story to tell."

Margaret turned away and walked towards the library. A minute later, John poked his head in and said that he was going to get ready.

Margaret put the palms of her hands flat on the desktop and slid them open and closed on the surface. *This is where he sits*, she was thinking. *This furniture has absorbed his essence. It is like being in his arms.* She opened the drawer and pulled out a sheaf of paper. It seemed to have the weight and coloring as her love notes. She had felt pretty sure that John was the sender, but he seemed to be enjoying it, so she didn't insist on his admission. No scissors were in the drawer. She would need those to cut the name cards to small sizes. She walked to John's bedchamber door and knocked lightly.

"John are there any scissors in the house?"

John stopped what he was doing to think about it. He remembered his mother using them to cut thread, but surely she would've taken her sewing basket with her. "I can help you in a minute. I think mother took them with her, but I have a way to trim the paper."

Margaret returned to the library and began to look over his collection of books. Most of them tended to be written on the subject of his work. There were books on building mills, mill machines, shipping to the world and many others. She did find one shelf which appeared to contain novels, although most of them looked like history.

John came into the room. He reached into his desk drawer and found a straight edge ruler. He simply laid the ruler flat on the paper and ripped it against the edge. It wasn't a fine cut, but this wasn't a proper dinner. "Will this do?"

"Perfectly. Do you want them addressed with their surname only?"

"How is it normally done?"

"Usually it is the whole name written out, unless the person is titled. Is Miss Hawkins titled in any way?"

"I really have no idea. Just put Miss Elaine Hawkins. Also put Mrs. Hannah Thornton. I hear Branson. I am going to go and help him.

Margaret set about her task, finding her hand less steady than it used to be. She had to practice several times before she could write fluidly. She finished the six name tags and brought them into the dining room, to find John with Branson.

"Hello, Branson," she greeted him cheerfully.

"Good day to you, miss. You seem to be improving every day."

"Branson, is it your place to keep confidences?" she asked, and then said to John, "John, you don't have to pay attention to this; go on with what you're doing. If I were to take you into my confidence, Branson, would you feel compelled to keep it confidential?"

"Miss Hale, just what are you up to?" John asked.

"I am up to nothing. I would just like to know if Branson would honor my private words as he does yours."

John looked at Branson, but gave him no instructions or no certain look. It was up to Branson to decide.

"Miss, anything told to me is always held in confidence regardless of who it is. Should I feel that a person is placing themselves or someone else in danger, I may seek advice. I don't actually have a confessional booth, where if you told me you murdered somebody, I would have to keep that to myself. If you think that, then you have overestimated me. I have never had any such hard decisions to be make." Branson bent down to get some glasses from the lower shelf. "However, I have foreseen a situation to which I don't clearly have an answer."

"What would that be," asked John.

"Sir, if you and Miss Hale were to marry and you told me to let you know wherever I had to take her and she might say, 'Don't tell Mr. Thornton,' well … you can see the problem that would cause me."

"Let me put your mind at ease right now." John said. "Whatever lies ahead, I trust Miss Hale implicitly. You will take orders from her as you do from me. That way you can maintain your honor and confidences without guilt."

"Thank you, guv."

Margaret smiled at John as if to say *thank you.*

"What's that cooking?" Margaret asked.

"It is my mother's favorite. It is liver." Seeing the look on her face, John burst out laughing. "I'm sorry–that was too good of an opportunity to miss."

Margaret walked behind John as he placed the nametags. He and Nicholas would be at the ends of the table. That was to be expected. To John's left would be Miss Hawkins, and next to her would be his mother. Nicholas would be at the other end of the table, and Margaret would be to his left, sitting next to Peggy. Margaret liked that arrangement. She could see both John and Miss Hawkins very well. And across from her was his mother and Margaret had Peggy and Nicholas on her sides.

John and Branson had finished setting up the libations area leaving a place for Cook and Maddie to bring up the serving plates. It had been agreed that the side dishes would be placed on the table, while the meat would be carved in the kitchen and placed on a plate to be set in front of everyone.

Branson left the dining room and went downstairs. John made one last check of the table and the drinks. He walked over to Margaret and took her hand in his. He guided her to the darkening hall that led to her bedroom, stopping to face her towards him. He took her second hand in his other one.

"Margaret, I am serious when I say you do not have to do anything other than be yourself. No matter what transpires or conclusions that could be drawn, nothing will change our futures. I really feel my mother wants to be close to you. It may be for my sake, but I truly think she feels she has done you an injustice. She knows she changed my life, causing your rejection a year ago. I am fully capable of ending my relationship with Miss Hawkins. I do not have any affection for her, and she knows we will never marry. What I'm trying to say is, please find a way to enjoy yourself."

John leaned down to kiss Margaret, and she stood on her tip toes to make the kiss more firm. She wanted John to know that she was not afraid of the evening to come. She could potentially have two people against her, but she knew she could brave it through. Whatever it took, John was worth any slings or arrows that came her way. John kissed the back of each hand.

"Margaret," John said reassuringly, "you look beautiful even with those sallow cheeks. Your lips are heavenly, your eyes are bright, your hair is shiny and you smell simply delightful. I must go and pick up Mother and then Miss Hawkins. I shall be but a half hour or a bit more. Sit down and read the paper. Don't forget I care about you more than anyone in this world."

John let go of her two hands and collected his coat. He popped on his hat and headed downstairs. Margaret went to the window to watch him leave. He looked up at her and she waved.

Margaret paced the room. While she appeared brave, she was actually quite nervous. She laughed to herself, thinking of taking one of those pills that made her talk funny, as John would tell her. He had told her to be herself, but Margaret wasn't so sure he would like what she was planning to do. Margaret was curious to meet Elaine Hawkins. Would she be beautiful or wealthy? Would there be a great difference between her and Margaret?

"Miss, would you like me to turn up the gas lights? It's becoming fairly dark in this room."

"Yes, thank you, Maddie. How long ago did Mr. Thornton leave?"

"The master has been gone nearly thirty minutes, mum."

Margaret knew she must have been there thinking about the night if she had to be told that it was getting dark in the room.

"Good luck, mum."

Margaret wasn't surprised that Maddie had already picked up on the situation in the house. Either she had been talking to Cook or she had overheard some conversations quite by chance. Margaret heard the coach coming to the house.

Chapter Twenty Nine

Margaret let out the breath she had been holding when she saw that it was Peggy and Nicholas. The reinforcements had come. Maddie was at the door to let them in.

"Oh, I'm so glad you two are here first. I thought I was going to be brave, but may need your support."

"Margaret, there is no competition. You have already won the prize. It's just that Miss Hawkins may not know it yet," Peggy laughed. "John knows precisely what he is doing. Never underestimate that man."

Margaret could see Nicholas smiling at her worries. "I know what you say is right. I'm just suddenly nervous."

"We only accepted at the last minute because we wouldn't miss these fireworks for anything." Peggy laughed louder. "Dear, I am only jesting. I see a little glassy sheen starting in your eyes. Now buck up and be the Margaret we all know."

As Nicholas was hanging his coat on the peg, he said, "They've just pulled in. Places, everyone." Nicholas was enjoying Margaret's discomfort because he knew she soon would find John's words to be real.

The door at the bottom of the steps opened. Mrs. Thornton came through the door first, followed by a rather attractive woman closer to John's age. Margaret was immediately struck with the fact that she must come from money. She, Peggy and Nicholas backed into the sitting room to allow the others room at the top of the stairs.

John did the introductions. "Mother I think you know everyone here."

"Yes, I do. Hello, Miss Hale. I hope you are recovering."

"Thank you. I believe I am. I took steps today for the first time." She looked back at John for the next introduction.

"Elaine, this is Miss Hale, I believe you have met Nicholas, and this is his lovely wife, Peggy. People, please meet Elaine Hawkins."

Margaret was first to extend her hand of welcome. Next came Peggy.

"Please, everyone, find a seat. Branson should be in to take your drink orders."

Mrs. Thornton sat on the end of the sofa where she had usually sat, while Miss Hawkins took the center and Margaret the other end. A chair had been brought from the dining room for Peggy, and the men took the overstuffed chairs. No one seemed to want to open the conversation. Finally Nicholas spoke up.

"Miss Hale, you do seem to have a little more color."

"You mean, I have more color than when you saw me only a few hours ago?"

Nicholas laughed, slightly embarrassed. "Margaret, you weren't supposed to say that. I was just trying to start a conversation." There was a smattering of laughter.

Margaret leaned forward to get Mrs. Thornton's attention. Miss Hawkins stared at her and finally asked if she'd like to change places.

"Miss Hawkins, I don't mean to inconvenience you. I just wanted to ask Mrs. Thornton how she was liking her new flat."

"Rather than shouting in my ear or talking past me, please allow me to exchange seating with you, Miss Hale."

Both ladies stood and exchanged places in front of the couch. Margaret was now in the middle and wished to engage Mrs. Thornton in conversation. She felt the invisible female claws beginning to show.

"Mrs. Thornton, I understand that Cook has prepared one of your favorite meals. I am quite tired of eating liver to boost my illness with anemia. What might she be cooking for you?"

"I'm surprised you haven't spoken with Cook, Miss Hale. She and I always discussed the meal menu for the week. I take it you don't like liver. If she really has cooked my favorite, the meat should be lamb."

Everyone seemed to be listening to the conversation.

"You are quite correct. I do not like liver at all. Lamb sounds delightful. As for speaking with Cook about meals, I am a guest and do not wish to intrude on John's way of doing things. If he would ask me to help, I would be glad to, but he hasn't. If your son ever leaves the Millworks, he would make an excellent nurse."

The laughter was a bit louder this time. Branson arrived and took the ladies drink orders first. There was light conversation between Peggy and Elaine, Margaret and Hannah, and the two men.

Cook and Maddie had set all the side dishes on the table and were beginning to bring the main meat plates to each diner. John called them all to the table.

Margaret watched as Miss Hawkins realized that she was sitting next to John. She gave him a charming smile. Margaret felt like removing Elaine's teeth.

One by one, Cook and Maddie placed the plates with lamb in front of everyone but Margaret. Margaret was patient, perhaps they didn't have enough room on the tray, but no one lifted a fork until they all had their plates.

Margaret was swinging her legs under the chair, and smiling, trying to not look embarrassed that her meal was holding up everyone.

"Cook, did you bring Miss Hale's plate?"

"Oh, sir. I apologize. I had no room. I will be back in a moment. The light conversation started again until Cook walked over to Margaret and set a plate of liver in front of her.

Margaret kept her head down because she knew people were looking at her plate. She looked to her left and Peggy had lamb, then she checked Nicholas and he had lamb. She wasn't sure if Cook had made a mistake, but didn't say anything. She raised her eyes a bit more and checked everyone's plate. She started to lift her fork when Nicholas passed her the boiled potatoes with butter and parsley. She took one.

The dishes went around the table and Margaret looked at John, seeing he had lamb. Why wasn't he eating liver? She looked up into his face and saw a contorted grin. Then he burst out laughing, as did everyone except Elaine. Cook leaned over her shoulder and swapped her liver with lamb.

"Margaret, do you think Cook would forget you?" laughed Peggy, we knew what was going to happen. I think John's been waiting all day to spring that on you. You looked so brave staring at that liver again."

"Nicholas thought I had gained some color. Do you think so?"

"Yes, a bit. You have a ways to go, plus you're still nothing but bones."

"John, do you think my color has improved?"

"I've seen you every day. It's hard for me to make the slight distinction like the others."

"Well, I'm seeing Dr. Donaldson tomorrow and taking him all the liver you have stored in the house. He can have it. I'll live on lentils or some beans."

Laughter by all but Elaine.

"Margaret?"

"Yes, John?"

"Would you mind if I told them your adventure the other night?"

"I believe you knew if you asked that question in the presence of everyone that I would be forced to say yes. Why not? It's probably all over Milton by now. I'm surprised it hasn't made the front papers."

"John, what is she talking about," asked Hannah.

"I believe it was Margaret's second night here. I had left the lavatory gas light on so she could see her way there in the dark if she needed to. Well, it seems she did. Being conscious of the cost of gas lighting, she turned the light out before returning to her room. She told me, she fell because there was no moonlight coming into the room as it had been earlier. She tripped over something. I'm not sure what it was, but she fell and injured her knee. I heard her call out and went to see what had happened." John stopped and looked at Margaret.

"He's making this up, I want you all to know that," said Margaret.

"I am not making this up. The following night, I exchanged beds with her. She slept in my room which is just a few steps from the lavatory. Again, I left the light on. I went to her room, but left the door open to listen."

Margaret put her two elbows on the table and covered her face with her hands. John laughed and pointed at her.

"Now comes the unbelievable part," John started laughing and began trying to get it out. That tended to make others laugh at his laughing. Hannah was stunned to see her son laughing.

"John, please go on," Hannah asked.

John's shoulders were going up and down as he laughed silently, hardly able to catch his breath. "Margaret you tell them. You know the story better."

"Me?"

"I can't help laughing, I will never get it out. Please tell it."

"I wish someone would tell it," barked Elaine. "Miss Hale, may we hear this story that has John so tied up he can't speak."

"I was sleeping soundly when I felt an arm lying across my waist, as if being snuggled. I paid little attention, thinking I was dreaming. But I started to awaken as the arm moved. A hand picked up mine and laid my hand on a breast. I was sure it wouldn't be John, and realized it wasn't a man's breast. I quickly flipped over on my back to find John's naked housekeeper. I screamed. She screamed. Apparently, she was going to seduce John. She was naked, and worst of all, she kissed me before we screamed."

Peggy, Nicholas and John were howling. Hannah was in shock, and Elaine didn't know what to think.

"John, what would you have done if it were you in the bed?" asked Elaine.

"What any gentleman would do."

"So you wouldn't do what comes naturally?"

Everyone seemed to stop laughing and looked at Elaine. Hannah was mortified.

Margaret continued speaking to stem the stares at Elaine. "John heard the screaming and raced towards his bedchamber, passing a naked woman on the way. I was … I was … I'm not sure what I was. Disbelieving isn't strong enough. John tried to calm me and was determined to find out what happened and if she had hurt me. He wanted to dismiss her immediately, but he didn't want to leave me shaking and crying. Branson showed up. John asked Branson to stay with me and started to leave the room when he noticed Branson had taken his place on the bedside. John told him to sit in another chair. Poor Branson."

"So what happened to the housekeeper?"

John took over the story. "Branson checked her room and all of her belongings including herself, were gone."

"Miss Hale, what an ordeal you had," said Hannah. "I am sorry that happened to you in this house. Where did she come from?"

"She lied giving her references and previous duties. She just wanted into this house or just wanted John. Cook has her own theory, too, but she won't share it."

"Oh, my. I think this has spoiled my appetite," expressed Hannah.

"Mrs. Thornton, no one was hurt. John was a gentleman. It was serious at the time, but it gets funny as time fades. I'm sure John would have liked to have been a fly on the wall when we both discovered who the other one was."

"No doubt," Elaine chimed in.

Finally everyone seemed to return to their plates, but there was little other conversation after that. It was the topic of the night.

Eventually, Cook and Maddie cleared the plates and brought trifle, while Branson poured glasses of port.

Margaret heard John clear his throat.

"John, may I make the toast," asked Margaret.

"If you wish."

She stood. "For the past few months, out of pride, I have foolishly put myself and my housekeeper in danger. After father died, bills began arriving that I found father had been paying by rendering services to them. With him no longer able to perform his trade, the bills fell to the small money that we had left. The only people whom I knew in Milton are at this table, but I was embarrassed to ask for help until we were starting to go hungry." Margaret paused.

Margaret saw John look at Elaine.

"I'm not making this as short as I had hoped, but with the hospitalization of my housekeeper, John and the

Higgins came to my rescue. I was too embarrassed to let them know we had fallen so low, but they all insisted they wanted to help."

Margaret paused and lifted her glass. The others were poised to toast.

"I cannot thank the Higgins enough for their great friendship and support. They offered me shelter and care. Thank you, Nicholas and Peggy. You will always be my dearest friends."

"Hear, hear," someone said. Margaret thought it might have been John.

"Wait, I am not done yet. John Thornton offered his home, as well, so I had a decision to make. I finally decided on his Marlborough Mills home for several reasons, one being he had spare rooms and there was an old misunderstanding to correct."

Margaret paused. She turned to John.

"John Thornton, you have been gracious, polite, concerned and caring. You took it upon yourself to take care of me through some potentially embarrassing situations. You watched over me, worried about my mental state, and lifted my spirits in many ways."

John was smiling at Margaret, waiting for her to finish singing his praises. He was embarrassed.

"John, to thank you for all you have done, I wish to propose …."

Everyone waited for her to finish.

"Yes, Margaret," John said. "You wish to propose … and …."

"And that's all. I am proposing."

John still didn't get it, but the others did.

Elaine gasped.

"Miss Hale, you are proposing what to me? That seems a simple enough question. We're all here waiting for what you are proposing." John smiled.

"John, I am proposing marriage to you. Will you marry me?"

The smile left John's face. "What?" he asked meekly.

"I think you heard me. I believe the others have."

"Wait. Wait. You, Margaret Hale are asking me, John Thornton, to marry you?"

"I can't wait any longer for you to ask. I don't want to wait in the long line of women who hope to become your wife. Miss Hawkins, you can save that evil look for someone else. I have asked ahead of you."

"Don't I have a say in this?" asked John.

"John, you don't have to answer her right away. Take some time to think about it," Hannah interjected.

"John, your mother is right. Do not answer me now. You have other obligations, and I do want you to be sure before you answer."

"Yes, and I'd like to speak with John, too." Miss Hawkins announced, standing.

"Miss Hawkins, please sit down and mind your own business," Margaret slung her fury at Elaine.

"This is my business, too, you know, Miss Pretender."

John seemed to have landed on another planet. He was too stunned to follow the two women. He had never been proposed to before. What did a gentleman do in this situation?

Margaret could feel Peggy holding her hand, holding her firm in her words.

"*Pretender*? Is that the best you can do, Miss Hawkins?"

"John, stop them," shouted his mother.

John finally caught up to the fact that two women were fighting over him. He decided to enjoy it. If anyone could hold her own, it would be Margaret. If this was her being herself, he couldn't be more proud.

"Mother, let them talk," he responded. "I shall make my own decisions, no matter what they say." He folded his arms and sat back. "Please, continue."

Nicholas was about to lose his dinner from laughing.

Hannah hung her head. "This would never have happened if I still lived here."

"No, it wouldn't have," John observed, "and I would have been sorry to miss this. Where were we? Oh yes, Miss Hawkins, I think it is your serve." John smiled and waved on Elaine.

"John, what's the matter with you? Are you going to sit there and allow this mealy-mouth bag of bones speak to me that way?"

John covered his mouth to stop showing his enjoyment.

"John, I believe you should take 'Miss Hawkins' home. She can't stand her own ground."

"Listen, sweetie …."

Margaret gushed out laughter. John's cheeks were ready to burst from holding it all in.

"Pardon me, Miss Hawkins. You were saying …."

"You wheedled your way back into John's life … and–."

"Wait a minute. You forgot the 'Listen Sweetie' part. I liked that. Go on," Margaret smarmed.

Elaine was becoming exasperated.

"Excuse me. Miss Hale, you have broken this man's heart once before and nearly broke his spirit, I have heard. Many know this. Do you mock him by proposing? Don't you think you will be an embarrassment to him … living near the Princeton area? Can't you see he feels sorry for you? He picked you out of the gutter."

"I cannot deny anything you say, but I am sitting here at his dinner table. Does it look like he cares where I lived two weeks ago? I'm not forcing him to marry me. He's not trapped. He can say 'No.' He knows I love him. Have you said those words? Look at him, does he look like his spirit is broken? Answer this, have you ever heard him laugh?" Margaret folded her arms, waiting. "I'm waiting, Miss Hawkins. With me he smiles and laughs all the time. I will make him happy. Can *you*?"

Elaine looked at John. He was transfixed by Margaret.

"John, she's going to make a fool out of you. The Masters will whisper behind your back. You will lose face among your peers. You will slip from your pedestal of being the lead Mill Master among hundreds. Your status will suffer. Tell me you don't care about that."

"I don't care about that. Apparently you do. If you took the time to know me, you would know that I shun the limelight. I am no different than any other man out there working."

"So … after a year of moping around, losing interest in everything, and now she reenters your life, what will people say about you?"

"They will say I am a lucky man."

"Have you ever thought that this may be pity you're feeling? Do you really think it is love which you have for her?"

"No. I don't think I love her, I know I love her."

"You bastard! You can both go to hell!"

"Bye," Margaret said, and she waved.

Elaine Hawkins threw her dinner napkin on the floor and stormed down the steps.

Nicholas stood up. "Miss Hawkins and Mrs. Thornton, I will escort you to my carriage and have my driver take you home. I can see that John isn't in any shape to stop this. Look at him. He's been bewitched."

"Thank you, Mr. Higgins. I will accept your ride home," quietly responded Mrs. Thornton.

"John, we will have Branson take us home."

“Margaret, the tables have turned. I believe he is the one that needs nursing. Evidently, he’s in shock.” Nicholas laughed. Peggy hugged her. “That a girl, good show.”

Chapter Thirty

"Mrs. Thornton, haven't you anything to say about your son's behavior tonight?" asked Miss Hawkins.

Hannah sat on the bench end with her hand holding onto the window frame. She was in deep thought. She could never remember such a sight at any dinner party in memory. "I'm sorry," she said, looking up at Miss Hawkins. "Did you say something?"

"Yes, I was wondering what you thought of John tonight."

"I have ceased interfering in my son's personal affairs. He has matured into an intelligent, compassionate gentleman. He can make his own way in life."

"Didn't you find Miss Hale forward and vulgar?"

"I was quite taken aback by her conduct, but I do believe she was prompted to react. I know where she was in her mind, though. She was protecting the man she loves. I can see why my son loves her. She is spirited, she is brave, and she is independent. I believe it is her spirited nature that John finds her greatest attraction. She is not of your caliber, Miss Hawkins."

"She certainly isn't of my caliber. She's only modestly pretty and has little to offer a man. I think John is just suffering a temporary blindness because she's in his house."

"You will forgive me, Miss Hawkins," said John's mother firmly. "I believe you did not understand me correctly. She is not of your caliber. She is *better* than your caliber. You embarrassed yourself tonight. If John felt any guilt concerning you because he was going to marry Margaret rather than you, you have certainly relieved him of it, and I thank you for that. Tonight I witnessed the two parts of a whole. They complement each other. They have loved each other for a very long time. I was the one who caused the interruption in their lives. I shall nay do that again."

The Higgins driver pulled the coach to a stop and jumped down. He opened the door and extended his arm for Miss Hawkins.

Before exiting the coach, she said to Mrs. Thornton, "Someday he'll be sorry he didn't pick me." Elaine turned and headed towards her door, with the driver trailing her.

Hannah Thornton sat back and returned to the evening she had just experienced. A year ago, she thought she had seen in Margaret an immature, thoughtless young woman. Tonight changed all that. John had recognized Margaret's spirit back then. Why hadn't she seen what John saw? Why couldn't she believe that he knew what was right for him? Hannah knew that he had tried to please her, as a good son would, though she had relentlessly tried to manage his life to suit her standards. She felt old. Times were changing, and she wasn't. She would gladly accept Margaret as a daughter-in-law without reservations. She had some new pillowcases to embroider, she foresaw.

Peggy, meanwhile, was quizzing her husband. "What did you think of tonight, Nicholas? What did you see that surprised you?"

"What did I see that surprised me? Where do I start? Let me see … I knew Margaret was independent and that perhaps she could be aggressive if she needed to be so. But the vehemence she displayed is another matter. She had quite a bit of self-control, as well. Miss Hawkins was crude at times, but Margaret didn't sink to her level. No one could doubt that she is deeply in love with John."

"Nicholas, you may find this hard to believe, but most women have that within them to protect their man. I think we know the lengths that a man would go to secure the love of a woman, but it is rarely expected from us. It lies in wait all of our lives and grows stronger when children come along."

"So you would do that for me?"

"Without giving it a second thought. It is a natural instinct. It was quite easy for a woman to tell that Miss Hawkins, although speaking a good game, had very little love for John. She wanted him as a husband as she would want a trophy or a medal."

"You saw that?"

"I am sure Margaret did not know if Elaine was truly in love with John before tonight. But as I saw the truth, so, clearly, did she. It became obvious how she saw John. Being on his arm, he would be showing her off, all the while the women would look up to her. Sometimes men are so dense," Peggy laughed.

"Don't ever underestimate John's knowledge of women. I'm sure many of the ladies in his company had the same thoughts. John instinctively knew that."

"I am sure you are right. What else did you see tonight?"

"I will save John until last. And I think I need no words on Miss Hawkins. Mrs. Thornton surprised me. Something has changed in her. I believe she was proud of Margaret's fighting for her son. Near the beginning, she was her old self, telling John not to make a decision quickly. But as the conversation continued, I believe there was pride in her eyes when she looked at Margaret. I think these two women will get on well together, after all. Now I must mention my wife."

"Me?"

"I did not miss the way that you picked up Margaret's hand and squeezed it. You were giving her support and courage to continue. We know how badly Margaret felt about her reduced circumstances. Some of the things that Miss Hawkins was saying to her may have hit home. Margaret could have buckled in spirit as she previously had in health. She might have done well on her own, but I think your taking her hand pushed her over the finish line."

"Thank you, my dear husband."

"I think we all saw a John that has never been known to this world tonight, not even to himself. He went through so many emotions that I laughed seeing him getting confused. First, well … none of us expected Margaret to propose, especially John. We all knew what Margaret was doing, well ahead of him. If I know John, he has probably practiced asking for her hand a thousand times. He just could not grasp what she was saying. From there he went to some euphoric place. He was not there with us for a few moments, and had a blank expression I've never seen on him before. I think he was dreaming about his future. And then the laughter and the smiles and the banter burst forth. He even shushed his mother. As any man would, he gloated in the fact that two women were fighting over him. And they weren't fighting for him over a date, or a dinner out, or some piece of time with him. They were fighting for ownership." Nicholas chuckled.

"I think every man must imagine that once in his life. But knowing John as I do, he believed Margaret would prevail. I am sure if he felt any harm could come to her, be it mental or emotional, he would have stopped the discussion. I'm sure this will always be one of his proudest moments of his wife-to-be."

John had turned off the dining room gaslights and all but one off in the sitting room, lowering it, instead. No words were said after the last person left. Margaret was at the window watching John's carriage carrying the Higgins home.

She was shaking so badly that her teeth chattered.

John removed his vest and walked up to Margaret and stood behind her. He lightly wrapped his arms around her waist, drawing her against him. "You overwhelm me." He whispered behind her ear.

Margaret placed her arms over his. She felt him nuzzling her neck. Her eyes closed eliciting a sigh.

John started kissing one side from ear to shoulder and then the other. "You were a firebrand tonight. My firebrand."

"Oh, John, I'm shaking."

"I know. Don't you think I can feel your body against mine?"

"What is a firebrand?"

"In simple terms, a firebrand is a troublemaker."

"Hold me tighter. My knees are going to give way."

John picked her up and sat in his big chair with her on his lap. He guided her head towards his chest after removing his cravat. Wrapping an arm around her, he unpinned her hair with the other and buried his nose in it.

"Does it smell like smoke?"

"Like smoke?"

"You said I was a fire something."

"I'm afraid you set me on fire tonight. Nothing will ever put out this flame you ignited in me. You will forever light my life."

John's words were whispers, low and soft. He was drawing in all of her essence as he spoke.

"You seem to be shaking more now than before. Are you afraid of me?"

"We need to talk about tonight before you muddle me further."

"Do you like what I am doing?"

"Far more than I should."

"Margaret, that's not possible. You should have every pleasant experience that exists. This is only the beginning." John turned her face towards him with the tip of his finger on her chin. In the moonlight from the window, he saw her frightened eyes looking at his.

With his bent finger he outlined her face, while she looked at him with her head in the crook of his arm. His fingertip slowly moved over her lips. He continued to trace her face, around her eyes, down her nose, and then ran his splayed fingers through her hair. When her eyes closed, he kissed her, holding the back of her head with his hand. He kissed gently over and over, on all parts of her mouth, until she began to respond on her own.

"Margaret, I love loving you," he whispered.

Margaret instinctively brought her arm up to his neck and held tight. She heard John moan while his lips were on hers.

He let her breathe while wrapping both arms around her, holding her tight against his chest. "Oh God, how I love you. I want to love you like this until you push me away."

Margaret gently pushed him back but remained sitting in his lap. "John, I need some answers before I can relax and receive what you wish to give. I'm not free yet to give myself either."

"By all means. Let's settle all questions now. I am not sure I can ever be as proud of you as I was tonight. You were incredible … no, not even that word is enough. I was stunned, yet at the same time in total awe of you. I love you for your spirit, and you outdid yourself this evening. I believe you impressed my mother–did we ever imagine that could happen? Go ahead. What are these questions that keep you from trusting yourself to me?"

"Can I get up and sit over there?" she asked, pointing to the other big chair across from his.

"Yes. Whatever makes you comfortable. I have a question myself."

"I will answer it if I can."

"Will you answer it honestly?"

"John, I will answer you honestly, not matter what pain the truth gives you or me I think we should know exactly where we are in each other's life."

"I strongly feel the same. I hope I have always been truthful in my responses to you. I might tease once in a while, but never when it means much to us."

"Yes, I noticed that tonight."

"In what way?"

"You didn't tell me I wasn't getting lamb."

John chuckled. "A few of us were in on that. We were amazed at how well you hid your disappointment. You smiled almost the entire time."

"Not inside." She smiled. "You had a question?"

John sat forward in his chair with his elbows on his knees. Touching his fingertips to each hand, he looked down. "I may have inadvertently led you to believe you needed to perform, as if on a stage, tonight. I hope you know that was never my intention. I just wanted them to know you as I do. To see what I see. To be yourself. Was anything you said tonight staged?"

"I had hoped I had the courage to propose to you in front of Miss Hawkins. Nothing beyond that, and I wasn't doing it to shock her. I was sincere. I thought you would be happy."

John went to her on his knees. "I cannot begin to tell you how that felt. It still hasn't found a place in my mind yet. I am taking it in by small doses. I want to talk about that with you at a later time."

"You never answered me."

"I realize that now. We will marry, and soon. There is no doubt about that. I am not sure my manhood and many hours of practicing can give up the fact that I am not the one doing the asking. Are you now convinced that, should I accept, I do out of love, not pity?"

"I don't know, really. I was afraid Miss Hawkins might ask. I didn't want to lose you."

"You do me much honor. Margaret Hale, I have looked for someone like you since adulthood. It was last year when I finally found you. Finding you after so long only to lose you was just about the end of me. I love you even more than I did then. I cannot only have you in my life, but must have you as my wife. Margaret Hale, I have no ring to give right now, but it would be the greatest pleasure ever known to me, if you would accept me as your husband.

"Can I think about it?" Margaret laughed out loud and threw her arms around him.

John unclutched her arms and pushed her back. "I want a yes or no answer, right now."

"Well … You know I will. Yes. And yes again."

John pulled her from the chair and lay her on the carpeted floor.

"Let's go to bed." John whispered. "We can just lie there and hold one another. We can begin to know each other. We won't do anything that you don't want. You could stand all night if you wanted, just let me hold you. I have waited so long to feel your warmth against me."

"I wasn't finished with my questions."

"What are they … and no, you can't sit up."

"Miss Hawkins …."

John kissed her to stop hearing that name.

"Wait. Wait. I must hear your words on this. She said words I cannot deny."

"Margaret, let me say this first, and then see if you need to ask about what you want to know. First, yes, you were in a low place. No, I do not care about that now, nor have I ever. I do not care if there is talk behind my back, though I sincerely doubt that would ever happen. I am proud of you. Marrying you will not affect my reputation or position in the mills, but I wouldn't care if it did. I would give up all of this to have you. I would give up my family, my home, the mill that is my primary source of income, if doing so were necessary for us to be together. Under no circumstances should you give any weight to what she said. She was not only rude but evil, if you ask me. Does that answer your questions?

"I think you covered all the points," Margaret smiled.

John stood and pulled her up to a standing position. "You may move where you please. I will not guide or lead you. Your wish is my command."

"My wish was to marry you, but you wiggled out of that command."

"Yes, Margaret. I will marry you. Next?"

"Will you visit Miss Hawkins tomorrow and exit that relationship better than how it went tonight?"

"Yes, I will."

"Will you talk with your mother and see what she now thinks of me?"

"I don't care what she thinks."

"I know you don't, but I do."

"All right. I will do so."

"And you will tell me the truth when you return?"

"As forever, I will."

"Will you hold me in your arms on your bed?"

"I thought you would never ask." He grinned.

Margaret sat on the edge of the bed, where John placed her. John bent down and removed her shoes. He sat beside her and removed his own boots.

"Margaret, I can feel you shaking. I am going to assume that it is nervousness, not fear. Nothing will happen. And do not think I expect anything at all. You asked me to hold you in my arms on this bed, and I could live my life happily on that privilege alone. So, lay where you will, and I will lay beside you. "

Margaret scooted to the other side and tried to get comfortable with all of her crinolines puffing about her. She lay on her back and clasped her hands across her stomach.

John moved next to her and asked, "Do you prefer my arm across your waist like this or would you rather lay with your head on my shoulder?"

"Does it matter to you?"

"I want what you want, but I will tell you a little secret. On my shoulder I can take in the fragrance of your hair and kiss the top of your head. With my arm across your waist, your lips stand a better than even chance of being kissed there."

Margaret let out a nervous twitter of a laugh. "And I have to decide this?"

"No, I could make the decision, but you have never been with me nor any other man before. I cannot know your wants or desires or fears. That is why I am letting you decide. In the future, I will usually make the decisions.

"You decide."

John held her to his chest with both arms around her for most of the night. She did roll away from him at one time, and he took the opportunity to close his door. With his arms wrapped around her, he could feel how restricted she was in a corset. He knew she shouldn't have done so, for corsets made breathing and moving difficult, all to attract a man. She would never have to wear one again.

Chapter Thirty One

John was up and dressed before Margaret opened her eyes. He thought the past evening's performance must have taken a lot out of her. He was glad to see she had finally slept well.

As he went down to get his paper, Nicholas caught sight of him and waved him over to the office. Being in such a grand mood, he trotted over.

"Good morning, John."

"Yes, it is. Truly the best morning in my life."

"Peggy and I wondered how Margaret was. That must have been a great strain on her last night. I can't tell you how much we enjoyed it. We were both so proud of her, as I am sure you must be."

"Indeed. We had quite a talk after everyone left. I still can't believe what she did. I had to propose to her myself. I think my male pride was slightly bruised, after waiting so long to say the words. It's very hard to believe that the day has come that she has accepted me. I haven't spoken to her since she fell asleep last night, but she should wake with no remorse. She has asked me to speak with Miss Hawkins and sever our relationship more clearly and more kindly."

"I cannot be sure of this, but I think maybe your mother was impressed by Margaret last night. Your mother had a look of awe on her face and no sign of the embarrassment she felt before."

"That is another of today's tasks; Margaret cares what my mother thinks, and would appreciate a sense of how accepting my mother may now be. Nicholas, I am going to speak with Margaret and see if we can have a small wedding in the very near futurc. Today I hope she will allow me to purchase a wedding ring. "

"I believe she has always thought that if her father could not give her away at her wedding, she would ask Mr. Bell. Is there still no word on him?"

John pulled a note from his inside pocket. It was becoming tattered, having been folded many times. "Read this. I received it just recently. I have been waiting for the follow-up letter from his solicitor before I spoke with Margaret. I have not received anything, as yet. I am not sure what to make of it."

Nicholas sat down at his desk. "This is certainly a sad letter and will affect Margaret considerably–though it would've been much worse, had she received it two weeks ago. She was in such a low state then."

"Do you think I should assume that he is still alive?"

"Only you can answer that. Whether he is alive or has passed on, I think you should share it with Margaret before you marry her. It shouldn't affect anything, but she should not think that you held something back from her. It's a cruel fate to have to give her potentially bad news on one of her happiest days ever. Another thing before you go–what should we do about the small cottage? You say you wish to marry very soon; it would seem there is no use for it now."

"We shall continue with our plans. My sister will marry soon enough, and I will bring mother back here if that is her wish. In fact, I think I will speak to her about it today. I just wonder how Margaret would feel knowing that she was only a few steps away from her in-laws, yet spoke with them rarely. Don't start anything until I have checked with my women," John smiled.

"I assume you will wait until Margaret is fully recovered?" Nicholas asked.

"I seem to doubt that."

"But she's so fragile."

"I think I know that better than anyone. Marriage would not be rushed just to consummate it. I just want to hold her and have her next to me. I must return."

Nicholas smiled as John went out the door. Why did he ever doubt the man? No harm would ever come to Margaret because of his own actions.

Margaret was awake and downstairs talking with Maddie and Cook. John rushed down the stairs to the kitchen.

"Good morning, ladies. Margaret, I hope you had someone assist you on the steps."

Maddie spoke up and said that she was with her and did very well.

"Good morning, John. The ladies tell me I am gallant. And if you wouldn't mind, we would like to continue our female conversation," Margaret smiled.

A warm, tender emotion rolled through John. It was as if she had settled in and was making a place in his home for her. In the past, he had worried that she would never come to feel this place hers. But it seemed he was wrong. He smiled to himself, imagining what the women were talking about. Of course, the topic of conversation would be her proposal and her resolute stance against Miss Hawkins' accusations. John decided that, while the events of last night were still fresh in his mind, he would write an account of the night as he remembered it.

John went back upstairs and into his library. He pulled out a sheaf of paper and sat there with pen poised going over the evening again. He laughed out loud when he remembered Margaret telling Elaine that she forgot to say "Listen, Sweetie." She was brilliant. He started writing about her facial expression when she received her plate of liver. John wrote for nearly half an hour before placing the paper back in his desk and attending the breakfast table.

"How did my woman sleep last night?"

"I'm not sure. Was she here?"

John sat back in his chair with his knife in one hand and his fork in the other, straight-armed, with the utensils pointing to the ceiling. "So it's going to be like that, is it?"

"Whatever do you mean?"

"Well, let's forget about her for right now. How did *you* sleep last night? "John said with a big grin.

"I could tell there was someone next to me, but I was pretty sure it wasn't another housekeeper." Margaret snickered.

John's quiet laugh had his shoulders shifting up and down. That answer was priceless. "How did you determine that it wasn't a woman?"

"Something kept wiggling. I could feel it against my hip even through all of these petticoats."

John put his hands behind his head and blushed. "Did he keep you awake?"

"He? Oh, yes. That is why I was so late waking this morning. I was up all night trying to figure out what was causing that."

"I am afraid to ask, but did you have any success in discovering what was wiggling?"

"I tried to get your attention, but you were sleeping soundly. I thought I had not better investigate. Eventually the movement subsided, and I was able to rest. Would you pass the butter, please?"

"I am sorry about that. Nothing was planned in that regard. That was uncontrollable on my part even in my sleep."

"What exactly was uncontrollable?" Margaret asked.

"Here's the butter." John went silent.

"Margaret, what shall you do while I go and bare my soul to these women you wish me to talk with?"

"Could you stop at Mr. Griffin's Mill and ask him to come calling?"

"Are you sure you are up to company?"

"I think I showed you that last night. Do we keep our engagement a secret?"

"I will have an announcement placed in the paper before we are to be wed."

"Really?"

"Yes. Do you mind?"

"Not unless it will embarrass you. I know you don't want me to think that or say that. I just need one more assurance that you know what you're getting yourself into."

"Don't be too long with Cecil. I want to buy you a wedding ring today."

"So early?"

"It may seem early to you, but not to me."

John was off. He met with Cecil Griffin first, who would make time that morning to see Miss Hale. Then, he continued on to visit Miss Hawkins.

The butler at Elaine Hawkins' residence that morning announced a familiar visitor. "Mr. Thornton, to see you, Miss."

"Well … show him in."

"Good morning, Elaine." John did not hand his hat to the butler this time. He held it.

"And what do I owe the honor of this visit? Was not everything said last night?"

"You have not heard my words." John said.

"Sit and please continue."

"First of all, I apologize for the way the evening went, for your sake. I had no former knowledge that anything like that was to take place."

"I assume it pleased you."

"Yes, it did. I believe I made it clear that I did not know what I was looking for in a wife, the last we spoke. However, I was honest when I said I hadn't found it in you. Talking and being in the company of Miss Hale since she left the hospital brought about the realization of what was missing in all other women. Perhaps you saw it for yourself last night. It is her courage, independence and spirit. I must admit, I was taken aback last night, though. We were able to resolve our misunderstandings from a year ago. Although we both tried to deny the other's existence, it seems our hearts never did. Miss Hawkins–."

"Please, John, spare me the details of what a wonderful woman I am, and how I will find the right man who will love me unconditionally, and all such nonsense. I don't need to hear it. I will tell you that I found you attractive and too polite. With your hard-earned wealth, good looks and community standing, I pursued you. I don't think I ever really loved you, either. I will deny this if you tell anyone, but I quite admired Miss Hale for her courage to propose. I should never have done such a thing. I think there is little more we have to say to each other. I wish you well. Good day."

Elaine genuinely seemed to mean her words, so John had no guilt when he said his goodbye. It had been over in minutes, and he left without scars and a clear conscience.

Still being a Magistrate, John stopped by the courthouse and began the paperwork for his marriage. The clerk was surprised and happy for him and promised not to mention it to anyone.

Before reaching his mother's flat, came the Milton Messenger. Branson waited for a fairly long time before his master reappeared. "To Mrs. Thornton's, Branson."

"Soon there will be two." Branson beamed.

"Two what?"

"Two Mrs. Thorntons."

"So there will. So there will."

When he arrived at his mother's door, Jane saw him in.

"Good morning, Mother, Fanny."

"Mother was telling me about last night. Were you surprised that she asked you? The nerve."

"Yes, I was quite surprised and think it was the best hour of my life. The nerve, as you call it, is what has held me back from marrying anyone else. I love her nerve. I love her wit, energy and everything about her. Now, Fanny, I would like to talk with mother. You may stay, but please don't interrupt."

John turned to his mother.

"Mother, I have come to say that Margaret and I will marry soon. An announcement will be in the paper within a few weeks. She is the woman I have waited for all my life. I would like your blessing, but Margaret is more concerned for your feelings than I think she should be. I would like to know how you feel about our marriage. Please be truthful. It will not stop me marrying her, but I would like to know what lies ahead for she and I and you."

"John, you can put your mind at ease, and Miss Hale's also. I saw your face last night. I saw the pride that you had for her. It warmed my heart to the girl. I've never seen such contentment in you since you were a child. I hope that she will forgive me, and that you will, too. I should have known that you knew what was best for yourself a year ago. I pushed you into that proposal, and it was the worst mistake of my life. I have had a year of watching your own spirit slip away. You have found it again. You are alive, and I see that. I see that she is the reason for it. I am sure we will get along grand."

"Mother, thank you. Your words overwhelm me. As much as I love her, I wanted you to love her too. She will not drive a wedge between us, as I have feared."

"No, that will not happen."

"I'm getting married soon, too, John." Fanny announced.

"I think I have known that was coming. Which puts me in mind, mother, that I am building a small cottage on the mill property. I thought it was going to be for Margaret, but she will not need it. Once Fanny is married, I hope you will consider moving there."

"Thank you, John. I will have to think about it. I am settling into this area, and have already made some friends. I think it might be hard to return to Marlborough Mills and live with all that noise. I know that is your home, and it must be Margaret's too. The two of you do not need me living next door. I'm not sure I would like knowing what my married son is doing with a woman in his home," she smiled. "I will always think of you as my son. I cannot think of you as a husband or father just yet."

"Mother, thank you. Margaret will thank you when she can. You have made us both happy. I must go. Margaret is expecting someone. I would like to be there when he arrives."

"He?"

"In her hour of need, she went searching for work. She found two weeks of clerking for one of the newer mill masters. He is visiting to understand how she will set up his books. She is extremely knowledgeable. Nicholas wants to hire her right away, but I think it will be after our marriage holiday."

"Have you any thoughts with that?"

"It's barely been 12 hours. We haven't talked about much yet. She was exhausted last night, so we did not talk into the night."

"Then it best you get home to be with her. Thank you for coming to see me this morning. I'm glad to hear your words on the subject that shocked us all last night. Oh, Miss Hawkins?"

"That was finalized before coming here. It was quite amicable."

"Good. Take care, son. I shall have the two of you for dinner soon."

"No, I shall take you two out for dinner."

"I will look forward to that."

Cecil Griffin was glad to see Margaret looking a little better. He had not known much about her weakness, but her paleness was quite apparent when he met her.

Margaret ordered tea and invited Mr. Griffin to spread his ledgers across the dining room table. He brought various invoices to understand her organization of expenses. They had been working on it for an hour when John returned home. He greeted Cecil and said he would leave them in private unless there were any questions that he could help with, as the Mill Works' current President.

At the moment Cecil had no questions, so John disappeared into his study and closed the door. He walked to his window, then decided to walk the mill. His time was soon going to be engaged elsewhere.

"Pardon me," he said as he passed through the room. "Miss Hale, I will be in the mill sheds if you need me. Send Maddie for me."

"Yes, Mr. Thornton."

"He tends to hover." Margaret told Mr. Griffin after John had left.

"I would think most of us men would do no different." Cecil smiled. "Miss Hale, this is very presumptuous of me and I know not the entire situation of your illness. I would like to invite you to the Master's Ball, as my guest, if you feel up to it. I wouldn't expect any dancing, unless you wanted to. You would honor me just keeping me company."

"You hardly know me. That is so kind of you. That lifts my spirits, but I am sorry to tell you that I have been spoken for by Mr. Thornton."

"Oh, I see. Well, I shall wish you a grand time of it, anyway. Perhaps some time in the future." He thought Thornton to be a kind man to offer to take her out.

It was nearing one in the afternoon. Margaret and Cecil concluded their meeting. Margaret was thanked profusely and Cecil left.

John had been mulling around in the office after walking the sheds, just waiting to go home. He looked about the room and imagined what it might look like with Margaret at a desk in the same room. He wasn't sure she would ever take to the sheds, but her use was going to be of great help in the office. Finally he heard a coach rolling away. He wondered when would be a good time to tell her about Mr. Bell.

Margaret heard John coming up the stairs. She began to waltz with an invisible partner, as she hummed. John smiled, when he entered the room, and walked over to her to take her hands and dance with her.

"Excuse us, Mr. Thornton. It is rude to cut in without asking." Margaret continued around the room.

John stood there with his arms folded, constantly watching and turning in her direction.

Margaret would occasionally mimic speaking and then listening and smiling to her partner.

John, smiling with his rolled up hand to his mouth, decided to tap the unseen gent on the shoulder and ask permission. Margaret dropped her arms, but stopped humming. John lifted her arms and looked at her face.

"Mr. Thornton, the waltz has concluded." She pretended to pencil him in on her invisible dance card.

Finally John laughed out loud.

"Mr. Thornton, you may have the third waltz."

"I am sorry, Miss Hale. I am engaged on the third and fourth waltzes." He chuckled, getting even with her.

"Oh, Mr. Thornton, I am sorry to hear that. It seems you will have to wait until the next Master's Ball unless you shoot someone ahead of you in line." Margaret's laughter gurgled.

John rushed over, lifted her and twirled her around the room with his lips upon hers.

After the two finished dancing and laughing, John set her down on the floor.

"Come, tell me how your visits went this morning."

"Must you hear them? I am smiling. Shouldn't that be enough?"

"Even so … your mother?"

"More so because of her. You have won her over and quite handily, I believe."

"I didn't embarrass her?"

"I think at first she was taken aback, but she was proud of you before it was over. She now sees and understands why I love you so much."

"Why do you love me so much?"

"Oh … perhaps on our wedding night, I will tell you. You'll just have to trust me." He preened.

"It wouldn't make any difference anyway. I would still love you, as I have, thinking you didn't love me. No one could have replaced you in my heart."

John pulled her to him and initiated a lustful kiss. He held her tight as he kissed her long and hard. His tongue searched for her opening. Finding it, he gently pushed the tip of his tongue through, parting her lips. He felt her brace to repel, but he continued on, holding the back of her head steady. Margaret relaxed.

To Margaret it felt intrusive and wrong, but before she could give that much thought, John was passionately taking his pleasure and giving her a new sensation. His body was invading hers. He had broken down the walls to take her as his own. It was more sensuous than she imagined. A streak of lightning from her mouth to her lower parts seemed to connect the two. She felt weak and powerless to change it. It was thrilling, which held embarrassment at bay.

John sensed her instability and stopped. He gently guided her backwards to a chair. "Margaret, that was so pure and heavenly. I'm almost shaking myself from the intense emotion coming from you. You accepted me. Next time I will seek more."

"Next time? I'm not sure what happened this time. Is that still called a kiss or something else?"

"Did you enjoy it?"

"I shan't think that *enjoy* begins to cover it."

"I hope to kiss you like that always when we are alone. I wonder if there were other feelings that you had."

Margaret blushed. John was chagrinned.

"That's why we wait to be alone."

"Because of …those …."

"Yes. I want to take my time leading you to your coming of age."

"I find no words."

"I know. I am experiencing the same as you. Love is powerful. It moves us, compels us to be one. We want to draw the very being of the other into us, here to live forever. When I tell you that you are my life, I mean I want your soul to dwell with mine beyond forever. We move toward a need to be sustained by one another."

"How do you know all this?"

"Because it is in my heart, right now." John lifted her hand and held it to his rapid heartbeat. He placed his own hand on hers.

"We feel it in each other."

Chapter Thirty Two

The delicate, intimate moment was interrupted by the sound of dishes being carried on a tray upstairs.

"What shall we be having for lunch today, Maddie?"

"Sir, today it will be a light meal of lentil soup and bread followed by a custard."

"Excellent. I'm sure Miss Hale appreciates that."

"She gave us very little choice. Neither of us wished to be dismissed if we fed her liver again." Maddie laughed, while Margaret snickered.

"You didn't really threaten them, did you?"

"In my own way," Margaret said coyly.

John smiled and seated Margaret at the table.

"Margaret, I have two important tasks to do today. One will be most pleasant, the other quite the opposite. You will be an intricate part of both. Are you particular about the way I proceed?"

"Let's save the pleasant one until last."

"All right. Let me preface the first one by saying, nothing is known for sure."

"Go on."

"About two weeks ago, shortly after your trip here for employment, I received a letter from Adam Bell."

"You did? The look on your face tells me it was not good news."

"That is so. It was a sad letter that presumed he was nearing his end. He would not be returning to England. He had waited too long. It did not sound like he knew of your father's passing, but I cannot be sure."

"Why did he write to you and not me?"

"He knew my feelings for you would always remain and that I would help you through his passing."

Margaret began to cry.

"He did have some private words to me," John continued, "about the two of us, which in the future I will let you read. I will say they were most complimentary."

"Why didn't you tell me before now?"

"There are two reasons for that. If you remember, you were in very low spirits. I worried to burden you with more. Mainly, the reason was that he said a note should follow from his solicitor for your inheritance after I received that note. There may be a chance that he did not die, for I have never received the follow-on letter."

"May I read it now, please?"

"Are you sure?"

"Yes."

John pulled the letter from his inside vest pocket. He handed it to Margaret. She looked at it and slowly pulled it from his fingers. Margaret looked down on it for some moments before she began to unfold it.

Her eyes welled immediately. John handed her his handkerchief as she sniffled through the reading.

"He knew about us more than we did ourselves, didn't he?"

"Yes."

"He was our family's closest friend, and now he is gone."

"Well, we're not certain of that, but forthcoming papers could take a while."

Margaret leaned over and cried into John's chest. He stroked her back and gave her comforting words.

"He loved you a lot."

"I know. At one point he was hinting at proposing. No one knew that. But he dismissed the idea, so that I did not have to be beholding or reject him."

"So, he was one of the men you spoke to about not knowing what to say when a man proposed?"

"Yes."

"I'm sorry. There was Henry Lenox, of course."

"Yes."

"Do you feel like good news now, or would you rather wait for a later time?"

"Give me a few moments."

"Take whatever time you need."

Margaret slipped into her bedchamber. She knew she needed a good cry.

John would let her go for only so long, and then he would go to comfort her. This was a time, he felt, she needed him. He wanted to be needed by her. That was an ingrained, God-given male instinct to protect his mate. He felt it very strongly at the moment. It was a new sensation to him. John felt at ends with himself. He paced the floor and periodically would listen at her door. He went to the lavatory for a cool cloth for her eyes.

Returning, he knocked gently and opened the door. Margaret was laid across her bed. He crossed to the side where her head lay and stroked the wisps of hair from her face. Her eyes, nose and mouth were running. John pulled her to his lap and wiped her face. The sniffles slowed as he cooled her brow.

"I love you, John Thornton."

John crushed her to his chest until she could hardly breathe.

Margaret needed that. She knew she wasn't alone any more. John's love would see her through anything. So far he had pulled her from poverty, illness and now this. She curled up in a ball in his lap and never wanted to leave the comfort and protection of her place beside him.

"I need you, John Thornton." She said, slinging her arm around him.

"As I need you."

"Thank you."

"Margaret, never thank me. It isn't a courtesy I am extending."

"I know. I mean … I know that. It isn't easy to understand these exceedingly deep feelings … to know they are for me and real."

"And there will be more to come for us. Get your bonnet. We're going for a ride. I need to get Branson ready."

"Where are you taking me, John?"

"I want you to pick out your wedding ring."

"Now?"

"We will be married quietly the day before the Master's Ball. I would like our announcement to come out that day. I want to show you off. Am I expecting too much to ask this of you?"

John saw her hands begin to shake. "I *am* asking too much. I am sorry."

"No, don't be sorry. I … I … just have doubts in myself of being a good wife to you."

"Is it fear of me?"

"No. Dear, no."

"Then what?"

"I find it hard to talk about ... my coming of age."

"I think I see. You will continue to fear that until it happens. That I think would be normal. A man has usually experienced that long before marriage. Will you let me prove to you there is only bliss that lies down that path?"

"Prove to me?"

"I will let your own desires guide you. I will not."

"Have you ever treated a woman like that?"

"No, but I am not afraid with you. I am confident that you still have much to discover about yourself."

"How do we start?"

"I will worry about that, not you. Just remember the feelings you had when I kissed you deeply earlier today. You thought that was pleasant, didn't you?"

"Yes, but I didn't do anything."

"Yes, you did. You reacted to me."

"Yes … but …"

"But, it's a place to start. We are not in a race. I am not in a hurry to know you that way. Whatever rumors you may have heard at school or growing up doesn't mean it will be the same for us."

John turned to Margaret as they sat on the coach bench. "Believe me when I say this. The pleasure I get is from the pleasure I give to you. Don't ever worry about my desires or needs. And I don't love you more for your feminine female body, I love you for who you are. Are you embarrassed or afraid to be alone in the house with me at night? It seems that situation has arisen."

"You're saying too much. I cannot understand it all. No, I am not afraid of being alone at night. Never with you. I would like to know if you will be satisfied with me as a wife is to her husband."

"That's all you need to say. I will take care of the rest." John leaned over and kissed her. "It seems we're here."

"Where?"

"At the jewelers."

"But this is the expensive place."

"I brought you here. You did not ask to come here. Can we go inside?"

"All right."

"Mr. Thornton, isn't it? This is a rare pleasure, indeed."

"We would like to look at wedding rings."

"I would be most honored to show you what we have."

Tray after tray, the jeweler set out rings by the dozens. "As you can see, we have various stones, cuts, sizes, old and new."

"Do you see anything you particularly like?" John asked.

"I would like what you pick out for me. Would you please do the honors?"

"If you wish. I would love to."

John went down the rows, skipping over the large gaudy and fancy stones. He knew they did not show Margaret's countenance.

"John, I want that one!"

"It's a pretty, rather simple ring. Are you sure?"

"Quite sure. Do you like it?"

"I would have purchased something with more fire to it, to show your spirit."

"I think that is my mother's ring. I do not remember coming across it when I moved. I assume father had to sell it."

"You will have that, regardless, but I will select a stone for the woman I am going to marry."

Margaret's eyes watered. "Thank you, John. It isn't too expensive, is it?"

"It is truly affordable. We will not allow a family heirloom to be lost." John handed the ring to the jeweler and proceeded to find Margaret in a ring. "There it is." John reached for a beautiful ruby, cut in a marquise shape with small pearls around it.

"What do you think?"

"If it's what you wish to see on me, then I love it. I have little knowledge of stones or jewelry. I will treasure it, though."

"Mr. Thornton, you have made a wise choice. It is a bold stone for a wedding ring, but it is known to be the most powerful gem in the universe, if you believe the tales. It brings contentment and peace. Rubies should be worn on the left hand, it is said. Given as a gift, the ruby is the symbol for friendship, love and protection."

"Margaret?"

"Yes, John. We shall have it."

John wanted to kiss her there and then, but withheld it.

Branson was waiting by the coach door when John and Margaret exited. "Are we having a wedding, sir?"

"Please keep this to yourself."

"Yes, guv."

Before sitting down to dinner, the second post had come and John gladly handed Margaret a letter from Dixon. "I hope she has good news for you.

John sat away from her but watched her expression as she read it. It seemed to cheer her, so he went back to his paper. "Good news, I presume?"

"Yes, she is coming along very well. She is seeing a doctor in Oldham. It says he keeps telling her to slow down, as she feels better than she really is. She is enjoying staying with her sister and being waited on. Her sister's husband is sickly, so Dixon attends to his needs, which costs her little strength. She is allowed to cook twice a week. She asks how I am doing."

"That must put your mind at ease."

"Yes, it does. But I am reminded that I have received no more love notes." Margaret smiled to herself, sure in her mind that it had been John all along.

John was struck with the fact that he had forgotten about that since Margaret's proclamation.

"I sent the messenger back today and told him to tell the sender that Miss Hale would not be receiving them." John snapped his paper pages straight as if signaling an end to the conversation.

Margaret wanted to laugh.

"You should have sent the last one back with him?"

"Last one?"

"Yes, you know. The one in your desk drawer."

John put his paper down and walked to his library. He opened his desk drawer and there was a love note in progress. He was chagrinned. He could hear Margaret tittering from the next room.

He walked back to his paper and picked it up. He placed the paper between his eyes and Margaret's. "How long have you known?"

"Known? I never knew for sure at any time. But, I believe it started with the first small bouquet. Now, I know it was you. That was terribly sweet and brightened each day."

"I smell beef."

"Oh, that subject is over, is it?"

"I think it need go no further."

"Embarrassed to be a flower-giver?"

"No."

"How difficult was it, John? Did you leave it up to the vendor or select them yourself? Did you look for the freshest cuts? Do you know each flower conveys a meaning? What caused you to select the bunched small bouquet over a massive centerpiece of colors?"

"Now you know why I have never been a flower sender."

"I suppose that is a rare occurrence here in the north. Not so where I came from. Must write that in my journal … northern gentlemen do not give flowers."

"Do you keep a journal?"

"I once did. Looking over it, I could see it was depressing, so I stopped."

John stood and walked to his library again. He looked over his shelves of books and pulled out a blank journal. Taking it and handing it to Margaret, "You must start a new one. I would especially like to know what you will write over the coming weeks."

"You give me a blank journal and then expect to read what I write?"

"Yes. I would like to see me through your eyes," he smiled.

"Is that pride or vanity?"

John thought that a question of which either answer sounded bad. "It will be guide as to how I can pleasure you more."

Margaret gulped. "I smell beef, too."

John chuckled.

Night had fallen, the dishes cleared away and the staff had left for home. They were alone. It was late summer, and the evenings were beginning to chill. John lit a fire.

From the darkened side of the room, he watched Margaret, under the gas lamp, scribbling in her journal. At the moment, she had too little to do that these moments when she was busy and unaware of her surroundings, John was fascinated watching her. His heart was full. He kept fearing he would wake up and find it never happened, but now, with a ring in his pocket, he knew it was real.

"Must you watch me?" Margaret asked without raising her head.

"Yes."

"Haven't you anything better to do?"

"Yes."

Margaret kept writing and decided not to pursue that further.

John chuckled to himself, knowing why she quit.

"When do I take you back to the doctors for your next check-up?

"I wasn't actually given a date. I could go tomorrow, I guess."

"We will go tomorrow, I know."

"You are getting bossy, you know? You will have to remember to treat me differently from your workers or your staff."

"I know that well enough."

Margaret flipped to the back of her journal where she could draw anything. Anything to keep her head down.

"Margaret, you may change the subject as often as you like, but it will still come back to the same thing."

"And what is that?"

"You are treading water and afraid to come ashore," he grinned to himself.

"I am sure I don't know what you mean."

"Would you like to read together?"

"Yes, that's a nice idea. I'll get my book."

"You stay seated. You are comfortable and under the light. I'll get it."

John went to Margaret's room and found Austen's *Persuasion*. Returning, he sat at Margaret's feet, as she had the only light. He removed his boots and her shoes.

"Before you start reading that, I want to say something. Last night I put my arm over your waist. I was upset to know that you must have been troubled with sleeping in a corset. Tonight, please don't do that. We can have a night like last night, with just me holding you, but not totally dressed as we were. Put on your night shift and your night robe, if you will. I'll be in this shirt and trousers. Would you care to do that before we start reading?"

"Are you sure no one will visit?"

"No, I can never be sure with the mill next door, but I will be presentable to answer the door. I only need to slip on my boots. You may head to your bedchamber should that happen. That's what Fanny would do."

"I suppose so. I've been trussed up for two days, and it would be nice to be free of it. I shall return in a moment."

"Do you need any help?"

"I believe I can manage on my own now until such time as you take ownership of me."

"I am counting the days."

Margaret closed her door.

John went to his bedroom and pulled down the covers. He removed his vest, cravat, and socks before slipping off his bracers. He removed any coin in his pocket and also set the wedding ring on top of his bureau. He walked back out and sat in his big chair where the light was shining. He stood back up and closed the drape near the chair, giving Margaret a sense of privacy.

He returned to the chair just as Margaret came out of her room. "How would you like to work this? You can sit in a chair and I'll sit at your feet, or the reverse. Or you may lay in my arms, as you did last night."

"On your lap?"

"You've done that before."

"I think I had a lot of petticoats on at the time."

"However you wish, my love."

Margaret stood there, rather bewildered. John said nothing. No coaxing or smiling, just waiting. Margaret finally looked at John with a reddened face.

"I think I will take a step closer to shore and sit on your lap."

John held his smile at bay and sat down. "Margaret you can sit up and rest your head on my shoulder or you may recline, and I will hold you in the crook of my arm. You may want to work it so that you have enough light."

John sat there with his arms poised to help her get situated. He watched as Margaret looked down and pondered something. He knew he would embarrass himself any moment now and he wished she wouldn't be watching.

Margaret decided to sit up with her head leaning between his chest and shoulder. As she sat, John adjusted her with his arms so he could hold her and not break anything below.

When they were both settled, John turned her head to kiss her. It wasn't a deep fiery kiss. He then reached for the book beside him and handed it to Margaret.

"You start."

John listened as Margaret spoke about Sir Elliott and his vanity. There was an introduction of the other Elliott relatives and ancestry. John tried in vain, but within ten minutes Margaret stopped reading in midsentence.

"What was that?"

"Is it my turn to read?" John was trying to change the subject."

"There it goes again." She pulled back and looked at John's face. "You are doing that, aren't you? You're doing that wiggly thing again."

"I'm sorry. I cannot help it. I can do that when I want to, but it's very difficult to stop if I do not want it to happen."

"Is there a book on this, so I don't get embarrassed with you explaining it to me?"

John couldn't believe she said that and chuckled quietly. "It will all become clear when you have come ashore."

"Just how deep is this water I am in?"

John started to laugh and the wiggling stopped.

"Are my feet at least touching bottom? No, wait. Don't answer that question about touching bottom."

John took the book from her hands. "I think it is my turn to read."

"I bet because I asked for a book that you think I don't know anything about what you're doing."

"Margaret, I know you are an intelligent, educated woman who grew up with an older brother. I have no doubt you know why that is happening."

"I am not quite clear as to why, but I do know what is happening. My dilemma is how do you do that?"

"Are we reading or do you need an anatomy lesson?"

"I think you are reading."

John held her with one arm and held the book away in the other. He began reading where Margaret had left off. Every time Margaret moved against him, it started up again. He knew Margaret was conscious of it, but she was staying quiet. Eventually, it seemed to John that she was intentionally moving in order to prove something. He finally burst out laughing at her antics.

John dropped the book on the floor and wrapped Margaret in both arms. He moved her into the crook of his elbow so he could kiss her unconditionally. He kissed her and licked her lips until she parted them for him. As his tongue swarmed her mouth, she instinctively wrapped her arms around his neck. Though his embrace was giving her no quarter, his caress was tender, loving, and inviting. As their tongues would meet, Margaret began to feel changes in her body. She realized she had the feeling of cessation as if she wanted to surrender.

John's one hand began to roam up and down her arm. She tilted her head back, allowing him access to her beautiful neck that he had thought about for a year. He suckled lightly several places and licked and kissed all of it. Margaret felt him nuzzling her neck with his nose. Still his hand roamed. It seemed like it was moving everywhere but her breasts and female parts. She could hear herself breathing heavily. John returned to her mouth and plundered. Margaret became quite conscious of the fact that he had not touched her breast. Even though it was improper, she had a desire for him to alleviate their loneliness. She finally reached out and steadied his roaming hand. She held it with her splayed fingers for a moment before she guided it where it was needed.

He moaned. As John was being encouraged to pleasure her there, his kissing became more lustful and rapid. He paused long enough to stand, holding her in his arms, while he turned off the gaslight and parted the drape. His heart was beating rapidly, and he could tell that Margaret's was too. He immediately returned to her round, firm breast and began to circle her nipple. He felt her legs tremor.

"Do you like what I am doing, or are you just putting up with me?"

Nearly breathless, Margaret said, "Like?"

"Do you love what I am doing? I love what I am doing."

"Yes, I love what you are doing, but I feel as though I shouldn't love it this much. I am greedy."

"Did you say greedy or needy?" John whispered into her ear.

"I don't seem to have any control over myself, and I'm not sure I want to."

"That's the way it should be right now, my love. Unconsciously you are in control. As much as I love pleasing you this way, I am withholding more that I wish to do. I am reacting to what your body is telling me."

"Do you mean to say that I am telling you to fondle me in this way?"

John didn't answer her because she shivered as he circled her hardening nipple. His lips returned to hers, and his hand slid over to the other nipple.

"Margaret, I can feel you are beginning to tense. That means you are starting to feel embarrassed because we are enjoying each other. This is a big part of our love. Since we are to marry, there is no shame in anything that we do. It will be a significant behavior in our lives. You are beginning to come of age. Learn to relax and allow me to discover your delicacies."

"I'm still offshore, right?"

"Yes, but we are not going to rescue you tonight. Let us just continue what we are doing."

"But, I am not doing anything."

John pulled his shirt over his head and dropped it on the floor. He lifted Margaret's hands and placed it to his chest. He couldn't help but love the sudden intake of her breath.

"Now you may do what I am doing. We are even."

"The wiggling hasn't stopped for a long time."

"I know. He loves this too."

John eventually had to back away from his seduction of Margaret. She was surrendering herself much faster than he wanted for her. All of this would only come once in their lives. Even though there had been much sex in his life, he had never experienced such intensity as he with Margaret. He sat her in the opposite chair.

"Have I disappointed you in some way?" she asked.

"I think you know the answer to that."

"If I had done this before, perhaps, I would be certain."

"No, you have not disappointed me. There is no way that could happen. I am stopping it because I feel I want to venture too far, and you might be willing to let me."

"And that is wrong? I must admit I cannot seem to keep my wits about me. I am not accustomed to my physical self dominating my mind. It must be shameful, even though you like that."

"Margaret, there is nothing shameful about it. It is what one hopes for in a mate. As long as you feel desire for my touch, I will be a complete man. It is more than a desire or need on my part. It is the urge to conquer, to make you mine in every way. I am overwhelmed to know that I please you to the point of wanting to continue. I think it is every man's dream."

"Then why am I sitting over here, now?"

"As I said, I wanted to wrestle the control from you. I truly love this slow, step-by-step process of knowing each other. Only once will we have these initial offerings. Seeing these new reactions on your face, these new movements of your body, is very pleasurable to me. I don't want them all gone in a moment of time."

"Have you moved so gradually with others?"

"Never in my life, and never again."

"So, you have to keep your distance from me in order to keep your self-control?"

"Yes. Another act of nature, I'm afraid. I can only go so far before the scale is tipped in my favor, and I throw us both off balance."

"So this is the end of it before I come ashore?"

"No, it doesn't have to be."

"Then there could be more before that?"

"Yes. There can be steps between now and sand under your feet. I want to speak with the doctor tomorrow, too."

"Do I need his permission?"

"I do." Said John.

"You?"

"Margaret, you are still recovering. Although you feel stronger, I don't think you are entirely healthy. Actions that could follow may exhaust you … pleasantly … but still, I need to ask. I could feel you tensing. Your muscles were starting to tighten, I think. Feeling your legs tremor are signs that … well, signs a man reads. Your body will become taught, which is … I can't believe I am saying this. I've never spoken such words, it's been instinctual, except with you. I fervently want to be at my best for you to give and be as tender as possible." John sighed.

"Enough of this," he insisted. "No more reading. Off to bed."

Chapter Thirty Three

Margaret decided to sleep in her room that night. Many thoughts roamed through her conscience. What was happening to her body to make her feel totally accessible to anything John wanted to do? Where did her willpower go? How could his touch weaken her, excite her nerve endings? That was when she needed more. It made her want to fidget as if to satisfy an itch where she couldn't reach. Several times she kept herself from crying out his name. No books, rumors, or school girlfriends had ever mentioned these feelings. All of her surroundings and sounds disappeared. She could only hear John's breathing, and in that breathing was his desire for her. She became mindless, while the rest of her craved more than she knew what to expect. Margaret knew where it all led to, but she had never, in all her adult life, expected such a journey to get there. She was brought up that marital relations were merely a wife's duty to her husband. No one told her she would love it, too. It was John. It wasn't just the process of getting to the actual intercourse, but John's finding a way for her to delight in the experience. Love had to be a great part of the journey. Her deep abiding love sustained her trust in him. He was wonderful and experienced. His attentions never felt superficial or hasty. Margaret smiled to herself. Most people saw him as tough, but fair. If they only knew how exceedingly tender he could be.

John stripped down to his undergarment. Crawling in bed, he put his hands behind his head, remembering the evening. He was enraptured with Margaret's emerging sexuality. He had not frightened her. John could tell from

Margaret's response that he was, indeed, only that which pleased her and which she clearly desired. He was surprised and delighted by her placing his hand on her breast. No doubt, he mused, she was thinking about this new delight in her room. But was she feeling shame at what she'd done, or looking forward to future delight? Would she instinctively know how their lovemaking would progress? These were, after all, her first intimate and passionate moments. John's prior relations had been with experienced women, and he had no idea how broad or deep the knowledge of virginal women was regarding intimate relations. Margaret had been disappointed when their intimacy stopped, causing John some concern regarding whether she understood the limitations of even the most ardent lover.

God, what a woman I have!

The following morning she was greeted with a kiss. "How did you fare last night with your thoughts? I had many, too, so I am sure you did." John winked.

"A woman never tells–isn't that what you say about men?"

"Margaret!" He laughed. "You don't keep those from *me*. We are one, or soon will be. We do not hide our private feelings from each other. You may have remembered your blissful request of me last night." Now, he'd made her blush. "It was magnificent to know you had boldness."

"You don't know how long I thought about that last night."

"I assumed that. Good. Let's discuss it."

"Breakfast is coming."

"Later, then." John proclaimed.

"I'm sure I can't discuss these things in the light of day."

"I can't wait to *do* these things in the light of day, much less discuss them."

"*Randy*. Is that the word? Are you randy?"

"Is this coming from one of your books?"

"Actually, no. Dixon asked me what it meant because she overheard staff at other homes use that word. I had to go to the library to find out what it meant. My brother wasn't around to ask."

"Margaret, you are making me laugh. I will choke soon."

John moved her away from where any staff could be. "It means sexually aroused. Any young male will become randy in response to the attentions of an attractive woman. This is a physiological response, and it doesn't need love to trigger it. So, because I love you, this word isn't the best choice, as it refers to a lower form of desire."

"What word would you use?"

"*Passionate, desirous*, perhaps."

"*Lustful*? Now, that is a word from my books."

"Yes, I would call myself lustful without the lechery. Except for loving you beyond my own life, I am no different than most men truly in love."

"Do they all do that wiggle thing?"

John cracked up and walked her backwards into his room, shutting the door. He fell with her under him onto the bed top. He passionately attacked her creamy white neck with kisses and sips and licks. Then he kissed her deeply, again and again. He placed his hand on her corseted breast. "This is lustful. Want me to stop?"

Margaret pushed him away, giggling. She felt for her hair still being in place. "All right. We will talk later."

John smiled as he pulled her to a standing position and walked her to the door.

"You're having fun with me. I'm like your dolly, aren't I?"

"Indeed I am, and indeed you are. Think of all the time I wasted on other women."

"What? What does that mean?"

"I don't know. You just make me so happy. I'm starting to babble nonsense. Really, I don't know. Perhaps, I was looking for the fun I have with you, but never found in them"

"Got out of that one, didn't you?"

"By a whisker."

"Speaking of which –"

"Yes?"

"No more kisses until some of that is gone," Margaret said pointing to his ever-increasing beard. "It's starting to scratch me."

John turned around and headed to his room, rubbing his chin.

As they were walking to the coach, John asked, "It's Dr. Price you see, isn't it? Not Donaldson?"

John helped her into the coach, then spoke to Branson. Margaret had her list of foods she was given. She was anxious to get rid of a few of them. John stepped into the coach.

"Do you have questions for the doctor?"

"I think so. It may be easier for him to explain how that thing wiggles than it would be from you. Perhaps a medical explanation would be more bearable to me."

"You are *not* asking him that!" John sighed. "What am I going to do with you?"

"More of last night?"

"*That* is understated. I'm sure I mean that literally, too." John smiled.

John and Margaret stopped at the desk in the front part of the hospital, asking for Dr. Price.

They were asked their names. "I'll have someone locate him. Please be seated."

"John, would you mind if I went in alone?"

"No, but know it's probably your last time alone with a doctor. I will see him after you."

"You really will?"

"I really will. I am taking no chances with you, my love."

A few moments later, John and Margaret were led down several corridors into the doctor's office. Margaret looked at John. "Dr. Price, I would like a word after Margaret."

"By all means."

John backed out of the door and closed it.

"I don't think it's been quite two weeks since you were admitted, but you look much improved in color. You have been eating your liver, I take it."

"Yes, and you can take it. I can't stand it anymore. Here's the dietary list you gave us. I know that's number one on here, but can we *please* erase that?"

"I'd say we can, just by seeing your color. How about the weakness?"

"I think I'm coming along. I've been down the steps unaided, though someone with me. I have had no trouble walking and riding in the carriage. I do think John Thornton is going to question you about that."

"In what regard, do you know?"

"I can only assume. We have decided to get married within two weeks."

"So quickly?"

"It's been a year in the making. We have just rekindled what we once had. It ceased due to a mutual misunderstanding. I believe real intimacy is not far off."

"Do you mean before two weeks from now?"

"Yes." Margaret blushed.

"Now, I see your color very well. That is a good sign. If you are going to ask me if there is anything going on with you that could prohibit lovemaking, I will remind you of a couple of things."

"All right."

"You are very near your time of ovulation, meaning you could become pregnant. That in and of itself is not a problem, but the beginning of a pregnancy would require bed rest for the first month or two, until you felt strong. Strong intimate emotions and feelings can exhaust you, but they surely will exhaust Mr. Thornton first."

"Can you promise me that?"

Dr. Price laughed. "No. Another thing to think about is that in two weeks, if you will have another woman's cycle this time, it should arrive about then. That does not mean that there cannot be intimate contact, it's just that some women refuse their husbands at that time. I haven't found many men that mind a woman's week."

"So, you are telling me I am well?"

"No, I am not. You are still weaker than you think you are. You'll have to take my word on that and don't test it. Also, we will take another blood sample and look at it under a microscope."

"A microscope?"

"It is a powerful magnifier, if you will. We can see the individual cells of your blood. Right now we are advancing science quite rapidly in improvements to these tools."

"I have never heard the word."

"The first one invented was in 1590, but it was only used for science. For the last hundred years it has been used increasingly in the medical field. That is how we knew you had anemia, as we could actually count the red blood cells. Your Dr. Donaldson is not trained in such science, so he wouldn't use it, but he can refer you to doctors who do."

"Fortunately for me. I wanted to tell you that I had a note from Miss Dixon, and she is doing very well and is happy."

"Thank you for letting me know. Will there be anything else?"

"When do you want to see me?"

"After your wedding. I should bring up that there may or may not be any bleeding when your maidenhead is taken. You are chaste, and I can confirm that to Mr. Thornton if he has doubts because you may not bleed."

"I'm not sure it would make a difference to him. We are deeply in love. Nothing will part us. I'll leave now, and let him speak with you, and will see you after our wedding."

"May I wish you the best of marriages? It sounds like you are off to a grand start."

"Thank you, Dr. Price. Good day."

The doctor opened the door for Miss Hale to leave, and John entered the office. Turning toward Margaret, he said, "Branson is around the corner in a waiting area. Wait a minute." John split the air with his whistle. The doctor laughed, then saw Branson rapidly walking toward them.

"Branson, please escort Miss Hale to the area you just came from."

"Aye, guv." Branson extended his arm and Margaret took it.

Dr. Price closed the door. "Quite a polite driver you have there. Seems very dedicated to you. Take a seat. How can I help you?"

John never spoke about his meeting with the doctor. Margaret was afraid to ask. She had asked to be alone, so he had the same right.

"Where are we going? This isn't the way to Marlborough Mills."

"Margaret, you will have to start referring to that place we aren't going to as your home. Say 'my home.'"

"My home. That's going to be hard, you know—feeling this it's mine, too."

"Once we are married, you can change whatever you want to make it be ours. By the way, we are going to see Mother."

"Oh, do I look all right?"

"You are fresh and lovely and beautiful."

"But what will your mother think?"

"Something close to that, I imagine. Can we have her for dinner tomorrow night?"

"Would that be stewed or baked?"

"It took John a moment to catch her joke.

"Would you like to extend an invitation to her for a dinner out with us soon?"

"Dine out?"

"Yes. You and I will do that frequently."

"We will?"

"You are repeating me again."

"I am?" Margaret laughed.

John kissed her.

"This is a nice surprise," Hannah said, coming into the sitting room. "Please sit. I will ring for tea."

"Mrs. Thornton, this is a bright and cheery room. The only sound is that of a horse and carriage driving by. Is the silence hard to get used to?"

"It's been delightful. Every day feels like Sunday, with the mill closed most of the day."

"Margaret, I think that was a joke. This is a cause for celebration. I've never heard her jesting."

"Should we call the doctor? Perhaps, she misspoke. I think being away from you, Mr. Stoic, she is learning a new and enjoyable behavior. Do you think there's a man in the next flat?"

"I wonder if her heart is fluttering," John said about his mother.

"You two, stop it." Hannah was smiling.

"Why the change, Mother?"

"I am convinced that Miss Hale is the ideal woman to make you happy. This has given me a peace of mind I had not known before, relieving me of a burden I had not realized I carried. This new home and new sense of happiness suggest there may be a new purpose to my life around the corner. Miss Hale, you really opened my eyes at dinner that night. I was shocked when you began, but very soon was rooting for you. Just watching my son's expression spoke a thousand words that I wouldn't have believed had he told me, and I am sure he did try."

"Mrs. Thornton, you cannot know the gratification your words have given me. I have always feared becoming a wedge between you and John. I should so be grateful, if we could be friends and start anew. Can we?"

Hannah walked over to Margaret and uncharacteristically hugged her."

"Oh, thank you, Mrs. Thornton!"

"It is I who thank you, my dear."

"This is a beautiful sight to see, my two favorite ladies coming together as friends."

"I think so, too. Now, we can talk about you behind your back and all the girl chat." Hannah laughed at that.

"I do have a few secrets up my sleeve," Hannah admitted.

"Since you're now friends, Margaret and I would like to invite you out for dinner tomorrow night. We will pick you up at 8:00 p.m. Find something other than black to wear. If you have to buy something new, charge it to me."

"Mrs. Thornton, I'm afraid he's getting bossy in his old age. I have plans for that."

"If you need my help, please call on me."

Teas was brought into the room and served. A conversation ensued as to Margaret's health and John's new housekeeper.

They spent much of the morning talking about Fanny's upcoming wedding, and John was relieved to hear that Watson was footing the bill.

John asked Margaret if she had asked the doctor about returning to a desk job.

"I didn't. I forgot."

"I did. We'll talk about it at home."

"Did I tell you he invited me to the Master's Ball?"

"No, you did not. What was your answer?"

"I told him I was otherwise engaged. Nicholas and Peggy will come, will they not?"

"I believe so. They have in the past." John hadn't let the word out, but it looked like a good chance that Bessy would be home that weekend.

Setting their teacups aside, John said, "I think it is time for us to depart, Margaret."

"Yes, I suppose it is. I was having such a lovely time. Mrs. Thornton, perhaps you and I could visit now and again?"

"I would like that. We will try to do so often. Be safe, the two of you. I will be ready tomorrow night.

"John, we still are not headed *home.* Now, what are you treating me to?"

"We are going to a café for lunch. We will discuss the type of weeding you wish to have and if you need a new frock made."

"Oh, that sounds wonderful! Carry on." Margaret looked out the window, enjoying the rare pleasure of seeing many of the city's sights from a carriage.

Chapter Thirty Four

Night fell much too quickly for Margaret. She had been anxious all day, and now she was nervous. John was sitting in his big chair reading his paper. She was doing nothing but waiting. She finally stood and walked the room looking at this and that, opening a few drawers and looking at linens and silverware, even running her fingertips across the tops of hanging pictures, looking for dust.

John was quite aware of what she was up to. She was waiting on his move towards her, but tonight, he decided, he would let her make the first move. He loved the cat-and-mouse game between them and tonight he would play the mouse.

Margaret walked into the dining room, turned on a light, and found her food list. On the back of the paper she began to suggest some meal ideas, which took all of ten minutes.

She sat back down in her big chair and wondered how long John would be reading. After an hour of passing time, she finally announced that she was going to get comfortable for the evening. John had a big grin hiding behind the paper.

When Margaret returned in her shift and robe, she found John had moved. She saw him sitting at his desk in his library.

She flopped down in her chair and felt defeated. This was so unlike the John she had known for the past two weeks, it made her wonder what the doctor may have told him. Margaret walked to his library door?

"Do you have much to do tonight?"

"Almost finished. Miss me?" He smiled.

"I miss having someone to talk with."

"I am sorry. I'll only be a moment."

Margaret walked to the sofa instead of her chair. John would surely come and sit next to her, but he didn't.

Within a few moments, as he had said, he turned off the gas lamp and came back to the sitting room.

"Are you reading tonight?"

Finally, Margaret felt she was getting somewhere. "No, I don't believe so."

"Thinking about our reading last night?"

"Yes. No! I mean no."

John turned off all the lights except one, which he lowered. Then, he returned to his chair. In the quiet of the room, he heard a small sigh. He suppressed his smile. "Would you care for a fire?"

"Yes, please."

The fire had been set by someone. It fell to Maddie, but Branson often helped with that job. John lit the fire and kneeled by it until he was sure it caught on. "Romantic, isn't it?"

"Yes. Quite romantic. A man and a woman in love and alone enjoying a fire in the fireplace. Another scene in a novel."

"And what happens in this scene?"

"The gentleman advances. The girl, his governess, shies from him, admitting she is cold and must go to bed. He wraps his robe around her and holds her close to him. He looks deep into her eyes and speaks with her."

"And?"

"She leaves for her own room," Margaret was forced to say in saddened tones.

"Do you feel romantic, Margaret?"

"Yes, but apparently I'm not very good at it."

John let out the laugh he had been holding back.

"You're laughing at me," Margaret frowned, feeling a little hurt and rejected.

"I am not laughing *at* you … well, I guess I am, after all. You fill me with amusement. Tonight, I am not going to be the one to make advances toward you. If you want to spark my attention and encourage my touch, you shall have to take the lead."

"Is this a game?"

"No. It is a lesson. Self-taught. I will give you a hint."

"And that would be what?"

"For the rest of my life, I will be wanting to love you in any possible way. It will surpass greed–a good kind of greed that is hungry to please both of us. But I will realize that I ask too much of you and will wait–wait for you to come to me so I can love you."

"So you are waiting now?"

"Yes."

"I thought the doctor warned you about me."

"Warned me. About you?"

"Yes. That I could get pregnant."

"Oh, I already know your dates. And it would be a miracle for me to get you with child with what we have been doing. We are beginning to explore each other. Slow and sublime discovery."

"So how do I start this?"

"You start by wanting to be close."

"Yes, but I feel that all the time. How do I tell the difference?"

"What difference?"

"Isn't there a difference?"

"For men, usually not. They are interested all the time. I believe women are not saddled with constantly having intimacy always on their mind."

"And you are?"

"Along with all other men. I'm afraid we're made that way. Women, on the other hand, are not driven in that way, and are given the sense to keep us men from over populating the world. We're here to continue the human race, while you're here to manage it. Our needs originate in biology and yours from something higher."

"How do you know all this?"

"I studied it. As men, it is very early in our lives when we have the desire to be with a woman. I wondered why. I wondered if it was our minds driving us. It's more than that. I think that is all you need to know for a long time."

"But … but how about men in the wars or at sea for a long time where there are no women?"

"Now, I *know* you've had all you need to think about. At least for now. Experience will bring you knowledge, Dr. Hale. Let us get back to you and me. Where were we?"

"I start by wanting to be close."

"All right. I am here by the fire, you are on the sofa. Right now, what do you want?"

"To be kissed by you."

"And how would you plan to get that?"

"I'd wait."

"Wait? Wait for what?"

"For you to want to kiss me."

"This is going to take longer that I thought. I am blessed. All right, you know that I want to be with you, touching you all the time, but sometimes I feel I am forcing myself on you, so I learn to control it. Now, you know this. What do you do?"

"It just doesn't feel natural for me to want you in that way."

"It is natural by God and nature. It's only the propriety that you have been brought up with that prevents you from thinking freely. Do you want to be near me?"

"Yes."

"Then come sit by me, or ask me to sit by you."

Margaret went to John and sat by him in front of the fire.

"The woman I love is near me, and I want to react to her. I will touch you in some way. I may kiss you. I may draw my arm around you and pull you closer. I may hold your hand or push a lock of hair from your face." John picked up her hand and kissed her wrist, repeatedly.

"Do you feel any physical stirrings inside of you?" he asked.

"Yes."

"Then turn your face towards me and look into my eyes or at my mouth. That tells me you want to be kissed. I will immediately oblige, or maybe I will let you initiate it because I would love that, too. I must warn you, though, a kiss usually suspends lessons and instinctual desire takes over. But now my love, you have a place to start. And I'm so glad you want to begin."

Margaret turned to him and began to untie his cravat. "You're smiling too much."

"I know," replied John. "I see in you a budding flower wanting to bloom."

"Shhh … I can't remember all these steps."

"Steps?" John threw his head backward and chuckled. "What was the last lesson you just learned?"

Margaret stopped to think.

"Margaret, stop thinking—react!"

She let loose of the cravat and threw her arms around John with closed eyes, hoping her lips would land on his. They didn't.

"What happened my love?" He grinned.

"I think I closed my eyes too fast. I missed."

"Perhaps, I should take the lead back until you become more acquainted with where my mouth is." John gleamed. The joy he felt was devastating.

John reached over and pulled her to him. Margaret seemed relieved. He laid her back on the floor and pinned her arms over her head as he straddled her waist. He nuzzled her neck and licked her lips. Then he stood.

John turned off the last light, pulled off his boots, socks, vest, cravat and shirt. That left only his trousers and undergarment. He lifted Margaret to a sitting position and removed her robe, leaving only her thin night shift.

He placed her as he had before, but he put some of his weight on top of her. Their faces were only inches apart. His eyes roamed her face while her eyes watched his. He titled his head and assaulted her with a ravenous kiss. He continued to do so until she participated on her own. His tongue slid out, down her neck and over to her shoulder. With his one hand he lowered the side of her night shift until a breast was exposed. John took it into his mouth while Margaret caught her breath. She was fidgeting.

Chills ran down John's back when she pulled her fingers through his hair. The action increased his libido and spurred him on to take the other breast as he had the first one. He suckled there, long, hard and deep. Margaret was trying to find his face to pull him away.

"John, I can feel that everywhere."

"I hope so."

"No, I mean it. I don't know how that does that."

"You don't need to know how–just lay quietly and enjoy it."

"It's not possible to lie quietly. There is a fire burning inside me. Kiss me, please."

John lifted Margaret to his mouth, but this time when he kissed her deeply, her back arched, touching the front of his body. He rested back on top of her and settled his erection between her upper thighs. "I want you to know me, Margaret."

"I do. I do. It's awfully hard. The fire is getting more intense. I'm having trouble breathing. Let me up."

John rocked back on his feet and pulled Margaret to a sitting position. "Those are the most beautiful breasts I have ever seen, and they belong to me."

Margaret gasped as she looked down. John was reaching for the shoulder straps of her shift and pulling them up. "Do you really think so?"

"Yes, I truly do. I believe they are as perfect as they can be, but I will need more time with them." He smiled.

John let Margaret sit there to find a calm within her. He went into his bedroom and removed his trousers, leaving his undergarment on. He slipped back down beside her, and she hardly noticed for a moment.

Margaret spied his hairy legs. "John, are you naked?"

"No."

"So you are wearing your undergarment?"

"I am. This is what I wear to sleep."

"How far along are we?"

"What do you mean?"

"In this … quest … this quest to discover the physical expression of our love."

"Hmm… I would estimate about a third of the way there."

"A third? Only a third?"

"That surprises you. Is a third good or bad?"

"Does it continue to escalate? Will I burn hotter?"

"Yesss …" John whispered into her ear.

"I won't make it."

"You will. I've never had this amazing teaching assignment, but I must admit, I think I'm doing rather well. What do you think?"

"I cannot judge it against anything. Nothing in my life has been like this. You have made me want more, so I say you're doing well. Shall I place an ad in the paper, as they do with horses?"

"Horses? You flatter me, milady. I shall be a disappointment to you." He chuckled.

"Thank heavens for small favors." Margaret replied.

"Well, I wouldn't go that far in saying small favors."

Margaret burst out with a giggle. She dropped her head because of her blush and something moved beside her.

John felt his own reaction and knew Margaret noticed it. She couldn't seem to raise her head back up. He made it happen again. She gasped that time and raised her head as she cleared her throat.

"Something wrong, Margaret?"

"Ah … ah … no. I don't think so. Are you feeling well? Everywhere?"

If John wasn't in the predicament he was in, he would have laid on his back, covered his eyes and laughed until he cried. "He loves you, too," was all he could think to say at that moment.

"He? He who?"

"Him," John said, pointing towards his groin.

Margaret gulped hard. "I'm not getting another lesson, am I?"

"Not unless you want one. Did you ask the doctor today, as you said you would?"

"I'm not telling."

"I thought not."

"I think it's getting late."

"I think you're right. You will be sleeping in my arms tonight and, I hope, for the rest of our lives."

"Bossy!"

"Yes, but you love me anyway."

"Tis true." Margaret feigned a swoon with the back of her hand to her forehead. "I am lost in the sea. I'm trying to make it ashore. I think there is a rope about to be thrown to me, so that I may cling to it."

John almost got sick, his stomach hurt so badly. It took him several moments to recover, and Margaret enjoyed seeing him so happy with smiles and laughter.

"I must leave first on that note." John said. He turned away from Margaret and stood. He walked to his room and called her name.

Chapter Thirty Five

The night was extraordinarily cozy.

"Margaret, I will go no further than we did tonight. You should not be surprised by anything I do. Most likely I will pull your back to my chest. I will tuck your bottom against me. I will hold your breasts."

"And I am supposed to sleep through this like it happens all the time?"

"We could easily reverse that position. You tuck your body against the back of mine."

"And where does my hand go?"

"Wherever you want it to go. If you want to be rescued you can reach for the rope," He chuckled inwardly. "Please, don't let me sleep through that, thinking I am dreaming."

Margaret giggled at that. "You face your back to me."

"Good choice." John said.

"Stop it." Margaret cuddled up against his back and threw her arm over his broad hairy chest. John laid his arm over hers.

"I see you decided to stay offshore."

"Yes. From where I am I can see a large bonfire guiding me to it. The rope would pull me too close to the flames. I would ignite immediately. I think I am safer where I am."

"How long can you float?"

Margaret was silent.

"I love you, Margaret. Good night."

"And I love you. Sweet dreams.

"Without a doubt."

A few moments of silence went by as they were still getting comfortable having another person in the bed and touching them, too. Margaret could feel the sheet gently move every so often.

Margaret whispered, "Can the rope swim?"

John whispered back. "I think someone threw you the rope to cling to, but you missed it. It is sinking. Poor rope."

"Well, the person who threw it will just have to pull it back to shore." Margaret could feel John shaking, again, in quiet laughter.

"John?"

"Yes, my love?"

"I know I'm being silly about this. Sometimes I pretend I don't know things, but this is a huge event in my life, and I am scared of it. Thank you for making it so easy and gentle and taking away the embarrassment."

John rolled over to face her. He placed his leg over her and drew her in. He kissed her gently and tenderly. He held her close with her forehead against his chest and sleep finally came.

Maddie came down the steps with an empty tray. She had been setting the breakfast table.

"Cook, did Miss Hale stay the night?"

"I would think so. I was told no difference."

"Her bed hasn't been slept in."

Cook grinned. "The master is truly in love. He's never had a woman stay over in this house. Now he has one in his room. It's about time."

"Why do you say that?"

"Look at the man. He's handsome, has some change in the bank and everything a woman could want in the perfect husband. But he's never found anyone he could love. It was terrible a year ago when he was happy seeing Miss Hale. Then, things went wrong and words were said.

They parted. It's been so sad watching him this past year trying to pull himself up. Then she came back into his life, almost accidently. He grabbed at that slim chance, and it seems he's won her."

"I am very happy for them. Should they get married, so you think?"

"I am sure of it. He would never shame a woman by taking her to his bed if she wasn't going to be his wife."

John went to the mills for work that day. At breakfast, they had agreed they wanted a small, private ceremony at the courthouse. He would let his staff know at the last moment, but would tell Nicholas today. John was willing to do whatever Margaret wanted, and she decided on a small wedding, since she had no family and no one to walk her down the aisle. John felt sorry for her in that respect. As a man, it made little difference how or where the ceremony was held or the people invited. But John knew it usually meant a lot to a woman. He thought about Branson being his best man, and Nicholas giving her away. He would ask her about that later.

Margaret spent part of the day responding to Dixon with her wedding news. She also went over all the dresses she had to wear. She had a simple wedding ceremony and a Master's Ball coming up very soon. Little was had if she wanted a dress for the ball. Simple elegance she still had from her school days in London, but no ball gown. She went to ask John.

Maddie stayed with her down the steps, which she had no problems negotiating, and then stayed on the porch watching her as she crossed the mill yard.

Margaret started up the steps to about half way when she had to sit down and rest. Maddie started towards her, but Margaret waved her back. She was determined to make it.

John and Nicholas had been talking inside when voices were outside the door. They paid little attention, expecting the voice to enter.

There was a knock. "Enter," shouted Nicholas. Both were surprised to see one of their foreman helping Margaret through the door.

"Sorry, boss. I just saw her sitting on the steps about half way up."

"Thank you, Randall. I'll take her from here."

"Thank you, Randall," Margaret said as he turned to leave. "I could have made it. I was just resting. Maddie wanted to come to my aid, but I waved her away. Randall didn't seem to pay attention to my shooing him away."

"I'm glad he didn't. He is paid to care for anyone on this property."

As John rested her in a chair, he asked, "What couldn't wait until I came home?"

"I don't have a ball gown, and there isn't much time to have one made. All the seamstresses are probably working on other gowns. Nicholas, do you know what Peggy is wearing?"

"I've never dared open my mouth where frocks and gowns are involved. They'll ask my opinion and when I give it to them, I am told I don't know anything."

John laughed. "Don't look at me. Fanny tried that on me a couple times, and I got what Nicholas got. Why do you think the masters all dress in black? It's because we don't know any better. I would say that I would like to see you in something that accents your figure, but doesn't give it away."

"Give it away?"

"You know what I mean."

"I suppose. Can Branson drive and walk with me?"

"I'm not sure how he'll fancy frock shops, but I guess there is no time like the present to try."

"Do you have any accounts set up?"

"Ah… no. But you can start one.

"John, I am a foolish woman. I didn't even ask if I could spend your money. My presumption is most irregular."

"Should I leave?" asked Nicholas with a smile.

"Margaret, I don't care about the money. Haven't we talked about that?"

"Am I being scolded?"

"No, of course not. We will talk more about that tonight. A new lesson for tonight."

"Oh."

"I will have Branson take you to see Peggy. She can give you an idea about Milton balls and gowns. We are not London."

"All right. It will be nice to see her. Is she home, Nicholas?"

"Yes, she is. I have the coach, so she must not have had plans for the day."

"Margaret, wait here. I will get Branson and then come back for you."

"I can make it, but I'll wait."

John left the office.

"I take it that you and John have settled your differences and picked up where you were."

"We are far ahead of where we ever were. He really loves me, Nicholas. He is sweeping me off of my feet. He makes me dizzy from his attentions."

"John's waited mighty long to do that. Whether it be his attentions or intentions, you will be safe with him."

Margaret blushed. "He's being very patient with me."

"I'm not surprised."

John was heard coming up the steps. "Ready?"

Branson assisted Margaret up the steps at the Higgins home. Peggy greeted her and went to take her arm, but Margaret declined.

"I am doing well, Peggy. Going up steps seems to be my next goal. I'm sorry I didn't send a note, but Nicholas thought it would be acceptable to see you on short notice. I was wondering about ball gowns."

"You're going?"

"I think so. I told John that Mr. Griffin invited me and I replied that John was taking me. It doesn't mean I will dance."

Peggy laughed. "You shall be very popular there."

"Why?"

"One … because you have hardly been seen by anyone in town. Second … you're with the President of the Mill Workers Association. Third, you will be the only woman that John has ever taken to the ball, although he is forced to go because of his leadership."

"I was wondering what type of gown I should have made, but John said this wasn't London and I should talk to you about how they dress."

"He was right in telling you that this isn't London. If you were fashionable, you would know that we are two or three years behind London as far as gowns and work frocks go. I shall be by and see you in a day or two and we will look through your wardrobe. I remember you have some lovely frocks. There will be one for our ball."

Margaret and Peggy chatted for over an hour. They talked of Bessy, the ball, marriage to a master, and Margaret's current health. Margaret thought she might have questions about the events yet to come in her life, but she knew John was handling everything gently and without fear.

"Look at the time. I believe I have missed my midday meal, but I should go home to lie down. We will get together often. I have so enjoyed my visit."

Margaret arrived home, and the coach alerted John to that fact. He started out the door, but he saw that she was in good hands with Branson, and so returned to his desk.

"It looks like Peggy convinced her to make a decision on the gown because Branson is putting the coach away."

"When is Margaret going back to Cecil's mill?"

"Only two more days. She's been doing quite well around the house, which doesn't seem to be much different than the office she will be in. As you saw today, she still struggles a bit going up the stairs, but I don't believe Cecil has any steps to his office."

John had thought on and off during the day about his evening with Margaret. She had such incredible belief in him. He had anticipated a few obstacles and questions to this point, but there were none. She put her complete faith in him. He had to govern his own control since she wasn't going to apply the brakes. He could almost picture her tonight as she sat patiently for the next lesson, waiting with a smile. John worried that the next step might take them over the edge. He did not want to withdraw himself at his own climax, but Margaret was passing into the days of conception. Living many years with her virginity, she probably never accounted for actual conception days. John's practice had always been to withdraw, which rarely gave him pause to think about it either. It now loomed large in their life. He and Margaret had never discussed a family, although he felt she would be as interested as he was. With her health not fully restored, he didn't feel this month was good for her.

The two sat together on the sofa sipping their last cup of tea for the evening.

"Margaret, I've never asked your opinion about having a child. It that something you look forward to in the future?"

"Yes. Perhaps more than one child. Have you given much thought to a family?"

"Quite a bit. I would like to raise a family and give them the benefits of a childhood that I never had. And before you ask, I have no preference. I am not a man that needs you to bear a son as an heir. I would enjoy a house full of little girls as much as little boys. I would welcome someone saying, 'Here comes John Thornton and his girls.' Mother had a rough life with my father, at least the years that I was aware, and Fanny, well you know her. I want some little girls like my wife. And you?"

"I only pray that I can carry and birth them. I want us to have a family very much. It would be nice to have a boy in amongst the girls to carry on the traditions and the empire that you are creating."

"I hope we can educate all of our children, but I will not expect any of them, even if I have a son, to take over what I have built. That would be 20 years from now and this is the age of machines. Many things could change and other factors could capture his fancy. He will know that it would be his, but he is not obligated to carry on Marlborough Mills."

"I'm glad to hear you say that. You may even have a daughter that would like to run the mill."

"Do you have any thoughts of how you will interact with the mill? Do you think you will have any interest in it at all?"

"Yes. I will take an interest. I will improve it for you, and I will seek better ways to help those that work in the mills."

John felt his own chest expand with pride. It wasn't until just recently, so blinded by her presence and health that he began to think of what she would experience as the wife of a mill master. Margaret had given him an answer that eased his worries. Whether it turned out the way she hoped it would didn't matter. She was more than willing to try.

John saw Margaret put her teacup on the table and then she slid over in his arms. His smile was missed by Margaret as he embraced her.

"Is it permissible for me to take the initiative? You taught me last night what I should do if I want to be close to you."

"It is not only permissible, but desirable." John noticed she had not turned her head to look at his eyes or mouth, so apparently she had more to say.

"To go from one third to one half is only one sixth."

John burst out laughing. So that's what was on her mind? He hoped she didn't ask about one sixth.

"You know what I'm going to ask aren't you? During my times alone today I have done nothing but wait for the night. Where would you take me tonight?"

"Oh. You have been thinking about tonight, have you?" He said with a grin.

"Don't embarrass me, please."

"I'm sorry. You just bring so much joy. Please continue."

"I think I've asked my question."

"I see. So what you were wondering during the day is where I would take you tonight? It has nothing to do with the one sixth, does it? I'm afraid I have never broken down lovemaking to a chaste woman in such fine detail. I do know that my passion and desire for you are controlled by you, yourself. Quite honestly, I had expected more hesitancy and demurral from you. On the other hand, had you been healthy and well and strong in body we might've had the entire experience in one night. I didn't expect I would love this teaching so much. Do you feel there is any part you wish to repeat?" John was having the most fun of his life with Margaret.

"Would we not repeat all that we have done before the next step?"

"Steps? Sixths? Please, don't put our love on a measuring stick. We can do whatever we want. I suggest for now that we begin the same way. I believe many men make a mistake in rushing to their own satisfaction, as they feel the woman is there to do her duty. I am finding a way to build the passionate desire within you which will entice you to look forward to being pleased by me. The fact that you seem to be eager tells me that I am right. You can't know how pleased I am. You are surrendering to me in the sweetest way possible."

Finally Margaret turned in his direction and looked into his eyes. John allowed the moment to sustain itself. It was magical. He embraced her and began kissing her face, her neck, behind her ear. He pulled the pins from her hair and let it cascade down. Then he kissed her deeply and fervently. He felt the fires ignite.

Leaving Margaret in somewhat of a dazed state, John rose and turned out all of the lamps. The room was dark, but he knew where Margaret was. He walked over to her, lifted her in his arms and carried her to his bed. He kicked the door shut with his foot, and setting her on the edge of his bed, he knelt down and removed her shoes and his own boots. He rolled down her stockings, removed his vest, cravat and shirt.

On her own, Margaret stood and placed her back toward him so that her garment could be unfastened. John turned her back to face him and delivered a very erotic kiss. He knelt down in front of her and slipped off two petticoats. He found the string ties to her undergarment, unleashing them. He heard Margaret's audible gasp. He collected her clothes from the floor and placed them over the chair in his room. When he returned, Margaret had her back to him. It seems she was anticipating and eager to go forward.

Surprising her, John knelt again in back of her. He slowly lifted her dress and shift until her buttocks were exposed. He began to kiss her there and lick the soft skin that awaited him. Holding her thighs, John could feel her legs begin to quiver, so he stood. He began with unfastening the buttons to her frock and let that gently fall and pool at her feet. Her shaking was getting more noticeable.

John whispered, "Do you want me to stop?"

In one harsh word Margaret said no.

"Just hold yourself steady for one or two minutes until I can get this corset away from you." John worked as fast as he could, loosening the long laces that bound her. Pulling that away from her, he picked up her frock and laid them on the chair, leaving her in a shift. Returning, he pulled down the covers and then he lifted her in his arms. He laid her gently on the bed and removed his trousers before he lay next to her. His heart was hammering. It all still seemed to be a dream. How many times had he seen this scene in his mind?

John rolled on his side and began with her beautiful lips. He kissed them gently before his passionate aggression intensified. His hands roamed her body while his mouth stole her breath. When he found the hem of her shift, he slipped his hand underneath to feel her skin.

Margaret could hear his heavy breathing. His desire was evident. When she felt his tender fondling under her shift, it began an insatiable need. Her nerve endings were starting to tease her. Suddenly John pulled her on top of him, encouraging her to straddle him in a sitting position. Once again he slipped his hands under her shift to massage her breasts.

"Margaret, I love you. I love every inch of you, and I will know it all soon. And you shall know me. This is normal and natural behavior for two people in love. I do not want you to think, I want you to react. You are to relax and feel no embarrassment. I need you to need me. I want to give you pleasure. Can you allow me to do that?"

"But how?" Margaret asked in a trembling voice.

"Does it matter? We will know each other intimately, without awkwardness or unease. You will abandon all of your shyness with me. I will come to know your body better than you."

Margaret felt her shift being pulled over her head. She was quite aware of John's arousal. Taking a bold step, she reached down and touched him there. She heard him quietly moan and his body stiffened.

"Oh God, Margaret. I wasn't expecting that."

"Did I do wrong? Did it hurt?" Margaret began to draw her hand away, and John stopped her and placed it back on his covered penis.

"It did not hurt. It was extremely pleasurable, and you can never do wrong by doing that. That was where we were headed tonight. Please, just leave the weight of your hand there."

Once again John reached for her breasts. He held them firmly in his palms, but could not hold them completely. She was endowed. He began to massage them and stroked her nipples. Whether she knew it or not, she was stroking his manhood. His hands gently traced the contour of her body, finding her small waist and then spreading out to her hips. His fingers roamed to her inner thighs and traveled upward with a casual touch to her pubic hair. He felt her stiffen, but she relaxed as he passed up to her navel and back to her breasts. As much as he didn't want to stop her stroking him, he sat up, laying her back on his up bent knees. He kissed her deeply, and then his mouth fell to her nipples while she ran her fingers through his hair. He adjusted her slightly so that her feminine little nub was resting on his hardened penis. She began to moan as he slowly rocked her against him.

With a breathless voice, she called his name. He continued to sip at her breasts and rock her harder against him. He knew he would spill himself, but he couldn't stop now because she was so near her first orgasm.

Again she called his name. "Margaret, just go with me. Trust me. Do not withhold yourself. Enjoy the pleasure we are both feeling."

Margaret felt like she was going to snap inside. She was a rubber band being pulled taught with every nerve in her body. She tried not to think about it as John had asked. "Don't think, react," she said out loud. Moans and sighs and soft cries she heard coming from herself.

"John, I cannot help myself."

"You are not supposed to help yourself."

As her voice grew, so did her breathing. "I am going to burst. My body is about to snap."

"We are both about to burst. Do not withhold the sound of your pleasure. That excites me to completion."

John reached down to her womanhood and touched her there. Her whimpering grew louder into a crescendo as John climaxed. He slowed down the rocking, but continued to feel her pulse at the end of his touch. Margaret continued on, not fully spent. John was euphoric to know that he continued to please her for a few more moments. She was incapable of pretending. His undergarment was wet with her and him. He held her through the completion of her crest. Laying his hand on her heart, he could feel the pounding of the beats and the heaving of her breath. John kissed everywhere he could reach. He stayed sitting up, but laid her back between his splayed legs. She couldn't speak, and neither could he. The emotional and physical fulfillment was a rapturous communion with each other. He laid his hands on her thighs, allowing her to float gently back to earth.

After long moments of quiet, Margaret finally regained her senses and her breath. "I've reached the shore, haven't I?"

"No, not yet."

Chapter Thirty Six

It was early Saturday morning when John awoke. He still had Margaret in his arms, and if someone could glow in their sleep, it was she. They had spoken only briefly last night after their intimacy, as both were completely overwhelmed and Margaret was exhausted. John had hoped to hear her heavenly words and was not disappointed. She had been enchanted, using words such as euphoric, blissful and enraptured. He was surprised, himself, that a familiar intimate experience could be so powerful and come from deep within. He knew it wasn't his own pleasure that made him feel this way—that it was Margaret's. They did not have sex: They made love.

He slipped quietly out of bed. He stood over her and stared. The sheet was barely covering her nipples and her hair splayed around her face across the pillow. He was looking at a work of art that no museum would have but himself.

He went to his bowl and pitcher stand and washed himself before shaving. He kept waiting for her to wake until he realized it might be a while. He had taken a weak woman and weakened her still. He dressed and went to the sitting room. Maddie came into the room, ready to prepare the table and was surprised to see him awake.

"Mr. Thornton, would you care for a cup of tea while you wait for your meal to be served?"

"Maddie, I know what this looks like, and you are right. This is to be confidential between you and Cook for a bit longer, but Miss Hale and I shall marry very soon."

"Yes sir. We need no explanation. This is your home and we keep all confidences to ourselves. Cook said you would be marrying her anyway, so we knew."

"Cook said that?"

"Not in those exact words. She said that you had never had a woman stay over in the house and now you have one in your bed. Cook was elated and said that you had finally won her."

John smiled. "Cook knows me rather too well. And so does Branson."

"Tea, sir?"

"Yes. Also tell Cook that I shall be taking dinner out tomorrow tonight with Miss Hale and my mother."

Maddie did a small curtsy and left the room. John went down the steps to retrieve his morning paper.

Margaret's eyes slowly opened to a ceiling she was not familiar with. She looked for John, but he wasn't there. Margaret lay back down on her back staring upward, recalling the events of only a few hours ago. She remembered losing herself. John had pulled her across his groin area. She was amazed to realize she had touched the most intimate part of John's body, something she would never before imagine herself capable of doing.

Margaret sat up and rested her back against the headboard. She believed she had acted recklessly. She put her hands over her eyes, too embarrassed to think of the boldness she had displayed. She remembered trying to remove her hand and John stopping her from doing so. He had loved her touching him. She couldn't admit to herself that she liked it too. It was thrilling to feel the part of him that is seen by no one. As he would say, he belonged to her, now. She felt a grin on her face. Every time she tried to stop doing it, it came back.

How am I going to keep my feet on the floor today?

John knocked lightly and opened the door. Margaret was sitting up, smiling, trying to cover it up. He closed the door and went to her side. Margaret opened her arms and welcomed him into her space. John embraced her while he ran his fingers lightly up and down her back.

"Do you know you can't go around smiling like that all day? People will know what happened to you?"

"What did happen to me?" she asked. "I got lost along the way. You made me completely senseless, yet yearning. I never knew that you making love to me would make me feel anxious, yet heavenly."

"You were never lost. I think you liked what we did last night."

"I know I loved what you did last night. Did you do it right? I mean … I was delirious for most of it, but I'm not sure if you … ah … nothing hurt like I expected."

"Do you mean did I take you all the way?"

"That's a good way to say it. I was stuck."

"There is no right or wrong way. Any way that I can pleasure you is right. No, I did not take you all the way. But you're only about ankle deep in the water. You had your first orgasm."

"And that's possible without you inside of me? Am I still chaste?"

"Yes, to both those questions." John wanted to laugh, but her face was so serious.

"Have you done that before with anyone else?"

"No."

"You just knew?"

"I just knew."

"Why didn't you take me all the way?"

"Because you're in your conception days."

"I am? I think I learned when those days are long ago. You will have to teach me, again."

"Apparently, I will," he smiled. "When were are married and decide we would like to start a family, we will not worry about those days."

"What did you mean when you said my smiling will tell on me? No one knows what happened."

"I am afraid to tell you that uncontrollable smiling can be part of the process."

"You're smiling."

"I know. I think we need to hide today," John chuckled. "However, it should be gone shortly when other parts of our life need our concentration."

"Will your Mother know?"

"I don't care if she knows. And you shouldn't either."

"Oh, I wish we could do it again."

"We?" John laughed.

"I didn't do anything for you, did I?"

"Quite the contrary."

"I don't understand."

"You pleased me, as well."

"I did? I really was delirious. I was on a cloud up high that has our name on it. I only touched you. I want to do that again, too. Just don't shoot me off to the stars before I study you a bit more."

John kissed her hard. His erotic tongue was heating the room. He loved her for saying that. Pulling away from her before he went too far, he said, "We will revisit that tonight."

"In the dark, I hope. That gives me courage right now."

"As you always wish it to be, it shall be. I think it's time for you to dress. Can I help?"

"No, it's daylight in here."

"I've already peeked, my love. It was only a short hour or two." John leapt off the bed when he saw the palm of her hand coming at him. "I'll be waiting for you."

Margaret felt like she could wake up like that every day.

John left the room thinking about her words, "inside of me." Would that day ever come? He knew it would, but just her saying those words thrilled him.

As Margaret dressed with everything except her knickers, which she would change in her room, she thought about how exciting married life would be. The romantic intimacy was going to be a big part of their marriage, but she still believed deeply loving and knowing John mattered most to her. To feel he was hers and she belonged to him was greater than anything.

John found it delightful when he would see Margaret pinching her lips to avoid smiling. He knew he felt as elated as she, but he could control his grin easily. Grinning had never been a behavior in his life until her.

"John, I would like to bathe today."

"Are you asking for permission?"

"No, but do I tell Maddie or Cook to prepare it?"

"Unlike me, you have your beautiful hair to dry and I suspect that takes a while. We will leave to pick up my mother at half seven. Yes, just tell Cook when you wish to take it. She has to start heating your water. Maddie will assist you. Do we need to purchase anything for you before then? You didn't sell your clothes, too, did you?"

Immediately, John realized he had said the wrong thing. Her spontaneous smile disappeared. Foolishly he had reminded her of her recent past which was a wound still unhealed. "I'm sorry. That was thoughtless of me."

"That is perfectly all right. I am good with that," she said, but John knew she wasn't. "I don't need anything."

"If something is bothering you about your low times, we need to talk about it."

"I said I am fine." Margaret rose from the table before she had finished.

"I meant no disrespect. I hope you know that, Margaret." John followed her to the sofa.

"I do know that, John. I really do. Now, that you have taken me in, nursed me and now are loving me, I realize how bad it was."

"You are making it sound like my actions were charity. Stop that. It never was that. If what happened a year ago had never come between us, we would have arrived where we are now many months ago. I've loved you all this time. I haven't pitied you."

"I do believe you. God knows what you have been through with me these last weeks has even convinced your mother. All around us seemed to know your feelings. I will get past this. I just feel …."

"Feel what?"

Margaret was silent, searching for words.

"Feel what, Margaret?"

"That your peers may pity you."

"What!" My peers may have once pitied me, but that was when I was unsuccessful in claiming your hand. They will be happy that I have achieved what I have always wanted in life … you. No more of this talk. I'm not afraid to spank you now."

The smile came back.

"How about coming to the office with me this morning? Look at our books. Then we will have lunch, before you bath and nap."

Nicholas had already prepared a third desk in their small office for Margaret. John introduced her to the filing cabinets, boxed receipts and an archive of years past.

"Would you like to listen to our morning talk before you look into things? See how we run our business, the discussions we have and the plans we make?"

"Yes, I would like that. I know I won't understand much, but it is the beginning of being married to a Master, don't you think?"

John wanted to kiss her, but Nicholas was there. This was going to be a bit difficult for the first few months or a year. He could see her, listen to her, she'd make him laugh, but he couldn't touch her.

John and Nicholas talked as if she weren't there for about an hour. He would have to indoctrinate her into the business slowly outside of work time. That hour in the morning with Nicholas controlled almost everything they did.

Margaret listened, finding some relief that she could follow some of their talk. At the moment it seemed preparing for the holiday buying season would increase the output, so orders had to be placed now. Margaret could already tell they were going to fall short. They had planned a low increase to their sales projections. She was anxious to find the past three years of purchases and sales, prices of raw goods and cost of inventory storage. Did they have room in their mills to increase production? Were there enough machines, people and workspace?

After lunch, Margaret bathed in the copper tub off from the kitchen. With a cloth wrap around her, she took the steps slowly, heading for her room. She looked about and thought how little she had been in this room of late. Had John a plan for her clothing in his room? He had never shared his room before now.

She went to her wardrobe, flinging open the doors. She still had many frocks left from her school days two years ago. Tonight was a dinner out with John's mother. She rifled through all the dresses to see which one would say "I am the wife-to-be of your son. She found one that she felt was perfect. It was simple, but still a frock for evening. She could also wear it to church. Before she lay down, she tried it on again. She was shocked to see how loosely it fit. Looking back through her wardrobe, she knew they would all be the same. Loosening her corset would do very little to fill out her gown. She had no choice, but perhaps a shawl thrown over her shoulders would hide her recent past.

Margaret had Maddie come upstairs and help her dress.

"Miss, your frock is quite loose. Are you sure you want to wear this one?"

"Maddie, I have little choice. If I were not expected to gain weight I would have them all tailored."

"My, you do have a lovely collection of frocks in the wardrobe."

"I am having dinner with John's mother tonight. Do you think this looks suitable?"

"Yes, mum."

"Is Mr. Thornton home?"

"Yes. I believe he is dressing, as well."

"Thank you for your help, Maddie. I believe you are excused for the evening. Shall I see you tomorrow?"

"Tomorrow is Sunday, Miss. Neither cook nor I will be here. She has made a plate of sandwiches and has the tea tray ready for the morning. Did you not know that we both had off Sunday?"

"No. I did not know. I wonder if I can remember how to cook anything."

"I have not been here long enough to know of Mr. Thornton's habits on Sunday. Cook tells me he dines out quite often."

"I hope we dine out tomorrow. I don't want to kill the man before I marry him."

Maddie laughed.

"Are you sure I cannot help you with anything else? You need a handbag, you need shoes and you need a shawl to go over that baggy waistline."

"I can take care of the rest myself. I will see you early on Monday. I return to my temporary job on that day."

Margaret entered the sitting around where John was standing. He looked beautiful in his dining clothes. His apparel was very much like his master's clothes, but a much more elegant fabric and the slim cut made him stand out. "John," Margaret observed, "I didn't think you could be more handsome than I've known you, but you look splendid in your finery. I can see why all the women wanted your company. I'm not sure I'll ever get over being the woman in your life."

John walked over and embraced her. It had been all day since he could kiss her, which he did. He stepped back from her, holding her two hands to take a full measure of her.

Margaret felt she detected disappointment in his face, but he still gave her compliments.

"I'm sorry. It seems it will be a few months before I fit properly into my clothes. Will I be an embarrassment to your mother?"

"You will never be an embarrassment to anyone, including yourself. Are you ready?"

"I just need to get my shawl, bonnet and bag."

Chapter Thirty Seven

Margaret waited in the carriage with Branson at the door, while John went to collect his mother. Margaret was nervous. She wondered how prospective grooms asked the father of the bride for her hand. It must be most intimidating. Someday she would ask John to tell her how he would have approached that. She was of age. She could consent on her own, but if following tradition, John would've asked her brother. Where was he, she wondered.

Margaret moved to the opposite bench, giving John and his mother the proper position inside the coach. The male owner always sat facing towards the direction they were heading. If she were married to John, she would sit next to him. But not being married, his mother came next. After that it made little difference unless there were a fifth person.

Mrs. Thornton was handed in and sat across from Margaret. As expected John sat next to her.

"How are you this evening, Miss Hale?"

"I am doing very well. This afternoon I was strong enough to walk all the way up the stairs unassisted. I shall have no problems meeting with Master Griffin on Monday."

"What exactly will be your duties for Master Griffin, Miss Hale?"

"I shall endeavor to set up his beginning ledger accounting. He is familiar with the process to an extent, having done it in his last mill, but never felt comfortable that he was catching all the figures that could help them examine his profitability."

"And you can do all of that for him?"

Margaret saw that John was smiling at her. She had a feeling that he was proud of her.

"Oh, yes. I shall do only the basic bookkeeping. I have explained to John that I learned much more in my class than just setting up the books."

"Mother, with Margaret only being two years away from her schooling, she has brought to our attention finer ways of looking at our business. Our accountants are older gentleman and may not have kept up with more exacting ways to look at our profession. Now Nicholas and I think Miss Hale is boasting a nice game, but in the coming weeks we are going to put her to the test. We want her to astound us and our accountants. She promises significant increases in sales. Isn't that right, Miss Hale?"

"Indeed. I propose a bet."

Mrs. Thornton was listening intently.

"And what would that be, Miss. Hale?"

"I believe I can find you another 3% above your expected increase. We are coming into the fall, and the new year will soon be upon us. As of now what is your year-to-date increase?"

"Miss Hale, we shall earn approximately 9% increase over last year."

"That is quite an ambitious number, considering what I heard from Master Griffin. You are that confident in your number?"

John folded his arms in his normal resolute stoic stance. "Indeed, we will."

"Miss Hale, I was quite involved in the mill until recently. I can vouch for my son that he is not embellishing his success. And you feel you can increase his success that he has slaved over for half a decade?"

"I do."

"And how would you go about this, Miss Hale?"

"I cannot give away my secrets until I know what may be my prize if I can accomplish it." She moved her eyes from Mrs. Thornton to John.

"I believe we will have to continue this conversation inside. We are here."

Branson opened the coach door on John's side, who handed out his mother and then Margaret. He stood between the two women and offered his arms to both. He especially wanted Margaret to hold his arm, as she was not steady on her feet on this uneven ground.

Entering, the owner came up to John, "Good to see you, Mr. Thornton."

"Good evening."

"How lucky of you to have two beautiful women on your arms tonight."

"Yes, I am quite honored this evening."

"I have your usual table prepared. Follow me, please."

"John, I didn't realize you had such fine dining tastes," Hannah Thornton said.

"This is lovely, John," Margaret added. "What a nice situation for your table. Are you treated special?"

"Yes. It seems that I am, but I have never asked for it. Being head of the mill Masters for the past couple of years seems to have entitled me to better service. I am not sure how I could stop this, so I have decided to enjoy it while I can."

Once again the thought of John's reputation among his peers unsettled Margaret. She couldn't believe that she ever thought he wasn't a gentleman, and she was coming to find out how greatly he was admired for his business prowess, leadership, along with his physical beauty. How did she deserve him? She had drifted away in her thinking when she heard John calling her name.

"I'm sorry. What were you saying?"

"What would you care to drink, Margaret? Do you see someone you know?" John couldn't help but notice she was staring off into the room.

"I was just admiring the decor in this room. I will have any red wine."

"For a moment there you looked like you were standing in the water looking towards a shoreline."

That brought Margaret back from her daydreaming with a little giggle. Mrs. Thornton was smart enough, as she watched her son smile, to know there was something being said between them. She was uplifted to see him happy.

"Miss Hale, I don't know what your bet will turn out to be, but that sounds like a very useful skill for a business to have. I hope you bring John and Nicholas more success. Quite honestly I hope I live to see this because I think John feels he's doing the very best possible."

The evening went well, John thought. There was discussion about the wedding and his mother seemed a bit disappointed that he and Margaret wanted a small affair. She was still enjoying her new flat, but she did miss Cook. Margaret asked her about a few items that she had found around John's home. It was more of an inquiry about whether she forget to take them or had left the items for them. Hannah Thornton asked Margaret if she had a sewing basket, to which Margaret replied that she had a small one for mending only. She did not do needlework. Hannah said that she would take the sewing basket that she left.

John returned to the coach, finding Margaret with her eyes closed. "Let's get you home and into bed. I was quite proud of you tonight. I think you have really won her favor." John pulled her into his arms so she could rest against his chest.

"John?"

"Yes, my love?"

"You forgot to mention that there will be no staff in your home on Sundays."

"Oh, did I forget to tell you that?" He grinned.

"You know you are taking your life in your hands with me."

"I certainly hope so."

"I may be the death of you, you know?"

"You are learning far too fast. I'm not sure I can keep up with these lessons at the pace you want to set."

"John! I'm talking about my cooking."

"You had me all excited there for a moment."

"You made me laugh at the restaurant about standing in the water. I wonder what your mother must have thought."

"I could see that she is happy for us. For me. She knows what you bring to me."

"Well, it's not going to be your breakfast."

John laughed. "What would you like to do tomorrow? Anything your heart desires shall be yours."

"Can I think on that?"

"Of course you can."

When they arrived home, Margaret went and changed into her night attire. John kicked off his boots, hung his jacket, and removed his vest and cravat. He sat on the end of the sofa and waited for Margaret. When she came out she sat beside him, resting her head in the crook of his arm.

"As much as last night meant everything to me, could we suspend the lesson tonight?"

"All right. I don't ever want you to think that I love you only for nights like last night."

"I would never consider such a thing. That would mean you were shallow, and I know you are not."

"You will sleep in my arms, won't you?"
"Only in your arms. I am now spoiled."

The following morning Margaret woke before John. As she slipped out of bed, she took a peek as John had said he had done to her. Even though John was in his undergarment, an erection was very much in evidence. "Oh, my God," she whispered to herself. Margaret smiled and threw her hands over her mouth to keep from squealing with surprise. She felt like a child peeking through a boarded fence. It was as if she were doing something that was not allowed. When she exited the room, she laughed to herself.

Thirty minutes later, Margaret had hot tea and biscuits on the table. With the door being opened, she knew when John woke. She hadn't thought about her condition as she started up the steps with the tray and a teapot full of hot water. She did not seem to have any trouble with that. She had not mentioned to John that Mr. Griffin's lavatory was on the second floor of his home. She did not want him to worry about her.

"Good morning, my love." John walked over and kissed her tenderly. "It looks as if you have prepared our morning meal. What more could a man want?"

"He could want someone else to do it."

John seated Margaret and then poured the tea. "Did you sleep well? Did you peek well?"

Margaret dropped her spoon onto her plate and looked at John. She was mortified. He knew what she had done. And obviously he had known the state he was in at the time. Margaret saw his shoulders start to rise and fall in silent laughter.

"I don't know what you are referring to."

"Sorry. I must be mistaken," John said as he continued to laugh.

"Yes, you must be mistaken. A lady would never do such a thing."

"Perhaps not. But I certainly hope my wife-to-be will find interest in me. What was that you said the other night? It was something about what you wanted to do before I shoot you to the stars next time?" John smiled.

Margaret blushed. "I believe I told you I was delirious. I couldn't help it that you made me feel that way. And I certainly have no recollection of saying whatever you think I said."

"I think that's what we should do today."

"In the daylight?" Margaret said with incredulity.

John burst out laughing.

"You are hurting my male pride, you know?"

"Is that possible?" Margaret twittered.

"So, you think I am too prideful?"

"To men or women," Margaret laughingly asked.

"Does it matter?"

"Naturally."

"Tell me, my love, where is the difference—oh educated one." John was anxiously waiting to hear her response. Love in the morning—that's what this was.

"You really don't see it?"

"I don't see myself as prideful, much less some difference between men and women. Is it pride when one tries to do the best that they can in any endeavor?"

"Let's start with your posturing. Around other men you stand tall, speak slowly and authoritatively. Because you are tall and intelligent, people pay attention to you. You like that a lot, but maintain a stoic demeanor so as not to look pompous. If rumors are true, men in general have pride in certain parts of their anatomy. And should it ever come to comparisons … well. Therefore, what I am hearing this morning from you about finding interest in you and that I'm not supposed to have any hesitation in this, makes me think you are very proud where you think it counts the most to me."

John was sitting back with his arms folded, giving Margaret his full attention. "And the difference with women?"

"Oh, where do I begin with this one? Your name alone brings pride because of your reputation with women. You're beautiful for a man, and you put on a sophisticated air to maintain the mystique."

John had his hand rolled up covering his grin.

"No doubt you charm the women into asking for your favors, but you can maintain your pride because they asked you instead of the other way around. With so many women, there again, you believe yourself to be prideful in your anatomy. I believe you wait for those delightful words, in the daylight, 'Oh, my God.'" Margaret was starting to laugh herself.

"You did peek, didn't you?" John almost choked from laughing.

John thought her cheeks were going to pop. Her face was red. They were both laughing hysterically.

"And aren't you the lucky one to finally marry *it*?" John snickered. The taunts continued.

"Lucky? Why … it's used. It's second hand … no wait. No telling how many hand-me-downs it has had, including your own. The polish of vigor, breadth, content must have been worn down by now. The intensity has diminished. It's nearly used up. Where do you find the audacity to offer it up? Awe … maybe it isn't up." Margaret chortled. "Was it supposed to be part of the suit you offered? When you asked for my hand, I had no idea what you needed it for."

John thought he was going to be sick from roaring "Bravo!!" He got up and kissed her hard, then returned to his seat. "You are not so nearly naïve as you pretend to be."

"So, it's all true?" Margaret looked disappointed.

"It's ludicrous … all of it."

"All of it?" Margaret asked.

"All except the 'Oh, my God' which I heard you utter under your breath this morning."

Margaret was glowing, and John was chuckling at her.

"Margaret, I give you fair warning. You will be ravished today. You have a few hours to get used to the idea." John left the table to collect his paper.

Margaret sat there staring at her plate wondering exactly what he meant by *ravished.*

Two hours later, Margaret was being led on a horse down pathways into the trees. John had brought the sandwiches that Cook had made, plus a canning jar of water. Earlier, he told Branson to take the day off after he saddled the horses.

Besides trying to find the stirrups so she could stay on the horse, Margaret was still working on the word *ravished.*

Did John have anything planned for this outing?

Margaret began to feel a little anxious for what the day would unfold. "John, I would like to enjoy this ride and rest easy that you have no particular intimate plans on a blanket somewhere."

"Does kissing you often worry you in the daylight?"

"No. Not at all. I am looking forward to that."

"Then rest your mind at ease. That is all I hope to do. Anything past that will be at your urging."

"Well, you see, that is the problem. The charm I spoke about is your way of creating my urges. I think your experience makes that a little unfair, don't you?"

"What would you have me do with the most precious person in my life?"

"Do you feel the need to pleasure her in the daylight, as in today?"

"I crave to pleasure her every minute of her life. And that is not a boast or an exaggeration. Once you are firmly planted on shore, I am hoping you will find the urge all on your own."

"If it is anything like the other night, I will seek it. Will you think less of me if I am not modest?"

John stopped his horse and dismounted. He tied the reins to a tree and then walked over to Margaret and helped her down. After tying her horse up, he guided her to a fallen log where they could sit.

"Margaret, you are still thinking of us as two people interacting with each other. It may take you a while to accept the concept that we have become part of each other. We have become one. With me, you will have no shyness modesty or embarrassment. Your body is part of me. I shall not worry that I am not protecting or providing for you. What happens to you, happens to me. Not only do I want to be a good husband for you, but I want to be a good lover to you, and I know that I will be. My body is part of you. Soon they will be connected and we will feel as one.

"Am I not wading fast enough?"

"No. No. That's not it at all. There is no time limit here. Your naïveté and hesitation are endearing and richly rewarding to us both as you surpass them. I just don't want you to be afraid of being aggressive or inquisitive. I will think more of you, not less. I can understand this daylight talk. It does not bother me. It will come. You were raised in a pious household and rarely subjected to endearments between husband and wife. Showing affection to the one you love is natural and good. Look, Margaret, I am going to love you no matter how the flower in you blossoms. I, myself, am finally starting to overcome my own fear of losing you again. I want you to know that we are in this together. We each have fears and hopes. I doubt we are much different from any other couple in love with the exception of having lost each other once. We are now slowly putting behind us the devastating consequences of our separation. You are going through magnificent changes in your life right now. I feel responsible that you come out on the other side with no uneasiness toward me. This is my responsibility, if you don't realize it yet. I've seen too many unhappy marriages, and I am sure it is because the husband did not take the time his wife needed to understand and enjoy this aspect of marriage, or because the wife was reluctant to share her own needs. Man's biological needs cause many to rush the experience of making love. The woman knows nothing of what to expect, and so lives with what she is given. Her only chance to know her potential is if she takes a lover. Having a good intimate relation with the person you will live with forever is very important–not everything, but an important part of the whole. Do you think I talk about this too much?"

As Margaret listened to John, she struggled to keep her tears at bay, wanting, in a mature attitude, to understand what John was saying. He was right. Although she never realized what was not taking place in her life, she was having to learn it all now. What had always been spoken in whispers or not even that, was a natural and instinctual act and should be regarded that way by a husband and wife. The small shame that she had been feeling because of a pre-marriage fulfillment seemed to float away from her just then. Margaret was gratified to know that she could meet the expectations of a wife.

"Margaret, you are very quiet."

"I love you, John Thornton. Do I think you talk about intimacy too much? No. I don't. As you spoke, I realized that I still held mistaken assumptions, such as this topic should be never be discussed, even with one's husband. Had I been with any other man, I believe I would have pushed him away to the point of having a bad marriage. You are so patient, tender and caring with me, that I feel I am truly blessed. Women are supposed to be the nurturers, but a great man will lead his love to the stars. I see my openness with you plays a large part in my development. It makes me wonder how many marriages are suffering or thriving because of the man's initial steps."

"I love you, Margaret Hale, beyond all reason. You are the most important part of my life." John said softly.

"Since we are baring our souls once again and on the proper subject, can you tell me exactly what 'ravishing' means?"

John thought how typical of Margaret. She knew how to bring a subject to a close, but not before it was warranted.

"Ravishing … let me see. Ravishing is to ravish." John was smiling to himself.

Margaret sat there quietly waiting for the rest of his explanation. But none was forthcoming. Margaret stared at the ground. Could it be that the great John Thornton did not understand the word?

"I don't believe this. You don't know yourself, do you?" Margaret replied.

"Do you think I would tell you that you would be ravished before the day was over and not know what I am doing?"

"Yes. I think you might use that word, assuming I know what it means. You could be tricking me into eating more liver. So, tell me what it means."

"I believe I shall show you later what it means."

"I think I am ready to get back on the horse."

"Why is that?"

"Well, you talked about understanding daylight, and now we're talking about ravishing. I believe I am ready to go on down this path and find a nice place for our picnic.

John laughed and then untied the horses and brought them over to where Margaret was sitting.

John and Margaret had stopped at one of John's favorite places. He had told her about it earlier, but she didn't want to go when Branson was driving. John didn't tell her this was his place. He laid out the blanket under a tree while Margaret strolled to the edge of the cliff, where she could see all of the mills. John watched her as he walked back and forth to his own horse collecting the sandwiches and water. She sat down on the log near the cliff edge and propped her elbows on her knees and her head in her hands. It seemed she was doing what he would do when he was there, and that was reflect.

John walked over and sat beside her. "Are you looking at anything in particular?"

"I was looking for Marlborough Mills."

John pulled his pocket watch out and read the time. "At this time of day the mill is shut down, so I cannot have you count the smokestacks. From the entire perspective that you can see, we are the third mill from the right. Our second mill is further down past Griffin's. Speaking of Griffin's, are you ready to begin work tomorrow?"

"I was thinking of something else tomorrow. Do you think Mr. Griffin would give me a couple more days before I start?"

"I am sure he would. I can speak to him tomorrow, if you want me to. What is it that you like to do?"

"I think I would like to marry you tomorrow. Would that show you that I am not afraid to be forward?"

"Margaret, you cannot tease me like this. I am a fragile man where your love is concerned."

"Well I'm not sure I can do it by myself. I think you have to be with me, don't you? Just the two of us and a witness or someone?"

John turned her around to face him. He looked deep into her eyes. "Margaret, look at me. Look at my eyes and tell me that you are sincere."

John watched her face intently. She took her hands and put them to his cheeks.

"John Thornton, will you marry me, Margaret Hale, tomorrow? But before you answer you must promise a ravishing tonight."

"Yes, I, John Thornton, will marry you, Margaret Hale, tomorrow. I had set the paperwork in motion, so I know that is ready. I will also see Cecil Griffin in the morning. And I think we should return home, as I have no appetite for lunch. I love your forwardness.

John quickly packed what he had set out. He knew he was living his dream. It was now within his grasp, and he found it hard to believe that the day had finally come. He put Margaret on her horse and they headed back.

Chapter Thirty Eight

Arriving home, John saw that Branson was on the property, so he turned the horses over to him. He carried in the sandwiches so they could eat them when they were hungry.

Margaret went to her wardrobe to choose a nice frock for tomorrow. Her head was swimming. She was finding it hard to believe that she had asked John to be married tomorrow. The only reason that the marriage was planned in two more weeks was because of her illness lasting for a month. She felt no ill effects from her illness any more, but her doctor told her to expect that she would feel better when she wasn't. However, having a wedding day sounded like good medicine.

John walked into her room and stood behind her as she gazed at her frocks. He wrapped his arms around her and nibbled at her neck. "Have you decided what you want to wear? We will be married at the courthouse by a magistrate such as myself. I know we had not planned on a very big ceremony but are you sure you want to have one with just you and I?"

Margaret was having difficulty getting the words out as John's attentions were increasing, causing her to drift.

"Hmm? You have not answered me," John persisted between supple kisses to her neck.

"I'm not going to be able to talk much longer if you continue that. If you want my answer, you had better stop."

John turned her around to face him and met her lips with fire. Margaret felt that to her toes as her body turned to jelly. John pulled back and looked into her contented face as he lifted her from the floor and carried her to her bed. He gently laid her down as he followed beside her. He kissed her repeatedly from tenderly to erotic. Margaret felt him nibbling her earlobes and kissing at the edge of her hairline in the back. She could feel the shivering beginning. John rolled over on his back, carrying her over on top of him. He held her face between his hands and pulled her to his mouth. He licked her lips and her nose while he un-pinned her hair.

"It is daylight, Margaret. I believe I will kiss you until it grows dark. Do you know what else happens tomorrow?"

"A ravishing?"

"No. Not a ravishing."

Margaret was now on her elbows trying to hold herself up so she could look at his face. "Not a ravishing? Do I … I … ah … come ashore?"

"Yes. You will come ashore and be initiated into the "Womanly Fulfillment" consummation ceremony."

"Do I get a framed certificate for that?"

John burst out laughing. He held the back of her head and forced her down to his mouth, where he took her breath away.

"You are going to be busy this evening, so I suggest a nap now, and we will have sandwiches when you wake."

Margaret sat up on the edge of her bed as John left, closing her door.

John started smiling to himself, when he remembered Margaret's comment about a certificate. He walked into his study, pulled out a sheaf of paper and began to compose the terms of surrender. As magnificent as it had been, stepping her through the experiences to become of age, she had quite enjoyed the game-like lessons. Instead of her final exam which led her to her womanly fulfillment, he was going to write a lesson plan called Sweet Surrender.

Across the top of the page he wrote in bold letters:

Terms of Sweet Surrender

I. *Caution is advised. Fears and embarrassment will be laid aside. A final commitment will be made by one giving to the other, their heart and soul, their body and mind. This is an unconditional sweet surrender.*

II. *You will accept the purity of my love and lovemaking of you today, leaving behind all that went before in my life, which has been neither, as I have loved no one but you.*

III. *This night you will endeavor to allow me the honor of escorting you onto the "coming of age" shore of consummated fulfillment.*

IV. *By rite and by law I may seek your approval to enter the sanctuary of your womanhood. Furthermore, you are permitted and encouraged into the realm of my manhood.*

V. *Be it known that I will make to cause the loss of your lifelong virginity as the greatest gift I will ever receive. I shall give in return a life of protection, sustenance, pleasure, and abiding love. I will give up my life for yours.*

VI. Be it known that I promise to give my all to you: my honor, the fidelity of a husband, my mastery as a lover, and my commitment and leadership as a father.

VII. Be it known that I will love you into the next life.

John returned his feathered pen to the ink bottle and rubbed his knuckles, not sure he wouldn't add to his list. He smiled looking over his musings. It didn't look like much on paper, but it seemed to have taken some time to form the proper words. He stared at the paper, disbelieving it. After loving her for many months, then losing her for nearly a year, she asked him to marry her tomorrow. He slipped the paper into his desk and walked back to the sitting room, surprised to see Margaret sitting in the big chair with her book.

"Margaret, I did not hear you get up."

"I didn't mean to be quiet, but you looked busy with something, so I just sat down to read. I'm feeling a little bit hungry. How about you?"

"You sit there and I shall bring us the sandwiches and some cider—or would you rather go out for this evening?"

"Even though I just woke up from a nap, I believe I would rather stay home and have some quiet time with you. We will be getting married tomorrow. Perhaps we have undeclared secrets or were hoping for something from the other that we have not mentioned or even thought about. It is time to be as honest as we possibly can because there is no turning back after tomorrow."

As John heard his heavy boots trotting on the steps to the kitchen he couldn't help but smile at Margaret. She should have been a solicitor. As he rattled around in the kitchen placing the sandwiches on a plate and pouring two glasses of cider, he wondered what he could bring up that would satisfy her that he had been thinking this over. It may be possible that he could make a misstep in teasing her. Placing the food on a tray he returned to the dining room.

"Would you like your plate and cider beside your table or would you care to come into the dining room?"

"If it is all right with you I would much rather sit in the chair here, in a casual manner, and discuss anything you feel is relevant before the official loss of your freedom. I believe the loss of a man's freedom and the responsibility one takes on in marriage are serious steps, even more for the man than for the woman

John set Margaret's plate over beside her and returned for his. He sat across from her, wondering where this was going to lead.

"Margaret, I cannot think that I have any secrets that need telling or questions I need answered. So you may proceed first."

"Well, if you insist. I would like to know, what is the secret to your ravishing?"

John just barely kept the first bite in his mouth as she surprised him. Not expecting that, he laughed so hard that he had to throw his hand to his mouth to keep his food from leaving it.

"Margaret, since you have declared a wedding tomorrow, instead of pleasing you tonight I will wait for the honor of our wedding night. It will actually be as it should be." John detected the slightest hint of disappointment on her face. "Your next concern or secret?"

"Do you snore?" Margaret began to giggle. Waiting on his answer, she took her first bite.

"I do not snore. I change my socks, undergarment and shirt every day. I even polish my own boots. I usually clean my plate like a good little boy. I do not cook. I bathe in the copper tub twice a week unless a special occasion arises and I need to do it again. I do not shave every day, but now that I have a lovely face to be near mine I will have to make it a daily procedure in the evening. Tomorrow night you will know that I am a normal man, not wanting to surprise you or disappoint you." John saw Margaret turning red, but he continued.

"I do not care for compliments except for when I pleasure you." Margaret set her plate to the table and walked around behind her chair to look outside.

John was shaking with laughter trying to make no sounds. He was not teasing her, but wasn't sure that she knew it. "I like to read and write and will love making love to you. In my spare time I will endeavor to keep six hundred people employed. Have I missed much that you would have asked? I do not believe I have anything in my past that would embarrass you. I have excelled at my work and been admired by the ladies, but you know all of that. I think you know that my early life was difficult, but I worked hard to regain the Thornton name. If you would like to hear the story of when my virginity was taken, I will be shy, but I will amuse you with the tale. I am not ill, I am not scarred, and I am strong. I am eight years older than you and stand over a foot above you. I am not sure that the two of us can fit into the copper tub at the same time, but we shall try. I believe this to be a true accounting of myself. I now think it is your turn in the witness box."

As Margaret turned away from the window, she laughed as John bowed to her. It had seemed as if he were on stage, enacting a performance for her. "Are all of your performances so grand?"

"They will be, henceforth." John said as he sat down.

Margaret didn't know what to say. She had started this little game not realizing how it would be, but when she saw John tapping his foot impatiently, she realized she would have to think of something. The smile on his face didn't help.

"I am embarrassed by the fact that you know me better than I know myself. You know my height, my dislike of liver, and you even know my days of the month, not to mention potential desires. I like to bathe more than you do. I am not a woman with a high regard for owning and wearing the best things affordable. I prefer a simple life, but I do not feel a woman's place is only in the home. One of the reasons I think I love you is because you know that about women. I have been proposed to four times in my life."

John sighed, wearing a frown. "Four?"

"Aside from some girlish pranks at school, I do not think I could be an embarrassment to you. I believe I will make a good wife, a good mother and with your guidance, a good lover to you. You have convinced me to look forward to that part of our lives."

"But will you hold it against me?" John laughed.

"Hold it against you? I don't understand."

"Never mind. Continue." John continued to smile.

"I do not believe I have any other confessions. I have no secrets. However, I do have a question." Margaret sat in her chair.

"Please, ask it."

"Did you ever think I would find my way to you?"

John crossed his legs. He watched his fingers intertwine in his lap. It seemed as if Margaret had grown serious. "I had lost all hope, though I had never stopped loving you. Every woman who came after you was compared to a Margaret Hale. Not only had I lost all hope of marrying you, but I had also lost hope of all happiness in life. I very nearly lost my will to live on. When I saw your face appear in front of me outside that window in the mill yard, I felt reborn. Even though your visit was mysterious and brief, I felt a spark of hope. You seemed to be in some distress, and you had come to me. Later, after you had left, the thought that you saw me as a savior in some regard, floated down through the layers of my heart and settled there. It was almost instinctual, but immediate, that I knew I must keep that small spark from dying out. You don't know the campaign I waged to know all I could about you and your situation. I would have helped you under any circumstances, but down deep I knew I was doing it for myself, too. If I could help you, I possibly could save myself. Just to have a look from you or nod or a word would sustain me. I believe I have won the war against myself. The dearest and most treasured person ever to come into my life now sits across from me, waiting to be my wife. You can't possibly know how that makes me feel."

John had looked up occasionally as he spoke, but for the most part he did not look at Margaret because he could hear her soft cries.

"To change the subject a bit, I should let you know that I have written a paper on the subject of your surrender." John looked up at her now.

"Surrender? Am I surrendering? I thought I was giving myself to you, open and freely." Margaret smiled.

"You spoke about a framed certificate, but instead I have written a document that is legal where I have dotted the I's and crossed the T's. You will read it and you will place your signature upon it. It does allude to your 'coming ashore,' and it also binds me to you."

"That sounds like it needs two signatures."

"Perhaps you are right. You will see this document tomorrow before our small ceremony. If you feel you cannot sign it, then I should think we need to spend more time on getting to know the other."

"Could I ask of you one more thing?"

"As long as it includes you and me together, the answer is yes. So what is your question?"

"Could we take the train into London and stay tomorrow evening? I would like to be out of Milton. I expect there may be many women that may want to come and stare at me, or ridicule me."

"Not for any other reason except I should've thought of a honeymoon myself. Yes, I would love to be away from Milton and be alone with you. We may stay several days. Tonight we will pack a small amount of clothing and I will write notes to whoever should know we are away. I am quite besotted that you have orchestrated this marriage and honeymoon. Tomorrow morning I will make a stop at the bank before we reach the courthouse. Plan whatever you would like to do in London. Have you ever been there?"

"Aside from passing through there on our way to Milton, no–I've never seen the sights. When we return, will there be room in your bedchamber for my clothing?"

"Had we married in two weeks, I would have had all of this planned out."

"Should Dr. Donaldson be told?"

John stood. "I will go and see him immediately. He could tell me something that would delay our plans. I must know if you are physically able to come ashore." John slipped on his coat and left to find Branson.

Margaret smiled to herself. She had hardly asked the question, and he had left to find the answer. She sat back in her chair and tried to put herself in John's shoes. What was he going through at this moment in time? Margaret's mind was filled with many plans to be made–where to stay in London? To whom should she write? There was the ceremony, the staff, the mill and the honeymoon. The honeymoon will occupy his mind until it arrived. Margaret assumed she should begin a list for the details that he would overlook.

It had been three quarters of an hour when Margaret heard the coach return. She had packed one extra frock, several undergarments, some stockings, but very little else. She heard John coming up the back steps, so she went to the sitting room. He was smiling. Margaret had seemed to have been holding her breath because she felt a sigh leave her mouth.

"Are you packed, my love?"

"What did the doctor say?"

"I believe that is for me alone to know. However, he did advise that you be examined by Dr. Price when we return. I told him I would take care of that." John burst out laughing. "I'm sorry, I was unable to resist that."

"That has been quite apparent for a long time now."

Smiling, John asked, "What is apparent, my examination or my inability to resist?"

"If you can separate one of those from the other, you're a better man than I."

John pulled her into his arms and kissed her for a long time. He could feel the weakening in her. Dr. Donaldson had said her physical condition, mixed with her desire and no doubt her sexual urge, would exhaust her rapidly. John was warned to take precautions with her frail condition. She was still lacking in substance, leaving her vulnerable to fatigue. John asked if there were any restrictions as a new husband. He was told that he would know if there were.

"You still seem to be smiling. I will assume that you are not off-limits to me."

"Donaldson only told me to let you out of bed once in a while." He couldn't help teasing her. "I hope you know that I jest with you. I am in such a mood!"

"Well, I am packed, and I am ready. I am prepared to marry you tomorrow and ravished by you tomorrow night."

"I shall pack in the morning, but I will write my notes now." John kissed her one last time and walked to his library.

Margaret followed him and placed her bit of paper with her list on his desk. He looked at it and said, "Thank you."

John turned out the lamp and left his library holding several folded notes. He was surprised to find that Margaret had gone to her own bedchamber for the night. She had closed her door. John thought that somewhere in her mind, it was making her feel more like a bride.

He walked quietly down the small hall and listened at Margaret's door. She was speaking to someone. Was she talking out loud to herself? Was she in prayer? John was curious, but not enough to interrupt her. He turned out the lamps in the sitting room and went to his own bed. He knew there would be very little sleep for him. He arose within half an hour and found the ring and placed it in his coat pocket. After returning to bed, he once again got up, went to his library and collected his Terms of Sweet Surrender.

This was going to be a long night. John eventually heard the clock strike 12:00 and told himself this was the biggest day of his life.

Margaret hadn't prayed in a long time. She took a few moments to talk with her mother and father and even Adam Bell, if he were there. She told them how happy she was, and she knew they were happy for her. She would have loved to hear them.

Chapter Thirty Nine

John finally rose out of bed at 5 AM. If he had slept an hour all night, he would have thought himself foolish for missing out on the excitement he felt to his bones. He heard Cook arrive before 6 a.m. He threw on his trousers and crept down the stairs to ask for water for a hot bath. He scared her nearly to death, as he never went into the kitchen so early in the morning. In response to asking what was going on, Cook was told that she would know shortly. John had long since packed. He had even shaved.

John bathed, and put on his trousers and shirt, but his hair was still damp, and he wore no socks or boots. He sat at the table while Cook puttered around in the kitchen. He was slipping on his socks when he spoke to her about their secret plans. Cook rushed over to him as he sat in the chair and hugged John with her happiness and best wishes for the two of them. She planned an extra special breakfast. He gave her some instructions for the next two days or longer about whether she or Maddie would have to come to work. Branson would know that he was in charge of the house and the staff. If Margaret was still sleeping when he heard Nicholas arriving, he would go and speak with him as well. He did have a note ready in the event he did not see him. John hoped that they could be at the courthouse about 9 a.m., have their brief ceremony and leave for London on an early train.

He carried his boots upstairs, setting them by his big chair, which Margaret had appropriated, then went to his room to finish dressing. John would put his coat on when he was ready to leave, but he checked the pockets for a ring and a piece of paper hailing a surrender. He was nervous. He held out both hands in front of him, and they were slightly shaking. Never in his life had he seen that. John knew it was not nervousness, just pure uninhibited joy.

In his wakeful hours during the night John tried unsuccessfully to imagine what Margaret must be thinking. He assumed that brides thought a great deal about the ceremony, the reception and the night. With the first being only minutes long and the second nonexistent, John wondered if their long train ride would be taken up with thoughts of the night to come. Leaving the service quickly, Margaret and he would be whisked away to a public train. Hours would pass before he could hold her and kiss her. Practically from the first day he had met Margaret, he had plans for their wedding night or the first time they made love. Tonight he could not make plans. After a year of fantasies and dreams, the night would be led by Margaret. He knew he had to be cognizant of her condition even though she would not be thinking about it.

John was pacing the sitting room at 7 a.m. when he thought he heard sounds coming from Margaret's room. He crept down the hall and listened at the door. He tapped lightly on it and heard Margaret tell him to enter. With a very broad grin he slowly opened the door.

"John, you're not supposed to be in here. Don't you know the groom is not to see the bride before the altar?" Margaret, still in bed, flopped on her back and giggled and giggled. John's heart raced. With her being out of his sight during the night, he worried that she may wake with a new perspective on being married. She could have talked herself out of it, but instead she looked radiant with happiness. He walked over to the side of the bed and sat down beside her.

Sweet Surrender

"Margaret, our day has finally come. Last night we discussed concerns because there was no turning back. Today you take my name."

"Yes, for the first time in my life, I will proudly sign my name as Mrs. John Thornton or Margaret Thornton."

John moved towards her to give her a kiss, but she backed away. "Since I cannot keep you from seeing me before the wedding, I can at least keep you from kissing me."

"I certainly noticed how you disappeared on me last night, but I understand. It does fill one with anticipation, though. Are you going to get up or go back to sleep?" John smiled.

"I'm sorry. What is sleep? I have been so nervous all night I forgot to sleep. I believe I have some hours on the train that could be put to use."

"Whether you close your eyes or not on the train, we will go to the hotel and you will nap before we dine out. The only real reservation that Dr. Donaldson had was that you would exhaust easily today. He said your lust for me will weaken you." John chuckled softly.

"My lust! I don't think that ladies ever lust, do they? Surely there is another word for such a manly emotion."

"I would think that word would be desire. That works well for both of us."

"How long before we are actually at the courthouse?"

"I would hope to be there within an hour-and-a-half. I would like to see us get the 10 a.m. train to London."

"That would tell me that any time between now and then, I will get to see my terms of surrender?"

"That would be your Sweet Surrender."

"Will that be sweet like candy?"

"It certainly will for me," John smirked.

Margaret started to blush, not sure what he meant by that, but it meant something different to him. “If you wish me to dress,” she said firmly, “you must leave the room. I will bathe at the hotel this evening. Please call Maddie to my room.”

“Can I help?”

“Not at this point,” she smiled.

Maddie had been made aware of the news by the time she entered Margaret’s room.

“Can you help me dress, Maddie? I am all thumbs.”

“Very good, miss.”

“Are you married, Maddie?”

“I am, miss.”

“Do you have any advice for my wedding night, tonight?”

Maddie was surprised she wasn’t past that stage, knowing that she had been in her master’s bed. “Oh my, I’ve never had to coach someone on such a subject before. This is quite thrilling. From the lack of improper rumors of Mr. Thornton, I believe he will guide you gently.”

“I’ve heard it will hurt somewhat?”

“Only slightly and very quickly. You will be caught up in such a world of … ah … romantic frenzy that you shouldn’t mind but a moment. You will have a sense of wanting more and more and faster. Oh, listen to me, like I have all this knowledge. You will at times be lost and spiraling. That is especially nice. You will be needful. You will be embarrassed, but not care because your body is urging you forward. Now, of course, your man is controlling this. It could be different from one couple to the next, but it is all good. Don’t blush, child. We are made the way were are. A good man knows what we want and what he needs. It is natural in all of God’s creatures.”

“Can I ask if you ever are forward in that way with your husband?”

Maddie put her hand over her mouth and giggled. "Probably more than I should, but he seems glad of it."

"What … what about …."

"Go on, ask it?"

"What about the size of him and the size of me?"

"If that were a problem, this world would be deserted." Maddie giggled again. "I know exactly your thoughts. I guess every woman fears that when she has seen what is going to be introduced inside of her. There again, a bit of discomfort the first few times, but nothing you cannot abide. Your body will have the willingness and the urge to accept him. Again, your man is controlling how that happens to you. All I can say, miss, it is grand."

"We have been a little playful, but I am still nervous for all that happens this evening. Did you ever wonder what your husband would think of your body when he saw it? Would he compare it to others?"

"If he loves you, as I am sure Mr. Thornton does, he won't care. He loves you for you, yourself. I know we all think like you do, but I have come to realize it was a waste of time to worry about. I wonder what they would think if the shoe was on the other foot? We were chaste women when we were introduced to their bodies and it seems unfair that they don't have that doubt like we do. But that is of their own making. They won't let you put yourself down because you feel inferior to others in their past. They will deny it, and they will be truthful. They aren't marrying you for what they can see. They are marrying you for what is inside of you."

"Yes that's how I've heard it to be." Margaret laughed

"I didn't mean that, silly girl. Let me tell you one thing, you can overdo things. My sister's daughter was taken to a doctor for an examination after her honeymoon. She was extremely sore. The doctor called it honeymoon fever. It seemed her husband was quite active with her and made her raw inside. He was sent to the barn for a week," Maddie giggled. "Just use common sense. If you start feeling sore or burning, just stop doing it. This only happens when everything is new. Do not worry, miss. Just allow your husband to please you, and he will."

John knocked lightly. "Are you ladies discussing world affairs in there?" John spoke through the door. He pulled out his pocket watch and read the time. As he started to speak to Margaret, she opened the door.

"For the last time I will say, Miss Margaret Hale, we have a wedding and a train to catch. Please, let's eat so we can leave."

Branson was standing next to John, waiting to collect Margaret's bag. She noticed he had a broad grin, so apparently his master had told him of their plans.

John pulled the chair out and seated Margaret, then himself, at the table.

"Are we really in that much of a hurry? Isn't there another train after the one you want to catch? Why are you so eager?"

John knew she was starting to tease him. "I wish to be at the courthouse by 9 a.m. so one of the magistrates can perform the ceremony before he has to go to his bench."

"Oh, I see. It would be their fault if we were held up."

"We could always wait until tomorrow or late this afternoon and stay in Milton tonight. Which would you prefer?"

"John, your nerves are showing. Calm down. One might think that you were the bride. Look at you! Your hands are shaking!"

John was faintly aware that his fork was rattling against his plate and making a tapping sound.

"I am not nervous. I am in a hurry. That's all. If you ladies had not discussed Britain's economic position, we may not be in the rush that we are in."

"I was using her as my mother on a woman's wedding day. Do you want me to go on?"

"I can tell you anything you need to know about your wedding night, but not until we get on the train. Here is your toast."

Margaret had never seen John like this. He was hysterical. "So where is this Terms of Surrender thing? You don't expect me to marry you before I read the fine print, do you?"

Both heard the arrival of the coach at the front of the house. John ran through his list in his head. He had spoken with all of his staff members and given Branson a note for Nicholas and Cecil Griffin. He could feel the ring in his pocket, and he had the paper for Margaret to sign, but that would have to be on the ride to the courthouse.

Margaret gaped as she watched John stuff the whole boiled egg in his mouth at one time. He swallowed it down with his coffee, then left the table to find his coat. Margaret was still buttering her toast when he came back and stood beside her at the table. Margaret wanted to giggle, but she was afraid she didn't have time.

"John, if you would please collect my handbag, bonnet, and shawl, I could use the time to wrap my toast in this linen."

Before Margaret could fold the napkin with her toast inside, John was back by her side, holding her shawl open. She could tell he was holding back words like *hurry*. There was little she could do now, so she stood and allowed him to cover her with her shawl and tie her bonnet to her head. He hadn't noticed that he was still holding her handbag. Before Margaret could take her first step down the stairs, John had her in his arms and carried her down. As he reached for his top hat, he noticed a handbag hanging from his wrist. Margaret burst out laughing. John finally realized what a fool he looked like and laughed at himself.

They were barely seated in the coach when John had his pocket watch out again. He seemed to breathe a sigh of relief. The courthouse was only a few moments away.

John turned to Margaret, and said "Do you still wish to marry me today?"

Margaret looked into his eyes and said, "I will, I mean, I do."

"No doubts that I am the man you want in your life?"

"No doubts."

"That is essentially your terms of surrender. You may read the document once we are on the train. I will also be available to answer any questions about the night." John finally smiled as they turned into the courthouse area.

Will be available to answer... Margaret shook her head.

Branson pulled them to the back door, where John was usually let out on his days in court. He took Margaret by the hand and pulled her towards the titling and deed room. He wasn't watching or aware that Margaret was having to run because of his long legs and hurried gait. Margaret was so confused she finally had to start laughing. She wasn't allowed to eat her breakfast. She didn't have time to read the important documents. She was rushed off her feet to wherever she was being taken, and John seemed oblivious to what he was putting her through. Only because John was in such a hurry did it make her laugh. She was still running when he stopped in front of one of the clerks, leaving her to run right into the back of him. Her forward momentum, slamming into his back, bounced her backward and on to her fanny. She was still laughing. She knew John missed that she was on the floor because he was still holding her hand talking to the clerk. If the clerk hadn't notified John that she had fallen, Margaret was sure he would have dragged her along behind him. John turned and surprisingly saw Margaret sitting on the floor.

"What are you doing down there?" He had the nerve to ask.

"I'll stay here, if you don't mind. You just run ahead and find the man to marry us and probably he'll stamp some piece of paper you have to sign. When you have found him, then you may come and get me."

"What happened?" John asked as he lifted her off the floor.

Margaret and the clerk exchange laughing looks.

"Magistrate Thornton, this woman was on the floor because you were pulling her behind you. She was running to keep up with you and then you suddenly stopped to talk with me. I saw this as you came down the hall. When you stopped, she ran into the back of you, which you did not seem to notice, and bounced back on her fanny. She could be injured, and you stand there asking her what happened."

"Oh Margaret, you are marrying the wrong man. I seem to be proving this to myself. Do you know where magistrate Markham is right now?" He asked the clerk.

"I believe he is in his chambers."

John walked slowly with Margaret at his side to some hall seating.

"Margaret, I am so in love with you that all night and this morning, I have begun to feel as if I have coerced you into loving me. I've been in a hurry before you see it, too. Suppose you were right the first time you rejected me?"

"Where is John Thornton? You are not he. He wouldn't doubt my words when I said I loved him. The man has nerves of steel. He is always resolute in his decisions. If he ever doubted himself in his lifetime, it would shatter Milton."

"Yes, you are right. Where has he gone?"

Margaret slapped John hard across the face. People walking nearby turned to see what was happening. John sat there with his head down, twirling his hat by its brim.

"There. Don't ever doubt my love for you again." Margaret told him firmly. "Find that John Thornton and be quick about it."

"Miss Margaret Hale, are you ready?"

"I have been ready far too long."

"May I kiss you?"

"Soon."

John realized that he had not kissed her yet, but she would want him to wait until the end of the vows. John found the chambers of Magistrate Markham. They talked for a moment and were told to take their places.

John escorted Margaret towards the judge's bench where the magistrate was waiting. Suddenly Branson was at Margaret's side.

"Miss Hale, may I have the honor of giving you away?" Margaret turned to John, and they both smiled.

"I would like no one better," Margaret replied. "Thank you, Branson."

The magistrate seemed to flip another page so he could include "Who gives this woman away." The vows were pledged, the ring was placed, and they were officially husband and wife. John finally kissed her like someone gave him the world, and they parted.

Branson kissed Margaret on the cheek while the magistrate shook John's hand.

Branson, Margaret, and John walked out of the room into the next chamber, which was John's. He pulled the paper from his pocket and signed it in front of Margaret. Covering most of the document with his large hand, he slid it towards her and handed her the pen. John removed some official-looking rubber stamp from his desk drawer and made a mark on the document. He folded it back into his pocket and said, "Let's go. We only have a few minutes to make the train." All of a sudden Margaret was being rushed off her feet again. John still didn't realize what he was doing until Branson grabbed his arm to slow him down.

"Master, I can whip up the horses, but you should not be dragging your wife behind you."

John turned to Margaret and noticed she was breathing hard. He didn't apologize. He just picked her up and carried her to the coach.

As Branson had said, he whipped up the horses to a trot that was more vigorous than it should've been in the main part of town.

"Mrs. Thornton, it is too late for you now. I have you. You are mine by law." John actually felt a weight lift from his body. The nervousness seemed to dissipate instantly. He held their signed wedding certificate, still, in his hands.

They arrived at the station within minutes. The smoke was huffing from the engine, preparing to release the brakes. John ran to the ticketing window while Branson escorted Margaret and their bags to an empty coach.

"Miss, I have never seen my master as he is right now. I believe once I close the door he will return to normal. I've been with him for quite a few years, and I know what you and this day mean to him. Here he comes."

"Thank you for everything, Branson."

Branson handed her in, then followed with the baggage, which he stowed overhead. John reached the door as Branson was exiting, and they shook hands. Branson congratulated him, and Margaret witnessed that their handshake was meaningful. Words were being passed silently to the other.

Branson waited on the platform until the train began to pull away. He waved them off.

John was a new man today, and their lives were just beginning.

Chapter Forty

Once out of view of the platform, John took Margaret in his arms and caressed her tightly. It had only been twenty-four hours, but it had felt like weeks since he held her. He gave her several long, loving kisses before he was ready to apologize.

John sat in the corner towards Margaret, who was wrapped in his arm. John looked down at the ring on her slender finger. He turned the ring around and around as Margaret watched.

"I almost ruined our special day. I have no excuse. Thinking all through the night and early this morning, I wondered if I really was the right man for you. I knew I was not making a mistake for myself, but had I encouraged you to believe something that you didn't really feel? You have never given me any indication that perhaps I had intimidated you into seeing a love of me. It was purely all in my head. I have never felt so desperate as I did last night. Several times I walked to your room, intending to talk about it one last time. I think you were right. I did feel like the bride, but not because I had any doubts of you. I wish we could roll back the clock one day and forget my foolish behavior today."

"John, I think that is about all the penance I can stand. If you weren't feeling so low right now, I wouldn't tell you how amused I've been since I began to dress for the day."

"Amused?"

"Oh yes. Let me tell you a tale of the last hour and a half. I was barely coming awake in a most happy mood when I hear a light knocking at my door. Allowing the knocker to bring me completely awake I permitted entrance. I knew it had to be my future husband, but had no idea of the anxiety you were going through. I was sure no one could be happier than I. I had to turn your kiss away because I did want some semblance of a proper wedding. I was gay and feeling light in spirit with a heart overflowing. Nothing was going to spoil my day."

"I asked Maddie to come and help me because I was giddy and perhaps a wee bit nervous. Since I had no sister and no mother, I asked her if she was married and she said she was. She was gay and smiling too. I continued then to ask her if she had any advice for tonight. She seemed quite complimented that I would speak of such things to her. You see dear, there are just some things that a woman wants to hear from another woman. I know you could tell me everything except how it feels to me. These were questions I could not put to you. These questions needed answers. So, I was bonding with our housekeeper. She was putting a lot of my exaggerated fears to rest. She probably saved you a lot of problems with me tonight. We were enjoying this conversation and laughing about the thoughts that women have. Suddenly, through the door, comes this somewhat harsh voice, essentially asking what is taking so long. That was when I was first amused. I knew you were anxious. Although I was anxious too, I've never seen you like that."

"Maddie and I hurried along, and when we opened the door, there you were standing with Branson at your side. To think that she and I could have been discussing something most private to women, and find two men who could have been eavesdropping, was a bit unsettling. But I laughed at that, being aware of the mood you must be in."

"We weren't eaves…."

"From the bedroom, I believe I was permitted a full thirty seconds to get to the dining room and be seated. As it turned out, thirty seconds was being kind." Margaret laughed again.

"Oh I am so forgetful. I forgot to bring my journal. This is just the type of incident that we would look back on and laugh ourselves silly."

"To continue, I had just put the linen in my lap when I saw you push an entire boiled egg into your mouth. You seem to chew once or twice and then gulped it down along with your coffee. Without saying a word, you left the table and returned with your coat. I had not even spread the butter on my toast. To keep you from hovering, I asked for you to fetch my bonnet, bag, and shawl. I think that gave me another twenty seconds to wrap my toast in my linen napkin and ready it for my bag. You had an egg for breakfast and I had nothing." Margaret pulled the piece of toast from her handbag.

John sat Margaret up and slightly away from him. He turned in his seat and placed his elbows on his knees with his head in his hands. Margaret watched this in continued amusement. She thought that any minute he would put his hands over his ears.

She placed her hand on his back and tried to soothe him as she continued laughing and speaking. "I think if you had three arms you would have applied my shawl and tied my bonnet at the same time, but, surprise, you wasted two seconds and tended to each one individually. The next part is most interesting."

"Even though I am well, you decided to carry me down the stairs rather than taking it slowly while I managed it on my own. I imagined that saved you much time, perhaps a full half minute. When we were on the bottom step, you still held me as you reached for your hat. I had to cover my mouth to keep from laughing as you had my handbag on your wrist as you put your top hat on. At least it wasn't forgotten. You then carried me to the coach."

"John, stop covering your ears," Margaret said pulling his hands away from the side of his head.

With a face of disbelief. "Margaret, you have to be making up a lot of this." John rested back on the bench with the look of utter defeat.

"We are now coming to the best part."

John groaned and looked out the window.

"Do you remember much about the courthouse only minutes ago?"

Margaret waited for an answer.

"I remember the vows. I remember you saying, "I do." I can see that I gave you the ring. I remember kissing you. I am not sure I can take what you are about to tell me. I seem to remember you sitting on the floor. Please don't tell me that I caused that. I am so ashamed I don't think I will recover from this." If it hadn't been for Margaret's wonderful smiling and happy nature through the telling of her tale, he would have been emasculated. He already knew he was an idiot.

"No, John. You didn't cause that, I did."

"But how?"

"You do know you are a tall man. You have long legs. When you are in a hurry, you take long steps. You had my hand in yours when you started off to where we were headed. In no time, I was forced to run or be dragged by you. You never looked back. You were so focused on our ceremony that everything around you went unobserved."

John turned once again and put his head in his hands.

"You seemed to recognize someone and stopped immediately to speak to them. Not being able to see through you I did not expect you to stop and ran into the back of you. I hit you so hard that it made me fall backwards onto my buttocks. I admit I felt a little embarrassed in front of the clerk. He noticed what happened, which seemed to alert you to turn around and look at me. Almost totally expected this day, you asked me what I was doing down there." Margaret laughed. "As you picked me off of the floor, the clerk and I looked at each other and almost laughed together at your comment. He proceeded to tell you what you had done. You had the nerve to ask me how it happened. I believe you know the rest of the story. There ends the tale of Margaret Hale becoming Margaret Thornton." Margaret sat back and began to eat her toast.

"I'm not sure I can ever make this up to you. You've kidnapped my life. I knew I wanted to lose myself with you, but I still wanted to be the man you loved."

"John, you are taking yourself too seriously. What I've seen today is a man very deeply in love with me, a man who has loved me and who lost me for a long time. Perhaps women never know the feeling of wanting to protect and possess a spouse, as men seem to need to do. Even though I was at somewhat of a disadvantage this morning, I quite found it fascinating to see a side of you that no one has ever met. Your actions this morning spoke more than the words I love you. Can you understand that? You were reacting from emotions deep within your heart and soul, almost to the point of the physical me being excluded. If I ever needed proof other than your words, of your love for me, you picked a good day to show it."

Margaret laughed. "Now, we will have fun with this. You will be teased, as there is no way we can hide this. And do know that it is very complimentary to both of us … but if you don't pull out of this pity for me, there will be no honeymoon."

"I'm not sure I deserve one."

Margaret turned his way, preparing to slap him again, but he was smiling. It appeared he was convinced that he had done no real harm.

The train finally arrived at the stop that John had ticketed. He let a porter collect their two bags and lead them to the waiting coaches. John mentioned a hotel to the driver, and off they went. It finally felt that they were on their honeymoon. John moved closer to Margaret inside the coach. He began with slow kisses until the coach arrived. A footman opened their door and a second footman took their bags, escorting them to the registration desk.

Margaret was awestruck by the huge beautiful surroundings. The lobby was large, its floor was covered with red, gold and black Oriental rugs. There were many potted plants of palms and other greenery. Around the room were many two and three seat private areas where people could talk in small groups. There was a small bar at one end and a spiral staircase at the other.

When they reached the reservation desk John asked if the honeymoon suite was available. He was told it was. Margaret sensed several porters disappearing as if the room were to be prepared. John was handed the pen and he looked down at the registration book. He stalled for a moment staring at the line and finally looked at Margaret. She thought his eyes were turning glassy as he turned back to the book and signed it Mr. and Mrs. John Thornton. He seemed to stare at his signature and then encouraged Margaret to see it. Somehow it seemed to make it all official. John was handed the key.

He turned to the Porter who was holding their bags and gave him the key and some coins. He told the young man to find them in the dining room when he was done. He looked at the man behind the registration desk, who nodded in the direction he wanted to go. Instead of holding her hand or giving her his arm, he laid his arm at the back of her waist.

"Mrs. Thornton, we have arrived. I think our original plan was to let you bathe, lay down to nap and then come to the dining room. I seem to be quite full from breakfast, but I imagine you are starving. It is nearing 5 p.m. Perhaps we shall have this early dinner and go to our room. I am sorry now that I asked for the honeymoon suite as it may be up several flights, far too much for you."

"I guess I will just have to stay there until we leave." Margaret gasped at the splendor when they walked into the dining room. All around were starched linen and lace tablecloths. Sterling silverware place settings and several crystal goblets each were waiting for patrons. The tinkling of china plates and early vintage Waterford glass rang in the room.

"John, this is spectacular. I've never seen a room so adorned with luxury. In fact all of the hotel is a fairytale. Have you been here before?"

"We have an annual Mill Owners National Association Meeting at a convention hall down the street. I have stayed in this hotel in one of the more basic rooms, but I've never eaten in the dining room. The men would rather go out to an alehouse and have fun after the long meeting day. Tell me, my love, how are you feeling?"

"Happy. More happy than I have ever been in my life. I am feeling quite well and sturdy for the night's main event," she smiled.

"Margaret, we're not going to a boxing contest, a horse racing derby, or an orchestral performance. Please don't call it 'The Main Event.' I have already suffered a loss to my self-confidence today. In the past I have worried about embarrassing myself in certain situations, and now I fear the reverse. You may have to be a temptress tonight."

"I bet you have been practicing that line. Well, I learned a lot talking with Maddie this morning. You may be missing some self-confidence, but I may have gained what you lost."

John raised his eyebrows and smiled. "I promise not to rush you through your dinner. I will not rush you through your bath, either."

"Now that we have signed a piece of paper, do I still get to lead because of my illness?"

"I bet you have been practicing that line," John laughed.

Suddenly John recognized a gentleman across the room. As much as he did not want to delay their honeymoon any longer, this would be a marvelous gift to Margaret.

"Margaret, come with me."

"Are you going to make me miss another meal?"

"I think I see a wedding gift for both of us. I want to show you."

They were sitting in the dining room and Margaret could not understand John's sudden excitement. He came to the back of her chair to take her arm in his. As they were walking through the tables, John purposely looked in the opposite direction because he knew she would be looking where he was.

They stopped at a table where a gentleman was reading the menu. "Excuse me, sir, haven't we met?"

The menu was laid on the table and Adam Bell rose from the chair, shaking John's hand vigorously. Next he took Margaret and hugged her and nearly swung her around in a circle. "John, Margaret, I was on my way to see you tomorrow. What are you two doing in London together?"

Against all propriety, John took Margaret in his embrace and kissed her in front of the world. Adam spotted the wedding ring.

He clapped his hands with joy and with a big smile said, “You two have finally married. What a wonderful coming home present this is. If you haven’t ordered, please do me the honor and dine with me as my guests.”

Adam pulled out a chair for Margaret as the tears rolled down her face. “We … we thought,” Margaret couldn’t get the words out.

“You thought I had died abroad.” Adam laughed. “Until very recently, I did have a very bleak outlook. The fever that I had suffered turned out to be misdiagnosed. At that time I had written John and told him of my wishes and my goodbye. Within a week my strength had returned, and I sailed home. I haven’t even been to the University. I wanted to get to Milton first.”

“I cannot tell you how happy you have made me. I had been worried for a long time about not hearing from you. John finally told me of your letter before we agreed to get married. I believe he felt he wanted no secrets between us. You missed your chance today, you know.”

“Don’t tell me your ceremony was today. Who stood at your side, Margaret?”

John was willing to let Margaret tell the tale. “We were married at the courthouse with just the two of us, and Branson surprised us by stepping up beside me.” Margaret went on to regale Adam with the entire story, including her low times, her illness, and her proposal to John.

Between the talking and the dining, it was nearly 8 p.m. before they reached their room. John carried Margaret up several flights of stairs.

Margaret thought she had stepped into heaven when John unlocked the door. John was impressed. The room was soft-looking with upholstered furniture, pillows everywhere, drapes around the bed, champagne on ice and a washroom for two. The room was warm with a large fire in the hearth and real wood stacked beside it. On the bed lay one red rose. At the foot of the bed were two night robes, one quite sheer and the other lightweight. Out of curiosity, John opened a drawer next to the bed where he found many new condoms in boxes. He didn't want to look on both sides because he didn't want to alert Margaret's curiosity.

"Look at this, John. Real ice. I wonder how long it will last?"

John paid no attention to that. He took off his coat and hat, walked over to Margaret and kissed her, first tenderly and then with his tongue and fire. He was a dragon breathing his flame into her. Margaret weakened and pulled away to sit on the bed.

"Too much, too early?" John asked.

"You never did get a chance to answer my question about my illness and being the leader."

"What was the question exactly?"

"Who leads?"

"Either. Both. We do what feel. We go where we are drawn. What exactly did you discuss with Maddie today? She may have you expecting things that I do not bring or perhaps, quite the reverse."

Margaret lowered her head and blushed. "Suppose I get my bath and we can talk through the door."

"Through the door?" John smirked. "We are in no rush, now. We have all night."

"That is one thing we did talk about."

"What about?"

"All night." Margaret turned away from John.

"My love, I know that is not for you. I'm not sure I am ready for all night, either. I won't mind trying when you want to, but not this early in our physical love."

Margaret grumbled about why she bothered asking Maddie anything. John flopped back on the bed and laughed. Margaret picked up her carpetbag and headed into the bath and lavatory area.

"Here, don't forget this." John handed her the sheer night robe.

"Will you be in that one when I come out?"

"Yes, and the champagne will be poured and the bed turned down. Can you take a moment before you go in there?"

"We are in no hurry, you said. What is it?"

John turned her back to him, pulled the pins from her hair and kissed her neck. "I've been waiting for this. Please, allow your husband to undress you."

"Can you lower that lamps?"

"How about the fireplace only."

"Yes, that will be fine. Wait a minute. Where is this document of surrender before I am past full commitment?"

"Oh, yes." John walked over to his coat and removed the official looking paper, which it wasn't. "Should I read this aloud so we can discuss it, or would you like to read what you have already signed?"

"I can read, thank you." Margaret was handed the paper and began to read.

Terms of Sweet Surrender

I. Caution is advised. Fears and embarrassment will be laid aside. A final commitment will be made by one giving to the other, their heart and soul, their body and mind. This is an unconditional sweet surrender.

"This first one seems to answer the full commitment question, but it's beautifully written."

II. You will accept the purity of my love and lovemaking of you today, leaving behind all that went before in my life, which has been neither, as I have loved no one but you.

Margaret swallowed hard. That would be on her mind for a long time. It was jealousy, pure and simple. Not much she could do about that.

III. This night you will endeavor to allow me the honor of escorting you onto the "coming of age" shore of consummated fulfillment.

“I hope I won’t drown before I reach shore.”

IV. By rite and by law I may seek your approval to enter the sanctuary of your womanhood. Furthermore, you are permitted and encouraged into the realm of my manhood.

“Sanctuary and realm. I’m not sure Jane Austen used those words, but they are exquisite.”

V. Be it known that I will make to cause the loss of your lifelong virginity. It will be the greatest gift I will ever receive. But so shall I give in return, a life of protection, sustenance, pleasure and abiding love. I will give up my life for yours.

“Yes. Hmm… this is the one Maddie and I discussed the most.”

VI. Be it known that I promise to give my all to you: my honor, the fidelity of a husband, my mastery as a lover, and my commitment and leadership as a father.

Margaret put her hand over her mouth to hide her smile about the mastery part.

VIII. Be it known that I will love you into the next life.

"John, this is charming and seductive, delightful and elegant. It goes in my journal. Thank you for making this for me."

"It's all true, from me anyway."

"Mastery, huh?" Margaret giggled.

Margaret turned out the lamp she was reading under. John extinguished the other two. Margaret went and stood in front of John and then turned her back to him.

John started on the buttons, the snaps, the corset and crinolines. When he met her shift and knickers, he left them on and pushed her towards the bath area.

Chapter Forty One

John didn't undress immediately. He lay on the bed with his arms stretched out, looking at the ceiling, but far off in his thoughts. His mind skipped merrily and some not-so-merrily over his time with Margaret. From the first unpleasant meeting at the mill, through the heartbreak of her rejection and then seeing her enter the mill yard only three weeks ago. Now, here she was in the next room bathing on their honeymoon night. It was a lot to take in, knowing it was no longer a dream. How many men, he wondered, found the perfect woman for them? Few, he thought, to the extent of his deep abiding love for the woman in the next room. Many times he had been in similar situation where he was in a lady's room while she changed into other clothing. Never had his excitement been as great as it was right now. His mind and soul wanted her as much as his body. Never had that feeling been with him. No other woman did he want to possess. No feelings past his loins had stirred him enough to look for a long-term interest. A giggle from the bath burst his silent reverie. He walked to the closed door.

"May I come in?"

"Wait. Let me move these bubbles around. They are fun to poke and pop. I've never had a luxury bath such as this. All right. I think I am decent."

As John opened the door, he said, "I sincerely wish you weren't." He looked at the drowned rat he had just married. Margaret's hair was wet, and strings hung down around her face. "You look like you've been wading in the water." She was exquisite. It was another masterpiece for his mind museum. If only he could sketch. He sat on the floor next to the tub and they talked.

"I'd like to ask my wife why she has changed since I knew her last?"

"In what way? I don't think I've changed."

"But you have, drastically. And you are changing me, as well."

"What can you mean?"

"You make me laugh and smile. You didn't do that even for yourself before. Why now? I can only imagine your upbringing in that household and I am sure it was full of love, but jesting and teasing … I think it could not have been that way."

"Now, I know what you mean. When I went off to school, I had a difficult time fitting in. I was dull and shy and too serious. Eventually, I began to be excluded from party invitations and group outings. It took me a year to see that I was the one with odd behavior, and the others were more normal for their age. A close friend knew of my pious household and told me what I was missing at home. On two different school breaks I was invited to the home of this friend. Her family was gay and lively. They had fun. It opened my eyes. I was able to convince myself that playing and teasing was not unfeminine or improper. I enjoyed myself over the other terms, but when I went home, it was back to a quiet existence. The first time you laughed at something I said, it inspired those feelings again. I tried several times to make you laugh, and you did. It did my heart good to see you smile at me. It has become a natural behavior in me now. Something lay dormant until you appreciated my wit. I'm afraid you are stuck with it now. Adam Bell does very well with his wit. Perhaps I learned at his knee."

"With you, I am fortunate in many ways, that being one of them."

John saw Margaret's knees pop up. He assumed she was rinsing her hair. He was going to ask to dry it by the fire. "I am sure your bubbles have moved, so I will turn my back and leave. I will be changed and pour the wine. I want to comb your hair dry."

Coughing and spitting water out of her mouth, Margaret responded, "Very good."

John hung his trousers coat, vest and shirt in the wardrobe. All else lay across a chair. He slipped on the lightweight robe, which fit well and hung to his ankles. John laughed, wondering if the robe had been made in light cotton so that his desire would never go unnoticed. He popped the cork on the champagne bottle and poured the contents into two glasses. A footstool was placed in front of the fire where he would sit as he brushed Margaret's hair.

Margaret opened her door a few inches and asked John to find her night shift in her bag. "I am not sure that the robe they provided was meant to be worn alone. There is nothing to it. I wish to start my evening a bit more respectable. Oh, never mind. I brought my bag in with me."

While waiting for Margaret to emerge, John walked over to the window. There was a full moon. His chest swelled as he stared at the bright luminous sphere. He heard Margaret open the door.

"My love, come here. I want to show you something."

Margaret set her clothes and baggage down. "Where are you?"

John moved the curtain. "Over here at the window."

Margaret walked over to him. She saw he had changed. He was looking at the moon, she supposed. "It is the moon?"

"Yes. I think it is our moon. It is full and bright and depicts a new phase that our lives are beginning." He pulled Margaret in front of him and held her to him as she looked on.

"It is beautiful. I don't think I've seen a full moon since moving to Milton."

"I guess you can imagine how many I've seen in my life. Very few, I should think." John whispered in her ear as he gently rocked her in place. "There is no need to tremble, Margaret. Perhaps, it's your wet hair making you chilled. Let me dry it for you. I have a place in front of the fire."

John took her hand and guided her across the room. "The stool is for me. You sit on the hearth rug. Where is your brush?"

John followed Margaret to her bag. He slipped her sheer robe off of her. There was no need for it with her shift. Margaret handed John the brush.

He turned her towards him and took her mouth and then her neck. Pulling away, John led her to the fireplace. He seated Margaret before he sat on the foot stool behind her. He began to brush her long hair. With it wet, it was so much longer than he realized. Margaret showed him how to start at the bottom and slowly work his way up the strands.

"Tangles will be easier to deal with that way."

They had a quiet hour of John brushing her locks, stopping often to take in her fragrance and kiss her cheeks.

John made sure he was covered well and then had her face him, so her hair was to the warmth of the fire. Margaret sat cross legged, as John reached behind her head to pull his fingers through her hair, separating the strands. There was only a little dampness left.

Margaret started to tremble again, but this time it was the way she was positioned in front of John. He wasn't playing any games with her. He was a gentlemanly husband, but curiosity was taking away her thoughts. She slowly reached under his robe and began to stroke his thigh. Then she retreated quickly. John had said nothing, although she felt him inhale deeply. He continued to seduce her hair. She tried again, this time stroking her hand a little further up. Feeling the hair on his legs tickled her fingers. John had stopped brushing her hair. She peeked up at him. His eyes were closed. She retreated again. A few moments later, he was weaving his hands in her hair.

John brought his hands around to the front of her face and lifted her chin. He bent forward and kissed her with deep emotion. The kissing became more enthusiastic by both of them.

"You are the temptress to my calm," John said. He lifted her from the floor and guided her to a chair that he took, bringing her down on his lap. The kissing started out gently until John entered her mouth. He placed his hand on her breast at the same time. He felt Margaret's heart speed up. They were both beginning to breathe heavier.

As John kissed her deeper and deeper, he reached for the hem of her shift. Margaret was so engaged in the wondrous kissing that she did not hesitate when John pulled her shift over her head. Immediately she felt his warm large hands roaming her back and buttocks.

He stood and carried her to the bed. There was very little light from the moon and the hearth through the sheer curtains that lined the bed, but there was enough for John to see her real beauty as he gazed at her lying there.

Margaret placed hear hands over her lower self in embarrassment.

"Margaret, this is your sweet surrender." John moved her hands away and looked at her while she shook. "Margaret, you are strikingly perfect. And you are mine.

What I see that you give me, is more than any man deserves. God, I love looking at you like this." While he stared down looking at the all of her, he unbelted his garment.

She watched as John removed his robe. Margaret immediately went back in her mind to the conversation with Maddie this morning. "I wish I had the same words you just said to me, but I am speechless."

John reached down and took her hand and put it upon himself while he stood there. If he were lying beside her, she wouldn't know him as he wanted her to. This way she could see and feel him.

"John, I don't know what I am doing. This … you …."

John crawled into bed next to her, and the fervent kissing began again. He brought her one hand to his chest and the other to his penis. He held the back of her head and began to explore her body. Margaret shivered. He loved that.

"Remember, this is our sweet surrender. No embarrassment."

"But, it's hard."

"It surely is." John kissed her while smiling before she could say anything. He moved his lips down to her breasts and nipples. He took his full measure with each one, pebbling her nipples into rose raspberries. "God, you're perfect, Margaret," He panted out.

Margaret could no longer reach where he had placed her hands, so she began to run her fingers through his hair. She noticed that his hand had moved down to her thighs. The yearning for more started to make her wince.

John gently lifted one of her legs over his hip as he moved downward, licking her belly and navel. He nudged her other leg over, encouraging her to open to him.

Margaret hesitated, and then gasped when he laid his palm between her legs. A fire had been building there, and now she was inflamed. She wanted his touch. He wanted to touch her. She became almost still when his fingers began searching. Margaret tightened, waiting for the hurt.

"Margaret, this isn't the part you are fearing. Just relax. I am preparing you for me," he whispered.

"Preparing?"

"Yes, my love. You are quite wet in this area right now. That is to ease the passing of me into you."

Suddenly, Margaret felt herself being entered with his finger.

"That doesn't hurt, does it? I believe it is a pleasant sensation?"

"Yes," Margaret gasped out.

"And this?" John removed his finger and began to massage her small little nub, as he called it.

Margaret raised her buttocks off the bed. "Oh, John."

"Say my name again."

"John, I think I am going to beg for mercy. That area is most sensitive and yet demanding something." Margaret began to struggle slightly.

Without leaving her womanhood, John placed himself between her thighs and placed his mouth where his finger had been. He moaned against her.

He slid off the end of the bed, pulling her down with him. "I want you to surrender to me, Margaret. I want the taste of you, the essence of you, the all of you." John began his slow lapping, licking and suckling, only grazing her most sensual area. John knew passing over that area only continued her sexual desire for more and more.

Margaret began to move more and writhe under him. "John, John, I surrender. I can't help it." A loud moan came from Margaret, and she threw her hand over her mouth.

"Don't hold back any sounds, just surrender yourself to me." John heard her second mournful moan. She began calling his name over and over between gulps of air. Her body was trembling, her thighs were twitching. It was time. He couldn't get enough of her. He wanted to take her into his own body. John began his final assault on her little nub, which was now swelling a little bit. He had brought her to her own erection. Suddenly, her legs stiffened out straight, and sound after sound escaped her. John could tell she was trying to be quiet. He loved her struggle. The intensity of Margaret's climax was unlike that of any other woman he had been with. Never had he a greater moment in his life. This was the epitome of being a man in love. Margaret was digging her nails into his shoulders. He wanted to smile, but that would have to wait. She was still reeling. She would tell him to stop when she really meant it. Her embarrassment caused her to push him away, which meant nothing except *I cannot take much more*.

"John, stop. Please … stop … I can't … breathe. I … surrender. Oh, my God," she panted. "I am shaking badly. This was much more extreme than the other night. The feeling is still with me. It's like a pebble thrown into a pond. The ripples will take a while to settle. It can't be like this for other women. It is has to be you. I would have heard about this before now."

John watched her heave for air. He climbed on the bed and pulled her up into his arms. She started to cry and rolled into his chest, hiding her face.

"I loved that."

"I know that very well. I felt and heard your partial surrendering."

"I can't believe it. Is that enjoyable to you or something you do just for me?"

"That is pleasure for us both. I could never explain what your reaction does to me. You make me solid as a man. Nothing else completes me except your response to me."

John and Margaret lay still for a while. He wanted her to float among the ripples. As he held her, he could feel the pounding of her heart and lungs.

"John?"

"Yes, my love?"

"I believe you said 'partial surrender.'"

"I believe I did."

"I'm not fully on shore, am I? We haven't done what I have always heard about. You have allowed me to soar to the moon alone twice."

"That is not entirely true, but it doesn't need discussing now. I wish for you to enjoy every last moment of your new experience before we begin again."

"Is there really going to be a '*we*' this time?" Margaret asked. "I feel like you are the hunter and I am the prey pretending I don't wish to be caught," she went on. "I feel selfish and rapacious. You know how to deliver me to real need. I want another pleasure. I want to pleasure you as you have me."

Margaret reached down to touch John's erection. It was hard as it pressed against her. John kissed the side of her face and pulled her closer to him. Before she knew it, Margaret was holding him firmly in her hand. She began to explore with the touch of her fingers. John moaned quietly in her ear.

"Whispering to her, John said, "Please don't stop. I love what you were doing to me."

Margaret slowly began to stroke him back and forth.

With great effort, John pulled her hand to his mouth and kissed it. "I have very little control left, and you are about to take it all away. Margaret, I should ask, 'How are you feeling?' I should be more specific. Are you feeling overly weakened? Do you feel exhausted as if you want to sleep?"

"I surmise you are worried about my illness. I love how I feel right now. If I tried to stand and couldn't, I would not mind. If you are thinking of stopping or waiting a long time, don't do that to me, I beg you."

John kissed her deeply while he easily rolled part of his weight on top of her. Every time he sought her lips she opened to him, allowing the embers to burst into flame. His tongue began a thrusting motion. His body moved against her. It was different than the other kisses. She could feel the hard ridge of his penis searching. As before, his kiss and lips and tongue moved down to her breast. As he continued downward licking and caressing her belly, Margaret began to tremble again. She didn't know if she did have the strength to sustain the nervous tension that he produced before.

John spread her thighs and felt Margaret tense up. He was expecting this.

In the softest tone, Margaret heard John tell her, "This is your final surrender. This time it will be my pleasure and your pain. It will last a very short time, and I will make it as easy for you as I can. All I need you to do is to relax yourself. Tensing will make it more difficult for you. I do this because I love you and I need you. I need you this way. I possess you this way. To be inside of you is the greatest gift we give each other."

Margaret whispered in a low voice. "Are you going to stake a flag?"

John was sucked out of his emotional journey that had been a lifetime in waiting. He couldn't help himself–he laughed, too. "Margaret, why are you not taking me seriously?"

"Possessing me. Being inside of me? You're the one coming ashore, discovering new lands. It … it … it just came out. I am sorry. I guess you'll have to start over and over again."

John rolled her on her side and smacked her bottom. "Did you at least hear every word I said to you? I exposed my soul to you, and you make a joke. I truly love your wit, but now I see you have problems with the timing. I should've said, 'Margaret, this is the part you have heard to fear.'"

John moved back to her lips and began again. He couldn't say it was any bother at all. Margaret was engaging and responding with her love. She was hugging him around his neck, their tongues kept meeting as the flames once again started leaping. As he began his descent, Margaret's trembling began again. He loved feeling that. Passing her breasts, she began to squirm and wince. John moved his hand to her entrance. As he slipped his finger inside, he felt Margaret jerk.

"Relax, my love. I know the anticipation is desirous and frightening. I will take care of you."

Margaret was as she should have been, very moist. He lowered his lips to her most sensual domain. She was beginning to thrash. He held her down for only a moment. She was needy. He began to position himself as he spit saliva into his hand and applied it to his penis.

He guided himself to her entrance and told her once again to relax. He pushed slowly and felt her fingers digging in to his shoulders. "Breathe, Margaret." John retreated a little bit and then pushed further into her. He repeated that again, this time finding her maidenhead as he inserted himself deeper. He heard Margaret sucking air through her teeth. He held still and kissed her until the discomfort passed.

"My dearest Margaret, I am going to continue." John was quickly losing any effort to sustain an easy rhythm with her. He thrust himself fully inside of her.

"Margaret, you feel like warm silk inside and I can feel your muscles contracting around me."

John's movements became faster and more intense. He was surprised when Margaret began to respond to his rhythm, and as she moved with him it seemed instinctive to her. He could hear in her voice the soft moans of expectation, the pitch in her tone rose and her breathing became faster. She began to call John's name.

"Now, sweetheart."

A few more deep thrusts emptied John of his seed, but Margaret needed more. Instead of stopping, he continued until she climaxed. In his mind, his virility claimed victory.

Gently, John withdrew and asked Margaret how she felt.

"Give me a moment, please. I am fine. Do you want to know how I feel right now?"

"I believe that is what I asked you."

"You will laugh. I feel like a turtle on its back. My arms and legs are weary, and I am completely helpless."

Only Margaret could have come up with that analogy at a time like this, John thought. "How do you feel inside?"

"How am I supposed to know that? It burns a small bit. If I had known the pleasure that comes with the pain was this wondrous, I would not have feared it all these years. I feel a bit squishy."

John laughed heartily at that. "I'm afraid that is my fault."

"I do know that much. So how many babies are swarming around in there?"

"You didn't learn that? Many."

"You said you would teach me. So, how many?"

"Should we count them?" John laughed.

"We can't do that, I don't think. The way I feel, it must be a couple of hundred."

John rolled out of bed to get a washcloth. "Margaret, there are probably a couple of million."

John washed himself in the lavatory and then brought several wet cloths and a towel to Margaret.

"Stay still, Margaret. I will tidy you." As John tended to Margaret, the first cloth came away as expected with a pink tinge to it. The second cloth was a little more intrusive. When he was done, he asked Margaret to move to the other side of the bed, and he placed a towel where they had lain. Never before had he taken a woman's virginity. The experience, along with the visual verification, was overwhelming.

John crawled in bed next to a contented, but exhausted wife. No greater love would he ever feel than he did right now.

"Margaret, you and this night could not have been more perfect. All the dreams and all my fantasies were fulfilled. All my plans were left behind, and I allowed you to lead me. I shall love you always and beyond."

"I may have led you, but being the man you are, I was willing to surrender who I am and follow you for the rest of my days."

"I believe our sweet surrender is the giving and accepting of our soul to each other." John whispered. "We are complete and we are one."

The End.

26175148R00306

Printed in Great Britain
by Amazon